DAVID DONACHIE was born in Edinburgh in 1944. He has always had an abiding interest in military history, including ancient Rome, the Middle Ages, the British navy of the eighteenth and nineteenth centuries and the clandestine services during the Second World War. He has more than fifty published novels to his credit with over a million copies sold. David lives in Deal, the historic English seaport on the border of the English Channel and the North Sea.

By David Donachie

THE JOHN PEARCE ADVENTURES
By the Mast Divided • A Shot Rolling Ship
An Awkward Commission • A Flag of Truce
The Admirals' Game • An Ill Wind
Blown Off Course • Enemies at Every Turn
A Sea of Troubles • A Divided Command
The Devil to Pay • The Perils of Command
A Treacherous Coast • On a Particular Service
A Close Run Thing • HMS *Hazard*
A Troubled Course • Droits of the Crown

THE CONTRABAND SHORE SERIES
The Contraband Shore • A Lawless Place • Blood Will Out

THE NELSON AND EMMA SERIES
On a Making Tide • Tested by Fate • Breaking the Line

THE PRIVATEERSMEN SERIES
The Devil's Own Luck • The Dying Trade • A Hanging Matter
An Element of Chance • The Scent of Betrayal • A Game of Bones

HISTORICAL THRILLERS
Every Second Counts

Originally written as Jack Ludlow
THE LAST ROMAN SERIES
Vengeance • Honour • Triumph

THE REPUBLIC SERIES
The Pillars of Rome • The Sword of Revenge • The Gods of War

THE CONQUEST SERIES
Mercenaries • Warriors • Conquest

THE ROADS TO WAR SERIES
The Burning Sky • A Broken Land • A Bitter Field

THE CRUSADES SERIES
Son of Blood • Soldier of Crusade • Prince of Legend
* * *
Hawkwood

A Crusades Novel

SON
OF
BLOOD

David Donachie

McBooks Press

Essex, Connecticut

McBooks Press

An imprint of Globe Pequot, the trade division of
The Rowman & Littlefield Publishing Group, Inc.
4501 Forbes Blvd., Ste. 200
Lanham, MD 20706
www.rowman.com

Distributed by NATIONAL BOOK NETWORK

British Library Cataloguing in Publication Information available

Library of Congress Cataloging-in-Publication Data available

ISBN 978-1-4930-7617-8 (paper : alk. paper)
ISBN 978-1-4930-7620-8 (electronic)

♾™ The paper used in this publication meets the minimum requirements of American
National Standard for Information Sciences—Permanence of Paper for Printed Library
Materials, ANSI/NISO Z39.48-1992.

To my Great Nephew Andrew,
rapidly approaching the age
to easily read it

PROLOGUE

No fighting man can go into the battle thinking of death, for to do so is to risk bringing on that very fate. The possibility must be accepted and set where it belongs, at the back of the mind, while the warrior concentrates on exercising what skills he possesses, though there are moments when such an outcome will come to the fore and all attempts to force it back to where it belongs do not suffice. This is what happened to Bonito of Alberobello who had, along with his fellow Lombard rebels, emerged from the fortified town of Noci to fight their enemies on the gentle, open and hard-earthed slope before the town gates.

The Normans, even although they were heavily outnumbered, behaved as though they were at little risk of losing, which came as no surprise; those heathens believed no Lombard could hold their ground against their superior fighting skills, just as no Lombard could be considered an equal. Yet the race they despised had withstood the repeated assaults of their ferocious cavalry, with Bonito aware that many of his compatriots had been fatally skewered on their lances. Having failed to break the line holding the approach, they had now dismounted to do battle on foot and Bonito was not alone in feeling his spirits soar at the prospect of the victory that would surely come and of the Norman blood that would stain the ground beneath his feet. Dismounted, they could not be half the warriors they were on a destrier!

As men had fallen the defenders closed ranks, so that Bonito moved nearer to the centre of the line, coming face to face with the most puissant of his enemies when battle rejoined, and that cheered him; perhaps he would kill an important leader and be in receipt of a just reward of gold or silver for such a feat. He was a doughty fighter, admired for that ability by those who had rebelled against the Duke of Apulia, a man they all hated with virulent passion, though they had never ever laid eyes on him. Robert de Hauteville, they were sure, was in concert with Satan; indeed, it was whispered he might well be the Devil himself.

To the Lombards of South Italy, even more to the Greeks over whom they had once held sway, the Normans were uncouth barbarians, little removed from Vikings, who hailed from the cold, misty lands of the north. Their only aim was to plunder and sack, being rogues who fought not for love of land, family or hearth but as greedy mercenaries. That was how they had come to Apulia, a fertile and rich terrain of vines, olive groves, burgeoning fields of wheat and fat livestock: invited by a fool who saw their fighting prowess as a way to throw off the yoke of their Byzantine overlords and restore Lombard independence to South Italy; in the end that aim had been thwarted. Byzantium was gone, but there had been no Lombard ruler

8

to take their place, for the Normans had stolen that ambition; one tyranny had been replaced by another.

Bonito's faith only began to waver when he realised that amongst the mail-clad knights advancing towards him at a steady pace, the fellow he would come up against was a monster who towered above him by a good three cubits; added to that, he was so broad in the shoulder as to be near double Bonito's girth. Normans were by nature taller and better built than Lombards and stood as positive giants compared to the Greeks who made up the bulk of the population. Yet even by that standard the man with whom Bonito would do battle made those confrères in his own advancing line look puny.

The Goliath's arm had a superior reach, rendering the broadsword in his mailed hand longer by two hands. The temptation to edge right or left was strong but impossible to implement – the line was too compact – and if Bonito did move he could not do so without exposing the flank of one of his compatriots, which would thus put him in peril. So with a whispered prayer to his one true god he resolved to do as well as he could, thinking perhaps such height and build concealed a weakling, for not all big men are strong.

The first swing of that broadsword, parried with difficulty, put paid to the latter notion as Bonito felt the effect of the blow run up his arm and jar his shoulder, this while he observed the unblinking bright-blue eyes that bored down into his own from either side of the nose guard, orbs that sat in unlined skin. Seeking to use the giant's height against him Bonito made to go into a crouch, hoping to get under his defence and hit him in the vital part of his groin. To achieve that he needed the split second of non-engagement that would free his own broadsword and that was not gifted to him, for his opponent's weapon was employed without pause. All he could do was hastily shift his blade to parry and his round buckler to deflect, aware that each time his shield was struck he was rocked back on his feet in seeking to contain the force of the blow.

Within moments that thought of impending death was no longer buried deep, it was uppermost in his mind; he could not do battle against this monster and he could expect no aid from his companions, for they were as deeply engaged as he. If that was the case, then there could only be one outcome, which brought to the fore the sole notion that nature allows as a substitute. It was not cowardice that made Bonito of Alberobello take one pace back but an overwhelming desire for self-preservation; in his action he fractured that cohesion which had held off the previous mounted assaults.

Those in the line to right and left sensed him giving ground. They, like he, knew that any open gap presaged doom for those who sought to hold their place, for they would be exposed on their flank as well as to their front, destined to do battle with two enemies, not one, so they too began to give way. The dent in the defence thus rippled along the entire Lombard line, with those who were too slow to react exposing their sides to deadly thrusts that, striking home, created even bigger gaps into which the Normans eagerly pushed, slashing right and left as they did so to widen it into a complete rupture.

The defence broke as each individual Lombard came to the same conclusion as Bonito: it was time to save themselves from a cause that was irretrievably lost. That they died in greater numbers for such a choice was the unintended consequence and fate did not spare the man who had first wavered, for there was no way Bonito could get out of the reach of the giant swinging his sword to cleave him. A last desperate parry saw his own weapon break in two, while his shield was now so mashed as to provide little protection.

The killer blow took him at the point where his neck met his shoulder and it cut through his mailed trunk as if his armour was made of links of wool, not metal. The collarbone was smashed, but the effect did not end there as his enemy drove his sword down and through his top ribs to the sound of screaming prayers for mercy from the victim, shrieks which died as the blade cut through the pipe that supplied wind to his gullet. The fount of blood that emerged as it progressed shot high into the air until eventually even the giant's great strength could sustain the effect no longer, compacted flesh and bone bringing the blade to a halt. Bonito of Alberobello died looking up into the still, unblinking eyes of the warrior who killed him, but not before he heard the man fighting next to him exultantly shout something in his heathen, incomprehensible tongue.

'You have your father's arm, Bohemund.'

There was no time for the speaker to say more and no time for the youth receiving the accolade to react. He had to extract his weapon from the limp rag of a body now collapsing to the ground, for there was much more killing to do as the defeated rebels broke completely and sought to get back through the city gate from which they had emerged to do battle. Amongst them now and swinging freely with his broadsword was Bohemund, a mere sixteen summers old, the bastard son of the devil-like Duke of Apulia, and he wreaked deadly havoc – so much devastation that he left behind him a trail of dead and dying enemies as well as most of his confrères.

It was Bohemund that got to the still-open gate first, and that same sword which pressed into the narrowing gap to prevent the double iron-studded doors from slamming shut, as those inside, sacrificing the fighters who had failed to make it in time, sought to secure themselves against what must surely come if they failed: outright

11

massacre. Alone for only a few grains of hourglass sand, the young warrior had to fend off attempts to kill him with only his long dagger and a mailed fist, but soon he had Normans by his side, their backs to the gate to force the surrender of those who were trapped outside their city walls.

As the Lombards dropped to their knees and begged in vain to be spared, Bohemund was joined by a mass of men pushing to open that narrow gap, enough to allow their compatriots to jab and hack at those seeking to keep them at bay. It would have needed a stout heart, strong confidence and great faith to get those gates closed, but that, so prevalent only a short while before, had now gone out of the rebels. Like those who had fought on the ground before the city they were concerned to save themselves as well as their families, a foolish notion given their leaders had refused the terms of surrender offered by the Normans, and thus by the laws of war had laid them open to rapine and sack without quarter given.

Pressure saw the fissure in the gate widen; fear of the consequence made those who knew they could not hold break and run. Soon the small force of Normans, with Bohemund to the fore, were doing execution in the cart-wide streets of the city, the blood from the slain flowing downhill on the cobbles of the roadway to that now wide-open gate – killing that would go on as the sun dipped and the light faded to darkness, so that torches were required, which lent a satanic hue to the continued butchery. If women and children were spared, and often they were not, it was only so they could be sold into slavery.

With seemingly no one left to fight, Bohemund could at last remove his helmet and ease his mailed hauberk off his sweat-soaked head and allow it to rest on his broad shoulders. To those with whom he had fought and killed, the sight, had they still eyes to see, would not have eased their souls into the afterlife, for they had not fallen to the sword of a scarred and experienced warrior. The fellow who stood in the central square of Noci was a youth of unblemished face, his blond hair cut short and his jaw showing little sign of the ability to yet grow even a trace of a beard.

It was there the man who had led the successful Norman attack found him; indeed it was his brother-in-law Ademar who had shouted that accolade in the midst of battle, for he had taken care that his relative by marriage should have by his side a warrior of long experience to ensure he survived his first real battle – too many young fools met their end early from an excess of zeal. It was only when Bohemund looked at Ademar's blood-drenched surcoat that he realised his own blue and white de Hauteville colours must now be hidden by the deep-red gore of those he had slain. Removing a glove, he lifted it and examined the cloth in the torchlight, sorry to see it was true, for he valued the right to wear these colours above all other things.

'Your father himself could not have done greater execution this day and I will tell him so.'

The reply was made doubly gloomy by exhaustion. 'Will my father care about any deed of mine?'

The hearty slap on the back would have moved a normal man; the recipient this time did not even notice. 'You will soon find out, Bohemund. Word has come that Trani fell four days ago and the rest of the towns in revolt have surrendered, all except Corato. Tomorrow we ride to join him there. Take that fortress and this rebellion against his title will be spent.'

CHAPTER ONE

Compared to the numerous towns and cities the Duke of Apulia had already either captured or forced to surrender, Corato was a pinprick of a place, a series of curtain walls joined to the four towers that formed the defensive whole, a construction that could be ridden around, even at longbow shot, in less time than it took to fill a quarter of an hourglass. Those dwellings that lay beyond the walls and the deep ditch which surrounded them, the kind that grew up around any citadel, had been razed to the ground in anticipation of a siege, the inhabitants now inside the walls with their animals, wine and portable possessions, some of them able to fight and support the knights who made up the garrison.

Ademar, Marquis of Monteroni and son-in-law to the Duke, knew that with the force he had at his disposal he could not hope to take the place even if, like at Noci, the defenders came out to do battle on the slopes before the main gate. Given that many of those inside were

Normans, better able to hold their ground than Lombards, added to the fact that he had been required to leave part of his force behind to secure and garrison Noci, while others had been detached to escort the slave survivors to Bari, the outcome of any fight was too uncertain to risk. His force now numbered no more than fifty knights, possibly less than the figure now sheltering in Corato.

'They might be tempted,' Bohemund said, looking back to where the men who had come with them from Noci were making camp, 'given our small numbers.'

'No, word travels faster than a man can ride, though only the evil spirits know how that can be. They will have heard that Noci has fallen and also have been informed, as were we, that your father is on his way from Trani with his whole army. If they decide to sortie out, Bohemund, it will be because they reckon defeat impossible, and since I am inclined to agree, we must spur our mounts and get away as soon as the gates open.'

'Run?'

Ademar smiled at the underlying disgust in the young man's response; that was only to be expected from one of his years. Added to his bloodline he had been raised to believe that he and his kind were near to invincible and his confidence was not misplaced; the Normans, no more than a few thousand lances, having arrived in this part of the world in dribs and drabs as mercenaries, now ruled over a population of Lombards and Greeks required to be counted in the millions, while their confrères back home in Normandy had not only held in check the King of the Franks and his Angevin allies who sought to occupy the duchy, but had recently crossed the narrow sea to invade and conquer Saxon England.

Bohemund de Hauteville belonged to a family, as well as a class of warriors, that when they were not engaged in actual fighting trained for combat on every day bar the Sabbath. Ever since he could wield a wooden toy sword and carry a straw buckler – and he had come to that at a tender age, being taller than boys who shared his years – Bohemund had been taught how to fight both on foot and mounted, to employ a lance, his shield, a broadsword and an axe. He had been instructed in the discipline and tactics of the ten-man conroys that ensured, acting in concert, and even outnumbered – they usually were – that the Normans had become the most feared warriors in Christendom.

'It is wise to run when the occasion demands it, Bohemund. There is no glory in a useless death.'

'We could try an assault under cover of darkness.'

'No.'

'There are those who would follow me.'

'And in doing so disobey me, their commander?' Ademar demanded, his voice hardening. 'When I say "no" that is what I mean.'

The glowering response that engendered, a youthful pout that spoilt a handsome countenance, nearly made Ademar hoot out loud and it was only regard for his brother-in-law's feelings that held that in check. Having had a hand in raising his wife's younger sibling he knew the boy to have a serious nature; indeed he was not much given to jesting, which Ademar saw as a pity – young men should carouse, jape about and get up to mischief. But then Bohemund had the burden of being his father's son as well as a family background that he seemed viscerally determined to live up to, for if the Normans had created much in Italy, the de Hauteville brothers had created the most. Bohemund's aim, never stated but obvious to a man who had watched him grow, was to be the greatest of that name, to outshine not only his father but every one of his numerous uncles.

'Our friends within those walls—'

The interruption was abrupt. 'They are not our friends, Ademar!'

'Whatever they are, they sit above deep wells that will keep them supplied with water and I daresay they will have butchered and salted enough meat to keep them for a year, and that takes no account of what they have still on the hoof. Their storehouses will be bursting with grain and oats, while their stock of arrows will run into the thousands, given they have been untroubled for months and have had endless time to prepare. I fear even with the full might your father can bring to bear we will be here and looking at those walls for some time.'

'Can we at least make a start on constructing ladders?'

'I have a better suggestion, given we too have to eat. Let us, you and I, go and hunt, for the forests round here are bursting with game. I'll wager you a skin of wine my lance finds flesh before your own.'

Robert de Hauteville, by papal investiture Duke of Apulia, Calabria and Sicily, known to all as the *Guiscard*, came in sight of Corato and the firepits of Ademar's encampment two days later, with the newly risen sun still low at his back. Close behind him rode the body of familia knights, his personal followers, men who would stay close to their duke in battle and, if called upon, sacrifice their own bodies to keep safe his – no easy task given their master was a dedicated warrior who relished combat and always led from the very front whether he was mounted or on foot. No man would employ his lance more aggressively or wield a broadsword with more effect, just as none of his followers would ever enter the breach in an enemy wall ahead of their leader.

For all his prowess in battle – and he was famed throughout Christendom for his string of stunning successes, often against seemingly overwhelming odds – Robert de Hauteville was best known for his tactical cunning; he was just as quick to deceive his foes into forfeiting victory as to beat them down by main force and the fighting superiority of his knights. Hence his soubriquet, which, to those who admired him, meant he had an abundance of guile; those who did not hold him in high esteem clung to the other interpretation of the appellation *Guiscard*, which could also mean that the man who carried it was a weasel.

Behind him, strung out over a line several leagues in length, came the rest of his force: first the Norman lances, then the Lombard and Greek levies on foot, each one conscripted to fight but usually content to be fed and paid, then finally in terms of warriors, the cohort of crossbowmen. The approach of the host was announced well in advance by the great cloud of dust that their marching raised above the tops of the trees through which they had progressed. To their rear would come the sutlers, the men who looked after hundreds of spare horses, the sturdy fighting destriers and broad-backed pack animals, for each mounted Norman required those as well as a cavalry horse, while their lord was obliged to provide replacements for any lost in battle while in his service.

The host travelled farriers, armourers, leatherworkers to see to saddles and harness, carpenters skilled in making siege towers, lesser woodcutters to erect shelters of framed animal skins, labourers who would dig the latrine pits, the concubines of the fighting men along to cook and wash for them, as well as the usual flotsam of urchins and layabouts that attended every army on the move regardless of their country of origin. The difference with the Normans was their ability to detach themselves from this trailing mass of humanity and become a highly mobile and self-sustaining fighting force; in short, they could maintain themselves in the field, move quickly and use surprise as well as ability to confound their enemies.

Ademar, standing with and dwarfed by Bohemund, executed a half bow as his liege lord approached, though he examined him carefully for signs of wear; the *Guiscard* was in his late fifties and had been at war now for close to thirty years, from his days as a near-bandit chief living from hand to mouth in the wilds of Calabria to the man who headed armies that dwarfed the one he now led. Yet apart from some grey in his long, red-gold hair and an increase in the lines on his cheeks there seemed little evidence of him being in any way diminished.

Tall and burly, his eyes still had a twinkle that hinted at his mischievous nature, for he was always game for a jest and a bout of good-humoured wrestling, which stood in contrast to a fearsome temper to which he could switch in a blink of an eye. Robert de Hauteville was mercurial, not much given to open disclosure of his thinking, and as brave as a lion, a man to inspire love in many and loathing in others, generous one second and as mean as the most grasping miser the next.

Now they were close, Ademar could see in the midst of the familia knights a fellow in a scuffed leather jerkin and woollen leggings, bareheaded, filthy and chained to the pommel on his saddle and his stirrups. To Ademar's mind Peter of Trani, who also held the title of Lord of Corato, deserved to be strung up to the nearest tree for his betrayal of his liege lord. It was Robert who had granted him every one of his possessions – the captaincy and high revenues of the important pilgrim port of Trani, as well as the demesne before which they were now assembled.

It was Robert who had shown Peter favour, raised him from one of his body of personal knights to a level to which all of his close followers aspired. The reward was to be betrayed while his liege lord was occupied in Sicily; Peter, in concert with other barons, raising their standards in revolt. Naturally, there were disgruntled Lombards, like those at Noci, who had taken advantage of that to launch their own bid for autonomy and paid a high price for their lack of fealty.

The look of disgust aimed at the prisoner was broken by the *Guiscard*'s gruff voice. 'I had hoped to see you inside those walls, Ademar.'

Was that a jest or a gripe? Ademar could not tell, yet the Duke could not fail to notice his diminished numbers. 'I prefer my head on my shoulders, not raised on an enemy spear.'

The *Guiscard*'s eyes flicked to the firepits where several carcasses were being roasted on spits – wild boar and deer – filling the air with their sizzling juices, and his tone was not benign. 'Yet I see you have attempted nothing but to fill your belly.'

'It was your belly I intended to fill, My Lord. We hunted hard so you would be fed on arrival.'

'Noci you have secured?'

'I presume my messenger informed you of that.' The Duke nodded and slid easily out of his saddle, one of his knights having dismounted himself to hold the bridle. 'He will also have told you of the bravery of your son, given I instructed him to do so.'

The ducal eyes moved to Bohemund and the leonine head nodded, though not with much fervour. 'A veritable Achilles, your man said.'

Robert de Hauteville was a giant in his own right, not accustomed to have to look up to anyone, but as he approached Bohemund he was obliged to do just that: he could not fail to be impressed by his build. Yet there was no way he was going to let that show and, given the youngster was not about to throw his arms around a father he was not sure had regard for him, that led to an awkward interlude.

As their eyes locked Ademar knew there had to be a whole host of thoughts chasing through both minds, for Bohemund was not a bastard by birth; he had been made so by a decision of his father to set aside and declare annulled his marriage to the boy's mother. The *Guiscard* would claim it was brought on by consanguinity – Bohemund's Norman mother Alberada had been too close in cousinage to her husband, and his father had sought intercession from a compliant pope to set her aside. The young man, as well as his elder sister Emma, would always harbour the suspicion that the marriage had been annulled for political concerns, not for any perceived sin against the strictures of Holy Church, for the gap between the annulment being granted and their father's marriage to a new Lombard wife had not been long in gestation.

'You've raised him well, Ademar.'

'I doubt I could have done otherwise, My Lord.'

'I have heard, Bohemund, that you are a paragon, that you do not act as do those of your age: light in the article of wine, not one to carouse and not yet taken up with women? If that is true I wonder if you can truly be of my bloodline.'

'I have never had cause to doubt I am your firstborn son.'

The words 'but not your acknowledged heir' hung unsaid. Robert had two other sons from his second marriage, as well as a wife who was determined that their firstborn child, not Bohemund, should succeed to the dukedom.

'Then it pleases me that you do not disgrace me,' the *Guiscard* replied, before spinning on his heels to look at the walls of Corato.

21

Bohemund, about to speak, felt his brother-in-law's hand on his arm and glancing sideways observed an imperceptible shake of the head. Robert having walked away to examine the defences more closely, Ademar could whisper for restraint.

'What you want to say should not be aired in public.'

'But it must be spoken of.'

'In private, Bohemund,' Ademar hissed. 'Your father is not a man much given to taking pleasure in public humiliation.'

'Have you demanded they submit, Ademar?' Duke Robert called over his shoulder.

'Of course.'

'And their response?'

'They told me where I could stick the shaft of my lance; far enough, they suggested, so I could taste wood in my gullet.'

That engendered a booming laugh, one that would plainly be heard inside those walls, this before the Duke called to one of his knights.

'Reynard, tell the Master of the Host to make camp, though I doubt he needs to be so informed. It seems we must prepare for a siege. Bohemund, when my tent is erected I require you to attend upon me so we can talk. Ademar, we will ride round the walls and when that food is ready my son and I will dine alone.'

'What about your prisoner?'

'Lash him to a tree, facing the sun, with no food and no water.'

'My Lord,' Peter of Trani protested.

That got him a hard look. 'Think yourself lucky I do not strap you to an anthill and leave you to rot, which is what you deserve.'

The ride around Corato was made to the accompaniment of endless jeers from the battlements, the usual insults heaped upon the supposed attributes of Robert's mother and the various creatures she had lain with to produce him, that added to imperfections of his own being, not one of which he had not heard flung in his direction time and again from stouter walls than these. Compared to some of the fortified places he had captured – Bari, Brindisi, Palermo and just a week previously Trani – Corato amounted to no more than a nuisance, yet it was an irritant that could keep his army here for an age.

The *Guiscard* had no doubt he could take the place, but the building of siege towers took time, ladders less, but they were not likely to be as quickly successful. This revolt by a number of his own barons had cost him too much time and money already and added to that high summer was coming, which in this part of the world meant a dangerous time to be campaigning, for nothing sapped an army like debilitating heat and the diseases that went with it. They would not come out to face him and Robert knew and told Ademar he needed a quick way to get them to surrender.

'Though I am damned if I can think of one.'

Ademar could only agree, though he did have a suggestion. 'Peter is their suzerain – perhaps he can persuade them to open the gates.'

'And what would he demand in return, Ademar? He would not do it without naming a price, which I would be honour-bound, once promised, to meet.'

The way Robert de Hauteville suddenly pulled up his horse surprised Ademar, who, looking at him, saw a twinkle in those bright-blue eyes, as well as the smile playing around the *Guiscard*'s lips. It was a look he had seen before, the point at which some stratagem occurred to his duke that would hasten him to the result he desired. That it was quickly and wholly formed was made obvious by the way Robert spun his mount and began to canter back to where his tent was being erected, the shouted commands to desist called out well before he made his ground.

'Gather the woodcutters and have them bring every animal skin that they have on their carts.'

Another known trait of the *Guiscard* was that he never explained his trickeries before they were employed, so all his fighting followers watched with deep curiosity as those woodcutters constructed, with saplings and lashings, throughout the morning and into the heat of midday, a long and wide frame, which they then covered with dried animal skins. Robert was in his element, overseeing the design, which he insisted required a strong central panel as well as grips at the rear so it could be lifted and borne forward. Completed, it lay on the ground, looking as flimsy as it undoubtedly was.

If he was happy, not many of those he led shared his joy, for it seemed obvious that their duke was constructing an object behind which he expected them to advance on the walls of Corato. It was true that animal skins, at the point where an arrow was losing its forward force, would stop the point penetrating to wound or kill those behind it, but that was a diminishing protection. Close to and just released from their bows, the arrows had such a high velocity they would punch through the hides, with those to the rear, unable to see them coming, in no position to take action with their shields to deflect them.

Duke Robert's whole army was not happy and that was only assuaged when he called forward his familia knights to tell them they would have the honour of carrying out the assault. There were no leaders as such in this group of elite warriors, but some had the ability to voice an objection, chief amongst them Reynard of Eu.

'As you know, My Lord, it is our duty to follow you wherever you go.'

Robert knew the meaning behind those words, which made his grinning response all the more worrying. 'And so you shall, Reynard, for I shall lead you from the very epicentre of the line we shall form up behind our wall of skins.'

That set up a murmur of doubt amongst them all, but again it was Reynard who articulated their concern. 'How can we protect you?'

'You will not be required to, Reynard, for I can call upon a much better safeguard than your swords and shields.' The *Guiscard* was in high spirits, amused, and he called to Bohemund, his tone larded with humour. 'Perhaps my son would care to join with me?'

Bohemund doubted the wisdom of doing so and it was evident from his expression; that he had no choice, that he knew he was being challenged to risk his body, was made plain by the way he stepped forward with purpose. 'I am at your command.'

'As is everyone here present,' Robert replied. 'But your first task, Bohemund, is to go to yonder tree, untie that wretch Peter who once had Trani, and bring him to me.'

The young man was confused, which altered his countenance, not that anyone else was much wiser. As he went to carry out his father's bidding he could hear him chuckling and, far from finding that annoying, he for some reason felt reassurance. He was not descended from a fool, not the offspring of a man given to uselessly sacrifice his person or the blood of others, but from someone famed for his guile, so it was with less concern he untied the prisoner and brought him to where his father stood.

'Those walls yonder are your walls, Peter, are they not, granted to you by me?' Peter nodded, unsure of what was coming. 'And those holding them are loyal to your title, for if they were not they would scarce hold them against me?' Another nod. 'Then I require you, in

25

duty to me, to order the defenders, your men, to open the gates.'

That allowed the one-time Lord of Trani, whose face had been concerned, a hint of a relaxation. 'You think they would obey me?'

'Have they not sworn an oath to do just that?'

'They have.'

'Then, of course,' said Robert in a jocular tone. 'You did the same to me and yet you broke it. Perhaps you feel your knights will treat you in the same manner.'

'They will not just yield to my entreaty, unless, My Lord, you offer them something in return.'

'Your body in freedom?'

'Would suffice if I would agree, but I do not.' Peter paused, as if what he was about to say had just occurred, which it had not; the thought had come to his mind almost on the first words spoken. 'Restored to my possessions once more, I might be able to persuade them.'

'Oh, Peter, I think you do not do yourself justice. Reynard, Bohemund, lash this wretch to the front of the frame, right in the centre where I have made it strong enough to bear the weight of a man.'

The laughter broke out as this command was obeyed, to reach a gale of amusement by the time Peter was tied hand and foot, spreadeagled over the front of the now raised frame like the blessed St Andrew on his singular cross. He was bleating before they even moved, but that turned to screams for mercy as the whole frame was lifted to progress towards the gates. The defenders, confused at first by the apparition, fired off arrows at long range, which landed in the ground before the lashed victim, to whom it was very obvious that they would soon be hitting the screen, and naturally his unprotected body.

26

His pleas for mercy from Robert turned to loud entreaties, and he ordered in increasing panic that those on the walls should desist and open the gates to the Duke of Apulia. The men carrying the frame walked right up to those gates and, crouching down, laid Peter at an angle from which he could look skywards and address his followers. They had only two choices, to kill him in seeking to force his enemies to retreat, or to open the gates and throw themselves and him on the Duke's mercy.

'You see, Bohemund,' Robert said, as the creaking sound announced that the gates were being opened, 'there is always more than one way to skin a cat, so that when we dine, it will be in Peter's great hall and in company.'

'But we will speak in private?'

'Later, yes,' his father replied. 'But for now I command you to go back and bring forward enough men to secure Corato.'

CHAPTER TWO

The need to examine the state of the defences in the company of Ademar of Monteroni was an excuse; Peter had spent his revenues wisely, the walls were in decent repair and Corato was not a really strategic and important location, more a secure castle with a small garrison to keep the local Greeks and Lombards in check and ensure no trouble when it came time to collect the taxes that filled the ducal coffers. It was also a fortress in which to store the things an army on the march might require to speed their progress on campaign. Robert wanted, before his private meeting, to ask Ademar about his son, to fill out in person those things regarding his upbringing he had received by written communication from the man in whose home Bohemund had spent his formative years.

'I have often wondered if he hates the very mention of my name,' he said eventually.

With the sun slowly setting, they walked the battlements. Ademar, smaller than Robert by two hands, had to lengthen his stride to keep pace with him, and with the night being warm and humid, felt his skin leak. Yet he replied with confidence.

'Not so, My Lord; if you were to question him about your exploits you would find he knows of your actions in detail and also that he recounts them to others with pride.'

'Your wife has not turned him against me, then?'

That induced a temptation to smile, which Ademar took care to hide, for it was a question he was disinclined to respond to; if anyone fulminated against the way she had been rendered illegitimate by annulment it was the Lady Emma of Monteroni. She was a woman who wore every opinion on her sleeve added to a disinclination to hold them to herself. Every time she encountered her father Emma would remind him, without anything in the way of grace, of the way he had abandoned her and her younger brother. Hence she was not called into his presence very often and invitations to visit his capital of Melfi were even more rare.

Robert pushed hard with both hands, feet splayed, at a stone block to check the strength of the mortar, satisfied that it did not yield. 'Yet I hope she allows that I found her a good husband.'

Ademar was known throughout Apulia as the 'Good Marquis'; a sturdy warrior, a captain careful with those he led, uxorious in regard to his wife and just as faithful to his liege lord in a world where the *Guiscard*'s vassals were endemic in complaint about anything they saw as a slight to their prerogatives, not least the need to pay him the assessments rightly levied on their lands. Too many were like Peter of Trani, now locked up in his own Corato dungeon, prepared to engage in outright insurrection rather than cough up their dues in either goods or gold. Ademar was the opposite: a steady fellow, content with that which he held and always quick to answer the call to aid his father-in-law and to put his possessions at his disposal.

The notion that Robert had found his daughter a good husband was risible; they had found each other in a genuine love match, the only curious actuality that her father had acceded to his illegitimate daughter marrying a man whose station at the time – no more than an ordinary lance – was scarce grand enough for the union. That had been rectified by the granting of his title and made more so by an extension of his present holdings around the old and at one time important Roman town of Licea, Lecce to its inhabitants, which having fallen into disrepair, Ademar was now reinvigorating as a regional centre.

'So tell me about Bohemund and not what you have sent by letter.'

In dealing with the *Guiscard*, Ademar had realised many years before that he was not a man for idle gossip; if he posed a question, as he had now, there would be motives behind the enquiry that he would keep hidden. What was he asking and what was he after? Ademar's first response was to be circumspect.

'The word I would use to describe him best is "diligent".'

'A quality, certainly, but is it enough of one in the times in which we live?'

That rejoinder gave Ademar a clue; Duke Robert had many who would oppose him if they could, and not just fractious barons. There were enemies aplenty bordering his domains and even more troubling ones further off in Rome, Bamberg and Constantinople, as well as Saracens in Sicily and North Africa. He was probably seeking to find out what use his bastard son could be to him in such a situation; in short, was he as good a fighter as had been said, was he a leader and most importantly could he be trusted to be loyal to his sire?

'He is much admired, even if he does not engage in debaucheries like his fellows. Out in the field he has, like you, an almost mystical ability to discern what cannot be seen beyond a hill, and when he hunts his eye for locating game is superb.'

Ademar had lost his wager the day they went hunting, but talk of forfeited skins of wine was not appropriate; he stuck to answering the question.

'Men, often those in advanced years to his own, come to him for his views and he is the arbiter of right and wrong with those of his own age and younger. In the training manège your son is paramount, an opponent even his seniors seek to avoid having to contest with, for he is not gentle in mock combat. At the same time he is the first to raise up and praise those he has bested and it seems there is little resentment for the heavy blows and bruises he hands out.'

'He sets an example, then?'

'I would say so.'

'You say he has followed my progress?'

'He closely questions anyone who has ever fought with you. I think you would be astounded by the depth of his knowledge of both your victories as well as your setbacks.'

The thought of the latter clouded the *Guiscard*'s brow for a moment; he hated to think of anything other than victory. 'There must be anger too?'

'If there is, it is well concealed. Your son is the master of his emotions, not a slave to them.'

Robert stopped walking and looked Ademar right in the eye. 'Even when it comes to my wife, the Lady Sichelgaita?'

Ademar took refuge by being ambiguous; he knew if Bohemund loathed anyone, it was a woman he saw as his own mother's usurper, to the point of never referring to her by anything other than an insulting soubriquet, the 'much-larded sow' being his favourite.

'I have never heard his opinion of her – it is not a name that he mentions.'

'I am minded to relieve you of the duty of raising him and take him under my own wing.'

Ademar had the satisfaction that he had guessed right. 'I can think of no place where your son would be happier, and as to raising him, Bohemund is now grown to manhood. Certainly there is bulk to come with added years but he needs no instruction in combat. Leadership, perhaps, but not how to fight.'

'You never call him by his given name of Mark?' the *Guiscard* asked, in an abrupt change of subject, as he began walking again, his shoulders hunched; the impression created was that he had been too open and revealed too much.

'It is not one he would answer to, even with his sister. You gave him the name of the mythical giant when he was a child and he wears it with pride.'

'He was a giant of an infant all right,' Robert said, stopping to face Ademar with a smile of reminiscence. 'Damn near killed Alberada bearing him. Too narrow in the hips, I think she feared to bear another like him.'

They had come full circle to a point above the kitchens and the great hall, from where they could see, now that the sun was near gone, the flickering fires that illuminated the main encampment which had been set up outside the walls, temporary home to the mass of Robert's forces, each blaze under a spit of roasting meat, the smell of which permeated the whole atmosphere.

'Then we shall talk, my son and I, but not yet, for my nose, as well as my grumbling belly, tells me it is time to eat.'

* * *

The great hall of the castle of Corato was neither grand nor overly spacious; this meant, given the number of knights needing to be fed in the presence of their lord, it was crammed. Added to that it was exceedingly noisy, rowdy voices echoing off the bare stone walls as men who felt sure their campaigning was over indulged in the copious supplies of the wine that had been hoarded to quench the thirst of the recently surrendered defenders. They would have consumed to excess anyway, but with no enemy to face the next dawn it was likely to end up with many rendered insensible.

At the high table, set on a dais to dominate the assembly and to his father's left, sat Bohemund, his expression benign and uncritical of what was happening before him. He nursed his half-empty goblet and was quick to put a hand over it when a servitor came from behind ready to refill it from the heavy clay ampoule. Likewise his father was careful in his consumption, if not as abstemious as his son, aware that if he was surreptitiously watching Bohemund, then the examination was mutual.

In between responding to the shouts of his followers, the Duke was working out in his mind what to say to this paragon and he had come to a reasonably swift conclusion that to seek to employ subterfuge, to make excuses or to dissemble would not serve. The boy had no reason to trust him and that was what he required, along with blind loyalty, so he would tell him the truth and watch closely to gauge how he reacted.

Before that could happen, both were obliged to sit through the acclaim heaped upon the mighty Duke of Apulia for his warrior prowess, as his knights sang his praises in drunken orations, their words interspersed with shouted toasts from their companions, each of which had to be responded to. Bohemund observed how his father

33

allowed his goblet to be filled time and again and, just as obviously to one sat close to him, poured the contents on to the flagstones at his feet before rising to drain what was a near-empty vessel in a show of excessive participation. Hours passed as the hall filled with the smoke from torches and their heat added to the crush of bodies, as well as the high night-time temperature, to leave the diners, even in light clothing stained with spilt wine, drenched in sweat.

Robert maintained his place, beaming and returning shouts, as some of his followers began to pass out, while others voided their belly so they could keep drinking and eating. One or two had begun to slip away, the attraction of a waiting concubine greater than the desire to stay and partake of the feast, and still the Duke sat there in what was a deliberate attempt to break his son's calm demeanour, to see him show even a hint of impatience. That he failed was half a cause for salutation, as much as being an irritant to a man who was known to have no fortitude in that area at all. Bohemund stood as soon as Robert did, underlining that he was waiting with some eagerness for what was to come.

The private chamber Robert had chosen was at the top of one of the corner towers, well away from prying ears, accessed by a trapdoor set in bare wooden boards, now closed, with *balistraria* on three sides and lit by tallow wads that smoked enough to hopefully keep at bay any biting insects. Peter of Trani's bowmen had manned these arrow slots earlier in the day; now they allowed a welcome breeze to run through and over the simple cot on which the Duke would sleep, for the *Guiscard* was not a leader who craved luxury.

His first act was to abandon his blue and white surcoat, which bore his ducal coat of arms, then the sweat-stained cambric shirt, to leave him bare-chested, the first and most obvious thing his son

34

observed being the number of red-to-blue weals and scars added to the dents of healed wounds that covered the flesh of his trunk. Then he went to stand by one of the *balistraria*, allowing the air to cool his body.

'You may sit on my cot if you wish. I have no need for you to stand in my presence.'

Bohemund's response was to half park his backside on the angled stones of an embrasure, his bulk completely blocking it, yet the crossed opening too allowed a draught of air to cool his back. Turning and observing where he sat his father frowned, as though he was witnessing an act of disobedience, then his face cleared and he waved his bile away. It was plain to Bohemund he was searching for a way to begin talking and when he did so it was several leagues away from the point the young man thought they must come to.

'When I was your age I was still in Normandy.'

'Driving my grandfather to chew his boots I have heard.'

'How do you know that?'

'Your brother Roger related the tale of your upbringing to my sister. He says Tancred saw you as a sore trial.'

The *Guiscard* grinned at that. 'Roger blathers too much, though what he says is true – my father and I never saw eye to eye.'

'Roger has it that you were too much alike.'

'Does that same blabbermouth tell you why I had to leave?' Robert demanded, leaving his son to wonder at his irritation; was it Roger talking too much or memory? 'Not that I was overly inclined to stay where I was scarce welcome and there was little chance of advancement.'

Bohemund did not reply, which made Robert curious, for the lad could hardly have failed to have heard that the leaving of Normandy had been forced upon him, nor could he be unaware of the dearth of opportunity that had brought his uncles south beforehand. Having been thinking of a way to approach Bohemund throughout the feast, his father now saw a route to entice him into a better understanding of his own life and actions, which might bind him to his cause.

How much of that family narrative did the boy really know, and was what he had heard accurate or part of the same embellishments shouted at him as Duke of Apulia in the great hall? If he had been at war with his father, Robert de Hauteville had not enjoyed one easy relationship with his numerous brothers, at home or in Italy, yet for all of the sibling disputes he was strong on family. Despite all their arguments, when danger threatened they hung together to avoid dangling apart, and to that, more than any other characteristic, could be ascribed their success.

Robert had faith in that as the means to keep secure and expand his possessions, but he was down to a single brother now: the others who had come to Italy had all passed over, while those who had stayed behind in Normandy showed no inclination to travel. In recent times the mixture of disputes and cooperation had been with the aforementioned Roger, the youngest in the family, and he had been leant on heavily when it came to fighting Byzantium, especially in Calabria. Now fully occupied in Sicily, he would only leave the island if the circumstances were so dire it was essential to protect their joint holdings and his line of communication.

'Did you know your Uncle Serlo knifed a high-ranking vassal of Duke William at his castle of Falaise, when weapons and their use had been expressly forbidden within the walls?'

Bohemund did not respond, forcing his father to continue and leaving him to wonder at what he had previously heard. 'To avoid the rope he had to flee for the deed and I was obliged to depart, sharing as I did his guilt by association, given I was with him when murder was done. Serlo went to England to fight with the Saxons, I came here to Italy and to a cold welcome.'

Robert laughed suddenly, filling the small chamber with the sound. 'My brothers were not cheered by my arrival. I was seen as a nuisance and shoved off to lawless Calabria where my men and I were reduced to living off my stirrup leathers. It was not a happy or glorious time.'

He paused then, possibly expecting Bohemund to comment, but the young man continued to hold his tongue as his father's mind filled with images of those years of struggle, of his crabbed half-brothers, never adding to his thoughts of them and the way he had been treated that he had been more than half at fault for his brash way of diminishing them – even William Iron Arm, the steady, shrewd genius who had first engineered the rise in the family fortunes, going from a mere mercenary lance to being called the Count of Apulia in a decade. William had been murdered, to be followed by the irrepressible Drogo, another brother destined to fall to an assassin's blade, unarmed while exiting a church that he had endowed and had built in memory of his favourite saint.

Next came miserable Humphrey who had succeeded them to the title they had taken, aided by compliant Geoffrey, the oldest, yet content to be subordinate to whoever held the honour. Not fiery brother Mauger; he had been bred for contention and died wrapped in complaint for being passed over in favour of Humphrey, who had won for the family acknowledgement of a title they had taken upon themselves, being granted his gonfalon by a reigning pope.

On his deathbed and with ill grace but shrewd judgement, Humphrey ignored his own infant son Abelard and passed the

37

leadership of the Apulian Normans, as well as his lands and titles, to Robert, the only man who could hold it. Finally Roger, the apple of Tancred's eye, now Count of Sicily, had come south, to be alternately a thorn in his flesh as well as Robert's right arm for years. Given everything the family held had been acquired, even as they squabbled in concert, right at that very moment, in the recollections of their joint endeavours, Robert felt alone.

'You're right to say my father and I were at loggerheads and it may be for the reason you say, though he was forever dribbling on about his exploits when in his cups, telling me about his campaigns against the Moors and the Saxons, though he seemed to spend most of my growing years in dispute with his most potent neighbour instead of finding positions that would ensure my brothers and I could raise ourselves.'

Which was necessary; Tancred had bred too many sons for the petty barony he owned: a few dozen fields worked by tenanted villeins, others for his horses and cattle, the lordship of Hauteville-le-Guichard, a small hamlet that lay beneath the manor house and wooden motte-and-bailey bastion into which all of his children had been born, that later turned into a stone tower paid for by those successful mercenary sons. He possessed the fishing rights on a stretch of the river as well as some salt pans on the rugged western coastline, and there was too the entitlement to appoint the parish priest, who was required also to tutor the family in Latin and numbers. Yet the whole added up to scarce enough to equip those sons with the weapons and mail they needed to call themselves knights.

'There's still scarce enough to feed the rest of the family who stayed behind, without I send them the means to maintain their inheritance.'

'Emma insists our grandfather was a good man, proud and upright, and she intends to name her firstborn son in his honour. She is, as you know, with child now and is sure God will grant her a boy.'

'He was only upright when sober,' Robert replied, seeking to avoid mention of an impending grandson, only to see what he intended as a jest not well taken. 'Certainly he was proud and not beyond reminding his own suzerain of his failure to honour the commitments made by his dead brother. I was present when he did so and you would have wondered, to hear him, who was Duke of Normandy and who was Lord of Hauteville.'

It had been a stony confrontation, just before a battle in which Tancred had led William and Drogo into their first proper engagement. The *Guiscard* could not claim to be a cousin to the Duke, he being from Tancred's second marital union, but William and Drogo, being born of an illegitimate sister to their suzerain, claimed that right. The promise referred to was to take them both into the ducal service as familia knights, from where they could hopefully rise to their own lands and titles by good and faithful service.

'You're named after Duke Robert, are you not?'

'I am,' the *Guiscard* hooted, 'and when I write to his son, I address him as "cousin" at every chance that presents itself, which I hope he chokes on.'

There was an unspoken truth hanging in the air, with Robert looking keenly at Bohemund to see if he would make reference to it, the burning tallow in the sconce at his side throwing gruesome-looking shadows over his face; William of Normandy, now styled King of England, was also referred to, if not in earshot, as the Bastard of Falaise, having been born outside wedlock, yet he had inherited fully his father's land and titles.

'Is it true that your namesake murdered his brother to take the dukedom?'

'What does it matter if it is true or false, given so many see it as likely? I think my father believed it to be true. He always referred to him as Robert the Devil.'

There was a temptation to elaborate then, to refer to Duke Robert of Normandy's then tenuous hold on his title, with so many of his vassals, like Tancred, suspicious that he had come to it by poisoning his elder brother Richard. On the day following the dispute with Tancred, prior to leading his host into battle, Robert the Devil had named his bastard William as heir to the dukedom and made every one of his vassals swear fealty by acclamation, but that was a slender oath to make to a child only five years old and one too easy to break.

Tancred suspected the Duke would not give employment to his sons for fear that they carried a measure of the same blood as William and would seek to usurp power if he died before the boy had grown to manhood. That is what came to pass, and who can say what would have happened if William and Drogo had remained in Hauteville-le-Guichard? Robert of Normandy was dead two years later and his bastard son, however successful he had been subsequently, had held on to his inheritance with great difficulty; given their bloodline and their subsequent rise to prominence, perhaps it was wise to refuse close service to the de Hauteville brothers.

'After that confrontation, and denied any prospect of service with the Duke, William and Drogo left for Italy, but know this: before they did Tancred made them swear never to raise their swords against each other or to do one another harm. It was at the time, and still is, I daresay, not unknown for brother to kill brother in Normandy without a desire for anything so grand as a dukedom. That oath he administered to each and every one of us who left the Contentin and it is one we held to, though the Good Lord knows sometimes it was a trial for me to keep my word.'

Robert slapped the cold stone wall hard. 'If we have risen as a family then to that must be ascribed much of the reason, but know this, Bohemund. There is not a Norman lance in my domains that sees it as a natural duty to bow the knee to a de Hauteville. They will not say it in my presence but there are many from families who hold that they are superior in blood to us. We have what we have because we have fought for it.'

'I have been told that it required a fair amount of cunning as well.'

'That too, and if I am known as the *Guiscard*, then the best of your uncles were just as crafty as ever I have been.'

'I look forward to hearing from you of their exploits.'

'Do not pretend to me you have not heard of them from others.'

'There is a difference as to the memories of one who shared their exploits.'

'Ademar speaks highly of you.'

'An opinion I would return in full measure.'

'All this talk of family, Bohemund, what does that tell you?'

'That if we are to hold what we have, Father, as well as extend it, that can only be achieved by the same combination which built the triple dukedom in the first place.'

That admission of his paternity, as well as the acknowledgement of the need for the unity of blood, rendered much of what Robert had intended to espouse unnecessary; his son had reasoned that his father wanted him by his side and he also had discerned why. The *Guiscard* was famed for never trusting anybody unless he was obliged to do so by circumstances. That was the way it had been with all of his brothers, all the way down to Count Roger, but if he ever reposed faith in anyone it was one who shared his blood. Could that be carried on through another generation?

'I feel the need to walk, Bohemund. My words come more easily when my feet are moving.'

CHAPTER THREE

The trapdoor was lifted and both made their way down the stone steps to the arch that led on to the wooden stoop that ran along the battlements, where previously Robert had questioned Ademar of Monteroni. The parapet was lit by flaring torches with a man-at-arms standing sentinel every twenty paces; the lack of a known enemy close by did not interfere with what was set practice for an assembled host. Likewise there were mounted pickets out in the approaches to Corato with orders to look out for threats; the Duke of Apulia had enemies in abundance outside those who had so recently broken their oath of fealty.

He began to talk of them now, taking no cognisance of what Bohemund might already know; best to have it all out to ensure he fully understood what his father had to contend with. The province of which Robert was overlord had been carved out, over twenty-five years of continual warfare, of possessions that had either been held by Byzantium, been fiefs of the Holy See or tenuously claimed by the Holy Roman Empire, and they had been hard won. Sicily was a separate affair, for on that island they had fought the Saracens under the auspices of a papal banner – the same holy banner that had been granted to the Christian monarchs of Spain – in what Rome saw as a crusade to push back the infidels who had invaded both Sicily and the Iberian Peninsula centuries before to desecrate churches and turn them into mosques.

Such a banner did not imply any love for the Normans or the *Guiscard,* him especially; it was more a piece of papal pragmatism that would allow any subsequent pontiff to claim to be the island's suzerain should the Normans of Apulia succeed in turning out the Saracens. Outside that campaign he was in constant dispute with Rome and suffering excommunication, not for the first time, over the jointly claimed Principality of Benevento. Added to that were the depredations of many of his followers in the Abruzzi, where it was said, thanks to their banditry, that no man was safe to travel for fear of being robbed down to his very small clothes.

Rome's demand that this cease had only been met in recent months because Apulia needed all its fighting men to put down the revolt, and it would shortly be resumed; as far as Robert was concerned, it was best if any of his unemployed knights sought their plunder outside his domains, not within them.

The bulk of that quarter-century of fighting had been spent in wresting the province they called Langobardia from the Byzantine Empire, who had not surrendered control without a long and arduous contest, while taking the great port cities had led to siege after siege. The one that ended with the capture of the most important, Bari, lasted four whole years and strained the *Guiscard*'s tactical genius to

44

the very limit. Every success had been followed with a reinvasion by an enemy that refused to lie down; cities and lands had been lost and recaptured for the very simple reason that the provinces of Apulia, Basilicata and Calabria dripped with fertile wealth, most notably oil from the endless olive groves. From Constantinople he felt he had, at present, little to fear if you set aside the gold they employed to bribe his vassals, of which the Eastern Empire seemed to have an endless supply.

'Thank God, since Manzikert they lack the leaders and men to trouble me on their own.'

When word came from Anatolia, that disastrous battle, eight years previously, it had shocked the whole of Christendom to its foundations; the flower of the Byzantine army utterly destroyed by the Seljuk Turks advancing inexorably out of Asia Minor, the reigning emperor, Romanus IV Diogenes, taken captive, which led to a coup in Constantinople and one of his generals, Michael Dukas, taking the purple. Having done so, he was in no doubt as to the weakness of the Empire and he had written to both Rome and Apulia seeking support.

'Michael Dukas sought from the Pope a Christian army that would fight the infidel, perhaps one strong enough to reverse the gains the Turks had made. The bait was his good offices to help to heal the rift between the two branches of the faith. The offer to me was more about holding his borders than pushing the Turks back. Three times he wrote and twice I did not reply.'

'Why?'

Robert laughed. 'If you had ever received a letter from a Byzantine emperor you would not ask; the language of flattery is enough to make a decent man vomit and if they have perfected anything it is the art of the vague promise. There were hints of high and profitable

45

office without any commitment. In the second letter ideas were again more floated than solid regarding an alliance by marriage to one of Michael's family. My silence forced them to be definite and the third time their letter included a proposal they knew I would be a fool to refuse.'

Knowing all this, Bohemund cut in to hurry his father on. 'The hand of one of your daughters, for Constantine, Michael's son.'

Robert had accepted that with alacrity, sending east his youngest, Olympias, a child of three, to learn their ways and to have her name changed to Helena as she was instructed in the Orthodox rite.

'Yet it was not an alliance, more a promise of future amity,' Robert insisted, as he took up his tale in a way that ignored the interruption, maintaining he was not concerned.

Byzantium now had too much on its plate, both internally and externally, to reinvade Italy, but they still had agents willing to spread around money to foster trouble, often with his vassals but especially amongst the Lombards, in order to keep a past and possibly future enemy off balance. Of that latter race the *Guiscard* was scathing; at one time the Lombards had been fierce conquerors of the land he now held. Over the five hundred years since they had crossed the Alps they had become not only flabby but racked by suspicion, mistrust and endless betrayal.

Never able to agree on a leader, the Lombards of Southern Italy had first been conquered and turned into imperial vassals by the Byzantine Greeks, then held in servitude while evincing a burning desire to recover what they had lost. They had fomented incessant uprisings under the banner of the western city states such as Salerno, Naples and Capua, only to find, when they looked like they might find success, their supposed leaders being bought off by enemy gold or betraying each other out of a determination to take over the direction of the revolt. After decades of crushing defeats they had sought help, paying the Normans to come south and win their battles, yet their disunity, in contrast to the cohesion and fighting skill of those they had engaged as mercenaries, meant that they now paid those revenues to Norman overlords who were more assiduous in collection than had been their Byzantine predecessors.

The other threat was a distant one, in Bamberg, the seat of the Holy Roman Emperor, where the heir to Charlemagne held his court. He could command a host large enough and of such abilities in combat as to make even the Normans cautious, but between Apulia and the Western Empire lay Rome, not only physically but also as a place that occupied almost the whole of imperial attention. The seat of incalculable wealth, the papacy had at its disposal vast spiritual power, but that did not go uncontested and such disagreements came to the fore in the election of the Pope. The Western emperors insisted that any candidate for investiture must have their approval; the more bellicose members of the Curia maintained it was a matter for them alone and none of anyone else's business, particularly a layman, however grand his title.

That was not a position agreed to by either the population or the senatorial families of Rome, ever ready to bribe the mob to support one of their blood to the highest ecclesiastical office, for the very good reason that it was the fount of prosperity, as well as the giver of wealthy benefices to the elected man's relatives. The result was too often a split, with two popes in contention, one either the Emperor's choice in conjunction with the Roman aristocrats, or the candidate from the Curia supported by those same elements who peopled the Roman Senate; they shifted their backing to wherever they saw personal or family advantage.

The so-called investiture crisis had been bubbling for almost as long as the Normans had been in Italy and showed no signs of abating. The ecclesiastical fight was led now by Archdeacon Hildebrand, a low-born but cunning Lombard who had risen from mere monk to become advisor to a succession of pontiffs. Strong in the cause of papal independence, he stood four-square against imperial interference in a battle the *Guiscard* had often thought those Hildebrand served might have let die down for the sake of peace. But the major difficulty was that men came to that office in their advanced years and were therefore inclined to expire instead of enjoying the long reign that might have solved the problem by extended negotiation.

If the Curia elected one pope, the Holy Roman Emperor would bring on the election of a rival, his preferred candidate, so it was ever a troubled responsibility full of splits and strife; Hildebrand's pope was likely to spend as much time under siege in the Castel St Angelo as enjoying the comforts of the Lateran Palace, either hiding from the wrath of the Emperor or the easily aroused Roman mob, while trying to deny the claims of the imperial antipope. With the last two pontiffs it had been Norman military pressure, given in return for the confirmation of their titles, that had allowed them to serve out their terms.

'It is that which keeps them from combining, Bohemund. I have no need to remind you, that if we wrested the lands we hold from Byzantium, the titles were granted to us from the papacy.' A discernible nod was all that was required in response. 'And you will also be well aware they were not originally granted out of generosity but unwillingly extracted from Pope Leo after Civitate.'

There was no need to relay to Bohemund anything about that battle, which for the forces of the papacy ranked with Manzikert. The

Normans of Italy, from both Capua and Apulia, under the leadership of Humphrey de Hauteville, had been ranged against and massively outnumbered by a combination of a Byzantine army and a papacy that for once had imperial contingents from Bamberg, as well as the rulers of Northern Italy south of the Brenner Pass, all combined to finally put paid to Norman depredations in Southern Italy.

Civitate is where the combined forces sought to force a decision, but the Normans got themselves between the arms of the enemy and kept them apart, which allowed them to fight against less daunting odds, though even then they had many fewer men than their opponents. But they had that one tactical gift their enemies lacked: cohesion, and the Norman victory was overwhelming – a powerful force of Swabians provided by the Emperor died to a man – and the subsequent rout resulted in the capture of Pope Leo. He was obliged, he later maintained coerced, into granting the Norman leaders legal rights to both the lands and titles they had taken by main force, this while the Byzantines melted away. The Battle of Civitate had secured the Norman place in Italy and formed the cornerstone of what Robert now held.

'And for all we laud it, let me tell you we must have had God on our side. If we had lost that battle every Norman in Italy would have been lucky to see their homeland again. More likely our bodies would have been hung from every available tree, as the Romans were wont to treat those they defeated. Every pope since Leo, instead of confirming us as they have, would take what we gained there back and see us damned if they had an army.'

'But they do not.'

'Which is not to assume they never will. If Leo, God rest his soul, once gathered a host to seek to dislodge us, another may do so again and that goat Hildebrand hates us as much as he hates Bamberg. I repeat, it is only dissension that keeps our enemies weak to both the east and the north.' There was a moment when Robert seemed to brood, as though disinclined to be open about the trend of his thoughts. 'What do you know of Richard of Capua?'

The abruptness of that enquiry startled Bohemund somewhat; it was like being back in the Monteroni schoolroom in which he had been taught Latin and Greek by the monk Ademar had employed, a fellow of short temper and an abiding love of physical chastisement when answers were slow in coming and spittle-filled fury when his charge refused to answer. Even with that memory uppermost there was no choice but to respond.

'He is all-powerful in Campania, is wed to your sister and was allied with our family at Civitate. It was with his uncle, Rainulf Drengot, that our family first took mercenary service.'

Robert nodded but did not immediately respond; it was as if he was pondering on that history. William and Drogo de Hauteville, newly arrived from Normandy, had first been engaged as lances by Richard of Capua's uncle, then styled Lord of Aversa, though as was common with Normans at the time it was a title taken, not granted by any higher power. William had risen through sheer prowess to become Rainulf's right-hand man; indeed it was he who had secured for him recognition of his Aversa gonfalon, in the process bringing about the fall of the Lombard Prince of Capua.

There had been scant gratitude for his efforts; Drengot had come to resent the de Hautevilles, now five in number and much admired, seeing them as a threat to his position, which had led him to conspire at their downfall with Guaimar of Salerno, Sichelgaita's father. William had cunningly outfoxed both to become an even greater rival to Rainulf's power and, in time, not only his equal but superior in the land he held and the forces he could muster. After Drengot's death his possessions and title had passed to his nephew Richard and for every time Capua and Apulia had cooperated there had been a dozen more times where they had been close to enemies, without either party able or willing to put the rivalry to the ultimate test.

'It has ever been our habit, we Normans, to combine when threatened, as we did at Civitate, though there has never been much love lost between us, even if Richard is my brother-in-law. Never forget he's a Drengot. I suspect in styling himself as prince, he sees us as somehow inferior to him, for he is stuffed with arrogant pride.'

That last opinion came out with a growl, causing Bohemund to pose the obvious question. 'Do you fear him?'

'Only in concert with another of our enemies,' Robert replied. 'We have ever held to our uneasy peace, but now I sense matters have shifted, for this revolt I have just crushed could not have been sustained without outside support and for once I do not see the interference of Constantinople.'

'Ademar was sure Gisulf had a hand in the uprising.'

'And Ademar was not mistaken,' Robert spat.

If there was one name to bring on deep irritation in the ducal breast it was that of the *Guiscard*'s other brother-in-law, the Prince of Salerno. Where Sichelgaita was steady and a helpmeet, her brother was a mischievous fly-by-night who hated him. Gisulf was an insect he could not quite swat, much as he would like to, for Salerno lay too close to the lands controlled by Richard of Capua and he would have to accede to any attempt to put the prince of that city in his place. If his wife did not hate her brother she knew him to be a dolt with an overinflated sense of his own worth, and she always sided with her husband when his follies were exposed.

'Gisulf lacks the means to create such mayhem, while all the information I can glean points to Capua.'

'Did the rebels admit this?'

'No, but priests and monks travel, and when they do, they talk with each other and with those they serve. Many of them serve me, or depend on me to endow their monasteries and churches, and if they cannot say with certainty that Capua is the villain, they have heard many hints to that effect.'

'So all you have is rumour?'

'It is enough,' Bohemund's father barked.

'Is it wrong of me to think proof would be better?'

'How do you find it? Richard would not become involved himself; he would keep it at arm's length, allowing stupid Gisulf to think it was he who was generating trouble, but consider this. If Capuan lands border mine they also border the papal possessions and Rome would very much desire that one seat of Norman power should seek to trouble the other, so in alliance with them he is a danger. There are many things to threaten what we hold, Bohemund, as I have just outlined, but at this moment I see my sister's husband, in combination with Pope Alexander and his slimy helpmeet Hildebrand, as the most pressing. What would be your response if I said that I intend that such a situation should cease to trouble my thinking?'

'Which means the power of Capua must be broken?'

'And that would require every lance I could muster, including my brother Roger.'

There was no doubting the meaning of that statement or the invitation it contained. 'It would be my honour to put my lance into your service once more.'

There was a touch of youthful bombast to that, which had the *Guiscard* suppressing a smile. 'Tomorrow I return to Trani to prepare an expedition against our overmighty and double-dealing neighbour. The task I have for you now is to ride to the borderland where my possessions meet those of Capua.'

'Under whose lead?'

'You shall have the command, Bohemund.'

'Not Ademar?'

'He advises me you are ready to act without him being present.' Seeing the shoulders square, Robert added, 'Choose your own lances, not more than thirty, and I would suggest men close to your own age, who are known to be eager for plunder and much inclined to disobey their elders. Feel free to raid Richard's farms, to burn his crops and interfere with his trade and do not hide that it is you who is the perpetrator. I will let it be known that I have forbidden such acts, but I will also let it be known that you will pay no heed to my commands. I want Richard worrying about you and blind to what is happening further east, to my preparations.'

Robert paused to allow his son to contemplate the action he would carry out, before adding, 'And if he seeks to recruit you to fight against me, which Richard will do, make as if to accept, but do so with no haste.'

'Will he believe that I would betray you?'

'Why not, Bohemund?' his father barked for a second time, turning to return to his chamber. 'You have cause enough, do you not?'

'It is not disapproving to be told that you should be careful what you wish for, husband.'

Sichelgaita of Salerno had strong hands and fingers, well able to ease the pains that assailed her warrior spouse. The bathing pool Robert was relaxing in had been in Trani since Roman times, and if many of his fellow Normans saw such immersion in cool water as risky and likely to soften a man, the *Guiscard* did not; he was wont to remind his followers that the consuls of Ancient Rome had conquered nearly the whole of the known world and bathed daily. A fear of water might serve in the cold and wet climes of Normandy, where it could bring on the ague, but here in Italy it was to be welcomed, especially now that it was edging towards high summer, when the midday heat made the body run sweat even when still and the beating sun could be enough to strike down a man wearing chain mail.

These were the weeks in which no one campaigned, for it was possible to lose a whole army to the kind of sickness that could assail them when the temperatures made the very earth seem to shimmer and the metal parts of a shield too hot to touch. Added to that the river courses dried up, which was no good for a mounted army and thousands of horses that required up to two *sesters* of water per day's march, and that took no account of oxen and donkeys; wells, the only other source, could be poisoned and frequently were by a retreating enemy.

The campaign, when it was launched, would take place once the weather started to cool and the rains filled the lowland rivers, so his conscript Lombards and Greeks could go about their daily occupations until the time came to assemble and be drilled before marching. Training, which for a Norman never ceased, took place in the cool of the morning, and that applied to a duke as much as it applied to the newest lance come south to seek advancement. Robert de Hauteville had been in the sand-covered manège, practising with the men on whom he relied in battle, both mounted and on foot, employing padded lances and hard wooden swords that, when they got through, left heavy bruises, now being soothed and kneaded by his wife. Opponents often asked why the Normans were so successful; such endless preparation was the answer – when it came to an actual battle they were at their peak.

He winced as his wife pressed hard on a long, bluish welt, given to him by one of his knights who had, and this was rare, got through his guard on more than one occasion to strike home. For once, that morning, he had not dominated the manège and even now he felt an unusual degree of lassitude, almost a desire to close his eyes and sleep, not made any less enticing by the way he was being nagged. Sichelgaita, of course, had enquired as to his health – she had noted his weariness – and had her concerns brusquely brushed aside, but he was not feeling himself and his response was tired to a woman whose opinions he usually inclined to treat with great respect.

'You seem certain Bohemund will be seduced by my brother-in-law.'

'The boy hates you, even if you are not told of his loathing.'

'I am told he admires me.'

'You listen too much to Ademar and he is blinded by his regard for his wife.'

From an open arch a breeze came in from the Adriatic, a hot wind from the east that did nothing to ease his lethargy. 'And you think too much like a Lombard.'

Sichelgaita laughed and it echoed off the tiled chamber walls, for it was no slight creature that sat on the pool edge, her feet submerged to the knees. She was a blonde Amazon who could stand toe to toe with Robert, was his equal in height and had a frame to match. Both being huge, it needed a stout bed to hold them and an even more robust construction when they engaged in carnal conversation, for when it came to enthusiasm and frequency in the bedchamber Sichelgaita could match her husband for gusto there too.

'What are you saying to me, husband? That Normans are more faithful to their overlords?'

Normally one to share the humour of such a remark, Robert just shook his head and began to haul himself out of the water, falling back as a pair of servants rushed forward with drying cloths. That was followed by a curse, then a more powerful effort, and once he was upright on the mosaic floor he grabbed a cloth and wrapped it round his trunk, making for the open arch, there to allow the warm breeze coming off the Adriatic to dry his upper body.

'Bohemund will be tested and he will either pass that test or fail it.'

That Sichelgaita prayed for the latter was no secret to Robert; she hated and feared Bohemund, for if his father had monitored his progress as he grew to manhood so had she, and for once it seemed more pressing than normal. To be so tired, so lacking in vigour was unusual, almost novel to the *Guiscard*, who was famous for rarely succumbing to the fevers and agues that afflicted others with whom he fought and marched. Yet at this moment he could feel the ache in his thighs and across his lower back that he knew to be the onset of some kind of malaise. Less normal was the feeling of morbidity, which he forced himself to suppress; he would suffer a few days of discomfort as he had in the past and would then, as usual, be back to his full and formidable strength.

Robert de Hauteville was not one to brood on his own mortality, even if he knew the number of his years and was aware that he was likely to expire before Bohemund and his legal heir. His son Roger, known as *Borsa* for his habit when a child of always counting the contents of his purse, was as yet physically no match for his older half-brother, which was odd given the brute size of his parents. Not that he was tiny; more that he was of an average height instead of a commanding one and showed no sign that he might put on a spurt to alter those dimensions. *Borsa* too had been in the manège that morning and he was, for his fourteen summers, a hearty fighter in contest against those of his own age, though in no way exceptional.

Such limitations extended to his manner, which was reticent where it needed to be bold, and to his father's way of thinking his son and heir was also too inclined to be swayed by priests; the boy spent far too much time on his knees. A pious man by his own lights, the *Guiscard* was of the opinion that God had to be kept in his proper place; no man, not even a pope – and that had been proved too many times to be gainsaid in their own venal bailiwick – could rule by the tenets of Jesus Christ. Robert worshipped regularly and was generous in his endowments, funding abbeys and building churches, while at the same time doing all in his power to spread the tenets of the Roman practice of the Christian religion with which he had been raised by, allowing monks sent by Rome to freely proselytise, but he refused to be a slave to faith.

This he did, notwithstanding his own present state of excommunication – was it the third occasion or the fourth he had been denied a state of grace by Rome? Not that he cared; it was a stricture that carried so little weight in the lands over which he held sway, for most of his subjects were Greeks and still adhered to the Eastern rite which they had practised for centuries. Likewise the Lombards, while those of his own persuasion owed everything they had or could hope for to him. In terms of worship things were changing among his subjects, but slowly and not without resentments that could be added to all the other grievances the ruled held against their Norman overlords.

The entrance of his chamberlain broke the train of thought he was following, a brooding both on his state of grace and his troubled relations with Rome. Here to see him was the man entrusted to ensure that what his master needed to know was put before him in terms that allowed for decisions to be made; his other task was to keep at bay the minor matters that fell beneath the ducal dignity.

'My Lord, I have the prisoner, Lord Peter, in your privy chamber, as you desired. Also there is a communication from Constantinople under the imperial seal that is said to be significant and is for only you to see.'

There was a moment when Robert felt like saying both would be required to wait, but it could not be. There would be much to consider on top of that, for after his chamberlain, and despite all his efforts to ease the burden of ruling, would come his treasurer, then the Master of the Host to report on the state of his supplies, then followed the various leaders he had tasked to plan the training of his forces. After he had dealt with those there would come a number of merchants and traders, ships' captains and guild masters, too important to ignore, supplicants seeking either favours or relief from the customs duties he demanded. Finally, in order that his subjects should know they had access to his largesse and the rule of law, he would need to listen to a whole raft of petitions from those who felt their lives blighted by either the principles he imposed, or the lack of his hand where it was weak.

'Let's deal with the flea first; I'll come as soon as I'm dressed.'

Trani must come at a high price. It may require you to spill your own blood in my service.'

'Yet redemption is possible?'

'All things are possible, including the notion that you might employ the truth.' He addressed his chamberlain, ignoring the look of curiosity his words had engendered. 'Have the armourer strike off his chains.'

Peter was on his knees, stumbling forward to take and kiss Robert's hand, swearing fealty as he did so. He would not have been pleased to see his liege lord's face, which showed just how much credence he put in such vows of faithful service. When Peter was gone, Robert was given the scroll, which bore the imperial seal of Byzantium. That he broke and rolled open to read the Latin therein, which told him that Michael Dukas, the imperial usurper, had been deposed and now languished in a dungeon – the import of that was plain.

Helena, his daughter, had been transferred from the palace to a convent, where he was assured she would be cared for, though not in the luxury to which she had become accustomed. There was no suggestion that she might be returned to Apulia, which was as good a way as any of terming her a hostage. The new emperor finished with a scrawl of a signature, which after much examination the *Guiscard* took to say 'Nikephoros III Botaneiates'.

The thought that Peter of Trani had been lucky was not paramount but it was there; had Robert read this prior to dealing with him, the fit of temper this scroll induced might have seen his liege lord strangle him with his bare hands. Added to that, all his feelings of partial recovery seemed to evaporate as well, leaving Robert feeling even weaker.

* * *

The receipt of that same news from the East caused deep consternation in the Lateran Palace, home to Pope Alexander and the seat of ecclesiastical power in Western Christendom. Not that it roused much ire in the Pope himself, old as he was and much troubled by the summer heat, which exacerbated the stink such weather and a lack of rainfall brought to the great city of Rome. He was content to leave matters to the man he had appointed upon his accession as chancellor to the Apostolic See, indeed the very man who had secured the highest holy office for him; Hildebrand had more than enough energy for them both.

For once the truth matched the depiction, for Archdeacon Hildebrand was truly a remarkable creature and an outstanding administrator. Born in low circumstances – many said he was the son of a peasant, the more generous born of a carpenter – he had risen over twenty years in papal service, by sheer ability and force of personality, to his central position, one in which he held within his hands the entire political and ecclesiastical reins of the most potent office in Christendom. The papacy sat at the epicentre of a web of money and influence: tithes, gifts, pleas for intercession to permit or annul marriages, to confirm or deny titles, never without the gold necessary to oil the wheels. This poured in from all over the continent of Europe to fill the Vatican coffers, while pilgrims of high rank and low came to the Eternal City to seek remission of their sins and were encouraged, if not obliged, to make offerings.

However unbecoming in a supposedly good son of Mother Church, the communication brought from Archdeacon Hildebrand a stream of curses, some of which were downright expletives, for if the message and its revival of a threat from the East had set a cat amongst the pigeons of Robert de Hauteville's proposed campaign against Capua, the words Hildebrand was reading destroyed at a stroke a carefully crafted and long-brewing policy. The archdeacon had many abiding obsessions, notably internal church reforms, like an end to the crime called simony – the selling of ecclesiastical offices. As well as that he was strong on the enforcement of celibacy upon the priesthood – a married priest was to Hildebrand no priest at all – apart from keeping his own position secure, and the church of which he saw himself as the protector safe from external threats or influence.

The first and most immediate obsession over those two decades had been to remove permanently the right of the Holy Roman Emperor to have any say in the election of the Pope, and that had been promulgated, if not universally accepted, by Pope Alexander's predecessor. Nicholas, in his declaration *In nomine Domini*, had laid out the rule which abrogated to the Church itself the right to decide on how a pontiff should be elected and who he should be. No more should envoys from the Eternal City crawl to Bamberg for the name of an appointee or be held to ransom by the aristocracy of Rome; the decision would be made by those qualified to judge the quality of the candidates: the cardinals, the senior bishops and the abbots of the great monasteries.

A second abiding desire was to bring back into the fold of the papacy the Eastern Church and to persuade the Patriarch of Constantinople, seen as the head of that communion, to acknowledge on behalf of his flock that in all matters of the Christian faith the Bishop of Rome was infallible and thus had ever been the head of both congregations – indeed there should never have been two – this being a prerequisite to his eventual ambition of a complete reunion. That centuries of dispute had ended in schism only spurred Hildebrand to work harder for reconciliation – at least, that was his term.

Unbeknown to the archdeacon, the church he controlled was seen as an intransigent bully with its insistence on the use of unleavened bread in the Eucharist; clerical celibacy for all ordained priests in whatever liturgy; that Latin, not Greek, was sole language of the Mass, and that the Patriarch required the consent of the Pope to his position and that same pontiff had the right to nullify his appointments, as well as excommunicate from the faith him and any of his followers, both clerical and lay.

Emperor Michael Dukas had seemed inclined to take on the difficult task of seeking that reunion, and there had been much communication in search of the form of words that would bring it about. Along with his good religious intentions came that request for an army to undertake a crusade to reverse the effect of the Battle of Manzikert: that knights from Europe should take ship for Asia Minor and form the bulk of the forces needed to push back the Turks. It was an appealing idea to Hildebrand, given it would kill two troublesome birds with one stone by removing the pestilential Normans, who he would ensure took a major part, from Rome's doorstep.

Even with the advance of the heathen Turks and the danger to their whole faith, what Hildebrand called reconciliation was not a notion that gained much favour with either the Patriarch or the Greek Orthodox flock, especially in Constantinople itself, where the mob was every bit as large and effective as they were in Rome. For any Byzantine Emperor who sought to impose a set of conditions that would please Hildebrand was to invite for himself instant and violent removal by that same congregation. Yet service to four popes had induced in Hildebrand the kind of flexibility that, once he had calmed his irritation, immediately had him seeking a solution; the overthrow of Michael Dukas was a setback to a policy, not the termination of one.

His first task was to pen for the Pope an immediate reply excommunicating the usurper Nikephoros – that he would pay no heed to this denial of the sacrament did not in any way diminish its effect in Hildebrand's eyes. Then his assistants were called, a dozen tonsured monks, the demand from their master that they find everything that was known about this new claimant to the purple. With many spies in Constantinople, plus a need to be aware of the shifting and tortuous politics of that sprawling empire, the details were soon being studied, this just after he had dictated letters to be sent to his eastern envoys to find out if what he had been told about the fate of Dukas – that he had been imprisoned – was true. It was not common for deposed rulers of that polity to retire in peace, indeed to survive at all; the least they could expect was that they would be ceremonially blinded to prevent any hope of restoration.

Pope Alexander was informed of what had occurred, the problem of the East was discussed and the conclusion of what policy to pursue arrived at. This, apart from the required excommunication, was the paramount need to wait until matters became less opaque. Byzantine was not a commonly used word for nothing; in that particular polity lay a tangled web of alliances and relationships that stood as a mystery to most observers, even those who were relatively well informed by their spies. In Constantinople court intrigue was endemic and had been for centuries, while the succession to the imperial purple was never straightforward – it was too often decided by coup, the secret blade or a doctored potion – and the wearer was often not the real power, for it was many times more necessary to calculate who stood behind the throne as to know who sat upon it.

'And the other inconvenience?'

'Progresses well, Your Holiness – the *Guiscard* blames his neighbour for his recent difficulties. He is, as we speak, gathering his forces to attack Richard of Capua and has even sent to Sicily asking his brother to support him with lances and foot soldiers.'

'And Capua?'

'Is, thanks to us, aware of the threat and arming at an equal rate to defend himself. Naturally he has been in communication with us to provide him with support, Apulia being the more powerful.'

The elderly pope gathered his hands before his lips, either in contemplation or prayer – Hildebrand could not discern which. A conflict between the twin seats of Norman power was as tangled with possible outcomes as anything else with which the papacy had to deal. That mutual destruction was the preferred outcome did not have to be stated; both Capua and Apulia were a concern it would be a blessing to be rid of and it had taken much time to manoeuvre both into a position of impending hostilities – the spreading of rumours, the use of Vatican influence, money and its many bishops, abbots and priests to foster and exacerbate an already existing mistrust between the Normans to the point where they were ready to seek a conclusion on the field of battle.

The hoped-for outcome was that both would be diminished and what the papacy had lost, like control of the fief of Benevento outside of the city itself, could be recovered, the banditti wracking their possessions in the Abruzzi should be thrown out of that province, and that both Norman enclaves should be so beholden to Rome that they would be more supplicants than bullies. Less welcome was the notion that one should utterly subdue the other, thus creating a more powerful single entity. Yet if both Norman overlords presented Rome with a problem, the greatest, at present, was Richard of Capua, for the very simple reason that he was the closest and thus the more dangerous – he could take the city of Rome at will – so it would help if the *Guiscard* clipped his wings.

For every time Richard had aided the papacy – and he had in the past acted as a saviour, not least in securing the position of both Alexander and Hildebrand – there were a similar if not greater number of occasions when he had been the most potent threat at the very gates, while his incursions into borderland papal territories to indulge in outright theft were so numerous as to be a commonplace. Yet if the Duke of Apulia crushed Richard completely, would he not become their neighbour and an even greater threat? The elderly pope had to put aside these silent considerations; Hildebrand was speaking.

'I have encouraged Gisulf of Salerno to continue to openly support Capua.'

'He is a feeble prince, Hildebrand; if his deeds matched his boasts it would be him we have to fear, every one of his and our enemies would be as dust.'

Hildebrand could only agree with that; Gisulf of Salerno was a shoddy prince, both a capricious ruler and a useless warrior who, despite his manifest failings, saw himself as a new Caesar. He was wont to conjure up in his imagination great hosts which he would lead to victory – the means did not exist in either the numbers he could actually raise, or in his ability to inspire them. Gisulf was a buffoon, more of a pawn in the chequered board of South Italian politics than a meaningful entity, and it spoke volumes of the lack of physical force the Vatican could bring to bear that it was necessary to seek his aid. Added to Gisulf's military weakness was his way of lining his pockets by what amounted to near piracy, the ships of Salerno combing the seas to attack trading vessels from the likes of Pisa and Amalfi, both of whom complained bitterly to Rome but to no avail – even if the papacy despaired of his depredations, Roman trading vessels from the port of Ostia were no safer.

'Whatever the outcome,' Hildebrand added, reinforcing the thoughts of the Pope, 'the contest is going to enfeeble whoever is come closest to victor, and that cannot but be a good thing.'

Bohemund had gathered his band of thirty knights, formed in three conroys of ten each, one of which he led personally, and had left Calore as swiftly as he could muster men, mounts and supplies; he had no trouble recruiting lances, for when it came to plunder, every Norman in the *Guiscard*'s army was keen to take part and many were disappointed to be left behind. The newly captured town was closer to Campania than Trani and there seemed little point in assembling there and having to retrace his steps. He therefore had no knowledge that events in the East had affected his role; with a new emperor in Constantinople and one whose disposition was a mystery, Duke Robert no longer felt comfort on that flank, which was alone enough to make him cautious about acting aggressively in the west.

To invade and conquer Campania he would be required to denude the Adriatic coast, so wisdom dictated that matters be delayed until the situation in Byzantium became clear. The notion of an invasion he could discount – this new emperor would have too many other troubles on his plate – but the loss of a possible marital alliance did mean that the Eastern Empire might, once more, be fully active in fomenting trouble amongst his quarrelsome vassals, and that he must guard against. Yet no message was sent to Bohemund; Robert did nothing to rein in his bastard son, keen as he was to see how he fared as well as offering a test of his loyalty.

Such ignorance of events found Bohemund and his conroys on

a small tributary not far from the eastern bank of the River Ufita, about to cross into the rolling and fertile uplands ruled from Capua. The aim was to destroy the smaller and less defensible outposts and watchtowers that owed fealty to Prince Richard, emptying his granaries, removing the stored ampoules of oil and wine, while letting run wild the spare mounts that were kept in his borderland stud farms, the very means by which he could mount and sustain a campaign in defence of his possessions.

On the first stage of their journey it was natural that when they rested they did so with the Duke of Apulia's vassals, but as they approached the border that ceased and they camped as if already on campaign. As soon as they crossed the Ufita the alarm would be raised; thirty strange lances and over a hundred horses – for each conroy had a quartet of young squires who would one day be warriors themselves – could not move without provoking a reaction.

'We must anticipate the local forces will gather to hunt us down. They will try to take us before we do any harm.'

These words had been spoken by Reynard of Eu, who led one of the conroys at Duke Robert's insistence – if his father had set Bohemund as the leader of these exploits, he was not dull-witted enough to do so without the inclusion of someone of more experience to provide advice; his son was, after all, only just turned seventeen. What Reynard had said could not be gainsaid, for Bohemund knew as well as his father's familia knight that such behaviour would not be allowed to go on unchallenged, and part of the young leader's task was to ensure that he took every precaution against being surprised by a superior force of lances.

That was a thought that had troubled Bohemund since the day they set off and where he could he had sought advice from those who had previously raided these territories, because for all Duke Robert's precautions, no invasion could be mounted entirely by surprise; Richard of Capua had to be too canny for that, so those border vassals would be on the alert for anything likely to affect both their security and that of their master. Against such a possibility they would, however, have limited strength; such frontier settlements had no great band of knights to protect them. The bulk of the Capuan forces, those Norman lances that would quickly coalesce into a powerful host, lay closer to their major possessions such as Aversa and Capua itself, while those on the extremities would be mainly locally recruited Lombards or Greeks with a small leavening of Normans to stiffen their fighting ability.

'Then let us make sure they seek us out, Reynard, with the certainty they know where we are.'

'You mean to bring them to a contest?'

'If I can do so, yes, but my ultimate aim is to create a period when we can roam freely and at will.' Before the older man could analyse what he was being told, Bohemund added, 'So before we so much as torch a farm we must do some careful reconnaissance.'

The maps Bohemund had brought with him were copies of those made by the surveyors of the Roman Empire, and no group had been more assiduous in ensuring the accuracy of what they recorded. Thus, if the nature of the landscape had changed through human activity – the Lombards had taken to themselves the best land, created bigger farms and also extended a settlement as well as built a strong fortress at Grottaminarda – the contours had not, so every hill and valley was recorded, as well as the locations of open country, forest and the streams that fed the river, the latter two features of paramount value to a marauding band. Thankfully, here in the uplands, those watercourses flowed well even in summer.

The local magnate, the most potent of Richard's vassals, would reside in Grottaminarda, for it was through there the trade routes ran east and west and the collection of toll revenues was both easy and profitable. It was a location too well sited and formidable to even contemplate attacking, but even if a force from there sallied forth to put a stop to their activities it would not amount to the whole available strength; no sensible commander would denude his main base of fighting men when it was essential it be defended and held. Policy dictated the man in charge send out a small body of fighters, backed up by messengers to the outlying forts and towers, taking a small contingent from each to make up a force of enough size to hunt down intruders and crush them.

Initially only a trio crossed the river: Bohemund and Reynard accompanied by a squire and one packhorse, leaving behind mail and helmets, dressed in the kind of dull woollen garments favoured by non-fighting men and walking as much as riding, never doing the latter with anything above a trot. Bohemund studied his maps and employed a natural eye for terrain that seemed bred into him. They stayed out of sight as much as possible, avoiding the lower ground where the farmers toiled, using the ridges to gain a view of their proposed pillaging grounds, which included the identification of places to raid as well as a good location to offer battle to those who would come to stop them.

A number of the elevated outcrops had a stone watchtower, built on the site of Roman predecessors and so rudimentary they could only be manned by very small parties of armed men, perhaps six or eight, with only half of them mounted, given there was scarce room to stable horses for more, which left them poorly equipped to defend the land around from banditry. That was not really their task outside petty transgressions; they were in place to overawe a less than contented Greek peasantry and also to ensure that a proper portion of what the farmers grew went to their overlord, and through him to their prince.

These watchtowers radiated out from a quartet of bigger bastions which they were careful to observe from afar, though none with a garrison above perhaps thirty to forty, while half of what they were tasked to protect lay outside the security of the walls: fenced-off pasture for horses and cattle, barns for storing grain and wines, these the very articles Bohemund and his party were intent on destroying. With great care, over three days, marks were annotated on his animal-skin map, working out a plan to both raid and fight; satisfied, the trio rode back into his father's territory.

CHAPTER FIVE

The following dawn the whole party crossed into the lands of Capua and made for a large farm within long sight of the chosen target, one of the outlying watchtowers. Having turned out the occupants – the tenant and his extended family, who held their land direct from the local magnate and no doubt bore down hard on their peasantry – they rounded up those working in the fields and invited them to loot what goods were stored in the barns. Then they were required to create a pile of hay higher than two men around the buildings, which was soaked with oil and, when laced with tar, set alight, sending, once everything was ablaze, a long pall of black smoke into the air.

Leaving twenty of his men to keep it going, Bohemund, proudly wearing his family surcoat and under his father's banner, led one conroy to a point at which he could cause the maximum fright to anyone coming from the watchtower to investigate, this a long and wide clearing, noted on his Roman-era maps, in which they would sight his men with enough time to turn and flee. It was close to a farce the way it played out; two slovenly horsemen in stained leather breastplates, armed only with short swords, rode out of the distant trees to see ahead of them a full conroy of ten Norman lances, who immediately dropped their points and began to trot forward, the sound of their battle horn piercing the air. For all the men from the watchtower were on low-grade mounts, they were animals more speedy than those of the men they faced, destriers bred for sturdiness in battle rather than being fleet of foot, rarely set above a fast canter.

Sure they had a good head start, Bohemund called a halt to let his other lances join him, they alerted by the very horns which had induced panic in the men who had fled, and together they rode, without haste, through the dense woods that surrounded the hill on which stood the target watchtower. The bulk of the force remained hidden while Bohemund took his single conroy on to the open ground before that less than formidable structure, there to dismount, remove their helmets and wait.

A quartet of swarthy, unshaven faces greeted their arrival, peering over the parapet, and sure that relief was on the way – if Bohemund had it right a mounted messenger would have gone to gather reinforcements – they were rudely defiant, with a couple balancing on the rim of the wall to show their bared arses. More importantly, one of the others, on sighting their approach, had immediately set light to a pre-prepared and smoky beacon, set in an iron brazier, that rose high above the parapet, the means by which they would alert their neighbouring towers that an enemy was at the door.

At a slow trot and bareheaded, Bohemund rode round the tower outside the range of a cast lance, as if looking for a point at which to attack, a foolhardy notion given the numbers on show. Since his lack of years was obvious at such close quarters he was subjected to many an insult regarding the need to be milk-fed and to have his arse wiped, jibes that were extended to his equally young band of warriors by men who knew they had little to fear. Not that he had any intention to initiate an assault on something an army would bypass; properly manned, even such gimcrack structures could take time to subdue, cost serious wounds and even lives in the taking, which could only be done with ladders or by undermining the walls.

The entrance to the main chamber was well above head height and the ramp that led to it had been withdrawn inside. From there a staircase rose to the fighting platform on top of the tower while an internal walkway led down to the stables and storerooms, probably with enough supplies to hold out for more than enough time to be reinforced. As if nonplussed about how to proceed, and to even louder mockery from the parapet, Bohemund withdrew his men into the woods until they too were out of sight, calling to his entire party to gather round him. Up till now he had not outlined his intentions even to Reynard – wise, given he had no idea if what he had calculated up till now would work. But the reaction so far had been what he had wished for; it was time to describe what he hoped would follow.

'Why light that beacon?' Bohemund asked, only to answer his own question. 'There has to be a local plan of defence that is triggered by any attack on any tower and it is my intention to turn that against our foes.'

As their leader explained his proposal to his young compatriots, he did so with the odd look at Reynard of Eu to see how his words were being received in that quarter. The familia knight did not speak, did not rush to say what the titular leader should do. In that he was following his master's instruction to give the boy his head unless he proposed something absolutely imprudent and likely to lead to disaster. Many would have accepted such an order and then disobeyed it, but the *Guiscard* had chosen his man well.

'The other towers have been alerted by that lit beacon and will be at this moment arming themselves to come to the aid of these fellows yelling insults at us, perhaps with half their number, but they will not just charge to the rescue. When the messenger reaches the castle at Grottaminarda, which must be his destination, the fellow who holds that for Capua will detach a small force that will pick up numbers on the way, sure by the time they reach this point they will be strong enough to drive us off.'

'Not if we give them battle,' one of the youngsters cried, a fellow called Ligart with flaming red hair who had proved on the way from Calore to have a touchstone temper, which looked about to flare up as Bohemund shook his head.

'Not here, Ligart – we will take them on the way, which is why so much time was spent scouting for the best site. This watchtower was not chosen at random; to get to it from the west any relief should pass through a deep-sided and heavily wooded valley and that is where they will meet us.'

'Thinking we number but one conroy?' Reynard asked, though in such a way that it was obvious he knew the answer; that was why Bohemund had only let that one group of ten lances be seen.

Bohemund just smiled, not wishing to say that if he was going to impress his father, then it was just as important to demonstrate tactical cunning as the ability to fight and win. 'That is what they will see facing them, one conroy, but in the trees on both sides, hidden from view . . .'

The rest was left unsaid, for the reason that to speak it was unnecessary, but Reynard thought he spotted a flaw and it was he who raised it. 'There must be a signal that tells the supporting towers the one we face is no longer threatened.'

'I agree,' Bohemund replied, 'which is why our squires will stay close and let themselves be seen from time to time wearing mail and surcoats. At a distance they will not look younger than the knights those buffoons on the parapet observed earlier. When the sun goes down they keep lit enough fires just inside the trees to indicate we are still present.'

'They may sneak out to investigate?' one voice proposed.

'No, their safety lies in doing nothing and waiting.'

Speaking softly he outlined the results of his reconnaissance, which included a calculation of how long it would take a hard-riding messenger to cover the nine leagues to Grottaminarda, using frequent changes of mounts from the watchtowers he passed, added to the time it would take to get the lances from the castle to where he intended to meet them, assuming that those that would join en route would be waiting at a prearranged rendezvous.

'It is close to a day's march and they may well not rush to get here. However, we must be in position before nightfall this very day, for if they come on with haste, at some time on the morrow they will pass through that valley.'

'Numbers, Bohemund.'

The young man looked at Reynard. 'How many men would you send to see off a band of ten?'

There was time to light fires and cook some food, to be both eaten and taken as rations; roasting and baking would not be possible again until the coming fight was over. While that was taking place every man not overseeing the cooking was set to gathering enough dead wood and brushwood, as well as splitting enough logs, to keep those blazing for a day or more. It helped that from the watchtower they would hear the sound of axes thudding into trees, indicating that perhaps timber was being cut for assault ladders. Once the wood stacks were high enough to satisfy Bohemund he led the fighting men and their mounts away from the tower on foot to minimise any noise.

If it was a warm night, it was one in the new encampment, found by the light of moon and stars, that went without a single flame and that continued after sunrise, for even if they could keep the actual fires hidden, the smoke would rise above the trees and excite curiosity as to their source. Much as he tried to keep it from view Bohemund was palpably nervous, which manifested itself in much unnecessary activity, pacing up and down, constantly checking the equipment of those who were well versed in the ability to maintain it, repeatedly asking about the alertness of the sentinels he had set at the head of the valley, until finally Reynard took him by the arm, hauling him well away from the rest of the men, and insisted he settle, given it could be a long time before any fighting took place.

'You have done all you can to prepare.'

'Failure is still possible. What if the relief force chooses another route?'

'Why would they?'

'A clever leader may smell a trap.'

'And if he does?'

'Then it is I who look the fool.'

'Fighting always carries that risk, Bohemund. If one plan fails you must conjure up another, and your father would tell you that. God knows he has been forced to often enough.'

Meant to reassure, it just underlined for the younger man the possibility that all his plans would come to nought, which was not aided by a day that dragged by with no sign of an enemy, which meant another night in which all his men could consume was the leftovers of what they had saved from their last cooking. Having called in his lookouts – the relief force would not come on in darkness – he sent them out again in the first grey light, with the feeling that if this day brought no sight of his enemy he must look for an alternative way to proceed. Luckily the sun was barely up before news came of the approaching relief force, added to the opinion they would enter the head of the valley within half a glass of sand at most.

'Numbers?'

'Fifty men, all mounted on cavalry horses but with only packhorses as led animals.'

No destriers – moving at speed, then, Bohemund thought, and relying on numbers to chase him away or take him, unless . . . 'Normans or Lombards?'

'Impossible to tell; they are all clad in the colours of Capua.'

'They cannot be Normans, Bohemund,' Reynard insisted, as he observed a degree of hesitation. 'Richard would not so use them.'

'If they are, I could have a short existence as a leader of men.'

That response was accompanied by a grin, to let everyone who could hear and see know that whatever the composition of those they were going to face, their leader was determined to fight them. Orders were unnecessary, given every lance knew where to go and what to do, those tasked to cross the valley floor departing as soon as their prayers were completed, again walking so as to leave no trace of their passing in the thick grass. Reynard, who would attack with his conroy from the left flank, took a hard grasp of Bohemund's gauntleted hand and wished him success.

'That depends on our enemies as much as me.'

'I have ridden into a fight with the *Guiscard* many times. This we are about to do has the stamp of his cunning upon it.'

Bohemund led his men, first through the trees and then, at the far end of the valley, out to take a line across the grassed floor. He was not about to assume whoever opposed him was a fool, and the location for his ambuscade had been chosen not only for the narrowness of the valley but also because of its length, which allowed him to ride forward as though he and his men were progressing to the westwards in search of places to plunder, mounted on their cavalry horses and leading their roped-together destriers and pack animals; it was his task to tempt his foe and break up any cohesion by offering them a tasty morsel they could not fail to consume.

How soon would they come into view? – an important consideration given timing was a guess. He needed to be at least halfway up the valley when sighted and with so few men he could spare no one to act as a sentinel and control his own pace to match theirs. It was therefore not surprising for those of his conroy who looked in his direction to observe his lips moving in silent prayer. In his favour was the strong morning sun at his back, so that he saw his enemy starkly before they could quite make out his party, though that was only worth a sliver of time.

He shouted to halt in a way that carried and, he hoped, conveyed surprise and shock, then immediately waved his hand to order a withdrawal as their superior numbers became plain, hauling his own mount round and kicking hard to make it gallop, his men doing likewise, dragging on their lead ropes to bring along his other two mounts, an act which naturally and dramatically slowed the turn. The next bit of his plan required that his enemy indulge in a swift pursuit and Bohemund's over-the-shoulder gaze was an anxious one.

Whoever commanded was not a man to allow a shapeless charge; down the valley floor the Apulians could hear echoing horns, accompanied by shouted orders as the enemy horsemen fanned out into two lines so that their flanks filled the entire space between the treeline on either side, their aim to ride down and envelop this inferior band. Before long those echoing sounds turned to thundering hooves coming on at a pace which would rapidly close the gap, one which Bohemund, still tugging on his lead rope, watched with concentration. For all the pursuit was swift, it was being carried out in an ordered fashion: if the front line of horsemen was not perfect, it was yet a row of lances acting in unison, getting dangerously close, and that had to be broken up.

The shouted command from Bohemund had his men let loose their destriers and packhorses, not that these animals ceased to dash along with the cavalry mounts, for no horse can see another run without they do likewise, that being instinctive in a prey animal. But roped together they could neither maintain the same speed, nor move in a straight line, so within moments a gap had opened and they were veering right and left, while in one case a pair went over with legs kicking and loud, panicked neighing.

The pursuit now hit that barrier of horseflesh, the riders obliged to swerve to avoid collisions, while they were now chasing men who, having abandoned their encumbrances, were riding as fast as they. With much shouting, the occasional jab of a lance point and even more pile-ups between various forms of horseflesh, the Capuans forced their way through what was now a confused and milling mass. In doing so they broke the continuity of their line and, having forced their horse barrier aside, became bunched in the centre. With all proper formation gone and control impossible by whoever commanded them, the pursuit turned into a ragged mass, in essence a wild charge, with a few lances well out in front of a seething body of horsemen.

The conroys that emerged from the trees let the front runners go by and hit the main concentration of bodies from each flank. Unlike their enemies they were in a perfect formation, moving at exactly the right speed on destriers, the right mounts to impose the maximum impact, while given the way their enemies had clustered into a horde they quite naturally had their lance points facing forwards. The Apulian weapons bore into the mass and drove it inwards, the whole made even more confused as every Capuan fighter sought to get his horse and lance into a position where he might defend himself, often impeding his fellows from saving themselves.

Bohemund's conroy had spun round and now came into the action as another cohesive force, not with lances but with swinging broadswords and axes, he amongst all of them doing massive execution, for the anxieties of the last days had disappeared and all his passion was in his right arm. Men went down to be followed by horses that fell or were tripped by their confrères and into that mass of flesh went weapon after weapon, jabbing, slicing and hacking, ignoring the futile attempts to either mount a defence or seek clemency; their victims died because a party that could not take prisoners could give none.

It took Bohemund himself to rescue the one fellow he wanted, a Lombard who shook like a leaf, sure he was going to be slaughtered.

'I will be that,' the youngster replied as he mounted his riding mare. 'But know this: if it appears I am tempted, I do so on instruction from my father, who told me this might occur and also advised me how to proceed.'

'And that is?'

'Slowly, Reynard, very slowly.'

That made Reynard grin, for he should have thought of that; when it came to being devious, few could play the game better than the *Guiscard*.

CHAPTER SIX

At the very moment when Bohemund was riding towards the parley, his father was lying in his bed, wracked by the effects of a horrific fever, his body shaking and sweat pouring off his naked frame, with Sichelgaita bent over him seeking to ease his discomfort with cloths which had been dipped in iced water, wondering whether instead of that as a remedy her husband should be shipped to the underground icehouse where there were still enough blocks left over from the winter supply to make it seriously cold. The Greek physician attending advised against that, convinced the malaise was escaping from the ailing body through a combination of perspiration and loose defecation; a cold atmosphere would not be beneficial.

The smell in the room was of overpowering corruption, for the mighty *Guiscard* had soiled his bed more than once like a mewling child, and the discharge by its colour and deathly odour indicated that the malady was horrendous enough to be fatal. Retching produced nothing but a trickle of bile, for without food there was little for his stomach to emit. He was dipping in and out of consciousness and gabbling, ranting in a way that sounded as though his mind was as troubled as his body.

Curses were heaped upon foes real and imagined, Robert speaking for and against them in a frenzied dialogue, some of the names human and known to those attending, others imagined creatures sounding like demons from the depth of hell as he screamed imprecations that made no sense to those listening, this while a relay of priests prayed continually for his troubled soul. For a warrior who had faced many battles in his time and had shaken off sicknesses as a dog shakes off water, it was clear this was one of the greatest challenges he could face.

His wife was in discomfort too, for, regardless of the heat of the day, she had ordered braziers to be lit and herbs to be burnt on them to relieve the malodorous stink, which she was sure was making her husband's condition worse. When torches, oil lamps and candles were added after the sun went down it turned the sickroom into an oven, for the drop in temperature was not great; a scorching day was followed, as clouds gathered to trap the heat rising from the baked earth, by a humid night. Her garments were soaked and her long blonde hair, normally braided, hung limp along her cheeks as she mouthed quiet prayers to all the saints she knew to intercede and make her man well again.

'Lady,' the physician whispered, 'a messenger has come from the Master of the Host to say that the sickness that affects the Duke is within the town and spreading. He has moved out the mounted knights to surrounding farms but he seeks permission to order outside of the walls every citizen of Trani their master has listed for conscription. He insists he needs to preserve the strength of the army.'

'Take back the message that he must act as he sees fit,' Sichelgaita replied, her cracked voice betraying her own near exhaustion; she had been at Robert's bedside for over eighteen turns of the glass and had not eaten or drunk anything in that time, ignoring the advice to rest lest she too succumb. Then, as the import of what had been said to her sank in, she grabbed the man by the sleeve. 'The sickness is spreading?'

'It is most rampant in the port, though I am told some cases have begun to surface in the upper town. The priests and mendicant monks are doing what they can, but for some it is giving nothing more than last rites.'

'Many have died?'

'Several dozen I am told.'

Sichelgaita had been bent over the troubled body, sometimes required to physically restrain her husband lest his writhing throw him to the floor, and as such she had addressed the physician eyeball to eyeball. Now she stood up and towered over him, her blue eyes boring into his, her sweat-soaked face flushed so her cheeks seemed on fire, and such was the effect of the flickering light and her own appearance that the man, no stranger to shocking sights and fearsome wounds, or even angry patients, took two paces back, alarm on his face.

'Never mind the conscripts; if death is around us we must get my husband and my son to somewhere that is safe.'

The Greek responded with a gesture of open hands, a signal that such thoughts were futile. 'Who knows where that is, Lady?'

'Is there any word of the sickness from any other place?'

'I do not think it has been reported elsewhere.'

The voice boomed out, with no particular person in mind, as Sichelgaita ordered the servants present to first find out, then to organise a litter and enough men to carry it in relays, plus a message to her eldest son, already outside the walls with his father's familia knights, to make his way to the road leading south, bringing them with him as escort.

'To move him could be hazardous, Lady.'

'To keep him here could be worse.' Then she yelled at those she had ordered to make arrangements, few of whom seemed to have reacted as she wanted them to. 'In the name of Christ risen, *move!*'

'Prince Richard asks that you accompany me to his castle of Montesárchio, where you will be received with all honour.'

It was notable to Bohemund that his uncle by marriage had sent one of his own race with the message, not a Greek or someone spouting Latin; was there some kind of statement in hearing the communication in Norman French? The fellow, however, did not look like a fighting man; the face was unmarked and smooth, more like that of a priest perhaps, even though he was armed with both lance and broadsword. Unheard of in Italy, he could indeed be a cleric, for the Norman divine saw no disgrace in being fighting men as well as members of the clergy. For such a breed it was in order to smite their foes and then see their souls into the afterlife.

'And my conroys?' Bohemund demanded.

'Will be accommodated as guests too.'

'How do I know Prince Richard won't just slit my throat, and theirs, once I am inside the walls?'

The smile was meant to point up the absurdity of such a notion. 'Nothing would bring down the wrath of your father quicker than

93

that his son should be in any way harmed, quite apart from the custom of our race that no guest can suffer indignity, regardless of how much he is seen as an enemy, when he is inside the walls of a castle by invitation.'

'And what does Prince Richard want to say to me?'

'I am too humble to even pretend to guess.'

'You don't look humble.'

That got a half bow, to acknowledge that his manner was, if anything, haughty.

'Perhaps if I was to outline the alternative, which is that you will be pursued until captured by a level of force you cannot overcome and taken into my master's presence in chains, while your conroys might suffer the fate of those who burn and plunder, the ignominy of dying at the end of a rope.'

'I would not be taken alive.'

The messenger, by the expression that appeared on his face, took that for what it was, an idle boast; few men chose death when life was possible. Bohemund wanted to tell him to return with a flat refusal, added to that a message to underline the difference between a threat and its implementation; they had not caught him and his band yet and it would not be any easier for them in the future as long as he kept moving and the peasants remained happy with free grain, oil and wine. But to do so would fly in the face of his father's instructions. That accepted, it seemed to him foolish to take his lances with him; even if the laws of hospitality were applied, as soon as they rode out to resume marauding Richard's possessions, their location would be impossible to keep from those pursuing them, for the Prince would have them closely followed, to ensure they left his patrimony and went back from whence they came.

'I will accept, my men will not.'

That got a shrug, as if his lances were of no account; was it meant to flatter him by making him feel important, or genuine indifference? Bohemund surmised he would never know, so he spun his mount to return to the messenger he had brought, a squire who held the reins of his packhorse and destrier.

'Go back to Reynard and tell him I am going to meet and talk with the Prince of Capua. I will rendezvous with him in four days by the River Calore, where we last camped seven nights past, and him alone – he is not to risk the conroys. If I do not, I leave it to him to either continue raiding or return to my father to tell him I am not at liberty to act as I wish.'

'And these?' the man asked, indicating the horses.

'Keep them. I am to be a guest of a prince, so they can provide for my needs and I doubt I will require a destrier on which to fight.'

It did not take long on the road to Bari for Sichelgaita to realise that, even on a well-maintained old Roman surface and with much care and frequent changes of bearers, her husband was suffering from the rocking of the litter. Hurriedly a messenger was sent back to Trani to requisition a galley to meet them at the fishing settlement close to Bisceglie. With great care and using two boats to form a wide stretcher, the Duke of Apulia was taken out and, after the making of a cat's cradle of ropes, a crane was employed to get him aboard and laid flat amidships. On pain that he would suffer as much as the patient, the master then had another rig made that left the board suspended and that took out the effect of the rise and fall of the sea, while an awning was added to keep the blazing sun off the Duke.

Sichelgaita had sent more than one message; she had despatched dozens by her husband's familia knights, calling on all of Robert de Hauteville's senior vassals to gather in Bari, and if she did not say why, once word spread of the Duke's condition it would not take a genius to work out what his duchess wanted. Riders had also been sent ahead to the destination with instructions to prepare to receive their lord and for every available physician to be in attendance, so by the time the galley passed through the water gate and drew up alongside the great stone quay a huge crowd had gathered to gaze at the still fevered body of their overlord.

'How many have come here hoping he is dead?'

That enquiry came from the *Guiscard*'s son and, as far as his mother was concerned, Robert's undoubted heir. Sadly it underlined a truth: that in such a Greek city as Bari his father was far from universally loved. It was not too many years past since many of those gathered had been reduced to near starvation by his four-year-long siege. Prior to that they had jeered at him from their massive – and they thought impregnable – walls and called him shoddy and a fool as well as many more and less flattering things besides. The siege had lasted so long because Robert, without a fleet, could not cut off access to the sea, meaning that Byzantium could resupply the jewel in its Apulian territory with all it needed to resist.

Most men would have given up after a year of no progress, but not the *Guiscard*. He found a way to cut off the city by ringing it with a wall of small trading vessels, all attached to each other by wooden gangways to form a solid and defensible bulwark. It had not held entirely when attacked but it had so diminished the relief efforts as to bring on hunger, disease and discontent, and that induced enough of the minds of those inside to see the only way to end it was to bow the knee to the Normans. To aid this Robert had his spies, as well as a small number of supporters within the walls, men who thought to prosper by surrender.

With a population close to revolt, those adherents took one of the main towers and that allowed the final Norman assault to prevail to the point where capitulation was the only option; the Byzantines in the garrison were obliged to flee. Robert entered the opened gates to a grovelling plea to be spared what their intransigence deserved: rapine and sack till not one body remained breathing. They had misjudged their conqueror – he was no angel of death, but a shrewd ruler disinclined to make enemies where it was unnecessary.

Not only did he spare them a massacre, but since the city fell their new master had been benign, allowing the leading citizens who had opposed him to keep their trades and positions, ensuring many of the privileges Bari enjoyed were maintained so that the port retained its wealthy trade and important revenues. In another setting the community would have been content but, as ever, it was religion that made true concord impossible; the Greeks resented the new cathedral Robert ordered built, for inside that would be performed the Latin Mass, conducted by celibate priests, while the monks and divines that came with the Normans worked hard to proselytise their version of the Christian faith.

'Odd,' Sichelgaita replied after a long pause, for she could not disagree with her son, 'that he loves a city in which so many loathe him.'

'Is that why we came here?'

'Partly; it was his favourite from the day he rode in to accept the surrender, but the best Greek physicians reside here too and they are much required.'

'And the other reason is?'

'Surely you have thought about what will happen if God takes him from us?'

'I try not to, Mother, and I shall pray that it is not so until he is well again.'

Few mothers see anything untoward in their sons and Sichelgaita was no exception with both her boys. She relished the piety of her eldest and saw his way of ever counting and recounting his purse money that had earned him his sobriquet of *Borsa* as just a harmless affectation, so much so that she employed it herself. But for all the maternal mote in her eye, she also knew that her son lacked the fiery spirit of his sire, and while he was a competent fighter for his fourteen summers, he was not amongst the first rank of his peers; in short, there were those of his own age who could best him in mock combat, and given the closeness of Norman training to actual battle, such a handicap was likely to apply there as well.

Experience, added to a few years, would make him more capable but he was not yet commanding by nature. Sichelgaita knew that if what she feared to happen came about, and her husband did not recover, then it would fall to her to protect her Roger until he could come into the qualities he required to hold his own amongst the *Guiscard*'s troublesome vassals. So be it; she had often stood in for her husband, indeed was seen by many as a co-ruler of the dukedom and was a match for Robert as a force of nature, understood the politics needed to acquire and maintain authority, all of which she would employ to keep *Borsa* safe.

'Come, let us go ashore,' she said. 'I desire you to go ahead of your father's bier and I also require that you smile at the populace. Look confident, *Borsa*, for whatever happens in the coming days, that is an attitude you are going to require.'

Robert had been craned ashore and laid on to a litter, to be surrounded by monks swinging thuribles of burning incense meant to ward off any malodours, with the crowd pressing forward as far as they were allowed to look at him, peering between the soldiers who formed an outer ring, seeing a much-diminished figure if you took account of the face. Gone were the florid cheeks and full red lips, to be replaced by heavily drawn features in which the bones of the jaw and the nose were prominent, while even his hair, which Sichelgaita had dressed, looked like used straw. Many just stared, but there were those, and this cheered Sichelgaita, who crossed themselves repeatedly and seemed to silently pray, hoping for his recovery, not saying farewell to his departing soul.

Massively walled, Bari also had a strong castle with a formidable citadel at its heart and it was to here that Robert was taken. His son made for the partially built cathedral, where he knelt with the priests and the congregation, many of them recently Orthodox in their worship, as the new Archbishop of Bari said Mass in the Roman rite to aid in the recovery of their overlord. Robert now lay peacefully in a private chamber, no longer the ranting, sweating victim of whatever assailed him, but in his wax-like appearance akin to an alabaster representation of the kind that one fateful day, mailed and with a sword in his hands, might grace his sarcophagus.

Bohemund was well beyond the reach of that and, in any case, heading further west. He had sight of Montesárchio a good while before they came to the base of the steep, cobbled causeway that led up to the castle gates. Once there he could not, as a Norman warrior, look at it from any other viewpoint than a fortress that required to be taken by assault. With his worship of family it would have pleased the young man to know that this was where his Uncle William had first won his spurs in the mercenary service of Rainulf Drengot, to know that the warrior who many years later became known as Iron Arm and Count of Apulia had bloodily fought his way up that cobbled causeway to the very gate through which he would be welcomed, and once inside, given the man commanding the expedition was wounded, taken it upon himself for the first time to act as a leader not a follower.

Constructed of cream stone blocks, the small castle of Montesárchio was set on a high hill, almost conical in shape, broad at the base but tapered at the top so that there was no glacis around the actual walls on which either ballista or ladders could be employed; thus the only route of assault was up the causeway, making it a hard place to capture. From its highest point – probably, judging by its aged stone, the original Roman tower – it overlooked the surrounding landscape, not least an old imperial road running straight east and west, which rendered it also near immune to surprise. From the pole at the top of the tower flew a red and black banner to tell all it was a fief of the Prince of Capua, though in size it barely suited his station.

Fearing that his horse would slip on that cobbled causeway, Bohemund dismounted, the reins immediately taken from him by one of the men on duty as sentinels. When he was halfway up to the open gates an elegantly clad group, some six in number, emerged and stood waiting to greet him. From the bearing of the man in the middle he knew he was about to meet his relative by marriage, who was employing the first step of what would be a long attempt to flatter him by the singular act of coming out to give him greeting. By his side was a lady who stood a good hand taller, whom he assumed to be his aunt, given he could see in her something of his sister Emma.

If the Princess Fressenda was loftier than her spouse – she had a measure of the de Hauteville build – it was natural that her nephew towered over him and by habit he sought to shrink himself by slightly hunching his shoulders to mitigate the effect. Bareheaded, the suzerain of Capua was stocky, small and balding, with cheeks that seemed puffy in a way that indicated he ate and drank well. An eye drawn to his midriff showed he had a paunch as well, which for some reason Bohemund found unbecoming in a Norman leader; if his father had bulk, it was muscle not fat. Try as he did, it was impossible to avoid the need for Richard to strain his neck to meet a pair of eyes now searching his face, the effort of forcing himself to smile obvious.

'Greetings, cousin.'

Bohemund turned to a more genuine smile, that of his aunt, and as she proffered her hand to be taken by his, he dropped to one knee to kiss it, saying as he did so, 'You do me great honour, Lady.' He would have been pleased to observe her husband's expression; he looked piqued that no such accolade had been addressed to him.

'It gives us great pleasure to receive you, Bohemund,' Fressenda replied, gently raising him up again, then stepping forward and forcing him to bend so she could kiss his cheeks. 'And it is to be hoped that you will stay as our guest for some time. I wish you to know that, for us, this is as much the bosom of your family as anywhere in Apulia.'

Looking down still, Bohemund smiled; there was no time-wasting here – that was the first round in an attempt to seduce him from service to his sire. A movement to his aunt's rear made him look past her, this as she stepped aside to introduce a young man who had recognisably de Hauteville features: broad shoulders, red-gold hair, blue eyes, a fair complexion and, not least, a height greater than his father, though like most men he was dwarfed by Bohemund.

'Allow me to name to you your blood cousin,' Fressenda said, 'our son Jordan. It is to be hoped that you will behave more like brothers.'

Jordan's eyes narrowed as swiftly as did those of Bohemund; how they would come to see each other, whether they would be friends, indifferent or enemies would not be dictated by blood but by the kind of rivalry that afflicts all young men.

'Come,' Fressenda said, turning to re-enter the castle, 'we have here dozens of men eager to set eyes on the youth they could not lay by the heels.'

CHAPTER SEVEN

While the Duke of Apulia hovered between life and death, those who owed allegiance to his person began to arrive in Bari, but the one face Sichelgaita longed to gaze upon was not yet present. Her husband's most potent vassal, she knew that his voice would carry most weight when it came to the succession and she had sound reasons to think him steadfast in her cause. Much would rest with Roger de Hauteville, Count of Sicily and younger brother to the *Guiscard*, after whom *Borsa* was named. He was on his way from the island, that she knew, for Robert had called upon his brother to bring to Apulia what forces he could muster to aid his campaign against Capua.

What she did not know, and her husband had prior to his illness suffered the same uncertainty, was how long he would take to arrive; there was no way of guessing the precise depth of his engagement against the continuing Saracen resistance to the complete Norman subjugation of the island. Boats had been sent out to intercept him on his way to Trani, to which he had been summoned, to ensure he changed course for Bari, which he must bypass on the way.

Meanwhile she could sense the atmosphere growing more febrile as the numbers who had taken up residence in Bari, and who had now witnessed for themselves the depth of their liege lord's malaise, turned idle talk into varying schemes.

All of these sought personal advantage and had only enough force behind them to last till they foundered on the aspirations of their equally ambitious peers. Naturally, those who had rebelled at some time were the most vocal, and noisiest amongst them and a perennial complainant was Abelard, loud in his constant protestations that he was the rightful heir to the dukedom and that it would be a double denial of his inheritance if the son of the usurper was considered as fitting to hold his title. It was a blessing he lacked the attributes to be a true leader of such a fractious polity.

Sichelgaita got minimal encouragement from her son; *Borsa* moved among those same vassals without the ability to engender much in the way of support, hardly surprising given his age. Too often, feeling either ineffectual or rebuffed, he took refuge in long hours of prayer with his personal confessor, without ever letting it be known what supplication they were seeking from God. His strong desire that his father should live was something he shared only with his mother and it was observed by her that when in the company of the men from whom he would require backing, few, when caught not looking at him face to face, gazed upon him in a way to produce encouragement. Quite often, in her fevered imagination, the looks aimed at his back had about them more a trace of the dagger.

Sichelgaita needed these men to pledge loyalty to her son and did much in the way of persuasion and sometimes outright bribery to increase that support, but with too many unwilling to confirm she feared to put an oath to the test; if the lords of Robert's domains refused to endorse *Borsa* while her husband still breathed there would be scant chance of them doing so once he had passed away, yet the longer she delayed increased the risk that some combination would be formed to thwart her wishes. Her pleas to the tribe of physicians for a clear prognosis fell on an equal amount of dissension: one would claim that recovery was inevitable only for another to insist that death could not be avoided and was hourly to be expected.

In the middle were those who hovered between being positive one day and the opposite the next but it was clear to even a medical layman that if Robert could not be fed, and being comatose that was hard to achieve, even if his vital spirit was strong it would weaken slowly until the end could not be gainsaid. So when the news came that a fleet of galleys had been sighted approaching the harbour from the south-east and that the lead vessel flew at its masthead a blue and white pennant, Sichelgaita could hardly contain her relief – Roger was here.

Looking from the deck of his vessel at the massive fortifications of the most populous port city in Apulia, Roger de Hauteville was astounded, even if it was a proven fact that his brother had ever managed to take the place. The walls did not just protect the port from the landward approach; what made it so formidable was that the entire inner harbour was enclosed, which, had it not faced such a cunning adversary, would have made it unassailable to a land-based assault. Also he wondered what he would face behind those walls, for if the boat that had intercepted him had told him his brother was seriously ill, there was no sign from his standard flying atop the citadel to say that he was more than that – it still flapped at the very top of the pole. Still, being by nature prudent, he had no intention of landing in force until he knew what lay ahead, evidenced by his call to his master of the fleet.

'Signal the other galleys to anchor in the outer roads. We will go in alone.'

Roger's sister-in-law, as well as his namesake nephew, were on the quay to greet him as his galley tied up and a gangplank was lowered for him to cross. Much as dignity was prized, there are few men who can move from a vessel to terra firma and quite hold their balance; after many days at sea their body has become used to the motion of the ship and some adjustment is required, so when Roger came off the gangplank he did so unsteadily. Sichelgaita was more concerned with the look in his eye than gait and that was firm, unblinking and meeting her own, so if others watching were unsure of his loyalty, she felt her own concern ease. It needed her two hands, both held in his, to make him feel steady as he kissed her cheeks and whispered his brother's name, the reaction of relief palpable when he was told he was still breathing.

Sichelgaita pushed him to arm's length and smiled. 'There you are, Roger, ever the most handsome of your tribe. You have no idea how glad I am to see you.'

That was greeted with a wry smile and a negative shake, for if he was indeed a fine figure of a man Roger did not possess the vanity to take the compliment without being dismissive. He turned to look at his nephew, whom he had last seen as a small boy; now he was close in years to manhood and while Roger was smiling there was in the eyes sharp examination – this lad could be a strong influence in his life and it was fitting that he make an assessment. Under his soft cap *Borsa*'s hair was the colour of charcoal, not the red-gold of a de Hauteville, and his face was olive-coloured, for it took the sun well, unlike the family tendency to reddish cheeks that suffered from overexposure. There was something about the boy that nagged at his mind until he placed it: he had about him similar features to his mother's brother, Gisulf of Salerno, quite natural given their relationship. It was not, however, one to encourage Roger, who knew only too well what a dolt was the boy's Lombard uncle.

'Do they still call you *Borsa*, nephew?'

'They do,' the youth said in response, before adding a shy grin. 'Though I am given to wonder if I might have more names to answer to than that.'

'If you don't have them now, you will.'

Sichelgaita killed any notion of what they might be as she made the ritual enquiry after a lady of whom she was fond, Roger's wife Judith, as well as his daughters, a diversion in which she could not but touch her boy, for if she too had four girls she also had two legitimate sons, *Borsa* and the ten-year-old Guy; Jordan, Roger's only male offspring, was illegitimate and without question so, therefore surely no threat to her hopes.

'Sichelgaita, I long to see Robert,' Roger insisted, when manners and the rituals of greeting allowed.

'And you shall, though I recall it was not always so.'

Her brother-in-law laughed out loud as they began to move from the quay towards the citadel, for there was much truth in that; it was hard to know if, in the last fifteen years, they had fought with each other more than cooperated, for even he had been forced to rebel against Robert over his brother's continual refusal to meet the obligations to which he had sworn. In moments of reflection Roger knew why his relationship with his older sibling was never smooth and it was not just a family trait – the *Guiscard* was conscious that in Roger he had a match, a de Hauteville with no shortage of the family genius in both war and statecraft, and it was a rivalry that he did not enjoy; he liked to think himself supreme in such arts.

'If he hears the sound of my voice he will stir for fear that I might usurp him.'

Meant as a jest, Roger was quick to see the effect on Sichelgaita was one of apprehension and if he knew it to be misplaced he also knew what was the cause: that should he contest the ducal inheritance with his nephew, then *Borsa* was doomed. Succession was not guaranteed by bloodline amongst the Normans of Italy; each de Hauteville brother who had succeeded had done so as much by acclamation as by a sibling gift and that had come about because of their unmatched abilities. It was necessary to reassure her.

'Then if he has any sense at all, he will know that I would never do so.'

'Roger, I am required to ask something of you.'

'I am Robert's vassal as well as I am his brother, and even if I were not constrained by that, I would never challenge him. I did not take the vow that others did. Tancred had passed away by the time I left Normandy but I hold to it nevertheless in his honour, and if I challenged Robert in the past it was only because of his chicanery over what I was owed.'

'That is not what I was about to solicit.'

'I can guess your other concern, Sichelgaita, and I beg you put it to rest. I made a vow to Robert I would look out for your son and that I will do.'

'Then you will support me when I ask that all Robert's vassals swear to him.'

'I will do what is needed.'

Later, sitting beside his comatose brother's bed, to the murmuring of priests saying prayers for his deliverance, Roger could too easily recall what he had called his chicanery, though he was forced to acknowledge that in his treatment he had not been singled out; many of Robert's vassals had been treated the same. Robert could not help himself, for he was devious as well as cunning; he would promise anything to get what he wanted, then wonder why he should pay up when his aims had been achieved, and that was how it had been in Calabria.

Roger had set out to subdue that Byzantine province on the pledge of being given the revenues of the fiefs and cities he took; his brother had reneged when he was successful. It had been necessary to rebel to get him to honour those undertakings and even then, when Roger had been required to rescue him from his own folly – or was it his hubris? – he had held out for an even share of those revenues. To this day the income from those possessions was split between them.

Together they had gone on to take the capital city of Reggio, which left them gazing over the single league that separated the Calabrian shore from Sicily, long an ambition of the younger de Hauteville. Once the *Guiscard* had been persuaded that if he joined with Roger an incursion could succeed, they had acted more in concert. The result was that even with their limited number of lances, never more than five hundred and often a third of that – William of Normandy's invasion of England had drawn off many of Robert's knights in the years '65 and '66 – they had overcome insuperable odds. First Roger took Messina by a *coup de main*, then after a decade-long campaign along the north of the island, which included more than one reverse and at one time threatened to end in disaster, in concert they captured the magnificent Saracen capital of Palermo.

If Robert de Hauteville was Duke of Sicily, that title granted to him by the late Pope Nicholas – really by Archdeacon Hildebrand in a rare moment when he needed the *Guiscard* on his side – it had been given to him when he did not have a single foot soldier on the island. Now it was clearly Count Roger's to direct and it was at the centre of his own ambitions. Yet he also knew that the path to complete control of the island was a long way off; there were still emirs potent enough, and in possession of cities and fortresses strong enough, to make subduing the island a task which could take another decade and he was wondering what support he could expect from his brother's ducal inheritance of Apulia and Calabria, regardless of who ruled, should that prove necessary.

'My Lord, the Lady Sichelgaita sends to say that she has assembled Duke Robert's vassals.'

Roger left the bedchamber and the whispering supplicants to make his way to the great hall of the Castle of Bari, which in its size matched the importance of the port and city. A long gallery, high-arched and well lit, it was crowded, mainly with men of his own race but also with a sprinkling of Lombards who had been granted power in a land too large for the Normans alone to control. Everyone who held a fief from Robert, however small, from simple watchtower to great baronial castle, had been summoned, with the Count of Sicily speaking for the entirety of that island as well as his and his brother's extensive and shared fiefs on the mainland.

Sichelgaita had taken up a seated position on the raised stone platform at one end, regally dressed in shimmering white silks, with her braided hair shining, occupying a place where normally her husband would conduct his public affairs and oversee the great feasts of which he was so fond. Her brother-in-law was obliged to admit, as he entered, that holding that place suited her. Behind her, in full canonical garments, stood the Archbishop of Bari and beside him two servitors with the means to bless those assembled and ensure that whatever vow they took, it was to God as much as to their suzerain.

Everyone in the great hall was aware that as a wife Sichelgaita held a position very different to the normal spouse of a great landed magnate; she was no mouse but had been as often Robert's right-hand helpmeet as Roger himself. When the *Guiscard* was absent from Apulia, indeed in the long periods he had spent in Sicily, Sichelgaita had acted fully in his name; in short the Duke trusted her to rule his domains as he would himself, and she had done so with great competence. Yet this was a greater challenge and it was telling that for all her imposing build and forceful presence, having her son by her side took away a portion of that, for in presence he could not match her.

'Count Roger, I would ask that you join me on the dais.'

'And I, Lady Sichelgaita, would not wish to elevate myself above the other lords present. I am content to remain at the level of every one of my brother's vassals.'

It was impressive, the way she dealt with that, for it was a potent response from such a powerful man and it was not an obviously supportive one, which was plain by the expression on the faces of the others present, though many worked hard not to react at all as they sought to filter in through their own feelings and deep-seated hopes. Sichelgaita, although she must have been both hurt and anguished, managed a beaming smile and spoke with enough sincerity to seem untroubled.

'Such an attitude does you great honour, brother. I hope that others present will see it as an example.' Then she paused, her eyes ranging over the assembly. 'You are all aware that my husband, your liege lord, is gravely ill and while we pray for his full recovery it must be accepted that our wishes and entreaties may not be answered.'

That set the archbishop nodding and naturally set up a murmur, but it did not last; all wanted to hear what they knew was coming.

'When I married Duke Robert there were reasons for our match that transcended the regard we found for each other as man and wife. I need not tell you Normans present that the lands he holds are peopled more by my race than your own, even more by Greeks than either combined, and that has only increased as he has expanded his possessions. If he has granted you lands and titles, he has also granted you overlordship of a less than settled polity. You will all be aware that in the last rebellion, it was not only his dissatisfied Norman barons who rose against him – some of whom are present and have been in receipt of his benevolence – it was Lombards too.'

Her eyes then, as they ranged around the room to pick out the mutinous, were like agate, and those of whom she was speaking had the good grace to look abashed.

'My husband realised that no Norman could hold this patrimony with the numbers he could muster, and he took me as wife as much because I am a Lombard as a princess of the House of Salerno. Also, when he has been absent it is to me he has given the reins of his power to wield, and I have used it to create harmony amongst a population that does not love you any more than they loved Byzantium.'

Abelard could not restrain himself; he stepped forward, tall and gangly, for if he had the de Hauteville height he had none of the physical substance. 'I will not be party to this. My uncle, whom I will not grace with any title, stole my inheritance. It is fitting that should he cease to lord it over my rightful possessions, then they should be mine to take by my bloodline.'

'I invite you to find support in this chamber,' Sichelgaita replied, lowering her voice to add a caveat. 'With a reminder that the *Guiscard* still breathes, as you have all borne witness. I would not want to promise that he would be magnanimous if those whom he has so recently forgiven their transgressions against him were to show a lack of gratitude. I would certainly counsel him against it.'

As a warning it was palpable; she had, at this moment, the power to act as she saw fit and would see hung, drawn and quartered any such ingrate even if Robert was against it.

'My claim is just,' Abelard cried, looking around for a pair of eyes that would meet his own; none were forthcoming and it was a sorry retreat that saw him seek to lose himself, after only a moment's consideration, back in the crowd.

'If my husband knew that to hold his fiefs required that the Lombards from whom he took power were appeased, who amongst you would dare to think yourself even his equal, and be willing to ignore that? Are there not men in this chamber that share my race whom he had promoted to that purpose? And is not the principle of any succession to maintain that which we now hold and do so in a way seen to be legitimate?'

She was never going to mention Bohemund's name, but that was as good a way as any of saying that he, as a pure-blood Norman, for all his supposed attributes – and they were as yet hardly proven – neither had the right, nor would be able to control such an inheritance.

'I therefore demand that you accede to your suzerain's wishes, which he would shout to the rafters if he were present, and swear, that should God see fit to take away that dazzling light, the only person who can hold tight what he leaves behind is his own beloved son, Roger, known to you all as *Borsa*.'

With that she looked very pointedly at the man after whom *Borsa* was named, but she was addressing them all. 'I therefore demand here in this chamber and on this day, in the presence of His Grace the Archbishop of Bari, that on your honour and at risk of the damnation of your soul, you swear allegiance to my son and his title, as the heir to the triple Dukedoms of Apulia, Calabria and Sicily.'

The silence that followed seemed to last a lifetime, with not so much as a whisper, not even from Abelard, from an assembly that could not number less than two hundred men who held, in their own fiefs, a degree of power. The Archbishop of Bari had stepped forward and made the sign of the cross and that allowed the knights to do likewise and murmur a small incantation, some of which would have been the mere pious request for guidance. That was when Roger, Count of Sicily, chose to move and the crowd parted to allow him to approach the dais, for he had remained at the back of the hall where he had entered.

Stony-faced, Sichelgaita observed his progress; her son was less in control, for he showed a measure of apprehension as he tried to read from his uncle's expression what he was about to say. Count Roger knew all he had to do, once he came close, was to mount that dais and declare his own right to the title; the Normans in the hall would erupt in approval and there were too few Lombards to contest with

114

them. Close to the archbishop he fell to his knees and crossed himself, and spoke in a strong and echoing voice.

'I, Roger de Hauteville, Count of Sicily by grace of my brother's trust, do hereby swear to be a true and loyal servant to his son, named after me at birth, and to attend upon his person as my liege lord when the time comes for him to rightfully assume his father's titles, may God strike me down if I transgress this vow.'

The archbishop, with some relief of his own, sprinkled holy water on Roger's head and said a prayer that bound the kneeling man to his words. Behind the Count of Sicily the others lined up, Ademar of Monteroni to the fore, to make the same vow and then kiss the out-held hand of the youth they were anointing as their coming suzerain. Standing to one side and watching, Count Roger finally met Sichelgaita's eye, to see there a feeling of hurt, for she knew what he had done; her son had been told, and so had she, that he held his titles only at the will of his powerful uncle.

But another message had gone out to those assembled and that was just as plain, for they knew to a man that Bohemund would not quietly accept such a dispensation; he would fight for what he considered his rights. Roger of Sicily had left a message for his absent bastard nephew to say that he would not stand by and let him overthrow his half-brother *Borsa*; he would, if need be, intervene to keep him in power.

'I wonder, Roger,' Sichelgaita enquired of him once the chamber was emptied. 'Would you have sworn that oath if you possessed a son of your own?'

'Since I do not, your question is not one I can answer.'

Sichelgaita could not hide the fact that she was reassured. Much as she would fight like a she-wolf for her firstborn son, and young

115

Guy if *Borsa* expired before her, she also knew, like Robert himself, that the laws of nature indicated she would die before either of them. However, Sichelgaita also knew that Roger's wife Judith, who had been fecund in producing daughters, was now past child-bearing age.

'You will remain with us?' she asked.

'Until my brother recovers,' Roger replied, smiling, 'and then I am his to command.'

The assembly had done that for which it had been called and most of those called to attend preferred to return to their own domains with their liege lord still not recovered. It was never possible to discover where the rumour began that Robert de Hauteville was dead, but it had begun to spread, perhaps either through malice, delusion or even wishful thinking. Suffice to say that it travelled in the wildfire way that such things do despite strong denials to the contrary from those who knew the truth, first through the city then out into the hinterland and beyond, snaking at walking pace up the trade routes, much more rapidly along the coast, carried by fast-sailing merchant ships to every port on the Adriatic and thence into the interior.

It was an irony that, as that news began to be promulgated across the northern Apennines, the object began to show the first signs of recovery – an occasional bout of consciousness, and a day or two later wakeful enough to take on the first solid food he had consumed for an age and with strength enough to ask that those miserable clerical supplicants disturbing his peace with their prayers be removed. He was weak and Sichelgaita kept anyone from his bedside that might trouble the recovery, even Count Roger, though *Borsa* and his younger brother were admitted to be blessed by a feeble parent. Sichelgaita took to nursing him herself.

'The rumour in the marketplace this last week,' she said, in between feeding him, 'is that you have gone to meet your maker.' Then she smiled. 'Or the Devil who spawned you.'

'I think I spoke with Satan recently,' Robert croaked.

'It certainly sounded as if you were at war with him in your fevers. But it would be well to show yourself, even in your diminished state, and lay to rest such rumours, which is the only evidence some folk will believe, for they can cause nothing but trouble and messengers must be sent out to suppress it in the countryside.'

'There is no risk here in Bari, surely?'

'No, all who matter know you are recovering and those who might want to profit by it have dispersed, while Count Roger has taken command of the garrison. He is anxious to speak with you, of course.'

The expression that crossed his face could not be the same as before; his eyes were too opaque to sparkle and the cheeks too drawn. 'A week, you say.'

'At least.'

The laugh began heartily enough, but soon turned into a hacking cough, from which Robert took time to recover his breath, but there was no mistaking the gleam of a coming prank.

'Then a few days will make no difference, for I am not yet recovered enough to be seen. Let the rumour run and let us see who seeks to make mischief with it.'

CHAPTER EIGHT

The Leonine City was in mourning: Pope Alexander, who had throughout his pontificate brought to the city a decade of something approaching harmony, was dead and once more all the demons that cursed the election of a successor were back in play. The Roman aristocrats looked at their extended families to select a possible papal candidate and counted the money in their coffers to calculate how much they could disburse in bribes to the mobs that often took control of the city, should they be able to conjure up some clerical support. The Imperial Prefect sent messages off to Bamberg to alert his master, the Emperor-elect and King in Germany, Henry IV, to a potential crisis, while other riders had spread out to the great monasteries and important bishoprics to call to Rome those whom Archdeacon Hildebrand knew would be required to both attend the obsequies as well as name and elect a successor.

Now the last of these divines had gathered, it was time for the funeral of Alexander to go ahead. Hildebrand was in the act of finalising the arrangements of the procession which would assemble the next day, when he received, from across the mountains, the news from Apulia. The cries of 'God be praised' echoed through the Lateran Palace, for Hildebrand was a man much committed to his hatreds. If it had taken action by the Normans of Capua and Apulia to secure Pope Alexander's position as well as that of his predecessor, plus their aid to defeat the machinations of an imperial antipope, it had come at the cost of confirming those demons in their ducal and princely titles in a ceremony that, when he recalled it, seemed to Hildebrand a form of nightmare.

Such concessions had been brought about by the expedient need to keep the armies of the boy Henry IV north of the Alps; easy when he had been a mere child with his mother as regent, it would be much more troublesome now he was grown to manhood and said to be wilful with it, so perhaps he would have to seek their aid again. If having to rely on the Normans sat ill with Hildebrand, it was not just them; he hated to have to rely on anyone. Surely that could not be the will of the omnipotent God to whom he continually prayed?

As the archdeacon saw it, the Church of Rome had to be the fount of all authority; how could it not be, given where its teachings came from: the very mouth of Jesus, the Son of God, as relayed through his disciples? No temporal power had the right to challenge that and it was his life's work, as he saw it, to bring to pass that such supremacy should be acknowledged. Emperors, kings, dukes and counts bowed the knee to the Pope, not the other way round, for that flew in the face of scripture.

But if the archdeacon was beset by his passions and his beliefs, he was ever the pragmatist, playing a weak hand with consummate skill as he sought to ward off all the perils that threatened the institution he controlled until the proper acknowledgments could be secured. Keep the Emperor-elect and his desire to interfere in Rome at bay, yet not so barred from influence as to allow the Normans free rein to do as they pleased. As a policy it had worked well sometimes and failed just as many, yet now some form of action must be taken. In the delicate scales of Italian politics, the death of the *Guiscard* altered the balance and might present an opportunity from which Hildebrand could profit, and a move towards his ultimate goal that acknowledged papal supremacy be initiated.

A message was sent to the religious home of the Benedictines in Rome, to summon into his presence his most trusted advisor – the divine who ran the great monastery of Monte Cassino, for if there was one man who would help him to decide what this portended it was Abbot Desiderius. His monastery bordered the lands controlled by the Normans of Campania and he knew the ways of the Apulians well; indeed none had been more troubled over decades by their depredations than that institution. Desiderius had dealt with them to keep Monte Cassino secure and his diplomacy had from time to time brokered an occasional amity – or was it a mere marriage of convenience? – between the Normans and Rome.

'News to gladden the heart, Desiderius – the *Guiscard* is dead.'

The abbot had not even got through the double doors of the chancellor's luxurious work chamber; tall, angular and simply dressed in his habit of undyed white, with his desiccated features that bespoke a life of much denial, he immediately crossed himself, then gathered his hands and said a short, silent prayer. Hildebrand was about to scoff but stopped himself, for he was in the presence of one of the few people who could make him feel inadequate in his love of God. Then there was his bloodline.

Desiderius had been born into a cadet branch of the princely family that had ruled Benevento prior to their being ousted by Humphrey de Hauteville, yet he had renounced all that brought in wealth and comfort for his faith and the simple life of a Benedictine monk. If both men were Lombards, they could be marked more by their differences than their similarities: Hildebrand was ill-tempered, dogmatic in his faith and intolerant of any perceived transgressions of the creed. Physically short and stocky, swarthy of face and with untidy black hair, he wore his canonical garments badly, managing, even in magnificent vestments, to look every inch the peasant many claimed him to be. The Abbot of Monte Cassino eschewed display, yet with his silver-grey locks, kindly, well-proportioned features and forgiving nature, looked and behaved like the aristocrat he was.

'We must pray for the soul of every one of Our Saviour's flock, Hildebrand, regardless of how much they have sinned.'

'The *Guiscard* won't cease to do that even in death,' Hildebrand snorted. 'He'll probably storm St Peter's very gates, prodding with his lance and demanding heaven submit; that is, if he ever gets to paradise.'

'He has endowed many places of worship.'

'And destroyed ten times more and he is an excommunicate. He deserves to burn in hell.'

'My friend, if I pray for his soul, I shall do so for you with as much sincerity when your time comes.'

That stopped whatever Hildebrand was about to say; the notion that he would need as many entreaties as a devil like the *Guiscard*

121

to enter heaven was a sobering one and enough to silence even his normally uncontrollable temperament.

'You know these heathens better than I, Desiderius. I need your advice on how to proceed.'

That made even the calm abbot look askance; Hildebrand was as likely to ignore him as endorse any opinion he put forward, but it was true he knew the Normans well and had dealt with them on numerous occasions, all the way back to Rainulf Drengot and William *Bras de Fer*. His aim had been to protect his monastery, which lay sandwiched between Rome and Campania, and in that he had been more than successful. Destroyed many times, not least by marauding Saracens, and rebuilt only to be diminished by Lombard-inspired Norman incursions, Desiderius had managed to secure it their protection, and that brought with it both peace and prosperity till the only rival it now had in Christendom, in terms of riches and prestige, was the mighty French Abbey of Cluny.

Naturally, with the news of Duke Robert's death came a report of the assembly called by Sichelgaita, its purpose as well as the conclusion. Desiderius was well acquainted with, indeed he had appointed, the personal confessor of the putative heir.

'This Roger they call *Borsa* is a pious young man I am told.'

'Which,' Hildebrand snapped, 'will do him no good at all if he cannot rule in Apulia.'

'The boy's mother is a formidable woman. If what we hear of this swearing of vows is true, I would surmise that while he may hold the title, it will be she who controls the reins until the boy reaches maturity.'

'What will Capua do when he hears this news?'

'Nothing, unless he had support from the Apulian barons, and they

122

have just been soundly routed. Richard lacks the strength to invade without that, and even then he would come up against the Count of Sicily now he has sworn allegiance to a legal inheritance. You know less of him but he is as good a general as ever was the *Guiscard*.'

'If he is so puissant a warrior why did he not take the title himself?'

'I surmise he is an honourable man.' That got a loud snort from Hildebrand; the concept of honour in a Norman was not one he could easily accept. 'If Roger *Borsa* has a difficulty it is with his half-brother, Bohemund, who is, I am told, a formidable young man.'

Hildebrand, when he replied, had no need to seek to appear cunning. His features inclined towards that naturally – his trouble was an appearance of sincerity. 'It could be in our interest to set them at each other's throats.'

'Would it not, Hildebrand,' Desiderius responded with a sigh, 'be better to bring them to a peaceful understanding?'

'Understanding, with a Norman?' Hildebrand sneered. 'No such thing is possible, but let us leave that aside, as we have other matters to consider.'

'I beg you not to go to them,' the abbot replied, for he had a very good idea of what was coming.

'I do not comprehend you, Desiderius. The Supreme Office is yours for the asking. Not a voice would be raised, even in Bamberg, if you assumed the papacy.'

'One voice would object most heartily, Hildebrand, and that is my own. I do not want it.'

'Well,' Hildebrand replied, in a way that did nothing to convince Desiderius he accepted his decision, 'I will convey that to the Curia, but do not be surprised if they do not accept it.'

'It is not an office that can be forced on any man.'

'What if it is the will of God?'

'How can one be sure of that, when it is expressed through mere mortals?'

'You should pray for guidance.'

'That must wait till tomorrow morning,' was the reply, as the abbot made to depart. 'Until then I shall do as I intended before you sent for me and sit vigil by Pope Alexander's catafalque. If my supplications have any value, which I doubt, then they should be employed to see that good man into the arms of Our Lord, not me into his vacant chair.'

Hildebrand went back to the arrangements for the next day's interment; having buried four pontiffs, it was a task to which he was well accustomed, but he had other concerns, not least how to persuade the man who had just departed that it was his duty to accept the mitre of St Peter and his own personal feelings had no bearing. If he felt it a burden all he would have, if he so wanted, were the trappings; Hildebrand had been running things for so long, down to the most tedious level, and he could continue to do so if asked.

Unbeknown to him, there were several conversations of the same topic being carried out in houses as well as palaces all over Rome, as the assembled cardinals and bishops met with the Roman aristocrats to see where they had common ground in the election of a successor to Alexander. What emerged took much overnight scurrying to and fro from meeting to meeting, as well as messages flying between the most important locations. In a city where plotting was endemic, the sole surprise was the speed of unanimity in coming to a conclusion between such disparate entities.

Those divines who had risen to high office in the last twenty years found, to their surprise, that they shared a desire with the leading

Roman families for an outcome, and given those same aristocrats controlled the mob, and they could with their coins direct them to carry out their aims, it fell to these families to make necessary arrangements to ensure the right candidate was elected.

Hildebrand was up long before it was light, first to say his devotions and then prepare for the coming ceremony, made sad by contemplation, because he had loved Alexander as a person as well as he had served and guided him faithfully. As that, he would have liked to lead the procession to the nearby Lateran Basilica where Alexander was to be interred, but even as Chancellor of the Apostolic See he must give precedence to cardinals, the senior bishops and abbots like Desiderius, now assembling with the clergy of Rome to perform the ceremony of consecration and burial. It was fitting that he fast this day, so with only a sip of watered wine to sustain him he stood while his servants robed him in his vestments, trying, and as usual failing, to make him look as noble as he should.

Outside, when he emerged, stood the Church of Rome assembled and his heart swelled to see their magnificence: vestments of heavy silk sown with pearls and jewels, crosses of solid gold, studded with gems, to be carried in procession, all the trappings that testified to the glory of God and his Vicar on Earth. In his lifetime the religion for which he had toiled so hard had been much reduced, and if his efforts had restored its pride he had also been instrumental in the restoration of its revenues to the point that there was no display of splendour it could not undertake. Yet for all that glitter, there was Desiderius, still simply robed as the monk he was, and the two exchanged greetings, an act repeated with all those whom Hildebrand had summoned to Rome. But no time was wasted and the bishop who would perform the Mass went to the head of the gathering to lead the catafalque and those who would follow it the short distance to the basilica.

A huge crowd of citizens had gathered, both high-born and low, and they fell in behind, the aristocrats naturally to the front. Most would be barred from the interior of the Lateran Basilica – space would not allow them all entry – but equity as well as sound policy dictated that a number of representatives of the guilds as well as the urban poor be admitted. For the rest, they would remain in the plaza yet still take full part in the Mass, conducted to them by relays of priests. Smoky incense filled the air as the bearers swung their thuribles and the plainchant of the accompanying monks rose in a slow but sweet dirge, which changed its note as it went from the open air and entered the high-roofed building, echoing off the rafters.

In a ceremony that would last half the day there was no sign of impatience; the congregations of Rome were accustomed to lengthy Masses as well as the stifling heat of packed humanity; there was no room for a communion wafer between the shoulders of the crowd. It was only when the final prayers were said over the coffin that the murmuring started, a beehive-like noise that made bile rise in Hildebrand's throat and his blood begin to surge, for it showed a lack of respect to the man being interred.

Then he recognised his name, first being whispered, then called, to be finally shouted, and he felt a frisson of fear. It had not happened for a long time, but it was not unknown for a Roman mob to string up someone they blamed for a real or perceived sin, and Alexander had been a much loved pontiff, added to which no pope died without rumours spreading through the seven hills and foul-smelling slums of rank deeds being involved in his passing. The noise grew, becoming universal, and it was only then he understood what it was they were yelling and that induced in his heart a feeling of cold fear.

Those close by, all clerics, parted to let through to him the poorer members of the laity, and it was their hands that took him and lifted him bodily to bear him out of the church where he was greeted by a screaming and packed mob. From being hustled along Hildebrand was suddenly lying flat on his back being passed over a sea of hands, he saying as he was transported a loudly expressed prayer to God that was drowned out by the cacophony all around him. They bore him to the Church of St Peter Viniculus, where Alexander had been crowned, the only pope to use that church, and still the cry went up to rebound off a second set of church rafters and, even if he did not know it, throughout the crammed streets and squares until it seemed the whole of the Eternal City spoke with one voice and the cry was: 'Hildebrand for Pope! Hildebrand for Pope!'

All those chosen to elect Alexander's successor had followed and were now in conclave, which gave Hildebrand some hope, for canonical elections in their progress were long, drawn-out affairs; opinions were canvassed, names put forward and rejected – sometimes days, even weeks went by before consensus was arrived at and a candidate accepted. The Curia elected Hildebrand in less time than it took to consume a full flagon of wine and such was the cheering that no one could hear him protest that he could not be pontiff, for he was only a monk in lesser orders, not a fully consecrated priest, even less a bishop, which the Pope must be.

That too fell on deaf ears; in the millennium since its foundation the Catholic faith had been proscribed and provided martyrs in the thousands, risen to a state religion and been overawed by emperors, seen its possessions, even its spiritual home, sacked and destroyed, and had brought it back to life and prominence. In that time it had become accustomed to both the necessity of compromise and need for expediency; when this objection finally got through to those who had elected him the solution was simple: Hildebrand was immediately ordained to be fully a priest and so entitled to hold the pontificate – his consecration as a bishop could wait.

'Your election was popular,' Desiderius insisted, to a collective and murmured assent as he chose to speak for the High Church dignitaries assembled inside what was now Hildebrand's Lateran Palace. 'Every voice in Rome from high to low is raised in acclamation.'

Seated by the desk at which he had worked for decades and slumped from exhaustion, Hildebrand replied with resignation, an unusual tone for such a passionate man. 'I never sought this.'

'Which makes you more suitable than most.'

'It should be you.'

'And if it was,' the Abbot of Monte Cassino replied, 'I would do no more, and pursue no policies other than those you advised. Better you do command yourself and are known to, than disburse the proclamations under another name.'

'What will Bamberg say?'

'They will fight you as Pope or whosoever we had chosen, for it would not be the Emperor's nominee, but your own.'

'Henry would have accepted you, Desiderius.'

The abbot wore a thin smile as he responded. 'Which surely makes me a very unsuitable candidate.'

As they had been talking, a clutch of clerks had entered carrying folders relating to those things which Hildebrand had been dealing with before his elevation, a list of appointments to the various offices of the Europe-wide Church, or at least approval or denial of same – William of England was being particularly difficult regarding the See of Canterbury. There were sheaves of letters, reports on everything, from what was happening in Constantinople to clerical malfeasance in selling benefices – neither encouraging – instructions to bishops to enforce celibacy or to defrock forthwith the deniers, and this applied especially in the regions ruled by the Duke of Apulia.

'Which reminds me,' Hildebrand said, as he beckoned one fellow forward, taking from him his folder and opening it to reveal on the top a finished letter, requiring only that it be signed. 'This I penned last night, a message of condolence to the Duchess Sichelgaita on the loss of her husband. Hypocrisy, of course, God forgive me.'

'If God will not forgive his Vicar on Earth, then who?'

Hildebrand looked hard at Desiderius then, for the abbot, despite all his apparent saintliness, was not beyond mockery. Speedily he read his letter again before reaching forward to extract a quill, which he dipped in his inkwell. Then he hesitated and looked up at Desiderius.

'How shall I sign it, for I have not yet decided how I will be named?'

'Now, Your Holiness, is as good a time as any.'

Hildebrand was startled to be so addressed. He sat for several moments in contemplation, then quickly bent and signed the letter. As soon as he did so another one of his clerks came to the desk and produced a stick of wax, which was held to a candle to melt. Then he put a red ribbon on the bottom of the missive, dripped the runny wax onto it and watched as the new Pope pressed home the ring with the papal seal that only he had the right to use. As he finished, Desiderius held out a hand, took it from him and looked at the name scrawled across the bottom, nodding slowly.

'Let us hope, Your Holiness, that Gregory is a name you can live up to.'

In Bari, the day before, the bells pealed out to announce that their liege lord had fully recovered, and to prove it to even the most sceptical and ill-disposed of his subjects he walked through the streets, on his wife's arm and trailed by his sons. Behind them came Count Roger and the leading men of his court and the garrison, heading to the cathedral where a Mass was said to thank the Lord for his deliverance. He was, of course, examined closely; was it truly the *Guiscard* and not some cunning ploy of a lookalike? But even the most doubtful had to accept the truth, for if his appearance could possibly be faked, his irrepressible manner and sheer presence could not.

Naturally the priests claimed it was their prayers that had saved him, the physicians equally certain their ministrations had brought about the recovery. Robert himself put it down to his own robust spirit, though he was careful to assuage the Almighty with several Masses performed in gratitude for his deliverance over the coming week. That was when the letter of condolence arrived from Rome, along with news of the election of a new pope and who had been elevated. Yet that was not what set him off; it had to wait till the seal of the office of the new papal chancellor was broken. When he opened and read it the *Guiscard* laughed so hard he nearly suffered a relapse.

The letter was full of duplicity; he was not an excommunicate, but *a dear son of the Holy Church*. The cardinals and the Roman Senate were grieving at his passing; indeed *they had been brought low by the news.* It said that Sichelgaita *in order that she should know of the perfect love we bore your husband* could take comfort from their permission for his son to succeed to those titles *which his father held from the Pope, our predecessor.* In other words, much as it pleased his wife when he read those words, remember he is our vassal!

'Gregory the Seventh, by damn!' Robert spat when he read the signature. 'You can't fault Hildebrand for ambition.'

'He may live up to the name,' Roger replied.

'I hope not, brother; the last thing we need is a pope who earns the right to be called Gregory the Great. Hildebrand was enough of a damned nuisance as an archdeacon.' Another of Robert's huge belly laughs followed that. 'Who knows, he might not last – he might go the way of Alexander when he hears I am still alive, which he will do from the messenger that will depart this very hour.'

CHAPTER NINE

With extensive possessions to control and the news circulating of the elevation of Hildebrand to become Pope Gregory VII, it was not surprising that Richard of Capua, having seen to the greeting and engaged in just enough conversation to be polite, had excused himself and his son, for he had much business to which he had to attend. Locally this meant a line of supplicants taking advantage of their lord's close presence, while mounted messengers came and went with noticeable frequency, carrying messages to and from the whole of Campania and very likely many places beyond.

In this industry he was aided by his son, Jordan, who gave an impression of taking a full part in ruling his father's holdings, and given the princess had retired from the midday heat, Bohemund was left to his own devices. If he was a prisoner not a guest – yet to be proven despite what that herald had said – then he was bound by silken cords, free to move around at will, both inside the castle and the immediate surroundings, but never out of sight of a watchful gaze from the many who attended upon his relatives.

He had grown up with people staring at him because of his height, but even taking that into account, the amount of attention he received from the Capuans amounted to an unusual degree of scrutiny and after a while he realised that one or a pair of them were observing his meanderings, if not always closely so. It was as if in his movement and actions they had been tasked to discern the very workings of his mind, while in conversation, when they did engage him, he was subjected to an unaccustomed amount of flattery. To hear them talk it was as if the prince's nephew had plundered the possession of some sworn enemy rather than that of their lord and master, for they were full of praise for his sagacity and his actions; no mention was made of those Lombard lances who had died in that narrow, tree-lined valley.

There was not much to Montesárchio, either in the way of extensive fortifications or the town itself, yet it had all those attributes that marked it out as a Norman outpost, not least a large training manège by which he stopped, with a battered false shield wall occupying one whole end, stout wooden stakes marked by the deep cuts from wielded broadswords, posts set in a zigzag pattern that required good horsemanship through which to manoeuvre at a decent pace, much of the guiding having to be done by the pressure of thighs and knees alone, for the hands would be occupied with weapons. There were straw-stuffed sacks set on swinging uprights to test a man's skill with the lance. It was empty now, being raked to remove all trace of what had taken place in the cool, early hours of the morning.

'You will join us on the morrow, I hope,' said one of the knights who kept popping up to converse with him. 'We will all wish to observe your obvious prowess.'

'Is it so apparent?'

'How could it not be when you have so recently run rings round we poor Capuans? We were given to wonder if the name Bohemund was another appellation for a chimera.'

The gap between flattery and falsehood is wafer thin; that sounded more like the latter to Bohemund, making him consider a less than encouraging thought. Had he been allowed to raid at will, had they let him plunder in order to aid the seduction to which he was bound to be subjected? If he hoped not, still he felt it best to at least consider it possible, given it is better to dent your pride than burnish it.

Walking on, he cast a professional eye over the quality of the extensive stud, many areas full of mares and foals – they kept well away from their sires – until he found the paddock with his own mount, who was grazing so contentedly that it ignored his calls. Still it had been well groomed and looked sleek, crest and tail well combed and the hooves shiny with oil. He would have liked to find his saddle and harness but that was not possible, given he was still under observation, and the thought occurred that if he needed to make a break he might have to do so riding bareback.

Lest they work out his thinking he moved away, examining the castle and its defences from every angle, until he came full circle to a point where the small town of Montesárchio abutted the bottom of the causeway that led to the main gate. He made to enter the first of the narrow streets, only to find his way blocked by a pair of fellows who by their gentle gestures – a hand on their sword hilts added to a minimal shake – made it plain that such a course was not open to him. Tempted to brush them aside and go his own way, he was stopped by the sound of the running footsteps of a servant; the message had been sent that the princess, now the sun was past its zenith, was eager to receive him.

Not doubting that her husband was keen that she should test the waters of potential disloyalty, Bohemund turned and made his way back up the steep causeway, realising as he entered the cool stone interior that, still fully dressed in his mail, he was sweating from even those less than exacting perambulations. Even if the sun had dipped, it was still baking, which made him long for one of those naked dips in a cool river which he had enjoyed in the company of his conroys when they were sure no danger was at hand – the last occasion had been many days past. No doubt for the same reasons of temperature, Fressenda, attended by a pair of ladies in waiting, sat in near darkness, the small east-facing room she occupied heavily shuttered to keep out the sunlight.

'Please sit, nephew, and tell me all about yourself.'

'What is to tell that you do not already know?'

'Much, I suspect, for if we are family we are not of the close kind. I have not seen you since you were a bouncing child and an appealing one at that, with your curls. You were of a size even then and restless, never still. Now, on the cusp of manhood you have your passions in check, but I wonder if there is anything of that boisterous babe still present?'

'I have not lost my love of mischief.'

That, an obvious allusion to his recent actions, made her laugh, and it had about it something of the *Guiscard*, though without the booming level of noise. Bohemund was frustrated by the gloom; he wanted to see her face, not just hear her voice. It is easy to dissemble when your features are hidden, much harder to be evasive when every word is accompanied by a facial expression, and, he thought, since she shared features and certain gestures with his sister Emma, Fressenda might give away more to him than she knew.

'Your father sent you to our lands?'

'No, I am here against his wishes.'

'His wishes, Bohemund? Are you defying him?'

'Word was sent that I was to desist and I was reminded that the Duke is your brother.'

'My much-beloved brother,' Fressenda replied, and it was not necessary to see her face to note the tone of irony. 'If you wish to defy him, would it not be best to plunder in his lands, not ours?'

'As a knight and a leader of men I must make my way, though I cannot ride alone and I must in all conscience have a care for those who attach themselves to my banner, all of whom are knights in his service. What chance of advancement if all my father knows of them is what they stole from him?'

'So you think that even in defying him, you personally will not be subjected to any retribution? It sounds more like an enterprise blessed than forbidden.' That was a suggestion best not replied to. 'When did you see your father last?'

'At the castle of Corato; he returned to Trani, I rode west.'

'And was he in good health?'

'"Robust" would better describe him.' Fressenda did not respond to that, and since she did not speak and he did not know what to say, a long silence followed, before his aunt added, forcefully, 'I am glad to hear it, but perhaps you are less inclined to feel happy that he is, as you term it, "robust".'

As an invitation to damn him it was obvious and given he had no intention of doing so, it led to another extended silence.

'You do not respond, Bohemund. Can you forget that he made a bastard of you?'

'No.'

136

'You, your mother and sister cast aside just so Robert could wed a Lombard and add to his riches?'

'That was not the reason given. He claimed to fear eternal damnation.'

'It does not occur to you that instead of asking the Pope for a dispensation of annulment, which was accompanied by several talents of gold to oil the wheels, that same bribe could have been put to the purpose of overcoming the consanguinity of his marriage to your mother? Why did he not choose that? It was driven by ambition, not fear, and if he can put aside the mother of his two children who will he not betray to gain his ends?'

His aunt's voice was irked, but was she really angry or just trying to manipulate his emotions? Without he could clearly see her eyes he could not tell.

'Do you hate him, Bohemund?'

'To do so would be a sin.'

'You are so deeply religious?'

'As I am sure are you.'

That held her in check for a moment; people with power tended to pay lip service to the Ten Commandments, relying on occasional and public acts of piety to ensure salvation, this while loudly exhorting those over whom they hold sway to trust everything to God. There were exceptions, his half-brother *Borsa* by repute being one, but nothing he had seen of his aunt, admittedly not much, made him suspect she was overly devout.

'Do you sin when you think of Sichelgaita and *Borsa*?'

'I rarely allow either of them to intrude upon my thoughts.'

That brought forth a low chuckle. 'If you wield your sword with the same skill as you do your tongue, nephew, you will go far.'

'I hope to do so.'

'Do you aspire to be Duke of Apulia, Bohemund?'

'If I did, it is not something I would openly admit to while my father is still alive.'

'It would be treason?'

'Foolish, more like, if he is as you say he is.'

'You can voice thoughts here that you cannot be open about in your father's domains.'

'Just as I can keep them to myself, wherever I am.'

'Even when help may be at hand?'

'You alluded to our family not being close, but you are of an age to have known all of my uncles, those who served with Rainulf Drengot. I would be eager to hear of their exploits and what kind of men they were; even more how they rose from humble knights to become great lords.'

'They were all de Hautevilles, is that not enough?' Again he did not need to see her eyes; the impatience at the deliberate change of subject was obvious in that reply. There was a rustle of clothing and enough light to see she had stood. 'Forgive me, nephew, I must prepare for our coming feast and so, I suspect, must you.'

'Meaning I smell like a horse?' Bohemund joked.

That brought forth another burst of real laughter. 'Not any horse I have ever owned; you're as rank as a pig.'

Like any great magnate, Richard and his wife ate in public, surrounded by a large number of their vassals, with, in this setting, the addition of jesters and musicians, which imposed as much strain on the limitations of Montesárchio as the Duke of Apulia had on Corato, while the knights that lined either side of the great hall were equally eager in their imbibing. There the similarities ended; there were no shouts of acclamation hailing their leader and victory, for there had been none, while Richard showed by his consumption of both food and wine why he had such a puffy face and a paunch; he overate voraciously and never let the wine servant go by without he drained his cup and had it refilled.

His conversation was stuttering because of that, though interesting originally as he told the youth rambling tales of his Uncle William's service with Rainulf Drengot, the very thing his wife had declined to do. These became progressively less controlled as the wine took hold and the number of de Hauteville brothers rose from two to five. It got to the point of nearly naming them, William Iron Arm most of all, as ingrates who had enjoyed Rainulf's kindness, then with Lombard help betrayed him.

'I would hope that you will hunt with us, Bohemund,' Jordan called, as the thoughts his father was harbouring made him look sulky and kept his face in his wine cup.

'That I would like, cousin.'

Bohemund responded as was required, but in truth he was thinking that this fellow, some ten or more years his senior, was the person who should be seeking to detach him from loyalty to his father. He was Richard's heir and time's arrow was more likely to find him holding Capua when the moment came to contest his inheritance, which he would most certainly do, even if he was not prepared to be open about it with those hinting they might help. Against that, Jordan had married a sister of Sichelgaita, making him also a brother-in-law to Gisulf of Salerno, a known hater of de Hautevilles, so his allegiance might lie in the wrong direction.

A good-looking fellow, with an intelligent cast to his eye, Jordan looked more the prince than his sire. The smile he was aiming at his guest seemed slightly enigmatic, though Bohemund had to accept that the impression was possibly brought about by heightened imagination and not judgement. Because he was abstemious, he had, while talking to the hard-drinking prince, been able to observe much and one thing had been obvious: Jordan had watched him the way a falcon observes an unsuspecting field mouse and the look had carried with it a hint of private knowledge, for he had also seemed, in some way, amused.

Both were then distracted by Prince Richard's fool, dressed in ludicrous layers of multicoloured rags, who was now bouncing around and jabbering in front of the high table. He had been making jests aimed at Hildebrand and Gregorian popes, but his tune had altered; now he was crying out that time had seen weasels and stoats back where they belonged, deep in the ground, with God to do the burrowing all the way to the anguish such creatures were entitled to get in the netherworld, for that was what they deserved.

Lords of the undergrowth one day, gobbling up mice and voles with low cunning in their supple hunt, meat for maggots the next. Beside him, Richard had begun to laugh in an inebriated way but his son was clearly less pleased. Yet it was not he who acted; it was Fressenda who threw the goblet that struck the poor idiot on the face, and with such force that it cut him. He staggered away from her and closer to Bohemund, his hand going to the point of contact and coming away with a trace of blood.

That set off a wailing and crying, for he was, like fools everywhere, a poor creature of dull wits who could, because of his afflictions, say things to the high and mighty that no other low-born person would dare to, for again, like all his breed, he was held to be much cosseted by God and that gave him protection from retribution. He fell against the table and turned, his odd-looking too-wide eyes fixed on Bohemund, showing his sad, flat face and yellowing skin. Then he cried out.

'*Mustela nivalis* is no more. Weep in the burrow!'

Then two servants grabbed the fool and dragged him away, with Bohemund looking round quickly to try and see who had given the instruction, just in time to observe Jordan sit back, his smile now looking more forced than enigmatic, this while the hubbub of noise in the hall dropped suddenly. He had to work just as hard to compose his own features, to pretend that he had not understood the message the fool had been imparting, this while the Prince of Capua turned to his wife in such a way as to present his back to his guest, so his face was hidden.

'I will have your horse saddled and ready at first light, Bohemund,' Jordan called once more. 'If that meets with your approval.' When the response was a nod, he added, 'You and I must speak with each other as much as you must talk with my father. I would have us be friends, if that is possible.'

To smile actually hurt. 'I am sure we will be that.'

'Wine!' Jordan cried. 'Damn it, my cup is empty and look to our guest.'

That was no sooner out than Richard turned back towards him, a lopsided grin on his face. 'And when you have hunted we shall converse, Bohemund. We have much to offer each other.'

Allowing his wine cup to be filled, Bohemund's thoughts were in turmoil; was that fool telling the truth? For with his damaged wits he was as likely to invent as to make jests that were truthful just as he knew the Latin tag for a weasel and that creature's relationship to his sire. How could he not when he had heard it used so frequently?

He could not ask, for in truth if the fool did have it right he was not sure he would get a straight response from anyone. Was it no more than a ploy to trap him into making some kind of arrangement? He must get away and suddenly that musing about riding bareback took on a more serious meaning. But he was going hunting and he would be gifted a saddled and harnessed mount, and surely, out in the fields and woodlands there would be a chance to break away.

The feasting went on for an age, his host becoming near insensible, which was a blessing since it saved him from too much conversation, and when Jordan or his mother took the opportunity to surreptitiously look at him now, it was with an air of enquiry which was matched in Bohemund's breast. Finally, at a signal from his wife, two servants took hold of an unresisting prince and aided him on his way to his bedchamber. With him gone, and most of his vassals as drunk as was he, it was clearly time to bring matters to an end. When Fressenda stood those who could follow did so and she swept out of the great hall with her son at her heels, Jordan avoiding Bohemund's eye, giving a mumbled message of, 'On the morrow,' as he passed him.

The morning was not cool, but it was mildly warm and pleasant as Bohemund, having struggled with his breakfast, emerged, dressed in the hunting clothes with which he had been provided – no doubt with great difficulty and the aid of a seamstress – after a less than peaceful night in which every possible avenue between truth and lies had been explored over and over again. He was greeted by a cousin who looked as though he had not slept well either, with neither willing to refer to the fact. Instead, both were quick to mount and in the company of a ten-strong party of Jordan's own familia knights they rode out of Montesárchio, heading into the sun and thus east at a steady canter, which was curious to Bohemund, given it was taking him closer to home.

Was it a standard, a signal or a prearrangement that had those knightly companions of Jordan's drop back out of earshot? There was no way to tell, but they did as almost immediately the heir to Capua began to speak about the new Pope and what troubles that might bring to both his father and Apulia, not forgetting to add that Pope Gregory had a strong desire, one he had often voiced as Hildebrand, that men such as Jordan and Bohemund could better serve their God by taking ship to Byzantium and fighting the Turks.

'There is too much that detains me here, Jordan – and you, I suspect – to even consider such a crusade. Our new pontiff is buoyed by the success of my Uncle Roger in Sicily—'

'And what had happened in Spain?' Jordan interrupted. 'They too are fighting and succeeding under a papal banner.'

'He thinks the throwing back of Moors and Saracens as well as their religion is easy, or should I say he sees it as the undoubted will of God, but what we hear of the Turks does not lead me to think they will easily succumb.'

'I think you right, Bohemund, and fear it would take more than we Normans to even attempt such a thing. If the might of Byzantium was destroyed at Manzikert, what force would it take to ensure we did not fall to the same fate?'

'What was that fool babbling on about last night, cousin?'

The abrupt change of subject and its effect went through Jordan's hands and body, making his horse jibe slightly, as Bohemund continued, 'I am not fool enough to be ignorant of why I have been brought to meet your father, but so far I have only hints from my aunt. It would be better if I had plain speaking and since I think you

143

know the prince's mind it would be as well from you as any other.'

Jordan did not respond immediately, with Bohemund remaining silent too, aware that if he spoke it would only allow his cousin to hedge his answer. When he did talk, and after the shock of what he said had subsided, Bohemund was amazed at his candour.

'We have been told that your father, the Duke, is dead at Bari of a fever, but we have no idea if it is rumour or truth. The fool spoke too soon.'

Bohemund sought to keep any trace of desolation out of his voice. 'You did not think to tell me of this rumour?'

'We thought of it and my father decided against it until it was confirmed.' Jordan hauled on his reins and faced Bohemund, who had automatically done likewise, the men behind them stopping too in order to keep their distance. 'I do not think I need to tell you why.'

'No.'

'You cannot begin to conceive of the times your name has come up in our talking these last weeks.'

Lost in contemplation of the news he had been given, and wondering how much it was fact, it took Bohemund some time to respond. 'I hope it was every hour of every day.'

'Every action was discussed from hanging you to throwing you into a dungeon and leaving you there till you rot.' There was a temptation to remind Jordan that they had failed to corner him and his men, but that was superfluous; best to let him speak. 'It was my notion to bring you in as a guest, in which I was aided by my mother.'

'And to what purpose was the invitation extended?'

'To offer you full Capuan support when you seek to take your rightful inheritance.'

'You're sure it is mine?'

'I think my mother answered that.'

'Did your father agree?'

'No, he thought we should balance out our aid to keep Apulia in turmoil, and when the time is ripe, to invade. He does not think, as I do, that such a thing is a malignancy, which is inclined to spread, not peter out. If your father could not contain his vassals, it is hardly likely we would do better and what trouble would that stir up in our own bailiwick?'

'Yet you just encouraged those very vassals to rebel and supported them.'

'We did not.'

'That was not the belief held by my father.'

'It would benefit him, or whoever now rules, to look a little deeper.'

'Are you saying you do not hanker after Apulia?'

'Only by invitation.'

'Which I would never issue.'

'Neither will your half-brother or any other de Hauteville. Apulia can only be taken by force, something my brother-in-law, Gisulf, writes to encourage me to undertake often, under his brilliant leadership, of course. First I doubt it possible, and very much impossible if your father still lives, uncertain even if he does not, and it would be a long, drawn-out affair in which we would bleed as much as those we fight. While we are busy fighting and killing each other, which we Normans have never before done here in Italy, what will our sworn enemies do?'

He had no need to mention popes or emperors east or west; they had been trying and failing to divide the Normans for decades – they would gather like vultures to consume the remnants.

'The only question which remains is, what will you do now?'

'I must find out if the rumour regarding my father is true.' The questioning look in his cousin's eye demanded a response. 'And if it is, I will be quickly back in Capua and not to plunder.'

Jordan used his knees to edge his horse close enough for the two to take each other's hand in a strong clasp. No words were added; they did not need to be.

'Go as you must, Bohemund,' Jordan said once their hands had been disengaged. Then he smiled. 'Odd that I hope the rumour is false – our world will be a sorrier place without the *Guiscard*.'

'I share that hope, which might surprise you.'

'No, it would be dishonourable that you should desire otherwise. If you ride straight into the sun you will come upon the men you led.' Before Bohemund could ask how he knew that, Jordan added with a grin, 'They were taken late in the very same day you were invited to Montesárchio, cousin. Without you to lead them they were easy meat.'

'Harmed?'

Jordan threw his head back and laughed, so loud that it had the birds flying in alarm from the surrounding trees. 'Not a hair, for who knows, you may need them.'

CHAPTER TEN

Having rescued his captured lances – they too had been in ignorance of the rumours – the party set off immediately for the borderlands with Apulia, their destination the ducal capital of Melfi, where Bohemund would find out the truth about the Guiscard. But there were other reasons to go there: that castle was one of the few places in his father's domains from which, in his possession, he could not be easily dislodged, while it was also the centre of the administration of the whole domain and in its vaults were the staggering revenues accumulated by Robert's tax gatherers, including those remitted from Calabria and the Norman parts of Sicily.

Naturally, on the way there was time to ask how his men had been so easily rounded up. The truth was sobering, for it transpired that Prince Richard – or was it Jordan? – had so covered the ground with their own conroys that escape became impossible. Reynard had jinked from one direction to another, taken refuge in a forest, which avoided capture on four or five occasions, only to find that whatever way he subsequently rode, there before him was an enemy, always Normans, more powerful in numbers, that could not be swept aside. In the end, in trying to break out of the encirclement, he had led the Apulian lances into a well-laid trap in which there were only two alternatives: to surrender or die.

'Which would have been foolish given we were offered safe conduct back to the River Ufita and that included what plunder we had on our packhorses.'

'To so box you in must have taken hundreds of lances.'

'Agreed, which means that Richard of Capua knows full well of your father's intention to invade and has moved his forces up early to meet him. Given the numbers we encountered, he was planning to cross the Ufita first.'

'You are sure it was not just me that brought them out in such numbers?'

'The river,' Reynard replied.

He said this pointing ahead and that hid the look on his face, a mixture of curiosity and a degree of concern; the one matter not discussed since they had come together had been what had been offered to Bohemund while he was a guest of the Capuans and what, if anything, he had agreed to. The familia knight had not asked and this stripling son of the Duke had shown no desire to enlighten him, while it was obvious that, should the rumour of the *Guiscard*'s demise prove true, they were riding into a situation in which Reynard himself would be required to make a decision about where his own allegiance lay.

The older man could not know the reason for Bohemund's silence, which was, quite simply, the need to seek some kind of reason for what had occurred at Montesárchio, and that included the Capuan leniency with his men, who at the very least should have been deprived of both their plunder and the means to ride – proper retribution might have seen them hanging from the trees. In that short talk with Jordan much had been implied that was left unsaid and that too had to be picked at for meaning; that no conclusion was possible nagged at him all the way to his destination.

Two days hard riding, in which no equine care at all was lavished on their mounts, brought them into distant sight of Melfi. As soon as the castle was visible Bohemund called a halt so that when they did arrive their horses would not be utterly blown – not a wise thing to do when he had no idea what he might face. They were unharnessed and allowed to graze while his men, tired as he was himself, were adjured to rest. Not that he himself could do so; there were still too many teeming thoughts in his head, and he walked a little away to examine a town and stronghold he had not seen for several years and to reflect on the fact that it was where he had spent his early childhood, before he and his sister had been packed off elsewhere.

Before him was one of the great seats of Norman power in the southern half of the Italian Peninsula, a de Hauteville possession ever since the days of William Iron Arm. His scrutiny was carried out, as at Montesárchio, with a professional eye as well as a sentimental one, for there was much to admire about both the location and the structure. Melfi had withstood every attempt to take it by main force ever since it had been built by the Byzantines, one of two unassailable bastions designed to hold the western border of Langobardia against incursions by Lombards, their Norman mercenaries and, should he venture so far south, the Western Emperor.

Melfi itself had expanded since William's day from a tiny and poor settlement to a vibrant and substantial town; how could it not with so much power close by? But it was the dominating fortress that mattered, standing on a high elevation and controlling the central route through the mountains from the east of Italy to the once powerful coastal cities of the west: Salerno, Naples and Amalfi. In a country dominated by defensive towers and fortified, walled towns, only one other location, also built by the Byzantines, could match Melfi for its ability to accommodate a force of mounted knights numbered in the hundreds and strong enough to be described as a host.

Added to that it was a place impossible to take by a *coup de main*, overlooked as it was by the even higher peak of Monte Vulture, the mountain topped by a watchtower. That too formed part of its defence; no substantial force could hope to approach from any direction without being seen a whole day's march distant, which gave the defenders the chance to both prepare their resistance as well as to send out a mobile raiding force that, using the surrounding mountains as a refuge, would render any siege a nightmare by the cutting off of communications with the coast, the interdiction of supplies and reinforcements, plus the fact that they could raid the siege lines in force at will.

Few men were needed to secure the walls and it was no easy task to even get close to them. A wide, winding causeway led up to the great gates, itself with a defensible wall. Imposing from a distance, with its great square keep and hexagonal corner towers, Bohemund knew from childhood memory how much more redoubtable it became at close quarters. A stone bridge spanned the moat to the twin curtain walls that contained a deathtrap between them, one that an attacker must cross to even attempt to take the main outer wall, this overlooked by a pair of tall, castellated barbicans manned by archers. Having done that they must somehow get open a double gate, only to be faced by yet another ditch with a raised drawbridge. Caught between the two they would be at the mercy of the defending bowmen and they would suffer greatly as they tried to subdue the defence.

Those walls and towers were made from the stone of the mountains in which the castle sat, rock so hard the walls could not be undermined, and they were well buttressed to withstand assault by ballista, while being tall enough to make firing anything over the parapet near impossible. On three sides lay steep escarpments that reduced the options for any attacker to a frontal assault up the causeway. The interior was spacious, with well-constructed accommodation that could house large numbers of knights, sufficient stabling for their mounts, with vaults below and lofts above that could store a quantity of supplies to sustain them for an eternity, added to which it had a water supply that could not be stopped: several deep cisterns in what was well-watered and fertile country.

Unbeknown to Bohemund the same examination was being carried out by his father, though he was riding, not stationary, and at the head of a long train of knights and all the paraphernalia that accompanied a great magnate on his travels, including, right behind him and also mounted, his wife and two sons. Also different was the emotion, for underlying Robert's examination was a sense of melancholy; he had inherited Melfi from his elder brother Humphrey and had no love of the location, unlike for example Bari, a place that had once thought itself impregnable until he proved the inhabitants wrong.

Melfi was not a place he had himself captured and neither had the two eldest de Hautevilles who had bequeathed it previously. A Lombard, Arduin of Fassano, given the captaincy by a foolish

Byzantine catapan, had taken the castle in an act of betrayal thirty years before, bringing into its walls a force of Normans led by William. It had withstood any attempt at recapture, becoming a base for their expansion, originally in the cause of Lombard independence, ultimately on their own behalf, and it had served the family well as a place from which they could not be ejected.

Yet now there was the question of its continued suitability: was it still an appropriate location to oversee an extended fiefdom that included the whole of Apulia and Calabria as well as, since the capture of Palermo, a good third of the island of Sicily, which would increase with time and his brother's efforts? In reality, Robert thought the centre of his administration, to be truly effective, needed to be on the west coast of Italy, not the east or even in the mountainous middle.

As against that Melfi was perfect as a place from which to launch any proposed campaign against Capua, for in this location he could gather his entire force and sustain them without, he hoped, it being obvious what he was planning. It was simple to cut any links to the west and keep his preparations hidden, as well as to disguise his route of attack. As these thoughts surfaced he wondered about Bohemund and how his raiding had progressed; he also wondered what he had heard, if anything, about his illness and supposed demise. He knew from his own experience, when plundering, that staying out of contact with the kind of people who might pass on such information was essential; they tended be those trying to stop you.

Robert craned his neck to look to the top of the high peak and to the banner on the flagpole. For several hours it had been a fluttering ochre, a sign to the garrison of Melfi alerting them to the approach of an armed party of unknown provenance; nonsense, of course, since messengers had arrived days before to alert them to the movements of their suzerain. Now the men that manned it could see his lance pennants they could confirm his arrival and replace the ochre with a long stream of blue and white, as if to say not even Duke Robert was permitted to approach his foremost castle without he must identify himself.

'Bohemund,' Reynard called, his arm outstretched towards the top of the mountain.

There was a long pause while Bohemund examined that long pennant bearing his family colours, wondering who did it signify, for it could mean that *Borsa* was approaching, not the *Guiscard*. If it was his half-brother, no doubt in the company of his fat sow of a mother, then he needed to get there before them, though the notion that he could then seek to hold it and keep them out was unlikely. What mattered more was that he was not barred from entry, so it was necessary to saddle up and move out quickly.

If Melfi was well defended from the east, the west was not ignored, and they were only halfway to the castle when a strong party of mounted men, fully mailed, closed at a rapid pace. Discretion demanded that Bohemund show no aggression towards them; he needed to halt and wait, which was frustrating, but he was not held up for long. If sometimes his height and build could be a burden, this was not one of those occasions; as soon as he put forward his identity it was accepted by men who very likely had never seen him before, so much had his proportions become the stuff of tales – he did, of course, look like a de Hauteville.

That was the first good thing; the second was the news that his father was alive and close by, less cheering that Sichelgaita and his half-brothers were with him.

*   *   *

153

Since Robert was in no hurry, Bohemund got there ahead of him and had time to join the knights lined up at the base of the sloping causeway to receive their master, a welcome carried out with some ceremony. He was obvious not just by being head and shoulders above the rest but by the filth of both his clothing and accoutrements, added to the ungroomed state of his horse, in contrast to the men of the garrison who had been busy with polish and oil to glitter and glow before their liege lord. A flourish of trumpets accompanied him as he rode along the line, greeting each man he recognised, for there were many in the garrison who had fought with him in years gone by and would do battle under his banner in the future. He must have spotted his son well before he came abreast – how could he not? – which must have given him time to wonder at his presence. Face to face he hauled on his reins and brought his magnificently caparisoned mount to a halt.

'I did not expect to set eyes on you this day.'

Partly it was the peremptory tone that made Bohemund respond the way he did – it was not a greeting with any degree of warmth – yet it was much more the glare he was getting from Sichelgaita that irked him, she having reined in behind his father.

'Nor me you, I was told you were dead.'

'Which you can see is not the case.'

'I wonder how such news was received?' Sichelgaita demanded, with a scowl.

'With sorrow, what else?'

'I can think of a dozen other emotions that might surface.'

'Where is Reynard?' his father asked, still without anything approaching a smile.

'Inside the castle with my conroys.'

Robert just nodded, kicked with his heels and that moved his mount on, which was as good a way as any of saying that he would talk to his familia knight before he ever spoke with his son. That thought was wiped out as Sichelgaita came closer, angling her mount, he thought, so her sons could get a good look at him. *Borsa* tried to both appear taller and hold a cold stare, but he blinked, which spoilt the effect. Guy was too young to do anything other than be amazed at his size, actually gaping, which brought from Bohemund a slight smile, given it was a look to which he was well accustomed, the cheering reaction the fact that it clearly annoyed his mother.

'Move on,' she hissed, spurring her horse more than was necessary and making its head rear back, a loud snort coming out of its nostrils. As his half-brothers moved away, he heard her say over her shoulder, 'Mark that man well, my sons, for one day he will serve to feed your dogs for a month.'

Not being called into his father's presence until the next day, plus knowing that Reynard had been summoned, caused frustration; it made him feel of no account, but there was one blessing: Sichelgaita had not come to Melfi to stay – she departed with a substantial train at dawn on the second day, on the way, he was told, to her prenuptial home of Salerno. It was later, well into the afternoon, when Bohemund was sent for, entering his father's privy quarters to another less than glowing welcome.

'So, are you going to tell me what you failed to pass onto Reynard?' Robert demanded. 'Did you commit yourself to Capua, did they even seek to detach you from my service?'

'There is nothing I can say in that regard that you will not guess.' The look he got in response was designed to show much doubt. 'But

I think I have learnt much that might be of use to you.'

That got the kind of raised eyebrows that acted as an invitation to continue. Bohemund briefly reprised his conversation with Fressenda, but laid much more emphasis on the exchange with Jordan, seeking to skip over his offer of aid while underlining the disagreement with his father Richard about how to deal with the supposed death of his great rival. He did not leave out his impression of a one-time warrior prince going to seed through overindulgence, or the advice that a deeper investigation of who stirred up the recent uprisings might point to a different culprit.

'Richard must trust him, since Jordan had no fear of his anger in letting me depart – either that or it was prearranged. I have had time to think since then and I cannot believe that what was said to me was anything other than a policy to which Jordan would hold. He claims to be continually prodded by Gisulf to bring you down.'

'You trust his word on my dolt of a brother-in-law?'

'I do,' Bohemund replied, with real feeling. 'As I do on many things.'

'This son of Capua has clearly captured your heart.'

'You mock me for believing him?'

'You talked to him but once and you trust him. You claim he has the confidence of Richard without proof. I like to see into a man's eyes myself and even then I look for duplicity, for the very good reason it is there more often than honesty.'

'What if he really does believe that a bloody contest between Capua and Apulia will only advantage others and will do all in his power to avoid it? And if Jordan is speaking with sincerity and Capua did nothing to stir up and sustain the revolt of your vassals, who, then, was behind the likes of Peter and Abelard?'

It was pleasing that his impassioned statement did not draw ridicule; instead his father looked thoughtful, though he remained silent for a long time, even holding up his hand when it looked as if his son was about to speak. Eventually the silence became too much.

'It could be Gisulf,' Bohemund said quietly.

'That fool! Even with the proceeds of his nautical larceny he lacks the means. The rebels had funds to pay their soldiers and that could not have come from their own money chests. And who armed those Lombards you slaughtered at Noci?'

'Gisulf is a Lombard.'

'So is my wife,' Robert barked. 'Leave me, I need to think.'

It was not often that Robert de Hauteville considered that he might have been duped, but he was thinking that now and in the background he saw the hand of the one-time Hildebrand. If Bohemund was right and Jordan was telling the truth, then there were only two other places the funds to feed the rebellion could have come from and he had already discounted Byzantium, while Bamberg was too distant and too disinterested. But if the cunning archdeacon were the gremlin he would work to keep his hand well hidden, so it was very possible that he had used Gisulf as a proxy. If that was the case, how much more trouble would Hildebrand cause now he was Pope Gregory; there was no comfort in thinking he might desist – the man was not like that.

Odd that in ruminating on such a conundrum, the thoughts he had mulled over the day before should resurface, melding into a set of possibilities that might solve several problems in one fell swoop. What emerged was the kind of tangled solution that the *Guiscard* loved, and in truth it had all the hallmarks of the combination of cunning and clear-sightedness for which he was famous; no one could pull the strings of the tangled skein like him. The call for messengers, when he had reached his conclusion, was as loud as that to which his clerks were accustomed.

'Messengers and scribes!'

For Reynard the notion of being a messenger was not one to make him feel elevated, but Robert had insisted that the message he was sending had to go with someone known to be close to him, so that its importance could not be doubted, and to assuage his pride the *Guiscard* had gone as far as to appraise him of the contents. This saw him heading back from Melfi in the direction in which he and Bohemund had so recently ridden, though at a less furious pace and on a constant change of horses.

There was no sneaking into Capuan territory this time; he went straight to the old Roman bridge and settlement by the Ponte Ufita where there was a contingent of soldiers to back up Prince Richard's toll collectors, stating his business and demanding free passage. Naturally, such a crossing was home to a hostelry where he could get food, drink and negotiate for a change of horses, his to be stabled until he came through on his return. It was while he was arranging this, as well as bespeaking a bed, that a knight of Capua, a tall, burly fellow in a red and black surcoat, came to talk to the innkeeper on exactly the same subject and since they were both Norman it was natural that they should fall into conversation over a flagon of wine.

'A messenger you say?' Reynard asked, for the fellow, who went by the name of Odo, had about him the air, as well as the build – not to say the scars – of a fighting man.

'To the Prince of Capua,' Odo replied.

'Can I say you do not look to be a mere messenger?'

That puffed his chest. 'I am one of the senior familia knights to Prince Richard of Capua, but it was felt that a communication of such importance required that it be carried by someone of my rank.'

'On what purpose, friend?'

From being affable, the look on the fellow's face made the appellation 'friend' seem out of place. He positively growled. 'I am not at liberty to share the thoughts of my prince.'

'What if I were to tell you that I too am a messenger, that I too am a familia knight, to the Duke of Apulia, and that he prevailed on me to carry a very important communication to Prince Richard for the very same reasons of standing?'

'Yet you will not know its contents?'

'Not the words, but I do the sentiments.'

There had to be something in the way Reynard said that, for Odo's eyes narrowed and he whispered, 'Peace?'

'And harmony between Capua and Apulia.'

'There's devil's work here, Reynard, for my message is the same.'

'Not the work of the Devil, friend,' Reynard replied, filling both their goblets then raising his. 'Maybe God's?'

Bohemund was allowed to accompany his father to the meeting with Richard of Capua at the Castle of Grottaminarda, but required to be discreet in his presence, for *Borsa* was there too and it would have been unseemly for him to seek to stand as the acknowledged heir's equal, added to which Sichelgaita was on her way from Salerno. Naturally, he and Jordan exchanged meaningful looks but to avoid suspicion they did not seek each other out for a private discourse. The two rulers greeted each other with a warm embrace; they had, after all, fought as allies against Pope Leo at Civitate many years before and if they had been very deeply suspicious of each other's motives since, and no doubt still were, they understood the demands of diplomacy and conversed as friends, while Robert graciously kissed his sister Fressenda's hand.

The arrival of Sichelgaita allowed for the very necessary great feast in which the followers of both magnates sought to outshine each other, while their wives sought, with less success, to disguise their mutual loathing, for Sichelgaita knew exactly what Fressenda thought of the annulment and her subsequent marriage. But important as both the spouses were, such dislike was not allowed to cloud the masculine bonhomie.

Richard, as was his habit, drank too much and had to be led off to bed, and a keen eye might have spotted the look from the *Guiscard* that followed him as he departed at a stagger; Jordan certainly did, and Bohemund, observing his father, saw that he was far from pleased, for it was not a benign gaze, rather one of pity mixed with calculation – the look of a plotter, not a companion. To Bohemund it only showed that his father too had drunk too much; he suspected he was normally more careful to disguise his feelings.

The outline of their discussions the next morning was perfectly simple: they would not fight each other but cooperate in those areas of mutual advantage, and part of that related to Robert's wayward brother-in-law, for Gisulf was as much if not more of a thorn in the flesh to Richard as he was to the *Guiscard*. The Prince of Capua's land bordered what little Gisulf still retained and if he had the power of a flea, they still nip and leave a mark, so when the suggestion was put forward by the Duke that both men should gain from the meeting it was warmly received.

'I sent my wife to warn him to behave and he laughed in her face,

Richard, and swore to bring me down. Even now I think him still in league with Rome, so I will countenance that no more. I intend, when the time is right, to chase Gisulf out of Salerno and make it my capital.'

There was a pause then, a look exchanged between Jordan and his father, which was held until the *Guiscard* added, 'And I will make no move to interfere should you wish to take Naples and I will also come to your aid with my fleet to enforce a blockade.'

Richard of Capua nodded; to take Salerno the *Guiscard* would wish passage for part of his forces across Capuan lands – he lacked ships to lay siege to a port like Naples. That was all that was needed, there being nothing put in writing: an air of amity they could show to the world, as well as an embrace made in public. Such secret arrangements had to remain that, so as not to forewarn their numerous enemies, while beneath the bonhomie, the mutual suspicion and distrust had not dissipated one jot.

CHAPTER ELEVEN

The news that all his plans in the south had come to nought sent Pope Gregory into another one of his teeth-gnashing passions; all his machinations through Gisulf were now exposed and the awareness of this saw a newly gifted chalice thrown against a wall of his Lateran Palace with such force that the dozens of jewels and pearls embedded in the solid-gold body flew free to roll across the floor because, sent by King William of England, it reminded him of those who were his enemies. He could not have the two great Italo-Norman powers in accord at a time when his other adversary, Henry IV, was weak; the Western Emperor-elect, a young unproven ruler of twenty-three years of age, was dealing with a revolt in Saxony and struggling to press home his imperial claims as throughout the Empire.

Desiderius was, as ever, the mediator and fount of knowledge when it came to dealing with Capua and Apulia. He was sent for and he advised Gregory of the obvious: that he must, in such a precarious situation, seek some kind of accommodation with the Norman rulers. That was easier with Prince Richard than the *Guiscard*, given the latter was an excommunicate and no pontiff could even dream of holding talks with anyone not in a state of grace, while papal dignity meant it could not be lifted without good reason. The first task as Desiderius saw it was to pacify at least one branch of the threat, not least in order to protect his own monastery of Monte Cassino, which overlooked the road from Capua to Rome and was thus likely to become embroiled in any dispute with Richard regardless of any wish to stand aside.

Envoys were despatched to offer a treaty of peace to the Prince of Capua in order to keep him quiet, with the granting of various benefits in terms of disputed revenues as an inducement. To initiate that was unsettling enough but Christ's Vicar on Earth nearly choked when it came to Robert de Hauteville. If compromise had been anathema when he had been Hildebrand, then as Pope Gregory it was even more unpalatable. Yet he had, on the pragmatic advice of Desiderius, to write to Roger, Count of Sicily, who was still on the mainland, hinting his elder brother could find his way back to the bosom of the Holy Church if he showed a degree of repentance. An offer that would have been declined out of hand by Robert caused surprise by being accepted; there was, after all, the future capture of Salerno to take into account and it would help if the *Guiscard* could persuade Gregory to disown the unreliable and foolish Gisulf.

After months of comings and goings, which must have taxed the body of a man well past his prime, and just enough give and take to allow the excommunication to be lifted, Desiderius got both the *Guiscard* and Gregory to Benevento, where the Pope had a palace, for if the Duke of Apulia held the lands of the principality, the city itself was still papal territory.

There this outburst of harmony stopped; Robert would not enter the city for fear of assassination, Gregory would not leave his palace for the dread of a further loss of papal dignity. Thus an encounter designed to make peace and foster concord did exactly the opposite and both went their separate ways without meeting. Gregory was already fuming when news came that the Duke Sergius of Amalfi had passed away, leaving only an infant son to inherit a city and trading port that had been in conflict with its nearest neighbour Salerno for decades, a conflict deepened by the fact that the Amalfians had participated in the murder of Prince Gisulf's father.

So, to protect themselves against the Prince of Salerno's oft-stated desire for retribution – he would hang half the citizens if he took the city – Amalfi asked the Duke of Apulia to accept the title. A letter from Gregory forbidding the Amalfians to allow Robert to accept was ignored and he was again excommunicated. But that was insufficient for the Pope, who decided he had to finish off the *Guiscard* once and for all. Hildebrand's memory of Apulian humiliations was long; he had served Pope Leo, only to see him humiliated by the de Hautevilles at Civitate – it was time to rectify that stain on the office he now held.

Since he was relatively secure in the north, and having that just-signed treaty with Richard of Capua that would, he hoped, keep him out of any conflict, Gregory sent out his envoys to those powers that he could count upon to aid his cause: Beatrice of Tuscany, her daughter and her hunchback husband who held Lorraine, to the port cities of the Tyrrhenian Sea, Salerno, Pisa, to Amadeus of Savoy, the Count of Burgundy and Raymond of Toulouse, all Christian knights in good standing with Rome.

Gregory was cunning in his appeal; the object of such a host, he insisted, was not to just spill Christian blood; indeed he desired that the gathering would bring the *Guiscard* to heel without a drop being shed. The prize was singular: once the Normans were subdued – Capua would be much more amenable if Apulia was humbled – the assembled forces would find themselves free to use the ports of the Adriatic coast. Given that access, they should not disband but proceed by ship to Constantinople to aid their Christian brethren suffering under the constant attacks from the followers of their so-called Prophet.

'Imagine it, Desiderius,' Gregory enthused, his eyes alight as he looked at a map of Asia Minor, his finger tracing the route from the Bosphorus to Palestine, 'a huge body of knights under a papal banner, riding in crusade to the rescue of the Eastern Empire, driving back the Turks and every other infidel. Can you not see a great Christian army entering the city of Jerusalem to celestial trumpets and bringing back under the control of our faith the very place where Jesus rose from the dead? Surely in doing that we could claim to be serving the will of God. And what ruler or patriarch, with our soldiers outside his palace, will deny the rights of the Bishop of Rome to universal hegemony?'

'Let us see to the *Guiscard* first,' the abbot replied; even if he too hankered after a great Eastern crusade he had been too long troubled by the Normans, had seen them slip too many a noose, to see what was coming as straightforward.

'My father declines to receive you, Bohemund,' Jordan insisted, 'for he can guess the errand on which you have come and he cannot agree to that which you are bound to seek.'

'It is simple: if we fall, so in time will Capua.'

'While the route to Apulia from Rome is through our principality,'

Jordan replied. 'If we contest the passage of Gregory's great host, the lands we possess will be destroyed much sooner by joining your father than standing aside and giving them free passage.'

Was Jordan uncomfortable? Bohemund could not tell; he hoped so, believing as he did that he had some regard for both him and his father. Yet he could not help but reprise the conversation he had shared with his sire at Melfi prior to allowing him to embark on this mission, for Robert knew very well the contents of the letters sent out by Pope Gregory, as well as the fact that his only potential ally was treaty-bound to his enemy. Capua had made no moves to show they might break that attachment and combine to meet the threat to Duke Robert. And he needed aid, for it would be potentially deadly to face on his own, as well as a serious risk even if he could repeat the alliance and the good fortune that was won at Civitate.

The army he might face was the largest to come south of Rome since a previous Emperor Henry had descended with all his imperial might to put in his place a previous Prince of Capua, a fellow named Pandulf who was unusually avaricious even for a Lombard. Pandulf had not only appropriated the lands of Monte Cassino and rendered beggars the monks who lived there, but had thrown its venerated abbot, a predecessor of Desiderius, into his dungeons. Count Roger, who had not long departed, had been summoned to return with every lance he could muster, for if Robert went down, Sicily would cease to be a secure Norman fief.

Increasingly allowed into his father's confidence, much to the disgust of Sichelgaita, Bohemund had no difficulty in observing that the *Guiscard* was worried; his assessment of the quality and quantity of the forces Gregory had managed to combine was alarming. Being outnumbered was always a concern, but a deeper concern came from facing a vastly superior number of warriors of a fighting capacity little short of those he could muster. Whatever the Normans put in the field as *milites* – and they would be inferior in numbers – it was his mounted knights on which he relied to win his battles, and if the reports he had received were true, then it was in that arm most danger threatened.

As well as learning how to use weapons as a growing boy, Bohemund, like all his kind, had been schooled in tactics, and the one paramount fact of fighting mainly on horseback was that it generally allowed the Normans to manoeuvre with more flexibility than their opponents and thus allowed them to choose the field of battle as well as giving them the ability to engage or decline contact at will. Quite naturally they wanted a slope down which to attack, preferably with at least one flank closed off by topography, a river or a steep hillside, a site on which their superior discipline counted. It was highly likely that such advantages would not be available to them.

'Then Capua must be persuaded, Father,' he had insisted, 'and I have a bond with Jordan.'

The reply had been cold. 'Do not be too ready to believe him, Bohemund.'

'I trust him and I am prepared to try to persuade him to work on his own, sire.'

That had produced an awkward pause; if they had never openly discussed the reasons Bohemund had for saying he trusted Jordan, it was no mystery – a shrewd mind would have little difficulty in seeing the outline if not the detail. Yet it seemed as if that knowledge had not acted to cause a breach; it was as if Robert had accepted it as a fact he could do nothing to alter and the subject of his successor was not one he was prepared to ever discuss. Perhaps it was because of the way he had come to the title himself, more, Bohemund suspected, because to do so tempted a fatal providence; he had a superstition that to talk of death might bring on that very fate.

'Father and son, Capua will always pursue a policy they think benefits them, just as I will always act in my own interest.'

When his father continued, his voice had an air of detachment, as though the outcome he was speculating upon had no bearing on him or his future.

'If Richard holds his peace with Gregory, what happens in Italy when this great host the Pope has gathered, having done that for which it was assembled, departs these shores on his mad Eastern crusade? Who then will be left to protect Apulia, and for that matter Rome itself? From being the inferior Norman overlord in the country, he leapfrogs to become the strongest, and unless our deluded pontiff can assemble another army to subdue Capua he will find himself at their complete mercy.'

'Is that Richard's thinking?'

'No, Bohemund, it is mine, but do not suppose that a nephew of Rainulf Drengot is any less calculating than a de Hauteville. My brother William learnt how to think and act from Richard's uncle and he also learnt never to repose trust in them. Remember, when William set out for Melfi he did so as a vassal of Drengot, and they would no more forget that the bond had been broken than would we. Deep in their hearts they see us still as their vassals.'

'Then why allow me to seek their help?'

Robert smiled and his reply was as enigmatic as the look. 'You should see more of your cousins, don't you think?'

He's tempting me again, Bohemund thought.

*   *   *

Following on from a wasted journey to Capua, it was even more depressing to join with and accompany his father to Benevento. Bohemund became part of a two hundred-strong escort of his most accomplished lances, a number that underlined his father's concerns; Robert still did not repose any faith in the Pope but this time he came as a supplicant, not an equal, which meant he would be obliged to enter the city to meet him at his palace and when he did so he wanted enough men with him to fight his way out again if he had to. A whole raft of communications in which he humbly begged to be told how he had offended his suzerain had preceded his visit, adding a wish to be informed of what redress he could make for slights he had never intended, none of which had softened the tone of Gregory's replies.

The *Guiscard* knew he was going to have to be subservient in the presence of a pontiff who would take much pleasure in his grovelling humiliation. To the north of the city was assembled his massive host, seemingly made up of half the knights in Christendom. Calculation had persuaded Robert to leave his own forces in Apulia, for no good would come of being thought to be playing a double game; it was time to extract from this meeting what he could and that might amount to no more than salvage – at the very least he knew he would lose the Province of Benevento.

In his palace Pope Gregory was ebullient and hardly able to contain his excitement; here, in the very same reception chamber in which Pope Leo had been made to eat dirt, he would make amends for the defeat of Civitate and extract from the Duke of Apulia a price so high he might be prepared to spill blood rather than meet it. Benevento would be his again and he had his eyes on depriving him the cities of the Adriatic coast, places he and his families had captured at such a high price. If he refused he would be crushed, but at the very least the *Guiscard*, whom, he was told, scoffed at the notion of a crusade to aid Constantinople, would be obliged to take ship under papal command and participate in a fight for the aims of Rome instead of his own.

Desiderius, in his last meeting, had sought to remind Gregory that for the trouble he had caused Rome, Robert de Hauteville had been a better son of the Church than for which he was being given credit. In every conquest he had made, the *Guiscard* had advanced the spread of the Roman rite, importing priests and monks, discouraging if not actually displacing the Basilian monks and Greek priesthood in their favour, endowing places of worship and contemplation, enforcing celibacy and even allowing his own Archbishop of Bari to be defrocked for refusing to set aside his wife.

'You cannot buy your way into paradise,' had been Gregory's magisterial response.

From the top of his palace the Pope could see over the walls of Benevento to the northern plain, and there the white and multicoloured tents looked as numerous as flakes of snow upon the ground mixed with flower petals of every hue. To contemplate the anvil on which he would forge a new dispensation in the south of Italy acted like a balm to his soul, and in his mind's eye he saw the swords and lance points being burnished, the foot soldiers being taught to employ the very basic manoeuvres required by *milities*, this while the mounted knights dashed to and fro to sharpen up their skills for the coming battle. That his imaginings turned to a field of broken and bloody Norman bodies did not trouble his soul; his God was a merciless one and those who did not obey his Vicar must pay the price.

In the command tent the leader of Pope Gregory's host, Godfrey, the Hunchback of Lorraine, was trying to broker an understanding – not easy with the amount of shouted insults being exchanged. On one side was Gisulf of Salerno, deeply unpopular with everyone, Godfrey included, for his insistence that such a host should be under the command of the best man to lead it, namely himself. But it was not his misplaced military arrogance that had brought about the present rift, more the actions of his ships over many years in engaging in downright theft of the possessions of the ports with whom his city of Salerno shared the Tyrrhenian Sea.

The most vocal in demanding redress were the Pisan soldiers of Beatrice of Tuscany, whose leaders were not only well trained and numerous, but made up a substantial part of the host. Their leaders, who were also ship owners, wanted not only redress for the losses they had suffered but a binding guarantee of future good behaviour; in short, that their vessels could sail between ports in safety and profit. Lacking that, they would not go into battle with such a cluster of thieves like Prince Gisulf and his contingent of slack foot soldiers, this while Godfrey and other leaders sought to get the matter put aside until the *Guiscard* had been dealt with. With agreement impossible, there was no choice but to call in Pope Gregory to mediate.

'Prince Gisulf, my son, for the sake of amity and our purpose, I beg you to accede to the Pisan demands.'

Gregory had not seen Gisulf for some time, years in which the prince's hair had gone from jet black to peppered salt, making a complexion that had always been sallow now look like a milk-based pudding. Also his taste for gaudy clothing, on a less than svelte figure, large in the midriff below a hollow chest and above extended haunches, was even more inappropriate than it had been when he had been a youth. The ability to pout like a spoilt child had not

171

changed, nor his lack of the facility to see himself as ever being in the wrong; at this moment, in the Pope's personal tent, he seemed deeply affronted.

'Surely you mean Pisan lies, Your Holiness?'

'They are good sons of the Lord, Prince Gisulf. Are you suggesting they would make up such accusations – claims, I am forced to remind you, made by others such as Amalfi and Genoa?'

The mention of Amalfi caused Gisulf's face to screw up, giving him the air of a gargoyle. Gregory looked and behaved like the divine he was, his face concerned and his manner composed, with no hint on his countenance of his feelings. In truth he was thinking this prince before him was a sorry specimen: duplicitous by habit, conceited to an almost unbelievable degree given his manifest failings, capricious in his dealings with his own subjects and those who would be his allies, always denigrating the abilities of others while erroneously promoting his own.

Gisulf's voice became a whine. 'How can they not be so, when they are the opposite of the truth? I have bent my back to near breaking to see that their vessels sail unharmed, have chastised with the scourge my own subjects who have disobeyed my instructions.'

While pocketing a good half of what they have stolen, Gregory was thinking.

'How can I make redress for what I have not done?' came the bleat. 'Do you not see their game for what it is, Your Holiness, an attempt to make poor my holdings, to raise Pisa up and to drive Salerno down into the pits of poverty and dearth? I would be betraying my subjects, whom you know I love as my own children, if I agreed to accept such falsehoods.'

Gregory knew full well that was hyperbole and nonsense, but he had more pressing concerns. 'We are engaged on a higher purpose, my son.'

The hollow chest, in its colourful doublet, puffed out and the voice, weedy as it was, declaimed, 'There is no higher purpose for a prince than to see to the needs of those God has entrusted to his care.'

'Let us pray,' Gregory responded, sinking to his knees and obliging Gisulf to do the same, in truth because he could think of nothing else to do. In a soft voice he asked God the Father, the Son and the Holy Ghost for guidance for his good and faithful servant Gisulf, noticing that the shoddy prince nodded at the compliment. Supplications over, he took his seat again. 'If for the sake of harmony I asked you to return to Rome and await me there, would you oblige me?'

'Rome?' Gisulf asked, merely to prevaricate.

'I will prevail upon Pisa and speak to them on your behalf,' Gregory said, hoping God would forgive him the lie he had just spouted and those coming behind it. 'And once they have been brought to see their error, and the devil we have come to put in his place has been dealt with, I would wish you to join with our host on their journey to Constantinople, where I am sure the chance will come for Gisulf of Salerno to become a name encrusted with glory.'

'I can only do that if I lead the host.'

Thinking he was a sly cur, Gregory said, 'That can be made to pass.'

'When would you like me to depart?'

'This very day would be best.'

For three whole days Robert de Hauteville had sat outside Benevento awaiting the summons, but none came, which he put down to papal malice. It made him a poor companion for anyone of his entourage, all of whom bore the brunt of his rage, not the least of them Bohemund, who saw a side to his father hitherto hidden. Being of an even disposition he never rose to the taunts and insults aimed at him, which only seemed to drive the *Guiscard* to a greater level of abuse as he gnawed on what might be demanded of him, in his imagination conjuring up torments of gigantic proportions, even to the point of having his eyes put out.

Dealing with Gisulf had obliged Gregory to delay the proposed meeting, but he retained his confidence that all would be as he wished. That was severely dented and he was obliged to rush back from his palace to the encampment of his host when he heard the news: getting rid of Gisulf had done no good, the protests against Salerno and its prince had filtered down from the Pisan commanders to their men and that had led to an exchange of name-calling between them and the soldiers of Salerno.

That in turn led to the first blow being struck, as one captain slapped another, only to see weapons drawn if not employed, as several knights from other entities intervened. Yet among those other contingents men took sides, often for reasons that they would never be able to explain, but common enough in an assembled army of conscript *milities* that was hovering on the edge of boredom, riddled with a concern for their continued existence and holding a strong desire to engage in battle, to get it over with so they could go back to their wives, their farms or their trades.

The first death was a secret knife at night, as a knight of Pisa was stabbed in his sleep. By mid morning there was a full-scale battle going on and much blood being spilt, with the aristocratic leaders of the contingents powerless to stop it. As an army fit to fight, Gregory's host fell apart in a blink of the time it had taken to assemble and march to Benevento, while no amount of papal pleading mixed with hurled anathemas could bring the encampment to order. The troops of Savoy rode out first, Amadeus leading his men away lest they turn into a rabble, the Count of Burgundy close on his heels.

The people who had watched in wonder this proud host march from Rome to Benevento, with flutes playing and banners waving, saw them straggle back with heads bowed. In the encampment they left, the bodies of men from Salerno and Pisa littered the ground, more the former, for Tuscany was so much more of a power than Gisulf's single city, while those troops left stood armed and between them to bring an end to the slaughter. Geoffrey, the Hunchback of Lorraine, sent off Salerno first then Pisa a day later, with a strong body of his own men to keep them apart until their routes diverged.

No more from the top of his palace could Gregory see that flower-petalled snowfield of tents; few remained standing, most left were torn and destroyed, the field now looking as what it was – a brown landscape devoid of men but rendered bereft of grass by the passage of thousands of feet. It was as desolate to look at as had become his dream and the time came, he knew, for him and his own followers to take the road back to Rome; he could not meet with and chastise the *Guiscard* now. The news of the falling apart of his papal army arrived in Rome before Pope Gregory, which found Gisulf of Salerno telling anyone who would listen, and they were few, that if he had been given the command, as he had demanded, this would never have happened.

A message had to be sent to t ie Duke of Apulia, but he already knew what had happened and soon found out why, and that restored his mood. Such an outcome made the ride back to Melfi a jolly affair and Bohemund was detached halfway to turn for Capua, and once there to request from Prince Richard that the Apulian army should be permitted to cross Capuan territory and to undertake the siege of Salerno, so much easier now that Gisulf, who had never had many friends, now had none at all. No one in South Italy had garnered to themselves so much hatred.

CHAPTER TWELVE

The city, the most populous in Italy south of Rome, had stout walls and was nearly as hard to crack as Bari; it was not a siege to undertake without serious purpose and the notion of it lasting for more than one year had to be accepted. Fortunately the land around the city was some of the most fertile in Italy, easily able to support the force the *Guiscard* mustered: Normans, Lombards and Greeks, as well as Saracens sent from Sicily. He had the soldiers, the skill, as well as the will to triumph, but his most important advantage lay in the nature of the man he was determined to depose.

Gisulf had been much hated for years by a populace whom he treated as a source to feed his vanity and fill his coffers with gold. He, of course, saw this very differently, perceiving them as a multitude of men and women who loved and were devoted to his person, willing to die for him at any time he required them to spill their blood or surrender up their possessions. If he was a man with a tenuous grip on his personal reality, he was not so stupid as to be unaware of the way others lusted after his stronghold, especially his brother-in-law; he had, after all, pursued an anti-Norman policy ever since coming to power, as much with Capua and Apulia, in what was a gift for making enemies.

Suspecting an attack could not be deflected he had demanded that his citizens, on pain of being thrown out of the city, lay in and keep topped up two years' supplies of food, reasoning, not without sense, that such a long campaign posed a threat of disease to the besiegers, which would go a long way to saving his city. This would have remained good sense if Gisulf had not, as soon as the Apulian forces appeared outside the walls and a Norman fleet occupied the great bay, sequestered one-third of those stores for his own personal granaries. Not satisfied with such theft, as summer turned to autumn he sent his soldiers round the city to seize the rest, or at least that portion those citizens had not so successfully hidden. Few complained at such larceny, for retribution was vicious; anyone who questioned Gisulf's actions was likely to find himself or herself blinded or to suffer castration if the mood on that day sent his malice in that direction.

Despite such impositions the population fought hard for Salerno, and it was before the walls of that city that Robert saw his bastard son in real action for the first time, leading his knights against the walls in an opening assault, which came close to breaching what were formidable defences by the sheer brio of the attack. Getting the siege tower into place was in itself a major task; built just out of arrow range by the skilled carpenters who travelled with the Apulian army, it was constructed from the massive wheels up with local timber – they and the axles were brought from afar, built in a workshop where the solid timber rounds could be iron-hooped and the connections greased to run smoothly. The outer body was lined with reed matting and on the morning of the assault soaked with water. From the base, internal ladders led up to the assault platform, which matched the height of Salerno's curtain walls at the point chosen for the attack.

The tower was pushed into place by those knights tasked to back up the initial assault, this made by a body of men already in place on the upper platform, Bohemund among them. In siege warfare this was the point of maximum exposure to risk but also the place of most valour. They had a high ramp to protect them as they approached, long enough to match the distance created by a surrounding ditch. This was riddled with long, needle-sharp spikes, which would drop onto the heads of any defenders too slow to pull back, and once that was down Bohemund and his men were required to rush across it and engage.

Above them another floor was occupied by bowmen, their task to drive the defence back from the parapet long enough to allow the chain-mailed knights to get onto the walls and stay there. They were obviously outnumbered, the only advantage being that the constricted space meant not all the defenders could mass against them, and if they could hold long enough, those knights who had pushed the tower from its start point to its place against the walls could ascend to reinforce them. Naturally the countermeasures were just as set: bowmen firing at an acute angle to skewer the *Guiscard*'s bowmen, knights with extended lances ready to spear their opponents, fire pots ready to throw, as well as tar-tipped arrows to set fire to the exterior screen of wetted reeds.

Bohemund led from the very front, employing in close-quarter fighting an axe instead of his broadsword. Even in the confusion of a melee at the top of the tower, those observing from a nearby hill, his father amongst them, could see him standing head and shoulders above his confrères, the weapon swinging, silver at first, a gleam that caught the sun, soon dulled by enemy blood. Given surprise was impossible, Bohemund and his men were up against the very best that Gisulf's captains could pit against them and no one expected such an early assault to produce a conclusion; it would take many of these to wear down numbers and the will of the defence. Behind the siege tower, manning long ships' cables, stood lines of *milities* whose task was, on their general's command, to pull the tower back once it was clear the assault had been contained.

Bohemund was now even more visible, balanced on the top of the wall; somehow he had acquired a lance, the axe having been thrown – probably a weapon he had dragged from the dying hand of an enemy knight – and he was using it like a mad fisherman, jabbing with furious strokes at a quite remarkable speed, half his strength, those watching surmised, required to remove it from the bodies and entangled mail of those he struck. He was still there when his father gave the signal to pull the tower back, yet he did not move as others alongside him did to get to safety, which led to an anxious moment. Only the length of his stride saved him, for on his own he would have succumbed regardless of his fighting skill. Where other warriors would have had to jump, Bohemund seemed to step over the now open gap, his final command a shout that carried, telling his confrères to pull the ramp back up to give them cover.

Never able to openly express his pride that a product of his loins should behave with such valour, Robert de Hauteville's gratification was evident in a palpable change of attitude; on his return to report, Bohemund was embraced then kissed on both cheeks, while also being subjected to much praise by a general keen to show him off to

180

his assembled forces. As the siege progressed he was more and more brought fully into his father's council, which happened despite the strong displeasure of Robert's wife, given it diminished the standing of her own son, *Borsa*, who was kept from combat for fear of loss.

As reward for his valour, and in front of the host assembled, Robert gave his bastard son the title of Lord of Taranto. No subsequent assault was launched without Bohemund's concurrence and it was he, not *Borsa*, who was despatched to Amalfi to bring from there the ships that would, by backing up the *Guiscard*'s fleet, finally block Salernian egress to the sea, cutting off their inward supply as well as any chance of escape. In another assault Bohemund stood shoulder to shoulder with his father as together they fought in a narrow breach the ballista had made in the walls, with Reynard of Eu on his other side. That they failed to break through did nothing to diminish any of them as warriors; even their fellow Normans saw this trio as supreme.

In the end it was Gisulf's insistence that his belly should be full, while others went without, that did more than valour to ensure his downfall. Winter brought hunger and that lowered morale for citizen and soldier alike; the population was reduced to eating their horses, dogs and cats. Finally they were reduced to rats, which was the precursor of full-blown famine, and only then did their prince open his bulging storehouses. Yet he did not do so to supply his subjects; he sought to sell back to them that which he had stolen at prices few could afford. With the choice of dying from hunger or Gisulf's greedy malevolence, a large number of the citizenry, seeing the Normans advance once more, opened the gates to the enemy and then surged out to pay homage to the man who would become their new ruler.

Gisulf, with the few still loyal to him, fled to the Castello di Arechi, the citadel that had been his family's refuge of last resort for decades.

Holed up in the home of his ancestors and with much of the food stolen from his subjects, they held out for a full six months, seeking terms from an opponent not prepared to grant him any, and he was only persuaded to give himself up when he was promised on binding oaths that he would be safe from his own people and be provided with both his goods and his treasure. Robert agreed because he wanted the city, not his brother-in-law's blood or money.

Gisulf and his family left Salerno in a line of covered wagons at night, with a strong, armed escort, so that his one-time subjects could not see him, for it was obvious to the *Guiscard* they would, at the very least, take the chance to pelt him with filth if not string him up from his one-time own gates. The Duke of Apulia, Calabria and Sicily, as well as Lord of Amalfi, now had a fitting capital. If it was not his first task, it was to the *Guiscard* an important one; he set in train the construction of a new cathedral, one of a magnificence enough to house a relic he had long desired to own, a tooth of St Matthew that had been in his wife's family for two hundred years and an object he had demanded Gisulf surrender. Naturally, the duplicitous prince had sought to palm him off with a fake; the message that persuaded him to part with the true relic was simple: surrender the real St Matthew's tooth or forfeit every one of your own.

Gisulf headed straight for Capua, there to seek the aid of Richard in recapturing his city. He found out then of the secret arrangement previously made: the *Guiscard*'s fleet was on its way to Naples to begin a blockade of that port in support of Capua, while his fellow Norman magnate had assembled his army to march on that city. Gisulf was sent packing, forced to resume his journey towards the Pope, the only friend he felt he had left.

* * *

Gregory was not in Rome but Tuscany, where he had gone so he could be close to confronting Emperor-elect Henry, who, in defiance of his instructions, had appointed as Bishop of Milan a married prelate of whom the reigning pontiff, with his insistence on celibacy, naturally disapproved. The new bishop was just as naturally beholden to the imperial right of clerical appointment while Tuscany was also a hotbed of simony, with offices being sold to the highest bidder so that the revenues of the Church could go to lining the pockets of the already wealthy, rather than being employed to carry out God's work.

Aware that he lacked the military power to curb young Henry's ambition, which naturally centred on his ancient rights, the Pope had alighted on the one measure he possessed to bring him into line. For the first time in the history of Western Christendom, on a February day, a pope pronounced excommunication on an elected King of the Germans. If this was an anathema that the likes of the *Guiscard* could live with, the effect on Henry was profound and even more so on his pious subjects. North of the Alps it was catastrophic, especially given many of his vassals were already in rebellion, but more so because the entire population over which he ruled were stout devotees of the Church of Rome and genuinely saw the Pope as God's Vicar on Earth; none of his subjects could obey or even show respect to a ruler who was not in a state of grace.

If that applied to the low-born, it was just as effective with the German princes who elected their king, especially to those who were ambitious for change. In an October meeting they joined with the religiously disquieted and threatened to designate another in Henry's place if he did not receive absolution. He was given a year and a day from the date of the excommunication to achieve this and a diet was called at Augsburg in February at which he must either appear before them forgiven or lose his crown.

For Henry there was no time to waste and notwithstanding the fact that it was midwinter he knew he must go to Gregory, where he would be required to abase himself, a necessity to keep his crown. With his wife and son in company he crossed the frozen Alps and eventually located the Pope at the fortress of Canossa, where Gregory was staying until the snows melted and the Brenner Pass cleared, at which time an escort would arrive to take him to the Augsburg Diet.

If Henry, holed up in an inn, suspected the Pope kept him waiting many days through a desire to make him suffer, he could not have been more mistaken. The last thing Gregory had expected was that the excommunicate would turn up on his temporary doorstep and he was at a loss as to how to respond. If Henry begged forgiveness then he could not in all conscience refuse him absolution, but that would release him to take revenge on those who had rebelled against his authority. Added to that there was no way of forcing him to hold to any of the vows he professed, or to ensure he would behave better in the future; once back in the bosom of the Church he would not only reassert his authority, but once more become a thorn in the papal breast.

Eventually he was obliged to relent and the deed was done; Henry mouthed those promises he needed to make, his excommunication was lifted and he immediately went north to deal with his rebels. Still intending to travel to Germany himself, partly to impose his moral victory and hold Henry in check, Gregory found that the Lombard magnates who controlled the Alpine passes, aided by their prelates, would not permit his passage.

After six fruitless months of trying, and much chastened, he returned to Rome and news that was even more depressing: Salerno gone to the *Guiscard*, Naples remaining under siege. Both Richard of Capua and his son Jordan were excommunicated, the latter for his banditry in the papal province of Abruzzi, but worse than all of that came the information that Robert de Hauteville had marched on Benevento and now surrounded the city. How feeble it seemed to make his excommunication a double one!

From being in the depths of despond, the death of the Prince of Capua changed everything for Pope Gregory. Richard Drengot, retiring ill from the walls of Naples, lay abed and sinking for a month before, having made a deathbed reconciliation with the Church, he passed away. Jordan was well aware that to inherit his father's titles as an excommunicate was impossible – it was a situation that could drag on for years and too many of his subjects, unlike those of Robert de Hauteville, especially those in the most valuable fiefs, were likely to listen more to their Roman priests than to a prince under anathema; he would have nothing but trouble and stood to lose everything. The siege of Naples was lifted forthwith, his plundering in the Abruzzi brought to a halt, and he headed immediately for Rome to make his peace.

The same news caused the *Guiscard* to worry because he was well able to read the runes. Jordan would do anything to get absolution and confirmation of his titles and that could include sending his forces to relieve the papal city. In an out-and-out contest he could best Capua, but it would not serve for the very same reason he had made peace with Capua before: the destruction brought on by such mutual enmity would only advantage their enemies. Yet for all his shrewd appreciation Robert failed to see how much pressure a ruthless pope like Gregory could bring to bear.

'Do you not see, my son, how I am bound by my lack of the means to enforce God's will?'

'I find,' Jordan replied, 'just being in your presence humbling enough to make me ashamed of my own recent behaviour.'

Pope Gregory knew flattery when he heard it, just as he knew that this heir to Capua was dodging the point of his question. 'You have committed serious sins, Jordan, and stolen much that was not yours to possess.'

'All of which I brought with me to Rome, Your Holiness, and it awaits only your decision as to how it is to be disposed of. Either returned to those who I have sinned against, or held here in Rome to do the work which you so tirelessly pursue.'

This one has a silver tongue, Gregory thought, so unlike his sire who had been a ruffian and abrupt in his opinions with it. But that bloodline argued a sharp mind as well, so there was no doubt that Jordan knew the direction in which the Pope was trying to edge him, in short into an open conflict with Apulia. He did not want to go there and it was a moot point as to whether he could be persuaded, for holding absolution over him could only go so far. Like Henry, if he asked for forgiveness it was the prelate's duty to grant it unless he could be absolutely sure such pleading was a lie.

'It troubles me that my city of Benevento is not safe, Jordan.'

The younger man was quick to latch on to that but he was not going to fight the *Guiscard*; as a way of losing his titles it was, in the long term, as near certain as refusing to beseech the Pope. He recalled how Bohemund had been brought to Montesárchio and what had been his father's suggested way of dealing with him. He spoke now, with that air which meant he was making an enquiry, not suggesting a course of action.

186

'Perhaps, Your Holiness, the best way to protect Benevento is to provide a distraction.'

'And what form, my son, would such a distraction take?'

'Encouragement in certain quarters.'

The new Apulian revolt did not break out for several months; it took Jordan, who was moving cautiously in any case, time to suborn the men who would rise against the *Guiscard*, as even those willing, such as Peter and Abelard, needed an excuse that would bring others to their banner. The thought of seeking to involve Bohemund was discarded; he had shown no inclination to rebel when he had no authority, now he was Lord of Taranto and one of his father's most trusted supporters, which led Jordan to surmise he would act to protect his father rather than seek to bring him down.

Capua needed an excuse and it was Robert in person who provided the pretext for revolt by demanding from his vassals, as was his ducal right, that they contribute funds to support the cost of his daughter's forthcoming marriage to a high French noble and in this he was a touch too avaricious, determined as he was on magnificence, if not willing to spend his own treasure. This aim for grandeur at the expense of others raised once more the spectre of a family getting above themselves, and the talk of bringing the de Hautevilles to a proper realisation of their true standing, from men who felt their bloodline at least equal if not superior, began to spread.

Good sense dictated they wait till the liege lord was absent in furthest Calabria with his familia knights as well as his two sons, both the bastard and the legitimate *Borsa*, before striking home – he was raising money there too to cover the wedding costs. Though the uprising was widespread, Peter was the first to move and constituted the most serious problem by retaking his old fief, sure that he could secure it and make it impregnable before Robert reappeared.

The restored Lord of Trani had reckoned without Sichelgaita, who was much more than a mere decorative duchess. Robert and Bohemund were tied down, having laid siege to Otranto, and both were too far off to help, so, gathering every available loyal lance, she descended on Peter at the head of her own army before he could consolidate his hold on the port city, and her siege tactics were so successful and speedy he was obliged to flee and join the other perennial rebel, Abelard, who held Loritello.

It took a long winter campaign to bring the rebels under control, involving siege after siege and march and countermarch to contain something which acted like a forest fire that broke out in unexpected places. His disgruntled vassals, seeing their liege lord occupied elsewhere, rose in revolt in Apulia when he was in Calabria and vice versa, each one doused. But it had an effect on their suzerain; while he was prepared to pardon these new dissenters, the *Guiscard* let it be known that this time the repeat miscreants like Peter and Abelard would pay with their lives – there would be none of the previous magnanimous forgiveness.

But there was one other problem that had to be dealt with and that was Capua; Jordan was clearly behind things, at the instigation of the Pope, but taking no active part when he had many opportunities to do so. Robert, when he felt that he had reached a point of real superiority, when the senior rebels had fled over the Adriatic to Durazzo, once more sent Bohemund to negotiate with him in the company of Desiderius, who, as ever, had tried throughout to bring them to an understanding.

'My father holds no grudge against you, Jordan.'

There was a close examination of the man as he spoke, to see if elevation to the title had made any difference. What Bohemund observed was a degree of reserve brought on by, he thought, discomfiture at Jordan having acted as he did, given he was not the only one present who knew the truth; Abbot Desiderius was just as aware of the hand of Pope Gregory in what had so recently occurred.

'And what does he propose?'

It was the Abbot of Monte Cassino who answered. 'That you renew the peace he had with your late father.'

Jordan addressed the layman, not the divine. 'He requires no indemnity?'

'He asks only that you cease to support those who would rebel against him—'

'Are there any left, Bohemund?' Jordan interrupted, showing just a trace of his old, more light-hearted nature.

'. . . and that you give those who are now fleeing no succour by allowing them to reside in your possessions.'

'And what, Abbot, will His Holiness say to this?'

Unbeknown to either of the others, Desiderius was in Capua as much to represent Gregory as the *Guiscard*. The Pope, now that his hopes of a successful Apulian rebellion had crumbled, had been forced to once more turn his eyes north, where Henry was succeeding in a way he had not foreseen: he was beating his rebels.

'It has ever been the task of Holy Church to promote peace, my son.'

It was a measure of their increasing comfort in the world of diplomacy that both Jordan and Bohemund took this barefaced falsehood without a reaction. Jordan knew that in the case of Desiderius, the older man spoke a truth to which he could hold, for he always had. Bohemund, having only just met him, thought he was as dishonest as his papal master. That counted for nothing; let him lie if he must, as long as he could return to his father with the right result.

'I might add,' Desiderius said, 'that I am here on behalf of His Holiness as well as Duke Robert. It is his strong desire that these disruptions should cease. He wishes Capua and Apulia to be at peace and has asked me to bend all my efforts to achieve this.'

'Why?' Bohemund demanded abruptly, breaking the air of diplomatic harmony.

'There can only be one reason, Abbot Desiderius,' Jordan interjected. 'And that is he has troubles elsewhere.'

Not wishing to admit that was true, the elderly abbot held his hands open, palms out, while on his face was a look of resignation. Whatever it implied, it was enough for Prince Jordan and peace was restored.

For Pope Gregory, matters went from bad to worse. Having put a cap on his own rebellion, the Emperor-elect called a synod of all those bishops and cardinals who both lived within his domains and quite naturally, for the sake of their continuation in office, owed him fealty. Along with those princes who had so recently threatened to depose him they proclaimed Gregory's election illegal and elected an antipope called Clement, putting the Church once more into schism. The next step for Henry, once more excommunicated, if this time ineffectually, would be to descend on Rome to have himself crowned Emperor by his own Pope.

Gregory needed the Normans and he required them to be united and on his side, more the powerful *Guiscard* than the Prince of Capua who had so singularly failed him. Ever an intensely proud man – he had stood on his dignity at Benevento seven years previously by refusing to meet with Duke Robert – he had to accept that there was now no time for such conceits. Yet he was not prepared to grovel and the melting of enmity took much time. Messages were sent but in a subtle way, as in an invitation for any magnate with grievances to bring them to his attention. As usual Abbot Desiderius was brought into the equation to smooth ruffled feathers until finally a meeting was arranged.

For the first time since Gregory's election, Robert de Hauteville walked into the same room as his papal suzerain, there to kneel and do homage as he had to Gregory's predecessors for his ducal titles of Apulia, Calabria and Sicily. No mention was made of Amalfi or Salerno; apple carts were required to remain stable not overturned, but in remaining silent upon them it implied a tacit agreement regarding their legitimacy. As he held Robert's hands in his, seeing how puny were his in comparison, and pronounced the required prayers over his bowed head, Gregory could be forgiven for enquiring if God was truly on his side.

If the places Robert had taken in defiance of Gregory were ignored there were still matters to discuss. Letters had to be composed and sent to Bamberg to let Henry know, without in any way sounding like an outright threat, that the *Guiscard* was concerned about the election of a pope to replace Gregory. Clement was a man in whom he could repose no faith – as good a way as any of telling the Emperor-elect that Rome was under Norman protection and that any attack on the city would be met with as much if not more force as any he could bring to bear.

Gregory had been satisfied on that concern but he still had all his usual concerns in the East. With the Holy Sepulchre in the hands of people he saw as heretics, problems were bound to surface. There were an increasing number of grim stories of Jerusalem pilgrims being badly ill-treated, denied access to the holy places, assaulted and robbed and even in extreme cases facing the enforced demand to convert to Islam. Had not Robert and his brother Roger dealt with that problem in Sicily by taking back the churches made into mosques? For all their efforts, the Pope was irritated that the infidels were still allowed to freely worship throughout the island, adding that he felt Count Roger could also do more to bring those of the Orthodox persuasion into the bosom of the Roman Church.

Robert brushed aside these concerns but got a blessing for what he proposed next, which would create difficulties for the still-excommunicated Emperor Botaneiates, who was struggling to hold his place in the face of constant threats and had also failed to shore up the Byzantine Empire. In the main it was a satisfied Duke of Apulia who left his suzerain; he had, after all, everything for which he had come. Gregory, still working hard on his notion of religious reconciliation between Rome and Constantinople, had kept up the pressure without once ever offering any concessions and what was proposed to him, nothing less than an invasion of Illyria, appeared a good way to concentrate minds in Constantinople.

It was irritating that *Borsa*, whom Robert had been obliged to bring along as his heir, seemed to incline to the papal point of view regarding both what was happening in Jerusalem, as well as the papal opinion on Sicily. He seemed willing to believe what he was told and less ready to give credence to his father's assertion that, when it came to the Holy Land, although pilgrims to the city faced difficulties – and how could they not? – much of what had been propounded was, as far as he knew, exaggeration. That it was so suited Gregory and his ilk; the spreading of this embroidery was used to drive home his desire for a great Eastern crusade, in which the whole of Western Christendom was being called to participate.

'It would be a noble thing to do, Father,' *Borsa* opined, as they made ready to take the road back to Salerno. 'To have in our possession the place where Jesus gave his life so that we could be saved.'

'All this blather about a crusade is so much stuff. Gregory talks as if the distance to Palestine is the same as crossing the sea from Reggio to Messina. You tell me how we are to get any army to the Holy Land and maintain it there?'

'Surely we would do that in concert with Constantinople?'

'Right at this moment, they could not swat a fly, never mind a Moslem.'

'With our help—'

Robert asked his next question gently, in a tone that he had to force upon himself. 'Tell me who is going to pay for this great expedition, for the Pope will not, in which, I will point out to you, there can be no plunder to meet the bill. We cannot sack Jerusalem as if it was any other city.'

That made his son think, which is what the *Guiscard* intended; he knew which levers to press in that penny-pinching breast.

'And when it comes to Sicily and letting Moslems worship in their mosques, ask Gregory how a few hundred Norman lances, which is all your uncle has, are going to rule a population in the hundreds of thousands if we force them into a form of piety they dislike?'

'So giving succour to the pilgrims of Jerusalem is impossible?'

'No, but it cannot be done in the way Rome proposes.'

That got an intrigued look from *Borsa*, who wondered what

it portended; he knew his sire as well as his father knew him. He was aware, if not of the whole purpose, that one of the *Guiscard*'s vassals, Count Radulf, had been sent as an envoy to Constantinople, ostensibly to enquire after *Borsa*'s sister. That was a tale in which it was hard to believe, given his father had shown scant interest in her welfare since the overthrow of the man who had promised her his son in marriage. That he was part in ignorance did not surprise the heir to Apulia; he was used to that, as was everyone who dealt with his father.

CHAPTER THIRTEEN

Ever since he had received that despatch regarding the overthrow of the Emperor Michael Dukas, as well as the transfer of his daughter to a convent, the *Guiscard* had kept Byzantium in his sights as a crumbling edifice ripe for future exploitation. In the time since, other matters had kept him fully occupied: first his preparation against Capua, the siege of Benevento and then his need to put down the revolt Jordan had helped to engineer. He had, of course, made protestations about the fate of his daughter, but they were not heartfelt – as far as Robert was concerned her continued presence in Constantinople gave him every excuse to push a problem into a rupture at any time of his choosing.

Now, with peace restored throughout his domains, he could at last concentrate on what to him was a prize of immeasurable potential – nothing less than the overthrow of the Eastern Empire, which with him at the head would become the greatest centre of Norman power in Christendom. He had fought and triumphed over Greeks, a race he despised, all his fighting life, so there was little doubt in his mind he could achieve such a great object. That it was what he hankered after had never been in any doubt, and while many might wonder at such vaulting ambition no one even thought to ask the Duke of Apulia whether such intentions were either wise or necessary.

The wellsprings of that were many and varied; no Norman warrior worth his salt saw what they held as sufficient, which explained the trouble Robert constantly had with his vassals, and he was no exception. As a race they were by nature's design committed to expansion and that was down to their Viking blood. Byzantium was a prize to tempt a saint, never mind a sinner, rich in a way that made even the *Guiscard*'s present possessions look feeble, and they used part of that endless stream of gold as a means to carry on a proxy war against him. Right now those like Abelard, who had rebelled and fled, both Lombard and Norman, were safe on the imperial soil of Illyria, just across the Adriatic, able to cock their noses at his demand that they be sent back.

Other reasons abounded, a less than noble one his desire to send a letter to William of Normandy as King of England, with the signature and seal at the base telling the upstart that he was being addressed by an imperial de Hauteville, which would pay back in bezants the insult the father of the Bastard of Falaise had heaped on his own family. Yet in truth the time was ripe; the Eastern Empire was weak both internally and externally, troubled on its borders by the pressure of Kiev Rus, the Magyars of Hungary and the Turks of Asia Minor.

Control from the centre was weak, with the man who had usurped Michael Dukas faced by constant intrigues seeking to depose him, this allowing the various satraps who ran the provinces to behave with a degree of independence, sometimes so barefaced as to have them acting like separate sovereign powers as they manoeuvred for an attainable imperial throne. If it was open to them, it was also exposed to the ambitions of the powers that pressed on its borders; someone might bring it crashing down – better that was himself, Robert surmised, than that he face a more potent power in its place.

The Duke of Apulia also had an unemployed army, a dangerous tool to leave idle in his own domains, as well as a fleet that he had built up to help subdue the numerous ports he had been required to blockade; that could so easily be transformed into an offensive weapon. Yet deep in his soul there was another pressing motivation and that had to do with his eldest brother, William. For all he had conquered and all he now held, Robert had still not matched in his own estimation the achievements of Iron Arm.

It was William who had founded their family prosperity, he who had created the base upon which successive de Hautevilles had constructed the holdings over which Robert now held sway, William who had defeated the Byzantines when they were a force to be reckoned with on the ancient battlefield of Cannae, so that he stood comparison with Hannibal, the previous victor on that field who had destroyed the legions of Rome. For all the songs made up in praise of his deeds, none, to Robert's mind, matched those dedicated to the warrior actions of William and that was a situation he strongly desired to change.

As ever, anything he desired to do was beset with problems that had nothing to do with combat, the first of which surfaced when he proposed to send an advance party across the Adriatic to secure for him a base for his fleet.

*   *   *

'Your rightful son should have the command,' Sichelgaita demanded. 'Not your long-legged bastard!'

For Robert this was tricky; how could he say to his faithful helpmeet and wife that he did not trust *Borsa* to lead the expedition? Even less could he intimate to a doting mother that the men who would go under Bohemund in his advance guard might not readily follow his heir with the same confidence? *Borsa* was not, as far as his sire could see, a leader of men; he lacked the ability to either inspire them or to instil such fear that they would obey his every command. In administration he showed ability – the appointment of officials, not least satisfying Rome with his clerical placements, added to an assiduous collection and accounting of revenues. These were his forte, so that his father had a bulging treasury – but then money had always been an attraction to the boy.

'It is not without risk,' he replied in a voice that lacked its usual force.

'What fight is not, husband?'

He could not help but think, even when being castigated, that an angry Sichelgaita was a magnificent sight to behold; near eyeball to eyeball with him, her hair was still burnished blonde, her shoulders square and her protruding breasts magnificent in their size and outline and even after the bearing of eight children she was a fine-looking woman. How he wished he still had the powers in his loins to engage in the kind of ferocious carnal coupling with her that they had at one time enjoyed, but that had not survived his near-death illness at the level he had once known. He had reached a point in his life where his vital spark required to be coaxed.

If, at sixty-five years of age, he felt his sword arm was still strong, the other parts of his body were subject to the terrors of old age. There was a stiffness in the joints when he rose from his bed of a morning and he was aware that in the manège he was no longer a figure of fear to the younger knights as he had at one time been; it was respect that permitted him to overcome them, not a superiority of arms. From now on he knew that, while he could still fight, his task was more to command than engage and not to lead by sheer example, which required that someone in whom he reposed faith should undertake that role.

In his son made a bastard he recognised those abilities he had for much of his life possessed: raw courage, a terrifying strength with any weapon he chose to employ, the cold blood and concentration needed to kill without mercy. But most important of all Bohemund had the ability to arouse in the Normans he led a passion that made them outdo even their known and famed skills. Added to that, he engaged in a way with Lombards and Greek *milities* which, his father had to admit, was superior to his own. Robert found it hard to disguise his antipathy to races he considered feeble, a disadvantage in a host in which increasingly they outnumbered his Normans.

'You would expose our son to the risk of death for the sake of an excess of pride? What if he was lost?'

'Then Guy would become your heir and he in turn will lead your army.'

That was a jest, but not one Robert dared laugh at; if Sichelgaita had a mote in her eye about *Borsa*, it was nothing to the regard in which she held his younger brother. Robert too was fond of him, for he was hard to dislike; Guy was a joy to be with, clever, witty, a bit of a rake, who had a legion of scrapes on his bedpost and a natural courtier manner, being well versed in the arts of diplomacy. But he was no soldier.

'No! Bohemund will lead.'

'And how will that be seen?'

'Sichelgaita,' Robert said, unusually for him almost pleading, '*Borsa* will have my titles, all of them, as well as what lands I possess, and if my planned expedition prospers that might be the imperial purple. But if he is the person destined to rule when I am gone, he is not the one to lead an army all the way across Romania and to capture Constantinople.'

'And Bohemund is?'

'Yes! As much as I am myself.'

Robert de Hauteville stood under the twin marble pillars that marked all that remained of a temple once dedicated to Neptune, as the galleys of a good proportion of his fleet manoeuvred to make their way out of the narrow neck that closed off the natural harbour of Brindisi. The temple had stood at the very end of the Appian Way since the time of Ancient Rome, a sacred place where the pagan gods had been beseeched to grant safe passage to both war galleys and trading vessels as they set out for the East from the Empire's premier southern port.

From here great Roman generals had sailed, much the same as Bohemund was doing now, to war and possible conquest: the likes of Pompey, Caesar and Mark Antony. Was it not from Brindisi that Octavian, soon to be Caesar Augustus, had set out for the decisive Battle of Actium and was not that an omen of some kind? Given this expedition had been blessed by the Bishop of Brindisi and all of his assembled clergy it was very hard not to feel so, to wonder if he too would rise to imperial magnificence?

'Right now, I think I need a slave to whisper in my ear that all glory is fleeting.'

'Only now, Father? I would have said you needed that in your crib.'

From feeling proud and regal, Robert's mood was reduced to a feeling of ongoing irritation. Bohemund's sister, Emma, come to see her brother off on his first independent command, had always possessed the ability to get under his skin. He turned to chastise her, only to find himself staring into the still, blue eyes of her six-year-old son, Tancred, which killed in his throat the shout he had been about to utter. What was it about grandchildren that so softened a man? He had never feared to bark at his own offspring, nor employ the back of his hand if they went too far, but somehow the gap in years made such a thing impossible.

'Give me the boy,' he growled.

Emma's reply was biting. 'Only if you assure me you are not hungry.'

Robert reached out for Tancred, who was given up without resistance and then raised to perch on his grandfather's shoulders, first kneeling, then standing.

'There, my boy, from such a height you can see the East and the future. Out on that galley is your Uncle Bohemund, the man to help me make it for us.'

Bohemund, as ever dressed in his family colours and standing on the poop of the galley, had a feeling that to look backwards was unlucky – Lot's wife came to mind – but he could not help but do so, for he wanted to feel that he had his father's confidence and somehow hoped it would be able to travel the distance between them like some raw animal spirit. He saw clearly Robert lift a boy on his shoulders, knew it had to be his nephew and that induced a pang of regret; he could not recall that ever being gifted to him, for if it had, he had been too young to recall it. Abruptly he cast his eyes to the harbour mouth, aware that such a sight actually pained him and made him jealous of a child of whom he was very fond.

There was much bellowing and oar work needed to get out safely, and when they finally emerged there was a moment of slight anxiety as the vessel hit the swell of the sea, for like all landsmen Bohemund feared to be sick; his shipboard experience to date had been the short trip across the Straits of Messina, another from Amalfi to Salerno Bay, both on very calm water. Here it was not truly rough – they would not have weighed if it had been – but there was a noticeable north-westerly breeze, which whipped up choppy waves that made the ship shudder when they struck. It made no difference that sailors often suffered from such an affliction; it was, especially to a warrior, too diminishing to be borne, too much of a blow to pride. With half his mind on his stomach, he addressed the sailing master, Lamissio of Viesti, the man who would control the whole fleet, as much to distract himself as to seek information.

'It would be of interest to me to be told the meaning of your commands. I am eager to learn the ways of the sea.'

The immediate if silent reaction to that request was one of scorn, quickly replaced by faux eagerness, for the thought, to the sailing master, of seeking to distil a lifetime of experience into few enough words to instruct one bound to be utterly ignorant bordered on the risible. Against that, this Norman was a Goliath, while he was a Lombard and, like most of his nautical breed, obliged to sail in cramped vessels, of necessity short and stocky even by the standards of his race. This fellow could pick him up with one hand and chuck him over the side. Quick as his change of expression had been, Bohemund

202

had spotted it; the master was aware of the fact and he sought to head off the blast he knew was coming. Normans were bad-tempered by nature, yet Lamissio was surprised by the calm voice.

'It will not suit either of us if I am totally in ignorance, will it?'

'No, Eminence.'

The gentle chuckle was even more unusual from a Norman. 'I am not yet eminent, fellow, so Bohemund will do.'

'I was about to send up the pennant that would have the fleet set sail, sir. With the wind on our quarter it favours us.'

'You do not require my words to make it so?'

'No,' Lamissio replied.

At Bohemund's nod he raised a wide-mouthed trumpet to his lips and bellowed his command, which could be heard on the nearest vessels, those more distant relying on the chequered flag that was run up to the masthead. Bohemund left the poop for the deck so that he could closely observe the men hauling on the lines that raised the great square, blood-red sail, and was even more keen to see how they lashed it off to the side of the ship at an angle so it billowed out as it took full advantage of the breeze. The heel as it did so nearly caught him out, the canting deck forcing him to hang on to the bulwark, the only sound to add to the wind whistling through the taut ropes the noise of a fair number of his knights voiding their guts.

The tang of the sea was strong in Bohemund's nostrils, his knees bending alternately as he rode easily the pitch and roll of the deck. The sky was blue and the surrounding sea, save from his own vessels, was empty, with the black ravens in their coops cawing now, aware by some divine gift that the sight of land was diminishing. He was thinking this was how his Viking ancestors had terrorised the world, pagan warriors sailing or rowing to destinations sometimes a year away – the cities of the eastern Mediterranean had not been spared – over endless seas out of sight of land, even up rivers to great inland cities like Paris and Tours, to steal, burn and destroy, and if that failed, to extract tribute for the mere act of withdrawal. As of this moment he felt at one with them.

If it was a mystery how the sailing master knew the direction in which to go in daylight; that was multiplied when darkness fell and the only sight of the fleet was the myriad flickering stern lanterns. The sky was filled with a million stars, numerous and strong enough to make up for the paucity of a moon, and by now Lamissio had realised that this commander was a different kind of Norman, with an even temper and a genuine desire to be instructed, amazed that to sail at night was easy for a man who had been at his trade from the age of five. Lamissio knew his constellations and the stars within them, and where they would be at any given time of year.

'Why, sir, it is as easy as walking an old Roman road.'

'When will we raise Valona?' Bohemund asked, in order to avoid agreement; he was far from sure he could ever learn to do that which Lamissio did quite naturally.

There was a pause while a concentrated examination was made of the heavens, Bohemund in the darkness having no difficulty in hiding a smile, for he guessed this was play-acting. 'We will be off the town before first light.'

'Could we sail directly in?'

The sucking of teeth was just as overdone. 'Depends, Your Honour. If the great lanterns are lit on the end of the moles, maybe, and even then we would have to risk them sealing off the harbour.'

'Chains and logs?'

The nod was imperceptible. 'Which would rip the bottom off any galley that tried to enter.'

'If the chain could be broken?'

'Don't see how, sir.'

Bohemund laughed, for a plan was forming in his mind. 'That is because you are a seafarer.'

There was no overnight rest. It took five turns of the glass to relay Bohemund's instructions, which saw the fleet of galleys drop their sails and close with great care till there was little space between the oars of those sailing abreast and even less between the bow and stern of the vessels following, a point from which orders to the fighting men could be relayed by shouts. Then they had to douse their lights, the only one visible that of Lamissio's ship, out ahead of the rest, where a bit of thick canvas had been rigged to cut off the light from the approaching shore, while beside it rested the sailing master's hourglass, the sand slowly dribbling through. Still too far off to be visible, it was the hankering caw of the ravens that told Lamissio they were as close to land as Bohemund needed to be.

An order was relayed to the ship of Reynard of Eu, who would take over command if what Bohemund was about to attempt failed and, satisfied that all was understood, the command was given to Lamissio's oarsmen to bend their backs and head for shore, their course made easier by the twin pinpricks of light that marked the harbour entrance to Valona, one of which they trended left and away from. Looking back, Bohemund could see the phosphorescent spill of the trailing galleys as they came on at a lesser and he hoped controlled speed.

Having been a sailor man and boy, there was scarcely a port on the inland sea that Lamissio had not visited at some time or other;

he knew them from the outer mole to the most deeply embedded tavern-cum-whorehouse and everything in between. He had been to Valona more times than he could count and he knew to the width of his own hand where the barrier that blocked off the harbour at night was fixed. Would they have armed men on that mole? There was no way of being sure but the possibility had to be accepted. The Duke of Apulia's intentions, a great fleet refitted for aggression and a huge army waiting to embark across a narrow stretch of sea, could not be hidden and the coastal towns of Illyria must be on alert.

Valona had been selected because it had an anchorage large enough to provide the *Guiscard* with a base for his fleet and it would not require too wise a head for the Byzantine governor to be aware of this, just as he would know that if his town walls were sound and would require a fully enforced siege to break, his Achilles heel was the harbour mole. Lamissio outlined the way they acted to protect that: apart from bowmen and pots of catapulted fire, sharp iron-tipped stakes were set into the stonework which protruded out far enough to snare any vessel at a distance from which they could not do harm.

It was the thought of his Viking heritage that had brought a solution to Bohemund and because of that, lying on a long plank protruding from the bows, he was the sharpest pair of eyes in the ship. The galley, propelled by a half-reefed dark-red sail, was approaching at a snail's pace, the oars used more to slow progress than propel, what the man in the bows could see passed back in whispers.

'My Lord, your surcoat will catch the starlight.'

Looking down, Bohemund realised that Lamissio was right; half of his family colour was a stark white and having already unstrapped his sword belt – the weapon for the coming task was an axe – it was flapping too, thus more likely to catch the eye. He whipped the garment off and rolled it so only the blue was showing, then tied it round his waist, eager to wear it into the coming contest. Just then a low call came back that they were approaching the first of the wooden barbs, its sharp point visible only because the metal tip reflected a small amount of the light. The call to his knights, who had been crouching in the bulwarks, was just as soft, though there was, he thought, an excess of carrying noise from knocked weapons as they stood to prepare.

Bohemund reasoned, and knew he would pay a high price if he was mistaken, that any guard detachment would not be stationed overnight out on the mole and neither would they be wide awake; they would have a shelter somewhere close to the quay and sleep in their mail and with their weapons beside them. That would mean a lookout, possibly only one on each side of the harbour entrance, and they would have been staring out at a silvery seascape for a long time, tiring to the eyes and inclined to induce slumber. He had used the lanterns to stay well away from the mouth, and the sailing master had also kept them out of the stronger streak of light provided by a sliver of moon now high in the sky. Could they get ashore unseen?

'Back the oars,' Lamissio called, bringing on a splash, thankfully covered by the sea slapping against the base of the mole. There was a thud as contact was made and so sharp were those metal ends that the galley shuddered to a halt as it embedded itself in the timbers. Bohemund had to admire the man in charge of sailing the vessel, for without being told Lamissio had got ready a grappling iron which was cast the short distance to another barb where one of the prongs got enough purchase to pull in the stern, and

Bohemund gave quiet orders to proceed when contact was made with the side of the ship.

To say that those he led had doubts was an understatement; not all of them so readily harked back to a Viking inheritance and one of his lances had made a very valid point when he suggested the barbs might be greased. The sailing master solved that by bringing up from below sacks of ballast, which contained grainy sand and, before the first Norman foot hit the protruding wooden poles, a pair of ship's boys went first, barefooted, nimble and who could both swim, spilling sand ahead of them on which they got their own purchase.

Now sure they could keep their feet, Bohemund led his knights in file along the same wide tree trunks – gingerly, for they were less sure of foot than the youngsters. If it was not an example of the old Viking game of walking the oars, it was close enough for the man in command and he was tall enough, when he got to the end, to hoist himself onto the wall that lined the mole, as well as strong enough once he was on it to reach down and help up his confrères. Within what seemed like a blink Bohemund had twenty fully armed knights ready to do battle.

That was not the aim; the target was the log and chain barrier and that was close by the nearest harbour-mouth lantern. Two men were there as guards and lookouts, though they failed in both respects, for they had seen nothing and were so surprised at the sudden appearance of an enemy that they could not even get their swords out in time. Both were clubbed to the ground while Bohemund used his axe to cut, with six powerful and noisy blows, the thick cable that secured the barrier.

There was no need for silence now. Bohemund shouted for the

covered stern lantern of his galley to be shown, that being the signal to those following that the harbour mouth was open and they were safe to point their prows at those twin lights and sail between them. A clever brain would have doused one – what was coming must have been obvious – but that too was lacking. All that could be heard were panicked shouts, but that was fading as the Normans made their way towards the point where the mole joined the quay.

Fighting men, roused from their slumbers, faced them, but they were Greeks who had never come up against Normans and very likely not of the highest calibre anyway. As soon as the front rank of three were despatched, a pair being cut at so hard they ended up in the water, the rest fled, this while behind them Bohemund's galleys were entering the harbour, making a hellish racket as instructed to strike terror into what defence could be quickly mustered. Chasing the mole defenders, the party of land-bound knights found themselves on the quay without an enemy, this as the first hint of light began to tinge the sky above the harbourside buildings.

Half the shouting now was from the inhabitants hurriedly fleeing their houses, shouting that the Saracens had come, a cry that did more to aid Bohemund than any sword or axe. The infidels who worshipped Mohammed had come many times over the centuries and they did not just come to plunder; they came to rape both women and men, to roast their captives over open fires and to destroy every Christian church they came across – the Saracens, in this part of the world, were the dread in the dreams of adults and children alike.

What soldiers the governor of Valona possessed made for the citadel, surrounded by fleeing locals. Meeting up with Reynard on the now dimly lit quay, Bohemund cautioned his men not to engage but to merely chase them into that defence. The citadel he did not need – that could wait, especially if those who might contest with him were locked up inside. It was the waters of the anchorage he wanted, as well as the long, low shoreline and the town. A fast-rowing galley was sent back to Brindisi to tell the *Guiscard* that he had a base for both his fleet and his army.

CHAPTER FOURTEEN

'Damn the Pope!' The messenger from Rome, a priest, was shocked at such blasphemy and it showed on his face, but the force with which the Duke of Apulia expounded his curse made him take a step backwards too. 'First he encourages me to invade Illyria, then he gets cold feet and demands of me that I desist.'

'He does not ask for that, My Lord,' the priest replied, in the kind of stammering tone that indicated he was in terror of the reaction. 'He fears that with you and your entire host absent from Italy, there is nothing to prevent King Henry from descending on Rome to force an election – that it is only the threat of your intervention that prevents such a calamity. He feels a substantial body of your lances on the edge of papal territory will act as a deterrent.'

'Benevento, you mean?' Robert asked, enjoying the discomfort it caused; that was a territory three popes had been trying to throw de Hautevilles out of for years. 'I thought Pope Gregory had excommunicated him again?'

'He has, My Lord, but it has not had the same effect as hitherto.'

'Then he's learnt something, perhaps from me.'

'A contingent of lances?' the priest asked, with the air of a man desperate to get back on to the subject of his journey.

'That won't stop Henry if he is serious.'

'That is not what His Holiness believes. He is of the opinion that such a thing will induce caution, for Bamberg knows that to harm one of your race is to raise anger in them all.'

With Jordan ruling Capua, Robert wondered if that was now something of a myth, but it was one he would still propagate. Yet it left him on the horns of a dilemma, for he suspected that in Illyria he would need every fighting man he could muster. Against that he was in vassalage duty-bound to come to the aid of his suzerain if the Pope required it, and at the risk of falling out with Rome at a time when it would be unwise to do so.

'Very well,' he replied. 'Return to the Lateran and inform Pope Gregory that I will do my duty by him.'

'Did you mean that, husband?' Sichelgaita asked when the priest had departed.

'I will give him a small detachment only and by the time he finds out I have only half fulfilled my duty I might have beaten whatever force Byzantium sends against me.' Seeing the look his son was giving him, one of deep disapproval, Robert snapped at him. 'When you come to rule my domains, *Borsa*, you will find that the truth is a movable commodity, especially when dealing with a man like Gregory.'

'I cannot but see it as a grave sin to lie to a pope.'

'You see sin everywhere.'

'For which I thank the Lord.'

Robert poked his own chest as his chamberlain entered. 'This is the lord you have to thank!' Then he turned and barked at the man, 'What do you want?'

'My Lord, a galley has just arrived from Valona, which is in the hands of the advance party.'

'What!'

About to say Bohemund had taken it, the chamberlain hesitated; the presence of Sichelgaita made that unwise. 'The force you sent has control of the anchorage and the town. Reynard of Eu is waiting to report to you on how it was taken.'

'Let him enter!' Robert whooped.

Then he looked at his wife and son as if to challenge them to say something. Sichelgaita, without a word, swept out of the chamber with *Borsa* at her heels, she having silently indicated that he must follow. His wife had no desire to hear how his bastard had taken in the blink of an eye a port that had not been expected to fall for at least a month and quite possibly not without his own presence as well as that of his army. Once he had heard the tale of Bohemund's exploits he was quick to command that both the Master of the Host and the Fleet be sent for; Robert needed to get both his vessels and his men over the water quickly to take advantage of this.

'Will you come too, My Lord?' his familia knight asked, for he had heard a rumour that, for the sake of the Pope, his leader might be delayed.

'Reynard,' the Duke responded. 'How can I wait?'

Bohemund had not waited either; his confidence was so high he felt he could conquer anything and anywhere merely by showing intent, so he sailed down to Corfu with a small portion of his force. Possession of the island was a necessary precursor to any invasion of Illyria, this to protect the southern flank from an incursion by what remained of the Byzantine navy, once powerful, now, due to neglect, a shadow of its former self. Yet any naval force, even a small and badly equipped one, could distract from the main purpose, and should they appear in Corfu they would have an anchorage too close for comfort to the rear of the Apulian operations, able to emerge at will from the narrows of the channel between the island and mainland to raid the *Guiscard*'s supply lines.

The initial target was the Castle of Kassiopi, one of the three Byzantine fortresses on Corfu, which covered the northern exit from the narrows. Bohemund knew the total island garrison to be tiny and poorly equipped – this information supplied to his father by Greek traders – which would mean insufficient men at Kassiopi to even hold all of its walls. The *Guiscard*'s plan envisaged securing the island by bringing his whole fleet to its shores as if that was where they meant to land, an armada against which the Byzantines could offer no meaningful resistance; faced with overwhelming numbers no blame would attach to the governor if he surrendered, but to take it without that would be a feat to equal or even surpass Valona. Bohemund wanted to gift his sire Corfu as a prize before he even set sail from Brindisi.

Without those numbers, the notion of taking any of the fortresses was based on bluff, it being more a case of asking them to surrender rather than threatening any action other than burning boats and parts of the towns over which they presided. Much bluster was employed to persuade the garrison of Kassiopi to open the gates; the Greeks just laughed at his threats, being behind stout walls, now crammed with the population of the town, who had fled to join them as soon as the Norman galleys were sighted. Somewhat disheartened, Bohemund was forced to withdraw and anchor his ships off Butrinto, across the Corfu Channel on the mainland, there to wait for the Duke and his armada.

It took days to get the army in its entirety into and through Brindisi, down to the quays and onto the ships, which included every trading vessel Geoffrey Ridel, his Master of the Fleet, could commandeer, and they were sent to the outer anchorage as soon as they had sorted out the mayhem and got men loaded. The less than perfectly trained *milities* were bad enough, the Saracen levies Roger had sent from Sicily much better, but that was as nothing to the bugbear that attended every Norman army making a sea crossing.

There would be horses in Illyria; Bohemund would have sent out parties from Valona to acquire as many as he could, but that would be nothing like the number the Apulian host would require. Roger first, then Robert and he in company, had experienced the problem in crossing to Sicily, an operation in which they had learnt a great deal from their Byzantine opponents, who were much more practised in the art of moving a mounted host. Also, despite his aversion to the Duke of Normandy, Norman solidarity, added to a close-to-pleading request, had obliged him to advise William regarding the transport of his horses over to England using the same methods and specially adapted vessels as were being applied now.

'And what did I get for it?' he would demand when the subject came up, which it did when his knights wanted to amuse themselves by goading him. 'Nothing, not even a brass groat, and this while he was handing out land to all and sundry, even his damned squires. If he had not had his destriers at Senlac, he would not have the crown of England and he would not have got them there without we told him how!'

He came down to the quay himself to watch the loading and to add his towering voice to the confusion, which was not always an aid. Horses had a terror of anything with which they were not familiar and that included moving ramps, and however generous, ships that were not steady either, even in harbour – broad-bottomed sailing vessels onto which they had to be loaded in their thousands, enough mounts for fifteen hundred Norman lances as well as the lighter Lombard and Saracen cavalry.

The destriers, bred for and trained in battle tactics, were the easiest to load, for they had been, through long training, brought to a pitch of fearlessness necessary to carry their rider straight at a shield wall of yelling adversaries waving swords and spears. The cavalry mounts were more skittish, and a stiff wind blowing sails and ropes about, as well as any loose bits of canvas, made it hard to get them to voluntarily walk up the gangways to the deck, which was as nothing to getting them down another narrow ramp into the dark hold and into the constricted stalls set up to keep them safe on the swell, each with strapping to run under their bellies in case their legs gave way.

In this they would kick and bite, as well as splay their legs to become immovable even with ropes round their flanks, which is when an equine found out just how much a Norman loved his horse, for many got a hard buffet on the snout from a less than contented knight. The packhorses, many of them mares, were the worst, neighing and rearing in panic, a goodly number only happy when hooded and rendered blind, others requiring a mix of herbs that Count Roger had learnt how to mix from Calabrian monks, a potion which sedated

216

them enough to allow them to be led aboard. Then came the donkeys and those who looked after them, that great trail of bodies of various trades and none that would bring up the rear of the host when it marched.

The same scene was being played out in the port of Otranto, lower down the Apulian coast. When the ships bearing both the knights and their mounts had departed for the outer roads it was time to load the supply vessels with everything the army needed, from bales of hay down to cooking pots, farrier's nails and shoes, hoof oil, curry combs, spare weapons, mail, bolts of canvas to make tents and salted fish and meat. That was a supply that might need to be maintained as long as the host was in Illyria; the Normans lived off the land where they could, but that was not always possible, especially when the force was numbered in the thousands.

The return of Count Radulf from Constantinople brought Robert back from overseeing the loading to his castle, but it did not bring to his master any joy or the information he sought – quite the opposite; what he was told sent him into a towering rage. In the first place the usurping Emperor Botaneiates, who was so unpopular Robert saw him as easy meat in any coming battle, had himself been overthrown, replaced by a claimant to the purple called Alexius Comnenus.

He was, according to Radulf, the nephew of a previous emperor and so had the right to the diadem. He was also a talented general, popular with the Byzantine mob and a soldier who could command respect in the imperial provinces. None of this came as music to Robert's ears, but what pricked Robert's anger most was the calm way his envoy informed him that Alexius was strong for peace. He was prepared to return the Duke's daughter or even allow a marriage to Constantine, to whom he had acted as guardian, his envoy adding that that young man's father, the deposed Michael Dukas, was still alive, happy making his way as an Orthodox priest, and that Radulf had even spoken with him.

Pope Gregory had sent Robert a fellow who claimed to be that self-same deposed emperor, a wretched-looking creature in a monk's garb who certainly did not convince many, and certainly not a sly judge of character like the *Guiscard*; his son and heir, *Borsa*, had openly scoffed at the notion that this might be the true Michael Dukas, and he was far from alone – not surprisingly, for Dukas had been, prior to taking the purple, a successful general and man of some standing, an able courtier to boot, who had all the attributes to go with his position. Gregory's false Michael was not quite an oaf, but he leant closer to that estate than towards the kind of grandeur of a man who had ruled Byzantium.

To Robert anyone would do, even if he was utterly unconvincing; in the tangled skein of imperial politics there would be those who still professed allegiance to Michael Dukas, and if he could claim that he was acting with and on the deposed emperor's behalf, how many men could be detached from their present loyalty and thus reduce the number of his foes? Gregory's man was a weapon, not a very good one but an asset nevertheless. The last thing the Duke of Apulia wanted publicly spoken about was that he was definitely an impostor, which was what Count Radulf was keen to prove.

'The coup had not taken place when I departed,' Radulf continued, his voice full of confidence. 'I heard it as I crossed Romania, but I suspected it was coming and spent time with Alexius Comnenus as though he had already assumed the throne. He speaks of harmony between Apulia and the Empire and would welcome the opportunity to talk with you in person and in friendship.' In making his report, Count Radulf had failed to see the effect his words were having on his master: the *Guiscard*'s already florid face had gone bright red, not least because it seemed his envoy had utterly failed in what was his true mission.

'Did you speak with those Normans who have taken service with Byzantium?'

Radulf responded with an airy wave. 'I did, but not to press them to come to join you, My Lord, since it seems we are to be at peace with the new dispensation.'

'So you have not brought back with you a single lance?'

Radulf finally began to realise his account of his embassy was not being well received. His voice lost its air of self-assurance and he began to stammer. 'A-as I s-said . . .'

He got no further, and if his master stared low in his rebuke, the voice rose inexorably to a pitch of saliva-spitting rage. 'You are a dolt, Count Radulf . . .'

'I—'

'Silence! A fool who has not for a second even begun to obey the instructions with which I despatched you to Constantinople. I sent you on the pretext of my daughter, not on an errand to see she was being well cared for. I sent you to get some sense of the forces Botaneiates could put in the field and to attract to my banner those Norman lances that, due to your stupidity, I might now face in the field, and then you come back singing the praises of another damned usurper, talking of him as though he is a companion of your bosom.'

The walls being stone, Robert's voice reverberated, but now he dropped it to an even more terrifying whisper.

'Know this, fool: when we meet this Alexius, which we will surely do if the seat of his arse on that purple imperial cushion is sound, it will be you who occupies the first line of attack, you who will lead in the first conroys and you who will be forbidden to withdraw even if I command the men you lead to do so. You will not be kissing this new usurper's cheeks, arse or face, but the point of his lance. Now get out of my sight!'

It was by torchlight and after two whole days that the last of the vessels was ready to sail and only then would Robert admit to the depth of his weariness. If he was tired, he was content, aware that in the coming days he would cross the sea to take command and begin a conquest that might well end in the Hippodrome of Constantinople with his being acclaimed as Emperor. Normally, when seen off on campaign by his wife, Sichelgaita was full of good wishes; not this time, for she had asked that he take their son as well and he had refused.

The last ship to leave the near-empty harbour of Brindisi was his own galley, with Robert very visible on the deck, his barrel chest covered with his colours, his red-gold hair flowing in the breeze. Cheered by his fighters as he made his way out to the open Adriatic, anchors were plucked as he passed by, sails set and oars dipped, each vessel falling in behind their leader in a pattern that had been worked out by Geoffrey Ridel. The war-fighting vessels were on the outer rim to protect the mass of supply ships lumbering along in the middle, each one with men hanging over the side voiding their guts.

Once they rendezvoused with the Otranto contingent, they changed course for the Corfu Channel, where Bohemund awaited them. The Byzantine governor of the island, on seeing the size of the forces now opposing him and knowing he could expect no aid from

Constantinople, readily surrendered all three of his castles. The tiny Greek garrisons were evicted to make way for Apulians and enough vessels were left to Robert's new governor to make any attempt to use the channel a costly one.

Bohemund now in company, the fleet set sail with undiminished confidence for Valona, there to disembark the backbone of his forces, the men needed to secure his base and keep his army supplied and their equipment in good order, the remainder then destined to invest and capture the great port city of Durazzo, once the capital of Roman Illyricum and a place from which ran a proper Roman road, the Via Egnatia, all the way to the imperial Eastern capital. Once Durazzo was his, it would be his base for his march deep into Romania.

It was almost as if the ancient pagan gods, who had been worshipped when that road was built, felt the need to take a hand, to remind even the most mighty warrior of the sin of hubris. The storm that suddenly and unexpectedly hit Duke Robert's fleet, coming out of the mountains of ancient Macedonia, was stunning in its violence, with a wind that tore sails from their eye bolts and waves of a size that, hitting galleys on their beam, had the force to so cant their decks that water flowed over the bulwarks and if they could not be quickly righted they capsized.

All Geoffrey Ridel's attempts to get the fleet facing into the tempest, to point their prows into the waves, were hampered by a system of signalling that was primitive and required good vision. The rain that came with the storm made that impossible, a downpour so heavy that he was unable to even see those vessels sailing in close company, while the screaming wind carried away from them any voice commands he could yell through his speaking trumpet. Down below on the transport ships the horses were in panic, neighing and snorting, kicking their stalls with such force that the timbers were being smashed, this while the men who would ride and fight on them sought, by whispers and endearments and holding their bridles hard, to calm them down, while at the same time being sick.

The storm died as quickly as it had appeared, leaving a still-heaving sea but clearing skies full of scudding clouds, the *Guiscard* now able to look out over a seascape of vessels in a sorry state: disordered, masts gone by the board, rudders smashed, galleys lacking oars, for so many had been ripped from the rowers' hands by the sheer weight of water that hit them as they tried to steer. It took time to reimpose any cohesion, and when they counted what remained, that established how many had actually foundered and what the bill was in terms of human loss. Some no doubt wondered if the Duke would see this as his hopes dashed and return to Brindisi; those who knew him better never doubted their destination would remain fixed.

At Valona the temporary disembarkation proceeded with even greater disorder than that which had attended the departure from Brindisi – hardly surprising, given as much damage had been done below as had been done that was visible. But as off Corfu, the sight of such an armada and the force it carried was enough to open the gates to the citadel once it was made plain that failure to do so would result in a complete massacre for those who had taken refuge. The ships' masters, especially those who commanded the fighting galleys, were endlessly harassed into getting the vessels back into good repair – there was no time to waste, for the speed of the Apulian attack was as vital as the level of its force; every day delayed gave the enemy time to mass to meet them.

If it was not as fine a sight as had departed Brindisi when they weighed, it was still a potent force and a leaner one, a fighting fleet with minimum transports designed to both blockade and take Durazzo, a city which would not only open up to the *Guiscard* the whole of the lands now ruled by this Alexius Comnenus, but would deliver into his hands all those rebels who had fled from Italy: Abelard, Peter and the others, a band of ingrates whom he was determined should decorate the walls of the newly captured city with their skulls.

The storm had been a shock, but even that paled when, as they rounded the promontory that enclosed the great bight of Durazzo, they sighted another fleet – dozens of fighting galleys of a similar size to their vessels, but also a high proportion that carried a similar shape to, but seemed an improvement on, Byzantine dromons. This was a type of ship much more potent than their own, with a taller mast that carried a huge lanteen sail, bigger hulls that could accommodate two hundred men, twin banks of oars added to higher poops and foredecks. They were sitting outside the harbour of Durazzo, between the Apulians and the prize they sought, and there was only one power in the Adriatic who possessed such vessels.

'Venetians,' Robert spat.

It was even more galling to find out from the local inshore fishermen that they had only just beaten him to the bay. Had not that storm delayed him, the Apulian fleet would now occupy a defensive position outside the harbour, instead of their more powerful foe – one from which, even with such ships, it would have been hard to dislodge them.

CHAPTER FIFTEEN

Durazzo stood at the northern end of a long bay, tucked into a fold of land that protected its harbour from the frequent storms that made their way down from the Alps, while a mole had been built out into the Adriatic to guard against most other eventualities. The greatest asset was the good and spacious holding ground outside, an anchorage that could accommodate hundreds of vessels, making it, as the end of the Via Egentia, the central point of the major land trade route to the East. Naturally, such an important city had well-built walls and towers, as well as a strong fortress, but if the port had a fault it was that the same long bay was lined with shallow sand, and that allowed an enemy to land in force well away from the ability of any local forces to prevent it.

That, along with a tight blockade, had been the *Guiscard*'s intention but the presence of the Venetian fleet and those dromons rendered that impossible. If he did land his army, that would leave his undermanned ships at their mercy, and once they were destroyed, his forces would be stranded; in order to keep up their siege strength and then advance into the interior they needed to be supplied from Italy. Without that line of communication his mounted knights, the best fighters on foot as well as on horse, would spend most of their time protecting foraging parties and they, should the investment of Durazzo be of long duration, would be required to search further and further afield for the means to feed the host, increasingly weakening the numbers he could pit against city walls.

Robert assembled the ships' masters as well as the men who commanded the soldiers borne on each vessel, to crowd out the deck of the ducal galley to discuss with them the forthcoming difficulties. They centred on the much larger vessels of the enemy fleet, not only because of their dimensions but also because of the higher number of fighting men they could carry, though he was not in doubt that the men under his command would fight regardless of such problems.

'We must overcome the dromons, then disperse the rest of the Venetian galleys before we even think of setting foot on shore.'

'A hard task,' Geoffrey Ridel responded, as was his right as Master of the Fleet. 'Even if the vessels we have can match theirs, Venetians are born to the sea, few of us are.'

'War is war, Geoffrey, and I would hazard we are better at that than are they.'

'Best to close with the dromons,' Bohemund added, 'and get aboard speedily. On deck we are more than a match for them. I would wager twenty Normans can best two hundred Venetians.'

Looking around the assembled faces as he said this, Bohemund could see that those Norman warriors were less troubled than the sailors; the former were conditioned to fight and would do so wherever they found an enemy. The seafarers held such as the Venetians in high regard, and given the well-trained quality of crews who spent most of their time at sea, that caution was natural. Against that these ships' masters had been working for months with their crews on battle tactics, the ability to manoeuvre quickly, the art of varying their speed to confound an opponent, seeking to perfect the ploy of bringing more force to bear at the right moment than any adversary could employ in return.

Many of them, Bohemund thought, must have wondered at why they were being so employed in that training, for they would have suspected that when the invasion of the lands of Romania were undertaken, they would be used as they always had been, to enforce a blockade. Perhaps now they saw such preparation as a sign of the genius of the man who led them, an act of foresight from a shrewd general who had anticipated what they now faced on this campaign. Bohemund knew better; they had been so engaged because his father had become fascinated by the art of naval warfare and the long-term possibilities it offered.

He wanted a fighting fleet because in the Western Mediterranean Sea only two other powers possessed one, the Venetians they now faced and the North African Saracens, and while he had seen no immediate purpose to it, given these were, he thought, distant and perhaps future enemies, he also knew that if he did take Constantinople he would likely need to be able to fight at sea to keep it. The fact that he now had something to oppose the Venetians in Durazzo Bay was more luck than prescience, but there was one question and that was simple – was it enough?

It was Geoffrey Ridel who responded to Bohemund's confident statement about competence and odds. 'You will have observed how much higher those decks are than ours and the dromons will be the vessels in the vanguard of any battle.'

'Then we must make a way to overcome them.'

'You can just jump, Bohemund,' Reynard of Eu joked, to general amusement. 'We mere mortals need wings.'

'Grappling irons and hooked ladders,' Robert proposed, adding a glare that choked off the mirth. 'We will distribute the bowmen to keep their sides clear and that will allow our conroys to use their hooks and lances to get on to their decks. I will guess these men are accustomed to fighting pirates, Saracens perhaps, not mailed knights and not Normans.'

'My Lord, there is a small galley coming down the bay with a truce flag atop its mast.'

'See!' the *Guiscard* cried, as he craned his neck to acknowledge the message from the lookout above his head. 'They know who we are and that is making them cautious.'

Geoffrey Ridel, without reference to Robert, bellowed orders to clear his deck, which sent those assembled over the side and into their waiting boats, Bohemund alone being asked to remain by his sire. The familia knights, now his own seaborne contingent of warriors, Robert lined up like a guard of honour, adjuring them to look as martial and fierce as they could without they insult his guest. The man they welcomed aboard came with ease across a gangplank strung between both vessels, a tricky manoeuvre given both were rising and falling at different rates on the swell. In doing so he underlined how easy he was on water, a statement that this, the sea, was a Venetian element, not a Norman one.

Dressed in soft leathers, covered with the kind of heavily embroidered silken cloak worn by high Byzantine officials, he also had a great quantity of gold and jewellery about his person: rings, a heavy bracelet on his wrist and around his neck a gold chain studded with precious stones. This envoy had presence; the only thing that diminished him in proximity to these Normans was his height, for he was short, stocky, with thick black hair and a face much marked and wrinkled by long service at sea. Aware that he towered over the fellow, Bohemund by his side even more so, Robert called for chairs to be brought on deck prior to making a greeting. He also whispered to a servant that the man he was promoting as the deposed Emperor Michael Dukas should be kept out of sight; this fellow may have seen the real one.

The fellow knew his manners; in the presence of a duke he doffed his hat and bowed to introduce himself. 'Maximian Palladias, My Lord, Master of the Fleet of Venice.'

'You do me much honour by coming in person, Maximian Palladias.'

'I could do no less to such an illustrious warrior as yourself, My Lord. To send a subordinate to talk with you would be marked as an insult to your person as well as your title.'

Two chairs having been brought on deck as this exchange of diplomatic niceties took place, Duke Robert indicated that they should sit, which they did, and a wave of the ducal arm saw everyone withdraw to give them room to talk in private, Bohemund excepting himself by remaining within earshot which, when the Venetian looked in his direction, got a nod from his sire.

'I hope you have not come to ask me to withdraw.'

'Would a man not be foolish to suggest such a thing to the *Guiscard*?'

Robert nodded at the compliment, without for a second giving it credence. 'Then what?'

'The Doge of Venice is a vassal of the Emperor of Byzantium—'

Robert held up a hand, which stopped his visitor speaking. 'I am curious to know which one that is, Maximian, given it seems to have been a troubled throne, and recently occupied by more than one person.'

That got a corresponding nod from the Venetian. 'The request to us to prevent you landing in Romania came from Alexius Comnenus, the man who now wears the purple and the crown.'

'And to him you are loyal?'

Maximian waved a hand that was intended to encompass his fleet, anchored to the north in an arc that covered the entrance to Durazzo harbour. 'It is a matter of some talk aboard our vessels.'

'Which means that there are those who see Alexius as a usurper?'

'My Lord, in any great domain there are factions. As of this moment it is impossible for me to know who, if any of those under my command, holds the ascendancy in terms of allegiance.'

'And your own?'

'Lord Robert, I would not be here on this deck if I was not a supporter of any man that can hold the Empire together. I see Alexius Comnenus as being that person by right of both his abilities and his bloodline. He is, after all, the nephew of a previous emperor.'

'Not Botaneiates or Dukas?' The response to that was no more than a raised eyebrow; this man was not to be so easily drawn. 'You must know that I have the Emperor Michael Dukas with me and I would see it as an obligation to consider that he has a right to your loyalty.'

'The news that you carry Michael Dukas in your train is part of the problem I face.'

'It has spread?'

'Such tales do.'

'It is not a tale, but a fact.'

'One that I may take leave to dispute, though not all of my captains agree.'

'So your command is not unified?'

'It is not in disarray,' Maximian insisted. 'But there is as yet a lack of the concord that might bring us to force upon you a battle; one, I would point out to you, you cannot win given our superiority in ships.'

'I am not accustomed to defeat,' Robert replied, for the first time in this exchange his voice carrying a hard edge.

'On land, My Lord.'

'It is not unknown for a land-based general to adapt to the ocean with success. I look to Ancient Rome and its consuls for such inspiration.'

'And,' Maximian responded, with a level of courtesy that was unctuously exaggerated, 'who would be more likely to be that person than your renowned self?'

'Maximian Palladias, I respect the fact that you have come in person to see me, which tells me you have a proposal to make.'

'I do, Duke Robert. It may be that elements in my fleet will not agree to do battle on behalf of Alexius Comnenus, which would seriously weaken my fighting strength.'

'You're inviting me to attack you as soon as you are back on your own deck and that truce flag is no longer valid.'

'Be assured, Duke Robert, that if you do so the outcome will not be in doubt, for there is not a ship's master or soldier aboard my vessels who will not defend their honour, and not just seek to preserve that, but to put to the sword and the bottom of the sea anyone seeking to besmirch it.'

'So?'

'It may be that a battle will not take place, that I will be unable to obey the Doge's instructions. In that case there will be no contest between us. What I am proposing is that we maintain our present positions, no anchors to be raised while the period of grace is in place.'

'And if you withdraw I will be free to land my army?'

'That is so. I suggest that I be granted a day and a night to seek to resolve my dilemma, and if it goes as I wish, I will send to tell you that we will prepare for battle, at which point I would, for the sake of saving lives and souls, advise you to withdraw, which you will be able to do unmolested.'

It was the *Guiscard*'s turn to use his eyebrows to make a point, that being he might choose to stay and fight, this acknowledged by Maximian with a wry smile as Robert enquired, 'And if it goes the other way?'

'Then, as I have already intimated, I will have no choice but to weigh anchor and take the fleet back to Venice.'

Robert dropped his chin to his chest, to give the impression of deep consideration, a silence that lasted for enough time to make Maximian shift in his chair. That was followed by a stare from the *Guiscard* that was deliberately designed to be hard to hold, though the Venetian was not to be compelled to drop his eyes or blink.

'A day and a night, Maximian Palladias, but not a grain of sand more than that. Should your dilemma be unresolved when the time is up, be assured that we will attack you and, perhaps for the sake of your own souls, you should avoid the contest. I will have Durazzo and more besides.'

'I have your word?'

'You do.'

Maximian stood and bowed, then without another word he made his way onto that swaying plank and back to his own galley. Robert watched him go and did not speak till he was out of any chance of overhearing his words.

'The fool has played into our hands, Bohemund.'

'How so?'

Robert hooted. 'He has given us time to prepare, to get those grappling irons out of our supply ships and to send a party ashore to cut timber for ladders and ready them for use. With the vessels he has he should have borne down on us as soon as he saw our masts.'

'They will be watching us, and even at such a distance they may see what we are about.'

'Let them, Bohemund, for they would expect no less.' Then he turned to Geoffrey Ridel. 'Call everyone back on board, they need to know what is proposed and what we need to do.'

In the subsequent discussion of tactics it was plain that those using grappling irons could not at the same time be fighters wearing mail; to haul up your own body weight was hard enough without both weapons and armour. Besides, hooked irons were normally used to haul down walls damaged by ballista by being attached by ropes to teams of oxen; it was rare that they were used to get a man onto a high defended wall for the very sound reason that a single slice with a sword would send him crashing back to earth. Ridel was of the opinion that the same problem applied on board ship and that such a means of approach should be used sparingly and more to lock the enemy alongside than to get men onto an opposing deck. Duke Robert was inclined to let what men saw before their eyes decide what use they should be put to, battle ever being confused.

Ashore, well-defended parties were cutting and lashing together timbers for short ladders, the blacksmiths using their forges to fashion metal hooks, the length of both the perceived difference in height between a normal galley deck and that of the higher Venetian vessels. Robert also had his woodcutters making double-thick screens to absorb arrows fired at long range, which the enemy was bound to employ, for they wanted to get onto the Apulian deck as much as their opponents. To Robert and his son, the answer to victory lay in putting Norman knights against men who had never faced the best close-combat fighters in Christendom.

All the next day, in bright sunshine, the best eyes aboard the Apulian fleet were fixed on the distant Venetians, not that such observations provided much in the way of what was happening; there was activity certainly, but what it portended was a mystery, for the distance was too great to discern any detail. All the Apulians could do was prepare for their own needs and wonder if indeed they would be called upon to fight at all, for that exchange between the Venetian and Robert was now common knowledge.

When men talked, those who had seen Maximian come aboard had much to discuss, for they had not missed the wealth he wore about his person and that led to speculation about what might be available to plunder inside those enemy ships. As the major maritime trading nation in the Adriatic and beyond, the Venetians, from their Doge down, were known to be affluent – how could they not be when they traded in valuable silks and spices of the kind that cost a ducal ransom?

Carried ashore, that kind of talk had spread in Norman French, Latin, Greek and Saracen, so throughout Duke Robert's fleet any lingering doubts about the wisdom of taking on the northern seafarers was diminished by the prospect of the abundant plunder to be had, an amount that grew with each exchange until every man was thirsting for a fight that they were sure would make them rich. With the truce in place, they went to sleep with that as the driver of their dreams.

The ringing of bells brought them from their slumbers and onto the deck, there to find those who had been set as sentinels pointing to the lights of those heavy Venetian dromons, now no longer distant pinpricks but flaring lanterns bearing down on them, their glow lighting the great lanteen sails. The Apulian ships' masters had to be quick to react, for there was no time to haul their galleys over their anchors and pluck them from the seabed. The cables had to be cut by sharp axes while the rowers were sent scurrying to their oars, this while the men on the transport ships ran to their ratlines and ropes to set some canvas and likewise get themselves under way; in what was coming upon them no one was safe.

Robert de Hauteville, in company with Bohemund and every other Norman in the fleet, was struggling to get into his mail so as to be fit to do battle, that carried out with an eye on those great sails, which seemed, on a northerly breeze, to be approaching at a speed which would scarce grant them enough time, only to see them disappear as they were furled, ready for the coming battle. In any other fighting force there would have been panic; indeed there was amongst some of his Lombard and Greek levies. Not with the Normans, for all the speed with which they were preparing it was done with the requisite amount of care, each man seeing to his confrère's equipment, like his leather mail straps to ensure they were as tight and secure as they needed to be for the coming fight.

There was no time to think about how their duke had been

deceived, no time to wonder at the chicanery necessary to break a formal truce, which for all his reputation for cunning the *Guiscard* had never done. The Normans, Saracens and, once they had been forced into position, his Apulian *milities*, lined their decks as the galley timbers beneath their feet began to groan with movement, the voice of the oar master loud and the thud of his hammer on the speed block slowly increasing.

'It's near first light,' Robert cried out, pointing with his sword at the first tinge of grey in the eastern sky. 'Geoffrey, try to get us with the sun behind us as it rises.'

On land, the Normans had a system of commands issued by horn, the number of blasts and their length determining which manoeuvre the conroys were required to perform. This had been adapted for sea by Geoffrey Ridel but it was not the perfect tool and nor was the element in which they were going to have to fight an easy one in which it could be employed; galleys were not destriers, turned by at thigh and a sharp tug on a single rein. Despite the best efforts of rowers and helmsmen they were slow to get up speed and even less adept at steering out of danger. Thus, when the first of the Venetian dromons got amongst the Apulian fleet they were able to take advantage of a great deal of confusion, putting several of Robert's galleys in danger.

'Look aloft, Father,' Bohemund yelled from his deck, which was close enough to the ducal galley for his voice to carry.

Robert de Hauteville followed his son's pointed gauntlet and it was there he saw why Maximian Palladias had asked for his truce. The Venetians had got to Durazzo just before the Apulians and they must have put to sea in haste, which indicated they had anchored off Durazzo before they were ready for a fight; Maximian was seaman enough to know what he faced and what tactics would be used against his vessels. He had needed time to prepare, time to get in place a weapon that would render all the notions the *Guiscard* had of how to get aboard the Venetian decks redundant.

The truce had been a ploy to grant him a huge advantage, for lashed to the high masts of the large enemy three-decked galleys were boats full of archers. The Venetians would have the ability to pin on his decks the men they feared, the Norman warriors, who would be so occupied protecting themselves from the deadly rain of arrows from above that any notion of taking the offensive would be nullified.

'Keep your shield above your head, Bohemund,' Robert yelled, 'for that is where danger lies.'

'The rest of the fleet?'

'Each vessel must look to its own, but we must lead them by example. Geoffrey, use that rudder and those oars to get me in amongst these swine.'

CHAPTER SIXTEEN

What followed quickly turned into a confused melee; there were no formal lines as in a land battle, no features such as rivers, forests or hills which could act as protection to a flank or provide cover for infiltration, not a single clear objective to which Robert could direct his men, quite apart from the very obvious fact he had been forced on to the defensive. Nor could he issue commands that had any hope of being obeyed, especially since his own galley was an obvious target for the dromons, massive in size now as they loomed up out of the increasing light, their aim to lop off the head in the hope the body would collapse.

In essence, while he could fight if they came close, his fate was in the hands of Geoffrey Ridel, and not for the first time in his life fortune favoured him, even if he railed against it, by granting him such a wily seaman, who had the wit to use his speaking trumpet while he could still be heard to ensure that the ducal vessel had around it a screen of fighting ships, one of which carried his bastard son, two of the others the crossbowmen.

'Damn you, Geoffrey!' Robert yelled, as he saw one of those dromons begin to close in on a galley. 'Get me into the fight.'

'Arrows!' yelled Reynard, as he saw the greying sky go black above the masts of the protecting galleys.

This had every man on deck immediately crouching, the familia knights using their shields to protect themselves, as well as their liege lord, from harm, no more than a trice before the arrows thudded into them to embed themselves into hardwood or clang as they spun off the metal frames or the central boss. A few, overflying and missing the shields, found the open hatches that led below to the rowing deck – there had been no time to put in place the covers – and the cry of more than one wounded man carried up to the deck.

As soon as he was upright again Robert de Hauteville was marching in fury to where Geoffrey Ridel stood on the poop, right by the great tiller and the men tasked to swing it on the Master of the Fleet's commands. Right beneath Ridel's feet lay a slatted hatch and underneath that stood the fellow who controlled the oarsmen, so the man in command could both dictate the speed of the galley and direct the course, if necessary by the use of both.

'Did you hear my command?' the *Guiscard* yelled.

Few people could look the Duke in the eye when he was in temper and even fewer had the ability to question his judgement, for he was a master of battle who could sniff out an opponent's weak spot before it appeared, or just by some sixth sense define the moment when resistance was about to weaken. That was on land, but being at sea Ridel had the upper hand; Robert could fight, and if age had diminished him he was still more than a match for those he was likely to face. But he could not steer a ship, nor did he have the wit to know when the combination of oars and tiller would work to advantage. This allowed Geoffrey Ridel to address his duke in a voice short on respect, indeed close to a shout.

'My task is to keep you safe, My Lord, just as it is the task of your familia knights.'

'I lead by example, man. I do not skulk in the background like some damned Saracen emir.'

'If your example is to be seen sinking beneath the waves, what then?' Ridel pointed to Robert's personal standard, streaming out from atop the mast, alongside the flag just raised that ordered every ship to engage, as though they had a choice. 'We must keep that standard flying; if it is cut down or this vessel is overpowered, then there is no hope of surviving to fight another day.'

'Survival? What do you mean, Ridel? We have to win.'

'My Lord Robert, against these great ships you cannot win, all you can do is endure.'

Bohemund was also blessed with a good hand on the tiller, a man who knew that the smaller galleys only had one advantage and that was their greater manoeuvrability; they could, if properly handled, spin in their own length, as well as swiftly increase and decrease speed. The dromons, with larger hulls and a vastly greater number of oarsmen, needed time to follow, which meant as they closed there was a moment of opportunity in which to avoid their intent to either ram or board, the latter signalled by the sudden withdrawal of the bank of oars facing the Apulian vessel.

Bohemund's master timed his tiller turn to perfection, but it owed as much to the quick reaction of the rowers that they managed to spin away from the Venetian bearing down on them: one set of oars held their way, the others backed hard. Not that such a manoeuvre provided security; the raised-aloft boats full of archers had a clear shot at the open deck as well as the warriors who occupied it and it was only a timely command by their leader that had a number of them fall back to the stern and use their shields to protect both themselves, the ship's master and the men working the tiller ropes. Speeding away from immediate danger brought momentary relief, but it was no more than that, for right in their path lay another dromon, its side lined with screeching fighters waving spears and swords.

'We need to get aboard one of these ships,' Bohemund cried into the master's ear. 'We have to show them they too are vulnerable.'

The look that got in response was not one to imbue Bohemund with confidence; clearly the man thought he was mad and had only one idea, to avoid contact and stay alive. About to castigate the fellow, albeit with respect for his skills, the sound of his name shouted loud made Bohemund spin round. Ligart, that redhead who had been so troublesome when raiding Capua, now a calmer fellow than hitherto, was madly waving his lance at a sight that no one aboard had ever seen. From the side of the dromon they had just avoided a pipe protruded, its spout inside the line of oars, and from that shot a bolt of flame, not aimed at them but at the hull of another galley that had been to Bohemund's rear.

'Greek fire,' screeched the ship's master. 'It is the Devil's work, we are doomed!'

The vision of the flames punching through water, even staying lit when they made contact, was not one to allow for Bohemund to call the man a fool. Even worse was to observe the side of the galley start to burn below the waterline, with flames rising up to ignite the timbers above sea level. If it brought fear to those who could see it at a distance, it was just as obvious that such a weapon, against which there was no defence, induced panic in those on the receiving end. Men, Norman lances included, were rushing about the deck like headless chickens. Some, easy to call them deluded when not in danger, were seeking to douse the flames with the buckets of water that lined the deck of every ship.

It was to no avail; the fire was impervious to such actions and soon the whole side of the ship was alight, with the dromon that had inflicted the damage drawing clear to avoid catching fire itself. In distress, the galley master had ordered his rowers to bend their backs, but could not see that by doing so he was creating a wind that fanned the flames and made matters worse. In the end it was not his folly that slowed the rate of fire but the panic of the oarsmen who, realising that they might be fried, let drop their sticks and began to rush on deck. From standing rock-still in amazement, Bohemund reacted to the screams emanating from the victims, many of them men he expected to fight alongside, who would be roasted alive if not saved.

'Steer for the open side, away from the flames.'

'You're mad!'

The master had responded without thinking. That he did as the giant before him bent over to press home his command.

'Do as I say or it will not be Venetians or Satan you have to fear.'

About to protest further, the scrape of a broadsword being pulled from its scabbard was enough to kill whatever objection he had been about to make. Now it was his men's backs that had to bend as he ordered the oar master to drum for full speed, before he yelled to the tiller men to haul hard and make the necessary turn. With both banks of oars working, that was made in a long arc that took them near the stern of the dromon that had spewed out the Greek fire, now with its oars raised just above the water, content to watch its victim burn and sink. Seeing that, Bohemund began to issue another set of instructions.

It was those same raised archers who alerted the commanders on the Venetian deck that the more manoeuvrable Apulian galley was about to make its way down their side, its own oars shortened so that it could get close. Bohemund had every man on deck on one knee, shield above his head, and another party with him on the poop to once more protect the master and his steering crew. Going at full tilt, Bohemund's ship passed the Venetian stern before those on its deck could properly react. The oars on the Apulian vessel disappeared and the master swung the tiller hard over to bring his galley into the line of Venetian oars. The sound of arrows from above thudding home was drowned out by the smashing sound of oar after oar breaking like a weak taper, while through the leather-covered rowlocks from which they protruded came screams as the men holding them, who could not see what was coming, were eviscerated, the ends being ripped out of their unsuspecting hands.

They could not entirely destroy the greater galley's ability to manoeuvre, but they did enough damage to reduce the number of oars it could employ, before steering far enough clear to get their own back in use. Bohemund had timed the arrow salvoes, which seemed slow. Then he realised that bows must take longer to load and aim on a swaying boat hanging from ropes, this caused merely by the actions of the bodies it contained. He had his men drop their shields and sling their lances up and over the side to the part of the deck where those commanding the ship would be standing, a crying sound telling them they had done damage to human flesh.

Getting back to full speed the ship's master swung his galley, using oars and tiller, past the prow of the stationary dromon, then deployed both again so that his vessel came round on a new course to bring it alongside his stricken consort on the far side. Bohemund was shouting instructions for grappling irons to be thrown so that the burning ship could be hauled close enough to get the warriors and crew off, aware that he had little time, for if he had by his actions slowed that fire-spewing dromon, it was far from ineffective.

Over the water he could hear the shouted commands to replace oars and oarsmen, to get under way with what they still possessed on a ship that could only have one aim, to close with him and perhaps once more use that Greek fire to set his galley alight. The desire to escape of those he was seeking to rescue did not aid him; some of the rowers jumped too soon, to fall between the closing hulls and be crushed or drowned. The Normans, however, even with roaring flames so close to their backs that their surcoats were being singed, showed great discipline, obeying Bohemund's command to clear the side and at the same time restrain those in hazard because of their panic.

Although Bohemund only realised it when they had got clear, what saved them was the way the two galleys came together in a far from gentle crunch, which swung the burning vessel right across the prow of the dromon and that prevented it from getting close enough to once more employ that deadly flame-throwing pipe at a range where it could do damage. The spout of flame shot out as before but it died in the water well away from Bohemund's galley. In seeking to manoeuvre for another attempt, while again avoiding the danger of catching light itself, the Venetians gifted those seeking to cross to

243

safety the time to do so. As soon as the last man boarded, Bohemund's master pushed off using boathooks, enough to get his oars into use again so they could speed to safety.

Robert could see three burning galleys, the flames that consumed them rising into a now sunlit sky, black smoke billowing too as the stores they contained inside their hulls went up. Yet what was most hard to bear were the screams of men being burnt alive, oarsmen trapped below and those warriors who delayed too long on the deck. Not that they were gifted a release, for they had only one way to douse themselves and that was to jump into a sea in which a Norman could not but drown; chain mail alone, even if they could swim, was too heavy to allow them to float and would drag them to the bottom.

Keeping him safe was that pair of galleys into which had been loaded the crossbowmen, originally intended for an aggressive role that had, thanks to Geoffrey Ridel and his speaking trumpet, added to a far-carrying voice, got between him and the enemy. With the longer range of their arrow bolts, added to their deadly accuracy, as well as by judicious and sparing use, they were able to hold off the pair of Venetian ships seeking to break through in an attempt to close with his flying ducal standard.

Apart from that he was and felt useless, but he could see that in other quarters his men were giving as good as they got; not every Venetian vessel was equipped with Greek Fire and it now appeared that those who did carry it had used up their supply, for no more of his vessels had been set alight for some time. Added to that, his preparations had not been entirely wasted and if one of his galleys could get alongside an enemy the grappling irons were doing good service to force them together at either the bow or the stern of the larger vessel. That achieved, Normans had both the courage and the skill to get themselves up his hooked ladders onto the enemy decks and fight there, and if they could not prevail, due to the disparity of numbers and the constrained area of combat, they could at least occupy the Venetians so that other galleys were allowed to close and support them.

That was what Bohemund was about, not least because he had on his own deck now double the number of fighting men, a tempting target for an enemy dromon and their archers. Casting his gaze around for a way to occupy them, he saw a line of lances strung across an enemy deck, shield close to shield, with just enough room between for their broadswords to do their deadly work. Behind them stood another conroy with their teardrop shields laid flat to cover themselves and the heads of the men in front, nullifying the attempts of the archers to rain down arrows upon them. His arm, in which he now held a huge axe, shot out.

'Master, steer for the tiller of that dromon.'

Even if he looked doubtful – the man wanted no more than to set his prow for safety and have his rowers bend their backs – he had long since reasoned that to question the orders of this Goliath was to invite a blow from that axe that would split him in two. As he issued his commands he could hear his giant doing likewise, making sure there were spare lances available, setting the grappling irons for use and arranging the ladders so they could be swiftly employed.

'The stern is higher than the deck amidships,' said Ligart, as they came close. 'These ladders of your father's will be too short.'

'Archers,' Bohemund replied calmly, causing both men to kneel and defend their bodies as he quietly answered that problem. 'Hook two ladders together and they are more than enough.'

Coming under the high stern protected them from the archers but their approach had not gone unnoticed on deck; there was a large and vocal party of Venetians waiting to oppose their boarding. Their attempt to discourage Normans by leaning over the taffrail and shouting imprecations at them was not only useless; it proved, for many, to be fatal. On the command, Bohemund and his double quota of warriors dropped their shields, stood upright and, after a slight pause, slung their lances. It was a drill they carried out daily, in the same way they rehearsed fighting on foot and mounted, so there was little wastage. Each man, in that short time they took to aim, had picked a victim, fixed that person for an instant before casting their lance. So many of their weapons found some flesh it almost cleared the stern, while the remainder, those who avoided a lance point, were so in terror of the sight of those who suffered wounds that they fled.

'Irons!' Bohemund yelled.

The grappling irons snaked over the now near-empty stern and the sheer weight of the subsequent pull had the galley crunching into the decorative fretwork hard enough to smash it to kindling, this as whoever commanded the defenders rallied them to contest the boarding. The ladders followed the meeting of hulls and within a space of a few breaths, swords and axes swinging, the Normans swarmed up with enough vigour to get more than half of them on to the poop, where their actions cleared the way for the remainder.

Bohemund led the way and with his reach and chosen weapon proved the most deadly. The deck planking was stained already from those thrown lances but that was as nothing to what followed – great spouts of red blood and gore, which shot forth as flesh was rent asunder by his axe, this added to by swinging broadswords in powerful hands on the end of massively muscled arms, while in maintaining close contact they made it difficult for the archers to fire at them for fear of hitting their own.

That security diminished as, moving forward, half pace by half pace, they began to drive back their opposition, which necessitated shield cover again, their progress slowed as more of the enemy came to reinforce the defence. Bohemund could see above their heads and if he only had half an eye – the remainder of his vision too busy at his killing, the only result of an axe strike – it was obvious they were winning their fight, while the party of Normans he had come to help were driving from the bows towards the mainmast.

Less cheering was the sight of two Venetian dromons bearing down on them from the shoreside, a development that had Bohemund stop to let the line in which he was fighting go on, it closing automatically to cover for his absence. A thud obliged him to quickly raise his shield, for they were still at the mercy of those archers; one of their arrows had just missed him and was now quivering near his foot. The feeling of anger at what the Venetians had done with their false truce, which had been with him and no doubt every one of his confrères since the first alarm, boiled up, and he rushed to one side where a line of taut ropes lashed round cleats set into the ship's bulwarks snaked upwards.

The swinging axe, honed and sharpened the day before in preparation for the coming battle, sliced through them like twine. He had no idea what his action would achieve, it being born out of frustration more than thought, but the yells from aloft indicated he had achieved an unexpected result, that confirmed when he spun round to see a body, one of the archers, his bow still in his hand, descend in flaying fall to slam into the deck. A glance aloft showed the boat in which they had been placed was now upended and hanging by one set of lines, not the many needed to keep it level, with other archers hanging on to anything they could get hold of and crying out for help.

That act alone doubled the number of his fighters, for now his men had no need of overhead cover, the result an increase in pressure that pushed back their enemies to a point where Bohemund found himself staring down a hatch, crowded at the bottom with unarmed men, who, when they moved fearfully away, set up a clanking sound. They had to be rower slaves, each one chained and thus no threat, so, calling to Ligart and two other lances, he shot down the companionway and into the gloom of the lower deck, where he sought another hatch cover which would, when lifted, take him below the waterline.

The stink of the bilge water stagnating the ballast rose to greet him and, breath held, he dropped down into what was a storage area for the things necessary to allow the ship to stay at sea, none of which was of interest; what he was looking for was a line of planks that, flat and affixed along the ship's side, provided a way for the carpenter to inspect for leaks in the hull. It was guesswork to swing his axe at the timbers below, and given the ship had a double skin, both of a decent thickness, it took time to smash his way through. The blow that split the outer hull produced an immediate flow of water; ten more heavy swings of his axe turned that into a torrent that immediately began to flood the vessel.

'Back on deck, Ligart,' he shouted as he eased himself out of that torrent and back on to the rowing deck. 'Pass the word to the conroy leaders to prepare to retreat – we have to get our men back into their galleys.'

Bohemund's axe was employed again as he made his way back to the companionway, smashing at those timbers that held the ring bolts to free the oarsmen. They were likely to die from drowning anyway, but his action at least gave them a chance to cling to what would soon be wreckage, for if all went well this dromon was going to sink; there was not a carpenter born who could fill the hole he had created. The cries of gratitude were drowned out by chains being drawn through rings, but he would have ignored them anyway, given he needed to be back up on deck to make sure his command was being obeyed.

The need that it should be, and quickly, was looming close; soon the Norman boarders would be in range of arrows fired from the approaching dromons, and if they remained fighting, the crews of those two vessels would get aboard and might overwhelm them. Even more worrying was that water now pouring into the hull, with Bohemund having no idea how long it would take to affect the trim of the ship; for all he knew it could cant over and capsize.

There was no horn to order a retreat, just his towering voice, and in any other fighting force – the Normans were, after all, pressing on their enemies – that command would have been questioned and quite possibly ignored. But the discipline that made them what they were held, and under the control of their conroy leaders they began to step backwards at not much more than the pace at which they had advanced. Bohemund's height allowed him to direct those who had come from the original galley to withdraw, as well as to tell them why; his Norman French made sure the Venetians had no idea what he was saying.

Getting off the ship while also fighting would have been difficult but for those slave rowers who, now freed, came up screaming that the ship was sinking. At first that merely caused the kind of confusion that eased the withdrawal, but when the sense of what was being imparted got home to the Venetian crew their desire to keep fighting evaporated, creating a gap by which the Normans could disengage. Bohemund's men piled aboard their galley, and the master, who had seen and appreciated the danger, got clear at ramming speed. As they drew off, the dromon on which they had been fighting began to settle in the water while those who had come to its rescue put aside any idea of pursuit and set to in order to try and keep it afloat. Dragging his eyes away from that sight, Bohemund could look around and what he saw did not cheer him; if he had scored a small victory, it was obvious by the wrecked galleys, added to one or two still burning, that the Apulian fleet had suffered badly.

At the masthead of the ducal galley that flag had changed; it was no longer a command to engage but the one that signalled the need to withdraw. It was, to his son, what it looked like: an admission of defeat.

CHAPTER SEVENTEEN

That the Venetians let them disengage without difficulty was the first surprise; the fighting and bloody withdrawal that the *Guiscard* had anticipated turned into an undisturbed retreat that took his ships back to the southern end of the bay, to where his transports had fled, while the enemy, having abandoned attempts to save the one dromon that had fallen to Bohemund's axe, made for the waters outside Durazzo harbour to anchor and no doubt celebrate. That one Norman victory now sat on the sandy bottom and as the sun faded, day turning to night, only the top of its mast still was visible, with the archers' boat hanging off of it; if that served as a consolation, it was a small one which soon disappeared into darkness.

The losses had been significant in both men and galleys and that took no account of the wounds, quite a number of them serious burns that rendered the victims so incapacitated that they were unlikely to survive. As they clung to life, the sounds they emitted, from mournful cries to outright other-worldly screams, acted as a melancholy backdrop to the deliberations taking place by the light of lanterns on one of the large transport vessels that had been designated as an infirmary. Robert had come aboard to visit the wounded and once that sad duty was done he went back aboard his own ship, having called together the men who led his warriors into such an unfamiliar battle, as well as those masters who by their laudable efforts had managed to avoid destruction, all of them exhausted by the day's combat.

'We fought well.'

These, the first words he uttered, were received as he expected, with cast-down eyes that told him agreement was mixed. Also the collective 'we' resonated with the man who employed it; Robert had taken no part in the fighting and if that could be understood on one plane, it sat ill with men who were accustomed to be led into combat by their duke, not observed and encouraged from afar. Geoffrey Ridel sensed the mood and felt the need to defend their leader from criticism.

'Know this, that our liege lord desired to get into the fight and it was I who stopped him, I who refused to sail his galley towards the enemy, and with good reason. If he had gone down, we would not be assembled now to talk of what to do next; we might well be raising our anchors and heading for Brindisi.'

'Not all of us,' Bohemund growled.

'What are we to do now?' asked Reynard of Eu, after a long and significant silence, not one of the commanders present wanting to be the one to first speak.

Robert aimed a grim smile at his familia knight, well aware and grateful that his man had only spoken to relieve a tension that

252

threatened to break into uncontrolled discord. He knew the difference between success and failure in battle, for, if he had enjoyed many more victories than defeats in his thirty years of warfare, he had tasted both. Winning brought harmony to a host; to lose, even on an element to which they were unaccustomed, could create dissension in any army and Normans were no exception. If anything they were worse; good fighting men and natural leaders were not sheep – they expected their opinions to be listened to and respected.

'The choices are simple,' Robert suggested, 'we can renew the fight—'

Geoffrey Ridel's interruption was delivered with acid certainty. 'A contest we cannot win.'

Bohemund spoke up again. 'We sank one of their dromons today.'

Now the Master of the Fleet was scathing. 'We need to sink all twenty, not one.'

'*Or,*' Robert emphatically said, 'we can disembark and lay siege to Durazzo.'

'Lacking a blockade, My Lord?'

'You say, Geoffrey, that we cannot fight their large ships with any hope of success. They – the one weapon we cannot overcome at sea – can do us little harm when we are on land.'

'Or,' Bohemund interjected, 'we could find another route to Constantinople.'

Reynard shook his head slowly. 'The landscape is not favourable, Bohemund.'

That caused a murmur of agreement, which matched the doubt in Reynard's voice; Illyria was not blessed with many routes through the interior. It was mountainous, full of deep gorges and unbridged rivers, while at those points at which progress was possible Byzantium had built strong defensive castles, which could not be bypassed by any army in need of a sound line of communication. In addition, this was ancient Macedonia, the heartlands of Alexander the Great's old kingdom, full of untamed and warlike tribes who not even the local Byzantine satraps sought to control; they were content to contain such folk in their mountain fastness with, when they raided too deeply into the civilised settlements, occasional bloody incursions to chastise them.

Bohemund was adamant. 'We cannot withdraw.'

'Nor will we,' Robert sighed. He was well aware that such an avenue reflected the general mood. 'But we are, to a man, weary. You all know me, and each of you is aware of what I have achieved. I expect you will believe me when I say that in the dark, when the day has gone badly, every difficulty becomes a steep hill to climb. Yet when the sun rises again it is often only a small and easy-to-overcome mound; so go back to your ships and reassure those you lead that we will prevail, as I hope I can reassure of such a thing come morning.'

Bohemund remained to ask the obvious question, one that was on the mind of everyone who had just departed. 'Do you have a plan, Father?'

'No, I do not, but I too must sleep and hope that God grants me in my dreams a way to overcome those Venetians, who, as of this moment, have me by the throat. If, tomorrow, they renew their attack, we must sail away from Durazzo as fast as our oars and sails can carry us.'

Sleep did not come easily to Robert de Hauteville; it never does when a problem is too thoroughly gnawed upon. Jaw tight, he tossed about for an age until he finally slipped into dreams just as troubled, so that a man who normally woke with the dawn was still in a deep slumber when the sun rose. Geoffrey Ridel woke him with a shake on his shoulder, holding a cup of warm and fresh goat's milk to ease his morning throat.

'My Lord Robert, the Venetians raised anchor at first light and are beginning to row north.'

'The whole fleet?'

'No, just the dromons, they have left their smaller galleys to mask the harbour and keep us out.'

Rudely awakened, Robert was slow to ask the obvious question, sinking his milk first. 'Why, Geoffrey? Is it some kind of Trojan trick?'

'I do not know.'

The *Guiscard* was off his cot and heading for the deck when he next spoke, Ridel on his heels. 'I expect you to tell me. You are Master of the Fleet, not I.'

Both men made their way to the poop, where the truth of what Ridel had imparted was clear. The dromons were stern-on and their gently stroking oars were taking them further away, while a line of smaller galleys had taken station across the harbour mouth, a scene that held them for several moments before Ridel responded, trying to ease things with a joke.

'I was not aware that anyone told you anything.'

The reply was a bark. 'Don't jest with me, Ridel, give me reasons as to why, when they have us in their palm, the Venetians should withdraw a weapon we cannot overcome. And why did they let us off so lightly yesterday, come to that?'

'They think us utterly beaten?'

'That is not enough.'

Seeing Ridel was seeking a proper answer, Robert had the good grace not to interrupt his thoughts; for a man who was a slave to impatience that was a struggle.

'It may be they cannot enter the harbour,' Ridel said eventually, with a slow and deliberate tone.

'Why not?'

'They draw too much water under the keel perhaps, but I think it is that they fear to be blocked in there.'

'Who can do that, for God knows we can't?'

'Size, My Lord!' the sailor responded, not hiding his ire at being pressed when he wanted to weigh his words. 'Even if there is depth enough, the access is narrow, so once inside they can only emerge singly . . .'

'Which means we could lock them up there?'

'Let us say it would seriously disadvantage them to the point where they might lose a vessel in driving us off, as they did yesterday in the fighting, which I would hazard shocked them. It was not in their mind to see one of their dromons sunk. By the same token, there is no security in anchoring in the outer roads for an extended time.' About to speak, Robert was stopped by a glare. 'Understand, My Lord Robert, that just as your lances are vital to you and your ambitions—'

'Those large fighting ships are vital to Venice!'

'They cannot afford to risk them on an open shore, for if a tempest arose of the kind we suffered on the way from Corfu, they could be driven onto land and wrecked. Such an event risks the major and most effective part of their fleet.'

'And lacking them Venice is, as a power, nothing?'

Ridel nodded and the silence that followed was a long one, one in which the dromons shrank in size as the distance between them and the two men on the Apulian galley increased to a point where they were mere pinpricks on the horizon.

'The question is, Geoffrey, will they return?'

'Why would they? I have told you already, they think us crushed.'

'Call everyone aboard at once.'

The subsequent battle was a very different affair and the loss of it for the galleys defending Durazzo was caused by the same failure to understand the Normans, and especially Robert de Hauteville, as had afflicted every power on the Italian mainland; they did not readily accept defeat and were only given to licking their wounds for a period long enough to either recover or allow fate, as it had now and had done many times in the past, to take a hand. They waited until those dromons were well over the horizon before launching an attack, one in which they were evenly matched in terms of the size, weight and number of vessels; what mattered was when they closed and engaged, where Norman fighting prowess did the rest.

As the sun began to set on the second day it was the Venetians who were obliged to cast an eye over their losses, many of them forced to do so from the shoreline onto which they had been driven by relentless Apulian pressure, there to watch their galleys break up in the surf. Out on the water they saw abundant wreckage where other vessels had been destroyed, or ships which had that morning been theirs, now in the hands of their enemies, with bodies floating around them of those who had been slain. For those that remained intact, all they could do was withdraw into the harbour and await what was bound to come, an assault coordinated with the advance on land, in which the possession of the harbour would be lost and the city they had sought to defend would be thus fully under siege.

The dromons did return, a fast six-oar and single-sail sandalion being sent after them, but which took time to find the fleet, but it was to see the Apulian army camped around the city and the mouth of the harbour blocked in a way that made it dangerous to attack, while staying offshore ran the risks of destruction by tempest outlined by Geoffrey Ridel. Venice had to have an intact fleet, not only to be a power, but also to maintain and increase that to which they were committed: their trade and wealth. Nothing Byzantium could offer would compensate for the loss of that.

Laying siege to a city was one thing, taking it another, and any lack of progress had as much to do with the man in command of the resistance as it had with the state of the walls and the cunning construction of the defences. Alexius had put his own brother-in-law in charge of holding Durazzo, but not because of a family connection; with George Palaeologus the reason was sheer ability. He was a brilliant soldier, an inspiring leader as well as a man not content to hide behind those stones, so the Apulian camp was on constant alert for the endless sorties in which he engaged. For all his own abilities, Robert de Hauteville was not slow to accord him the accolade of a worthy opponent. But there was another reason Durazzo held out and that had to do with the *Guiscard*'s tactics.

'Yet you do not press home the assaults,' said Sichelgaita, an observation that got a silent and furtive smile of agreement from her husband.

It was Bohemund, now openly acknowledged as his father's second in command, who replied. 'To do so would entail great loss.'

The sneer on the face of the Duchess of Apulia was undisguised; Bohemund's elevation was the reason she had crossed from Brindisi.

'I can accept you might fear to expose yourself, but not my husband.'

'Peace, woman,' Robert growled, the smile now gone to be replaced with a look of resignation. 'I have none braver than Bohemund.'

'And none so stuffed with ambition, husband,' she snapped, her face going red with anger, 'which you seem blind to.'

That made Bohemund smile. He was always happy when Sichelgaita was upset and she was not a woman to let her emotion remain hidden – it was not just the skin colour, added to that was her expression and right now she looked as if she had swallowed a hornet. If he was privy to this exchange, Bohemund had not been to the berating his father had received when she arrived. *Borsa*, who to Sichelgaita's mind should occupy the position Bohemund now held, had been left behind in Salerno, given no good would be done to his pride to be in the presence of his half-brother while forced to defer to him on anything of a military nature. Robert's reaction had been to admit that his possessions were in good hands, but he refused to dismiss his bastard in favour of his heir for the very simple reason he was going to have a battle and it was one he wanted to win.

'As of this moment, Alexius is marching towards us with a relief army and his brother-in-law has one task, which is to hold Durazzo until he can get here.'

'He would still come if you held the city.'

That riled Robert. 'Allow that when it comes to fighting I know what I am about. I need to bring Comnenus to battle and I need to defeat him, and for that I cannot risk losing men to take a city that will fall to me anyway. What if I can repeat Manzikert, destroy his army and take him captive? The road to Constantinople will be mine, so when you think of our son, which you seem to do above all other things, think of him clad in imperial purple.'

That got Bohemund another glare; he was sure, in her mind's eye, she could see him dressed in such garb, towering over an empire of millions of subjects and her family, and it was not a vision to bring much comfort. She turned back to her husband, her voice now silky with irony.

'I thought the intention was to restore your Michael Dukas to his throne?'

'That booby,' Robert spat, for he had long ago lost faith in his impostor monk; his appeal to the defenders of Durazzo had brought nothing but derision, none more than from his own renegades, Peter and Abelard, who had baited him from the safety of the city walls. 'I would fain put him on a privy as a throne.'

'Alexius is two days' march away, My Lord, and he has in his army a strong Norman contingent.'

That got Count Radulf, who was in the command tent with many of the other *battaile* commanders, a glare; these were the men he had been sent to Constantinople to recruit.

'The imperial bodyguard?' Robert asked.

'They are with their master, as always, made up of the men of Rus as well as an even larger number of Saxons who fled from England and are eager to avenge themselves on you, since they cannot do so on King William.'

'Remind me,' Robert intoned, in a voice larded with irony, 'to send my cousin my thanks for letting me fight his battles.'

The messenger, sent from the cavalry screen he had put out to keep him informed, had seen the eyes of the *Guiscard* narrow at the mention of the men of Rus. Just as he had his familia knights, Alexius would have his faithful bodyguard, called Varangians even if they had ever been made up of many elements. The name referred to a body of warriors originally sent to the sitting Emperor decades previously as tribute by the ruler of Kiev Rus. Of Viking stock like the Normans, the men of Rus were a formidable enemy to fight: tall and sturdy axemen who never left a field of battle unless victorious.

When faced with defeat they would die to a man rather than withdraw and in the process they always took with them enough men to outweigh their loss. It was a force that had been led, in William Iron Arm's day, by the late King of Norway, Harald Hardrada, killed at Stamford Bridge in the same year that William of Normandy had conquered England, and it would not be lessened in either bravery or ability by the addition of the bitter Saxons who had fought at Senlac Field for Harold Godwinson.

'It is more important, Father, that we find out what the Emperor intends. The composition of his army we cannot alter.'

Sichelgaita, who was also present, nodded vigorously at that, which obliged Bohemund to acknowledge that she was no military ignoramus, quite the reverse. She knew, as well as he did, where the greater danger lay – in the notion that Alexius might refuse battle and besiege the besiegers. To supply everything the Apulians needed from Italy, with winter approaching and the Adriatic, never predictable, even less so with seasonal storms, was to ask a great deal. Hitherto the *Guiscard*'s army had foraged the Illyrian interior at will to support the siege lines with food and timber on which to cook it. If Alexius cut them off from that source of sustenance, he might make life very difficult indeed.

'If you can see into his mind, Bohemund,' Robert said sharply, 'then do so, for I cannot!'

That pleased the Duchess, for if it was a mild rebuke, a way of telling Bohemund who was in command, it was enough of one for a woman who so rarely ever saw her husband check his bastard.

'We will set out the bait of battle, while leaving open a way through to Durazzo as temptation. Let us hope he accepts it.'

'If he gets in there, husband, you will never get him out.'

Robert emitted one of his great laughing whoops, as usual going from gloom to gaiety in a blink. 'Sichelgaita, if he gets to Durazzo, it will be over my dead body.'

The intake of breath was sharp, to indicate the tease had been taken at face value; she feared the loss of Robert for love of him, but also because, when he was gone, Sichelgaita would have to deal with Bohemund.

It was not bait that obliged Alexius Comnenus to do battle, more that he had an army made of so many elements: Normans, Saxons, Pechenegs, a body under the command of the King of Serbia and even renegade Turks. He harboured severe doubts that such a disparate force could be held together through a winter siege and up against such a puissant enemy. If he had never fought Normans, he was a vastly experienced general and not ignorant of their tactics, for he had in his ranks men who had fought many times with the *Guiscard*. Disinclined in any case to accept Robert's bait of an easy entry into Durazzo, the leader of his Normans advised that to present his flank on line of march to the Apulians was to invite disaster.

Robert had drawn his arm back from and to the north of Durazzo and had lined it up facing the city with his right flank on the seashore, leaving a second tempting possibility that Alexius could expect support from the garrison if he could pin and hold the Apulian army, thus increasing his offensive power at a critical juncture. Split into three parts, with the Duke of Apulia holding the centre with half of his knights and the Sicilian Saracens, Bohemund on his left, inland, with the rest of the Norman lances and the Greek conscripts.

Sichelgaita had demanded she be in command of the right wing, and if it was thought strange that a woman should hold high authority, no one in the Apulian army questioned it. That served too as a way of telling Bohemund that he faced more than her son should he prove to be too ambitious. Robert's wife, fully armed and wearing chain mail, as well as a helmet from which protruded her flowing blonde locks, was as much a soldier as any, and besides, the men of whom she had been given charge were of her race; she was a Lombard princess and they would follow her with spirit, where they might not a Norman.

CHAPTER EIGHTEEN

'That, *autokrator*, is the wing to attack. There you will face Lombards and they are not men to stand against your imperial bodyguard and nor is a woman in command, however large she is in body. If we can take and hold the shoreline, with George Palaeologus breaking out to help me attack the Norman left, then we may be able to force the *Guiscard* to run for his ships, for he will not risk destruction.'

'This Bohemund, what do you know of him?' the Emperor asked.

'He's a doughty fighter by repute, a paragon of chastity I am told, and a good head taller than any man with whom he serves. Should he appear, you will not mistake him.'

'As good as his father?'

'Better now his sire is an old man.'

Alexius was looking at the map on his table, not wishing to share eye contact with the subordinate proffering this advice and information, lest he show that he had doubts about anything emitted from between those lips. Geoffrey de Roussel was Norman but he was also the least reliable of men, a charming rogue, silver-tongued yet also a stout fighter who seemed able to wriggle out of difficulties that would see other men drawn and quartered.

He had left Italy under a cloud of an unknown nature and, having entered Byzantine service, he had betrayed that trust more than once, declining with the Normans he led to support an army of which he was part, then turning his coat to join the Turks they were fighting. That was an obligation likewise cast off; Roussel had cheated the Turks and set up as ruler in his own right. It had taken Alexius, at the time an imperial general, at the head of another Byzantine force, to catch him and drag him back to a Constantinople dungeon.

Yet here he was in the field again and to Alexius he was a living, breathing and walking reminder of the way he had to scrape the imperial barrel to field an army with some chance of winning, while trusting him now was a case of balancing where Roussel's interest lay; he had no love for the *Guiscard*, that was known, and he had only been released to lead a Norman contingent that would follow him where they might not another. Alexius had to presume that the man's future fortune, at least his immediate aim, favoured loyalty to the Byzantine cause. Putting all that aside, what he was saying made sense, for it was a staple of good generalship to attack an enemy where they were weak, so as to create confusion where they were more steady.

The question that had troubled him was Roussel's suggestion, the early commitment of his Varangians; such a fearsome unit would normally be held back until Alexis saw a point in the battle where to insert them was to break the enemy resistance, for they had the ability to smash through any defence, added to the power to destroy everything around it once it was rendered disorganised. Against that, he was facing Robert de Hauteville and that required him to be bold and enterprising, given he was such a canny opponent.

'And you would wish still to mask this Bohemund, Roussel?'

'I would wish to pit Norman lances against the same. There can be no catching me unawares when I know every horn call of command and you are right to see my task as to hold them, not defeat them, to keep them away from the main arena where the day will be decided – that is until I receive support from Durazzo, by which time I may be able to be a decisive element in the contest.'

An experienced warrior as well as a commander, Alexius knew that the first act of any battle brought on a fluidity that could not be planned for in advance and that applied to his enemies as much as it did to him. The last thing the Duke of Apulia would expect would be his Varangians to be committed to an initial attack, and being aware of their worth, such a tactic might throw him off balance. Added to that, once they had dealt with the Lombards they would hopefully face the flank of the Norman centre and be eager to attack it, their natural valour underpinned by a deep Saxon loathing of their opponents.

'Even this giant of yours, if he knows of them, will fear my axemen. When they have finished with the Lombards let us hope they will run to kill the same kind of men who made them exiles.'

Watching as the Byzantine army marched into position, Robert de Hauteville knew he was going to get the battle he desired, but just as Alexius Comnenus had knowledge of the hazards involved in battle, so did he. Thus offshore and behind him sat his fleet of broad-bottomed transport ships, while the waters in between were full of their boats. The requirement to tempt Alexius meant accepting a position with certain disadvantages but that did not mean throwing caution to the winds, so a line of retreat was essential. With a keen eye, added to what he had already gleaned from his cavalry screen, he knew that in numbers they were evenly matched. He also accepted that he was facing a general who could match him in skill, for he had questioned anyone who knew anything of Alexius's previous campaigns and what he had heard was impressive.

In essence the Apulian position was defensive, which left the initiative to his enemies; the *Guiscard* commanded an army just as heterogeneous as that he faced, albeit better trained. He wanted them to come on to him, working on the assumption that having been hurriedly raised they would lack the kind of cohesion necessary to launch and press home an assault, which would open up opportunities. A good general may be surprised and often is, but the art of command is not to allow that to induce alarm, so when Robert saw the Varangians moving along the rear of the Byzantine army, from their place in the centre around the imperial standard, to their left where they would face the Lombards, he reckoned it a feint to get him to move his lances to assist Sichelgaita and that would be followed by an attack through his weakened centre.

He was disabused of that when they filtered through the contingent that had occupied the left wing and began to come forward at a fast, disciplined jog that did nothing to rupture their tight formation. Opposite Robert the drums began to beat out an aggressive tattoo and the trumpets began to blow, with much movement of men, which only served to reinforce his view that the Varangians would stop rather than engage Sichelgaita and her Lombards and that he was about to be attacked by the forces now manoeuvring before his own position.

'Count Radulf,' he said quietly, as the Varangians broke into a run, screaming like banshees and, even at a distance, frightening with their horned helmets and huge gleaming axes. 'Go to Bohemund and tell him what is happening here, so that he may know his lances might be required. I will send word if they are and he must come with haste whatever he faces on his front.'

From the angle at which he was observing matters unfold Robert had a good view of the way the Varangians hit the line of Lombard *milities*, their great two-handed axes swinging to first smash the bucklers held up by the defenders, followed by great swipes aimed to sweep aside or decapitate their lances. Their weapons were then raised high to shatter into heads or shoulders left unprotected, this made more dangerous by the fact of the Lombards being generally small; they looked like dwarves when set against those they were fighting, for the Saxons had the height of Normans and the men of Rus had the dimensions, as well as the appearance, of their Viking forbears.

Much time had been spent training his Lombard subjects; likewise the Greeks and the foot soldiers had been taught to stand against Norman conroys seeking to break their line, while the mounted Lombards had been taught the skills of Norman warfare in order to support their fellows. Nothing could prepare a warrior of any race, however brave, for what they were required to do battle with now. Robert recalled that even his brothers had feared to meet these men in close battle and he was being shown why.

First the line of Lombard foot soldiers was in difficulty; then the cavalry rode into action, only to find that people they expected to break from a well-delivered attack with a rigid line of long lances not only stood their ground but advanced to engage. Then the horsemen too began to suffer and it was not the rider, it was his destrier, who could no more stand against a swinging axe than any human; they too went down with great gashes or legs broken or amputated, forcing them back. As he watched, the whole *battaile* both mounted and on foot began to buckle as too many fell. Looking to his front he saw that for all the activity of marching to and fro, it was no more than that; he had been deceived.

'Reynard, go to Bohemund and tell him I desire that he take his conroys, as well as his *milities*, across my rear to support my wife, but he is to seek to mask the manoeuvre. I will secure my flank with the Saracens, who will extend across his front, which will allow his rearguard to follow him.'

'My Lord, the Lombards have broken.'

The turn to look was slow and studied – never let those you lead see you are concerned – even if what he observed was the unpleasant truth of what he was being told, only worse than the bland word 'broken'. The Lombards were being routed, fleeing for the shoreline and the boats, a mass of men and mounts in total disorder, leaving a gap between themselves and the Varangians. In their midst he could see Sichelgaita on her huge horse, sword flashing above her head as she used the flat of it to slam into her people. She was shouting, that he could see, but what she was saying he could not hear.

'Cowards! Ingrates! Would you let a Norman see that you are no match for them, you curs?'

The following expletives were full of spittle, for she was in truth incandescent with rage; being married to a Norman did nothing to lessen her Lombard pride and she pushed her horse towards the line of surf, riding through the routed mass to get ahead of them. Once there she swung face on, and even at a distance her husband saw her as a magnificent sight, standing in her stirrups, sword raised like some Biblical prophet, haranguing her people and miraculously beginning to rally them. In a very short time she got them into some kind of order and then began to bring them back into the battle.

Having stopped once the Lombard defence broke, the Varangians were now reordering their ranks for an attack on the Apulian centre from what was a now open flank. To Robert's left the Normans, led by Geoffrey Roussel, were beating against the Sicilian Saracens he had sent to his left wing, men who had been personally trained by his brother Count Roger and well knew how to withstand the efforts of Roussel's conroys, who beat against their line in vain.

'My Lord,' shouted Count Radulf, now returned to join his liege lord, his arm outstretched towards the walls of Durazzo. 'The gates of the city have been opened.'

'Palaeologus will come out, Radulf, it has been anticipated.'

Robert was still watching his wife as Sichelgaita brought her Lombards in a series of compact lines back into the killing zone, which disrupted and surprised the Varangians, now obliged to wheel back to face them. Sword waving above her head once more, Sichelgaita led them into the fray, and if they suffered for their assault as much as they had previously, they were valiant in the way they pressed on, even as men and horses fell in increasing numbers. He was still watching this with admiration when Reynard rejoined him.

'My Lord, Bohemund is in position.'

'The horns,' Robert commanded. 'Blow the retreat.'

The high notes rose above the sound of fighting, the cries of men hurt or dying, of horses neighing in panic or pain, the bawled-out curses which aided the efforts of swinging arms and jabbing lances, even the clash of metal on metal and the noise of many things being broken: shields, swords and human bones. Afire with battle lust Sichelgaita still heard and obeyed those horns, quick to lead her Lombards out of contact. In doing so she passed through the line of Bohemund's lances, men sitting at ease on their destriers, eyes fixed forward on either side of their nose guards, as if the day was peaceful. As soon as the Lombards were through and reformed, Bohemund called forward the crossbowmen, who took up a position before him, each going down on one knee, then raising their weapons.

The first bolts hit the Varangians at a distance from which they could only retaliate by attacking, yet when they did so they were advancing into a maelstrom of short, deadly arrows. If they looked over their shoulder for support, which should have come from the renegade Turks and the Serbians through whom they had so recently filtered, it was not forthcoming. Wisdom dictated that in the face of an assault they could not counter, they withdraw; martial pride and the tradition of the imperial bodyguard made that anathema.

For the majority of the Imperial Guard, all England's exiles, Robert de Hauteville's ducal gonfalon was visible right by where he sat on his horse, unmistakable given his frame and colouring, a Norman rag to a Saxon bull, and the Varangians – regardless of their bloodline, for the act became collective – broke into a charging run to get at the Duke of Apulia and slay him in place of the bastard William of Normandy.

That was when Bohemund moved, bringing forward his conroys at a steady trot, lances lowered and couched, a new tactic he had developed in training outside Durazzo to unite the impact of both horse and man. They hit them obliquely and drove them back upon themselves. Axes notwithstanding, they went down in droves, which checked their forward momentum, which might have given them an advantage if the mounted men had still been engaged. They were not; Bohemund's conroys had broken off contact at the sound of a horn and retired. Not that there was any respite for the remaining axemen; – now they were, once more, at the mercy of the crossbows.

What followed was a savage, silent execution, for the Varangians could not come forward without facing Norman lances and nor could they stand still and survive the arrows which were fired at such high velocity and such short range that they smashed through their hardwood shields. Slowly, inexorably, their ranks thinned, yet still they stood tall and defiant, refusing to retreat. From being a magnificent sight they were reduced to a group of ragged individuals, few of whom were lacking a wound, which brought on the point for which Robert had been waiting. With a wave of his own sword, and the blowing of the horns, he ordered a general advance on the Byzantine line to counter an assault that had been launched to drive in what the Byzantine Emperor thought were two broken flanks, only to realise, once it was in motion, they were in fact holding.

Alexius had misjudged but was not undone; he had miscalculated but that was an experience he had undergone before. That the Serbians and Turks had not moved to support and help his Imperial Guard was enough to bring on an apoplexy, but that fury had to be kept from showing for the same reason as the *Guiscard* acted as though the opening attack had been no surprise: a general must at all times appear calm and in control. So, discounting them, for if they had yet to move it was not likely they would ever do so, he urged forward his magnificently caparisoned white horse and rode out ahead of his advancing army, to cheers that ran all along his line. He too used his sword to speed the advance and his men moved forward at a faster pace to meet the Apulian enemy, both hosts clashing in a cacophony of human sound.

The leaders were in the thick of the action and both were brave and skilled, the *Guiscard* confident that he would prevail, Alexius Comnenus the more desperate, for his rule and the Empire were at risk if he should fall. Sichelgaita led her Lombards against the Pechenegs while Bohemund was embroiled with the Byzantine soldiers Alexius had led before assuming the purple. Head and shoulders above his confrères, he was visible to Alexius, who knew that he would never get through to Robert de Hauteville with his familia knights forming an arc around his person, trying and failing to keep him out of the thickest part of the fight.

The Emperor was not wholly without personal supporters, and gathering them he pointed out the very easy to spot Bohemund and set his horse towards him, unaware that Count Radulf, whom he had so charmed in Constantinople that the Apulian envoy had forgotten his purpose, was eagerly manoeuvring to meet him and remove what he saw as a stain upon his standing with his liege lord. Eyes fixed on his quarry, Radulf took Alexius unawares, giving him a blow that nearly knocked his helmet from his head, leaving a gash that soon leaked blood into the imperial eyes.

Half blinded, Alexius turned to meet the Norman and their swords met with a force that sent a shudder up their arms. Seeking to manoeuvre a horse in an area that was fully occupied with fighting men was near impossible and Radulf, having been forced to turn his back on the Emperor, got a deep gash across his left shoulder, though the blow lost force by the fact he was moving away. Time and again they met, only to be forced apart by the need to expose anything vital and that was when Geoffrey Roussel rode into view yelling like some kind of satanic phantom.

'The Pechenegs have broken and are in flight! *Autokrator*, the day is lost!'

Alexius either did not hear or chose to ignore what he was being told, but in even acknowledging the arrival of Roussel his concentration was diminished enough to let Radulf through his defence. The Norman sword was thrusting to its full extent and would have ended its travel in the imperial gut if Roussel had not struck it down with such force he nearly unhorsed Radulf. The one-time envoy was now at risk and Alexius swung his own blade to take off his head at the shoulders. Roussel, hauling on his bridle, pulled his horse just enough to allow the blade to whistle past Radulf's nose and the Emperor was hauled out of the fight, even if it was against his wish.

In truth, blood boiling, Alexius had ignored his duties. All around him his host was breaking up and brave men were dying for want of a command that would save their lives and maybe aid them to fight another day. Wiping the stream of blood from his face, Alexius ordered the trumpets to sound the retreat, telling his soldiers to break contact and seek safety, which was only achieved by his own personal example. The Byzantine Emperor, in Greek the *autokrator*, rode time and again into danger to personally command his men to fall back and to lead them to a place where they could disengage, the order then to begin the tramp back to the East.

Robert de Hauteville kept up only enough pressure to make them run and soon it was his turn to sound the horns that would bring his host to a halt – all except those trying to capture George Palaeologus and stop him from getting back inside the walls of Durazzo. In the end that was only partially successful, Palaeologus being forced to retire with his brother-in-law, leaving the city without its best defender. Not that the *Guiscard* was disheartened; with no possibility of relief the fall of Durazzo was only a matter of time, while between him and the imperial capital there was nothing left to oppose him.

So tenacious was the defence, the siege of Durazzo went on for four more months, and while they were fighting to overcome those walls, Alexius, as well as trying to raise another army, was employing that well-worn Byzantine tactic of spreading trouble using a seemingly bottomless supply of treasury gold. Added to that the Apulian traitors got out of Durazzo and across the Adriatic without being intercepted and once there, with money and discontent to distribute, they had fomented yet another uprising, which broke out just after Durazzo fell and the Apulian army had begun to march up the Via Egnatia, with Sichelgaita insisting that *Borsa* needed help to contain it.

'Let us see how good my son and heir is,' Robert barked. 'He will have to leave off counting my treasure and learn to employ his lance.'

Sichelgaita was not a person to be shouted at without replying in kind. 'All you have to do is show yourself, husband, lop off a few heads, and the revolt will collapse.'

'Are you mad, woman? I have Alexius Comnenus by the throat.'

'What use an empire if you cannot hold your dukedoms?'

'You wanted *Borsa* to be tested, this is his chance to show his mettle.'

'You must send him the means.'

'I will, Sichelgaita, I'll send him my best general – you!'

In the end the *Guiscard* relented and sent Sichelgaita back with two hundred lances under Reynard of Eu; his jest to send Bohemund to command them was not a tease much appreciated. Having garrisoned

Durazzo he set off east for Kastoria, the site of another impressive castle and one that he was told had been left in the hands of Alexius's best remaining troops, with another sturdy and clever commander to hold it. In truth, these men surrendered the castle as soon as he demanded they do so, leading everyone in his army to assume the Empire was collapsing so rapidly it would fall into Apulian hands like a ripe apple in a high wind.

Robert de Hauteville had enjoyed good fortune throughout his life, but there had been setbacks too and, just as he thought he had the greatest of prizes in his grasp, it was snatched from him by both his duty and a greater threat. First, the revolt in Apulia was too dangerous to be left to Sichelgaita, but there was worse to follow. The call came from Pope Gregory demanding that he, as a papal vassal, come to the rescue of Rome, threatened by an imperial army led by Henry IV, bringing with him in his train the imperial antipope.

If it had just been Gregory, the *Guiscard* would have been tempted to leave him to his fate, but it was not. Jordan of Capua had deserted Rome and sworn allegiance to Henry, creating that combination of foes that always threatened the de Hauteville position. With nothing to fear from Capua the Eternal City might fall and Robert could not countenance Henry in possession of Rome, and nor could he have on the throne of the Supreme Pontiff a pope who would question the validity of his titles and might act to remove him.

Alexius Comnenus and Constantinople would have to wait. Handing over command to Bohemund, with an instruction to keep up the pressure without risking the host, Robert de Hauteville, with a heavy heart, headed back for Durazzo.

At one time, only a few months past, these men would have laughed at Radulf's jest; now they looked grim and in truth it had been delivered in a sour voice.

'On your honour, hold until I return, that is all I ask.'

No sooner had Bohemund left than Geoffrey Roussel appeared under a truce flag; Alexius had spies in the Apulian camp that told him of the departure of his opponent. Roussel, being Norman himself, knew that the men the de Hautevilles commanded had only one object and he came with the means to satisfy it, or at least the promise. Before their general embarked for Apulia his lieutenants had agreed the terms by which they would accept Byzantine bribes, had collected their sacks of gold coins and were occupied leading the men they commanded back out of Thessaly. Alexius followed them, and now thoroughly demoralised it took no great effort on the *autokrator*'s part to recapture Macedonia and push the remnants of the Apulian army back to the Adriatic shore.

Gold was not the only article Alexius had with which to raise the stakes against his enemies. To get those Venetian dromons to sail to Durazzo and take on the *Guiscard*'s fleet had cost the Empire dear – a waiving of their tax burden; now he needed to offer them more, and being a wise fellow he knew which key to turn. The Doge was offered trading concessions and even a section of the imperial capital through which they could import and export goods without duties. That, worth a fortune to tempt Croesus himself, was enough to send the Venetian fleet south again, carrying a well-armed complement of soldiers, to retake Corfu and besiege and recapture Durazzo, this while the Duke of Apulia was marching north towards the Leonine City with the largest host seen on Italian soil since the time of the legions of Ancient Rome.

Bohemund did not accompany him, depressed by the fact that everything they had gained in Romania had now been lost, furious that some of the men he had trusted to stay near Larissa were now back in Italy, part of his father's army marching to meet the new installed Emperor Henry, having been forgiven for accepting the Byzantine bribes. He retired to his sister's castle of Lecce, where Ademar, the good Marquis of Monteroni, had made his home and which was close to his own fief of Taranto, that subject to a flying visit. This was a part of the world in which he could curse his father and fate with impunity, for even a son who loves and respects his sire can often be baffled by his actions, or to be more honest, the lack of them.

There was confusion about the *Guiscard*'s intentions and no conversation with him brought enlightenment; if you speculated that he had put aside all thoughts of conquest in Romania for a war against Henry and the title of King of Germany, all you would receive in return was a sly look or maybe a winking eye. Suggest that the campaign against Byzantium be resuscitated and pressed home with even greater force and Robert would nod sagely without ever stating a preference; he had got to his present eminence by being guarded about his intentions and not even for Sichelgaita would he break that habit.

'How can you trust him?' his sister asked, as ever suffused with fury when any discussion came up regarding their parent. 'You are his firstborn son and even though, from what I have been told, you are his helpmeet in battle, he will not declare for you to inherit his titles.'

'He has not declared for anyone.'

'He does not need to, his fat sow of a wife will ensure that *Borsa* succeeds unless our father indicates that his preference is for you.'

The slight shuffling sound made Bohemund turn to look at the door to the chamber; in fact he was thankful to end a conversation too often aired by Emma. There stood Tancred, his nephew, just eight years of age but already showing signs of that height which was a de Hauteville family trait, though at present he was gangly rather than stocky. His uncle knew that to the boy he was an object of much admiration, not least because his mother was wont to sing in praise of her younger brother, regarding his purity, his prowess and his innate kindness as traits to aspire to.

'Do not tell me, Tancred, I am keeping you waiting?'

'I have no right to your time, Uncle, but I would be grateful for it.'

'How polite you are, Tancred; one day you will make a good envoy, a man to send to soothe ruffled adversaries.'

'I would rather be a soldier.'

'Well said, my son,' Emma responded. 'I am sure, too, my brother would rather be in the manège with you than here in my chamber.'

'Talking endlessly of outcomes the like of which we cannot know, sister.'

'I would make you ruler of all Italy if it were my choice.'

Looking at the boy, Bohemund was about to laugh, not in derision but merely because what Tancred had proposed was absurd, yet the solidly serious expression on the lad's face precluded mirth; he would not comprehend it.

'And what do you see for yourself?'

'First to serve as your squire and then to be in battle your equal.'

'Then,' Emma said, laughing, because as a mother it was allowed, 'you had best get Bohemund down to the manège and be busy, for to match him, my son, you have many leagues to go.'

The boy was keen to learn, fighting with a skill beyond his years, which reminded his uncle of his own youthful precocity. They were not alone in the manège; it was full of youngsters honing their skills, for their seniors were off fighting with their duke, Ademar included. As an adult Bohemund would have stood out anyway, but given his height he was an object of massive attention, so he found himself continually surrounded either in instruction or in relating the tales of Norman and Viking exploits going back into the mists of time.

But there were practical lessons too: in swordcraft, the throwing of axes so that the spinning edge ended up embedded in timber, using the new tactic of the lance couched under one arm and how to change grip and throw it so that it found its target. There were ponies of every size needed on which to teach the skills required to manoeuvre a horse with only the knee and a single rein, as well as how to care for a horse without forming a sentimental attachment to any beast.

'In the end,' he explained to his wide-eyed and seated-on-the-ground audience, 'your horses are no more than a means to get you into a fight and, if it goes badly, the instrument by which you can escape. Treat them well, but never let any animal command you, for they will if you are weak. And, if all else fails, what you are riding will feed you when there is no more meat to be had. Now, harness and saddle your mounts, and let us once more learn the calls of the horn.'

When Ademar returned to Lecce it was with a sorry tale: the *Guiscard*'s huge army had fought no great battle, even though the Emperor Henry, refused entry to the Leonine City, had come south with the intention of meeting the Duke of Apulia in combat; clearly he had no idea that he was outnumbered thirty to one. What saved him from annihilation were the people of Rome, who having denied him entry for months, suddenly decided to surrender to the imperial host, which sent it back north without ever making contact.

He did not stay long; when Henry found out the numbers he faced, a hurried departure became the only choice and he took his own pope with him. Foolishly, Rome, or rather a large proportion of its citizenry, whom Robert de Hauteville had come north to save, having so suddenly and stupidly plumped for the Emperor who had now deserted them, closed its gates against him. Three days went by, which tried the Duke's patience until he could stand it no more. A night attack on the Flaminian Gate got his troops inside the city, and foolishly those same citizens who had voted to allow in the Emperor tried to contest with the Normans, only to pay a price that saw the streets running with blood. They could not resist and within the day Robert had rescued Gregory from the Castle St Angelo and had him carried in triumph back to the Lateran Palace.

As he had in Illyria, Robert had increased his numbers by the inclusion of Sicilian Saracens and the sight of them alone inflamed the populace, for these men were the stuff of nightmares; had they not sailed up the Tiber hundreds of years previously and pillaged the city? Were they not the legions of Antichrist? If that became a problem, worse was the plunder, for the soldiers of Apulia, of whatever race, had never seen such wealth as existed in the one-time city of the Caesars. While Pope Gregory and the *Guiscard* were saying Mass in the Church of the Lateran the looting started, and one group, having seen their confrères loaded with their booty, soon set off to match them and the pillage began to get out of hand. If the Saracens were the first to enter sanctified churches and steal the gold and silver ornaments, the Normans, Greeks and Apulian Lombards soon followed until the whole city – churches, palaces, private houses, as well as the centres of the rich guilds of merchants and artisans – was being sacked.

The city rose in fury and this time it was not just the adherents of the Emperor who came out to fight – it was the entire population of Rome, and such were their numbers, in many instances they overwhelmed Robert de Hauteville's men, who retaliated by setting alight those places they had been so busy plundering. Worse, a mob surged around the Church of the Lateran screeching for the blood of the man who led them and a magnate who had chased two emperors now found himself trapped like a rat. It took *Borsa* at the head of a thousand lances to break through and rescue him.

'But,' Ademar said, concluding his tale, 'the city was by then alight in so many places the fires were out of control.'

'Could my father's men not have put them out?' Emma asked.

'Wife,' came the sad reply, 'they were the ones who started them. We went north to save Rome and ended up near to destroying it.'

'My father must regret it.'

'If he does, it is not apparent; as far as he is concerned, the city got what it deserved.'

The Apulian army had left with Pope Gregory almost as part of their baggage, the destruction visited upon Rome becoming the event to mark the abiding memory of his pontificate. The same people who had hailed him and borne him aloft to the Church of Saint Peter Viniculus eleven years before were now howling for his blood and would have torn him apart had not the Normans, Saracens and Apulians still controlled the smoking ruin of his once magnificent city. As he departed, his rival, the antipope Clement, was making preparations to come into the Leonine City, there to be hailed by a deliriously happy mob.

'Where is he now, the Pope?'

'In Salerno with your father.'

'Then that is where I must go.'

'Why, brother?'

'You know why, Emma. To my sire I must stay close, to him I must bring home that I, not *Borsa* or even amusing Guy, am the man to hold his possessions together when the fate that awaits us all comes to him. I need him to acknowledge me, which he will not do at a distance; and there is too another reason. Our father has an army, the biggest he has ever assembled, which he must employ if it is not to cause him trouble throughout his domains, and there is only one place that can be.'

'Illyria,' said Ademar; it was not a question.

'He has already resolved to return.' Ademar nodded emphatically. 'I failed there and that is a stain I would remove.'

'Take Tancred.'

Bohemund gave his sister a look full of doubt, one matched by the boy's father. 'He is too young.'

Bohemund's reply had Ademar vigorously nodding again.

'But he worships you, it will break his heart.'

'Then tell him to work hard in the manège for the next two years, for when he is ten summers in age I will happily have him as my squire.'

Bohemund was right about Robert and his army: to leave so many knights with time to think, plot and revel was dangerous and he had no other enemy to fight than Byzantium. The Western Emperor had his title and had been chastened and scared off; Jordan of Capua, having now regretted bowing the knee to Henry, had, through the ever-diplomatic Abbot Desiderius, made overtures of peace. Though it was suspected that the *Guiscard* was tempted to wipe him from the face of the earth, the greater prize still had a firm hold on his imagination; his magnificent host, in any case, would be wasted on his Norman neighbour.

By the time Bohemund reached Salerno the orders had gone out; the Apulian army would return to Illyria and this time it would not just be Robert and Bohemund – if it was not something to cheer his illegitimate offspring, Sichelgaita had got her way. Going with them would be *Borsa*, his younger brother Guy, as well as their mother. Pope Gregory himself blessed the proposed invasion in the newly completed cathedral Robert had caused to be built on taking the city, and it was on the steps of that church Robert made a pronouncement to his firstborn son.

'We have a proper papal blessing, Bohemund, for Gregory has termed what we are about as a crusade to bring back to the Mother Church those Greeks who have strayed from obedience to Rome. In such a cause, how can we fail? We are crossing the Adriatic and not coming back. I have promised our pontiff he will soon say Mass in Latin and in Santa Sophia.'

If Robert de Hauteville had a near-permanent advantage, it was that his enemies never seemed to learn. His first task was to retake Corfu for the same tactical reasons that had previously existed, though this time it was better defended, especially in the naval sense, with a combined Byzantine and Venetian squadron controlling the Corfu Channel. Also against him was a run of bad weather that trapped his own fleet in Butrinto for several weeks. When he finally emerged to do battle he was up against those same problems that had existed off Durazzo – ships too large to overcome – and so he was soundly beaten twice in two days and forced to retire with his ships battered and leaking, while the losses in men had been even worse.

So confident were the Venetians, who made up the bulk of the combined squadron, that victory had been achieved, they sent off a body of fast-sailing sandalions to carry the good news to Alexius and Venice. Even with ships near to being wrecks that was a foolish thing to do when fighting the *Guiscard*; those departing messenger vessels did not escape his attention and nor did he struggle to discern what intelligence they might be carrying. Many an ordinary commander would have struggled to raise the enthusiasm required for another assault, but that did not apply to Robert de Hauteville and once more that luck which had attended him all his fighting life resurfaced.

Not only had his enemies assumed him beaten, they had taken out of the fight those ships the Apulians most feared, the dromon-like galleys which had pummelled them previously. Having been at sea for a year, waiting for and then fighting the Apulians, they had bottoms covered in weeds and were in need of careening to deal with that, as well as the worms that, left to burrow, would rot their hulls. Prior to careening, in which the vessels must be carefully hauled over to expose one side of the hull then the other, it was necessary to remove the ballast – the weight that kept the vessel stable at sea.

Thus the dromons were sitting high out of the water when the men on board spotted the supposedly beaten Apulian fleet leaving Butrinto for another bout. Unable to raise anchor, for in any kind of sea they risked being capsized, they became easy targets for Robert's galleys – indeed two of them turned over in their Corfu harbour merely because the crews rushed to one side to fight the approaching enemy. This time the Apulians took full revenge for Durazzo: the destruction of the fleet that had ruled the Adriatic was total and without that the island was indefensible.

* * *

That conquest completed, Robert, much to the chagrin of Bohemund, gave *Borsa* an independent command. He was sent south with a sizeable force to take Cephalonia. Hardly had he departed when sickness struck his father's host. It was not unknown; men crowded in cramped encampments, naturally unsanitary, were ever at risk – how many besieged cities had been saved by such an affliction to their enemies? In this instance the outbreak was sudden and ravaging in its intensity, striking down men in substantial numbers and afflicting the normally strong and robust, not just the weak.

Bohemund fell victim quickly, for such a sickness did not spare leaders, and Robert, fearing for his firstborn and defying his wife, quickly determined to send him to Bari, home to those physicians, the most accomplished in his domains, who had cared for him years before. Before the transport ship departed his sire came aboard to see him, despite concerns that he was exposing himself to the malady. In the last two years of his seventh decade, the *Guiscard* shrugged off such concerns, sure that he was immune – had he not been visiting the overflowing sick tents for days without succumbing? – and in truth, sitting by the cot of his weak and feeble son he sounded as hearty as ever.

'You won't expire, Bohemund, I won't allow it.' Seeing his words had not been received as he hoped, Robert added, 'I wonder sometimes if I do not have a direct line to the Almighty, so lucky have I been, so take note of what I say.'

'Pope Gregory would not have approved,' Bohemund hissed, trying as well to smile, though what he produced was unconvincing.

'Poor Gregory, gone to meet our Maker, eh! I wonder what they made of him in paradise?'

Robert shook his head and sighed. 'He was his own worst enemy and never ceased to be crabbed Hildebrand even when he was granted the mitre. He could have had me as his protector all his life if he had but asked, yet he could never accept that all our conflicts were caused by his own intransigence, not mine. And what does he end up with? A miserable death in exile.'

'And no crusade.'

'A foolish notion, Bohemund, as you have heard me say many times before now. The Byzantines at their height could not hold back Islam and I think any army that carries the banner of Christ to fight them will end up as did Byzantium, dead in the sand.'

'For a good cause,' came out a wheeze, followed by an effort to produce a stronger tone. 'And if you had Constantinople?'

'That would alter matters, it is true, but I would march into Palestine for land, not the faith.'

'Father?'

'Don't ask me, Bohemund, for I can see the pleading in your eyes. I will tell you now, that I put your mother aside for a necessity. I could not hold my territories without a Lombard wife, but I will also tell you that Sichelgaita has made me as content as a husband can be, which, when you wed, you will find out is not without shortcomings, for women . . . well, they are what they are . . .'

The voice trailed off and Robert sat for a moment in silence.

'I cannot give you what you want, Bohemund, but when I am gone I cannot stop you from trying to take what you believe to be rightfully yours.'

'Nothing will stop me, bar death.'

'There are many things that might, God only being one of them.' Robert hauled himself up, his voice once more booming. 'But recover, for with what is coming I need you fighting by my side. Let providence take care of the rest!'

CHAPTER TWENTY

'Your father felt the sickness come upon him as he sailed to join *Borsa*, and so quickly did it diminish him that Sichelgaita ordered his ship into a Cephalonian bay in the hope that on dry land he would recover. He died without speaking a word, even to Sichelgaita.'

Still weak himself, but feeling better, Bohemund saw tears in Reynard's eyes and esteemed him for it; having been a faithful knight in his father's service for so many years he would feel the loss keenly. Yet he found he could not weep himself, for if he had a high regard for his sire, the kind of love that has the grieving tearing at their garments was now, he realised, not part of it.

'The body?'

'Is on the way to Venosa, to be buried where Duke Robert desired to be interred.'

'With his brothers?' Reynard nodded, as Bohemund added with a sad smile, 'No doubt he wants to dispute with them in death, as he did in life. Heaven will be a troubled place if they meet there.'

Love him he might, but Reynard obviously thought the chances of Robert de Hauteville or any of the tribe ascending paradise was unlikely, notwithstanding the abbeys they had endowed and the churches they had built. Yet of more vital import was the fact that the host of which they had both been part had quickly lost cohesion and like Reynard they were streaming home; it had been Robert's iron will that had got them across the Adriatic and without that the purpose faded. There was another reason to abandon the expedition: with Bohemund in Bari, possibly fully recovered and able to raise the standard of revolt, keeping a powerful army on the Greek Islands was unwise.

'Were you sent to me, Reynard?'

'No. I came because it is not fitting that you should hear of such a thing as if it were marketplace gossip.'

'Tell me, what will happen now?'

'Sichelgaita will do what she did with the army on Corfu and call upon every one of your father's vassals to renew their oath to *Borsa*.'

'And will they?'

'Most of them, yes, for he has the means to reward them.'

'You mean his mother does.'

'It amounts to the same thing, Bohemund, and there is not one of them who will not be pondering of their own personal advantage in the new dispensation. Think! It will not just be in the grant of land or titles. Duke Robert left a bulging treasury as well, which will be used to ensure that *Borsa* is supported.'

'Whereas I have nothing.'

'You have your name and there are men for whom that will carry weight.'

'I am forced to ask if you are one of them?'

'Why do you think I came to you?'

'And do you have advice for me, Reynard?'

'You need lances and I can think of only one place that will provide them.'

'You recall what I said about Capua the first time we rode together?'

'When you are a beggar, Bohemund, it ill begets you to examine the alms you are given to see if the coins have been clipped.'

'I will go to Venosa first, to see my father interred. Besides, I want to look *Borsa* in the eye.'

The de Hauteville family church of Santissima Trinità had been started by Drogo de Hauteville and not finished by Humphrey or Robert, so it was far from a grand edifice, nothing like the latter's great cathedral of Salerno, but it had a resonance for the family name and that was enough. It was not the *Guiscard*'s body they interred in the vault; a storm at sea had swept his coffin off the deck and the water had so corrupted the corpse when it was recovered that the heart and entrails had been removed and brought in a casket to Venosa.

As the priests intoned the words of burial and requiem, not every head could remain bowed, for there was an undercurrent: what would happen now that the man who had created the triple dukedom and held it together was gone, and with him the overwhelming personality that many reckoned irreplaceable? Sichelgaita eyed Bohemund as a cat examines a bird just out of reach of its leap; *Borsa* would look away when his half-brother's eye caught his but there was no missing the sentiment of trepidation mixed with loathing.

Guy, for all his supposed careless nature, was the most honest in the directness of his stare and what it meant; left to him, Bohemund could expect nothing but a pauper's grave – there would be no de Hauteville vault for him – and it would not be long in coming. Half-sister Emma returned that feeling to all three of them in full measure, which lent an icy mood to the whole occasion.

Robert's senior vassals, who had sailed with him to Corfu, were there, including those he had seen as his most reliable lieutenants, and it was to these that his bastard son gave most of his attention; his half-siblings and their mother were known quantities but these men mattered, for if they pledged loyalty to *Borsa* it was not from love and even less for the de Hauteville name. When questioned, Reynard had related that the way *Borsa* had been hailed by the army had lacked conviction, especially amongst the Normans, many of whom had at some time in the past either participated or led revolts against one of the brothers.

Now their suzerain, if he bore a name to which they bowed the knee reluctantly, also had, to them, a taint and that was his despised Lombard blood, added to which he was not the leader either in war or personality his sire had been. These were men who needed a strong hand to control them and even with that they took every chance presented to them to slip out of its grip. It was a sound guess that many would stay loyal only as long as it suited them and that *Borsa* would find that, as time went by and resentments festered, it was not only his half-brother who would cause him difficulties.

Could he hold the triple dukedom together? The missing factor was Roger de Hauteville, now called the Great Count of Sicily, who might not even yet know, as his brother was buried, that he was dead.

Messages had been sent to Sicily to summon him from the siege of Syracuse – if not to Venosa, to the capital Salerno, where *Borsa* would be installed as his father's rightful successor.

Those same vassals, who had been present at Santissima Trinità, this time with Count Roger, attended that ceremony, held in the great hall of the Castello di Arechi. He had brought with him all those who could be spared from Sicily, men who held their fief directly from the Duke of Apulia, but Bohemund stayed away, for here every vassal would be required to swear allegiance and that was not something he was prepared to contemplate. His powerful uncle noted the absence – it could hardly be missed by a man who knew what it portended and was not slow to touch on the subject when he met with *Borsa* and Sichelgaita in private.

'Did your sire ever tell you, *Borsa*, about our adventures in Calabria?' Roger enquired, once the polite formalities had been observed. 'If I had not come to his rescue, he might have been food for the dogs.'

'I told him,' Sichelgaita replied, though it did not, judging by her expression, provoke a happy memory. Her brother-in-law knew she had been amused at the time; it was what the recollection signified that troubled her.

As always the *Guiscard* had made a promise, then regretted it as too generous, which meant Robert and his younger brother had fallen out. Roger might have ended up in a dungeon but for a stroke of luck; good soldier as he was, he could not field the number of lances needed to beat Robert. Foolishly, while pursuing him, Robert had, on his own and unarmed, entered a Calabrian town called Gerace, only to be captured and confined by the inhabitants. Roger had rescued him – in truth the good folk of Gerace had not known what to do with such a powerful prisoner – which if nothing else brought peace between them. But not harmony; the next month had been spent arguing about who was owed what revenues.

'You see, even I rebelled, nephew,' he said, when the outline of the tale had been rehashed.

'That is in the past, Uncle, but I am sure you will be faithful to his memory now.'

'I doubt Bohemund will be.'

'We have the means to deal with him,' Sichelgaita snapped. 'Right now my husband's subjects are lining up to pledge allegiance.'

'So you are sure that every vassal who swears allegiance to *Borsa* will hold to his word? If that is so he will surely outshine my late brother.'

This was the crux and all three knew it; there were men who would make a pledge to him this day, then ride off immediately to join his half-brother, while others would go back to their demesnes only to plot rebellion. The new Duke looked at his mother, as if seeking advice, but Roger knew they must have discussed the matter without him being present.

'Naturally, Uncle, we would look to you for support if they did not.'

'And you shall have it, nephew,' Roger replied.

That was delivered after a long and pointed pause, with a smile that lacked warmth, which left both nephew and his sister-in-law in no doubt that there would be a price for his aid. That being true, in turn it led to a great deal of fencing that lasted for hours – not the swiping and sweeping of broadsword blades, it was more delicate than that, but just as deadly in intent – until Roger felt he had extracted his price. As well as the shared revenues of Calabria, Roger got transferred to him some of the fiefs his brother had held as his own in the north of Sicily, though not Messina and Palermo.

It was not greed that prompted this but the feeling that since such domains were only kept secure by his efforts, the money they earned should be paid into his coffers, not those of Apulia. *Borsa* sought to talk down the demands and so did Sichelgaita, but they were in no position to argue; the new Duke was negotiating with the one person who could by a gesture, as he had at the gathering in Bari, unseat him.

'Where is Bohemund now?' Roger asked, once the negotiations were over.

'In Capua,' Sichelgaita replied, 'raising lances.'

Prince Jordan had always felt keenly the fact that he was a weaker magnate than Duke Robert, just as he harboured resentments that went back beyond his father's time to that of Rainulf Drengot, who had sworn till his dying day that the de Hauteville brothers had betrayed a sacred vow made to him as their suzerain. The last time they had made peace he had not been cheering; Jordan had been almost obliged by Abbot Desiderius to crawl in order to divert the *Guiscard* to Illyria. Now, with his nemesis gone and a fight about to begin for the title, he was presented with a chance to increase the power of Capua at no risk to his own domains. Apulia, in a family war for who held the right to inherit, was never going to have the means to invade his territories.

But the outcome was uncertain and while he was pleased to supply Bohemund with the men he needed to fight his cause, the last thing he wanted on his borders was a Duke of Apulia as powerful as the *Guiscard* and gifted with a matching military prowess. The dream was of a neighbour so diminished, a weakened *Borsa* or a Bohemund so needy, that he would bow the knee to Capua, leaving Jordan as the senior Norman leader in the south of Italy, acknowledged as such by the Pope, confirmed in his titles by the Holy Roman Emperor and seen as the more powerful prince by the subjects of the triple dukedom.

A kingly crown was not too much to wish for, though much time and a great deal of political manoeuvring would be needed to gain such a prize. All very tempting, but he knew that care had to be exercised and certain pieces would have to be removed from the board; the last thing Jordan desired was that he should so threaten Apulia that Count Roger, who could unite all three dukedoms as one, would see it as necessary to intervene with such force as to provoke a war to the death. But he, like Robert, could not live for ever and his son eldest was unfit to govern, being an imbecile, while Simon was an infant.

'My lances must be free to plunder, Bohemund, you know that.'

'I will direct them to those places where they may do so freely, for I have let it be known that those who decline to come and fight with me, even those who stand aside, will be as my enemies. It is therefore fitting, Jordan, that they should suffer.'

Standing outside a Capuan manège, Jordan and Bohemund were watching the knights he would lead go through their exercises. There had been some scoffing at using a lance couched instead of loose until he had shown them how easy it was to unseat an opponent by the greater power it produced, so now they were competent at it. This would be a war; not one of massed armies but one of lance against lance, which also meant on many occasions it would be Norman against Norman. If they had tended to avoid doing each other harm in the past, such a restriction could no longer hold; there was for

Bohemund too much at stake, for he had few illusions about what would happen to him if he fell into the hands of *Borsa* and his family – the least he could expect would be to have his eyes put out.

It being common knowledge throughout Apulia and Calabria he intended to contest for the title, that brought to his side a number of his father's old familia knights, men who were the companions-in-arms of Reynard of Eu and who were accustomed to serve a warrior, not a woman or someone they regarded as not much above a counter of beans. Then there were the endemic malcontents, men who had caused his father so much grief, lances that joined any rebellion which presented them with the opportunity to advance themselves, or to plunder the property of the more respectable.

Others of a more personal value travelled to Capua to offer their swords, such as Ademar of Monteroni, who did so out of family loyalty and brought with him not only two conroys of his own followers but his son Tancred, now approaching twelve summers old and beginning to look more the man than the boy. Still to fill out, he had nevertheless the air of a true de Hauteville about him, the red-gold hair, the height and that look in the eye that hinted at a nature both serious and mischievous; though not as tall or as florid as the *Guiscard,* he did remind his uncle of his late father and Tancred was quick to request the promise previously made be fulfilled.

'You know your duties?' Bohemund asked.

'I do, My Lord. To keep your horses groomed, your harness polished and your weapons sharp.'

'I need food in my belly, boy, and the rust kept from my mail.'

'Your stockings darned and the moth holes in your clothing repaired.'

'You can sew, Tancred?'

'No, My Lord, but I know how to find a woman who can.'

Bohemund grinned. 'Make sure that is all you ask of a woman, the use of her needle.'

Those who witnessed that remark made little attempt to disguise their curiosity; it was well known that their leader was more than abstemious in that area and for many, less saintly in their own lives, it was a cause for speculation. Well past the age at which he should be married, Bohemund showed no inclination to do so and did not deign to explain why that should be so. Yet he gave no inclination of any other proclivities that might diminish him in the eyes of his men, so that concern was put to one side, because he was above all what he needed to be, a superb warrior.

'You will already have formulated a plan?' asked Ademar, when they had a chance to talk.

'I have, and with you I will share it, but I do not want it talked of openly, especially with Jordan and his Capuans. I have been open with Reynard but no one else who has come from Apulia.'

'The distrust is so acute?'

'As of this moment, Ademar, I do not know who to have faith in and who to suspect. Jordan has been playing a double game for so long he may be unable to stop himself, and any of his knights I confide in will pass on to him anything I say.'

'His support will not be wholehearted.'

'True, but only time and my success will winkle out his true intentions. As for the Apulians who have come to me, well, even you must suspect that some of them have been despatched here by Sichelgaita.'

'So they all must be deceived regarding your intentions.'

'Yes.'

'Then don't tell me anything lest I talk in my sleep.'

Bohemund gave Ademar a reassuring pat on the shoulder. 'The only person sharing your chamber is your son and if I cannot trust Tancred you had best take him back to Lecce. The obvious point of entry into my late father's domains is to retrace the route by which we came here on my first raid, yes?'

Ademar nodded, though his eyes carried the truth. 'But you do not intend to go that way?'

'I intend that everyone should think we are going that way until we have left Capua and are far enough away to implement what I truly intend to do. I want *Borsa*'s lances to be deceived too, so they are in no position to impede our progress.'

'Where is Reynard?'

That induced a wide smile, for it was clear that Ademar, probably no mean conspirator himself, had discerned that the absence of a man Bohemund must have come to rely on was significant.

'The route of march I intend to pursue is a long one.'

'And he has gone ahead to secure the necessary supplies.'

'He has gone to identify where those supplies may be taken and used. Unlike *Borsa* I do not have the means to pay for them.'

Ademar frowned. 'Plundering your way through *Borsa*'s domains will not endear you to his subjects.'

The response was brusque and demonstrated to Ademar a side of his brother-in-law he had not yet seen. 'I will make it up to them when they are my subjects, and if they still choose to whine I will take from them all they have down to the hay.'

'I have one request to make, Bohemund – a kindness if you like.'

'You of all have the right to ask for it.'

'My son is headstrong and he will want very quickly, possibly at this very moment, to seek to be more than just your squire.'

'He will want to get into the fighting?'

'He will put himself at risk and I want you to forbid it.'

'You are his father, you can forbid it.'

Ademar laughed out loud. 'What son listens to his father in these times, Bohemund?'

The leave-taking at Montesárchio, to where the conroys had moved prior to the incursion into Apulia, was attended by much ceremony: the castle itself bedecked with wind-whipped banners, the presence of Jordan and his court dressed in all their finery, the Archbishop of Capua along to say the required Mass and give the expedition his blessing, each lance, near three hundred in number, first confessing before lining up to receive the wafer that represented the body of Christ, and finally an array of trumpeters to attend the actual departure, this after their prince had made a rousing speech.

It was as if Bohemund was the rightful Duke of Apulia going off on campaign, yet not holding that title required a gesture to acknowledge his benefactor. Prince Jordan would have, no doubt, liked Bohemund to kneel before him and seek his blessing too, as a vassal does to his suzerain and as he had done to the high cleric. It was evident, his disappointment, when all he received from the mounted leader was an across the chest salute, that followed by a wave of the arm as he led his knights out of the small town, heading east.

The squires had taken the packhorses, destriers and spare mounts out beforehand and were waiting for their warriors. Bohemund had been strict on other things: there were to be no women and none of the usual artisans. His column was designed to move at speed and

Reynard had mapped out the route to be taken, not only for where they could plunder meat for their bellies and oats for their mounts, but also the places where they would find both water and pasture and, hopefully, no serious enemies.

The route initially took them to Grottaminarda, where a pre-warned lord of the castle entertained and fed them, consuming copious amounts of wine while talking eagerly of how it would be pleasant to follow in their wake with his own band of knights to plunder the borderlands through which they would pass. Such sentiments were heartily endorsed by an ever-abstemious Bohemund, ready to agree that it was possible that his line of march must tempt him to look into Melfi, to see if that great fortress might declare for his banner without a fight.

'Will it, My Lord?' asked an eager Tancred, when he raised a subject he had overheard at a table to which he had been admitted by his family name and rank, not his present position. Most squires ate outside the kitchens.

'Outside Salerno, Tancred, it is *Borsa*'s most important possession. It will therefore be manned by someone he trusts absolutely.'

'William Iron Arm took it by a trick, did he not?'

'He took it because a Lombard betrayed his Byzantine master. I do not have either of those.'

'It would be a fine feat all the same.'

'It would be a distraction, boy – now go to your bed and allow that I can go to mine.'

The Lord of Grottaminarda was as wedded to ritual as his prince, so it took another Mass and another blessing before they could ride on, trailed by everyone in the town who was so idle they had nothing to keep them inside the walls – the sons of knights and their squires mainly. Bohemund had to wait until they tired and turned for home, indeed well beyond that so he was out of their sight before he could, at a necessary halt to rest the horses, consult a man even more frustrated than he. Reynard produced his jottings, made on the first of another map from the days of the Roman Empire, and laid out the route they must follow as well as the demesne they must first raid.

'It is still on Capuan soil,' he said, 'and so owes fealty to Jordan.'

'Then,' Bohemund replied, with a grin, 'he will be happy to surrender the supplies we need just to please his prince.'

Waiting till his lances had mounted and knowing they would follow his lead, Bohemund rode due south. Behind him men were looking at the sun, wondering why they were heading right into its high and glaring orb rather than having it warm their right shoulder. No one asked until finally Tancred could contain himself no longer.

'Where are we going, My Lord?'

'To my castle of Taranto, Tancred.'

CHAPTER TWENTY-ONE

There was no possibility of Bohemund cutting a swathe through *Borsa*'s domain without that being drawn to the attention of Count Radulf, the man who had been sent to the borderlands to either prevent him crossing or so inflict on him a defeat that the only option for the rebellious claimant was to retire. Given the nature of that border it could only be looked after by small pockets of knights dotted at intervals who would observe in their own locality, and once they had hard information regarding the route of the incursion, report back to the hill town of Candela around which Count Radulf had his main encampment.

When the information came to him that the invaders were heading due south he had no choice, having sent word back to Salerno and Melfi, but to set off in pursuit, seeking to cut an angle and so intercept Bohemund, which he would succeed in doing if his quarry was moving slowly. Radulf soon discovered his foe was not dawdling, found that he was well behind and that he would struggle to close the gap even if he pushed his men and mounts beyond what was judicious.

Farmhouses and small outlying castles that had already been plundered once found Radulf and another large force of knights on their land demanding that they and their mounts be fed – a hard request to fulfil, for where the owners and lords of the manor had been unwilling, Bohemund had ordered everything they possessed to be either taken or destroyed; those who opened their granaries and wine cellars were spared once, but not twice, for if they had been seen to indulge one party, they were at the mercy of the other.

'He should have torched everything,' Radulf growled, as he watched burn the barns and outbuildings of a villein who had clearly been welcoming to those he was in pursuit of; the main house was already a cinder, its floors dug up in the search for hidden possessions and the family that had provided sustenance hanging from the trees that had been used to shade it from the sun. 'As an invader Bohemund de Hauteville is too soft.'

'If he had, My Lord,' asked one of his knights, 'what would we eat?'

Radulf grinned but it was a look to chill, not cheer. 'We could roast their children, could we not, instead of stringing them up?'

His man crossed himself.

Ten leagues a day was considered the maximum at which armed knights could move and that often had to be tempered by the terrain; to exceed such a distance was to risk the horses breaking down. Bohemund was glad he had insisted on no tail of camp followers to slow him down, especially as he was much of the time moving through the high, rolling country that rose from the eastern coastal

307

plain to create valleys and hills that took time to traverse, and which only eased when they reached the River Gravina and were able to follow it for a long way as it flowed towards the Ionian Sea.

Yet that left men without women, which was dangerous, and he had already hanged from the rafters of a barn two of his Apulians for the rape of the daughters of a farmer who had declined to aid him; burning his field crops, cutting down his vines and olive trees, as well as smashing what could not be carried was acceptable; the carnal abuse was not. That such an act led to their confrères being disgruntled – it was a blessing they were not Capuans he had strung up – was something he just had to accept, working on the hope that the prospect of months of plunder would outweigh any loyalty or feelings they had to their dead companions.

It was not morality that made him act in that way; every army on the march committed such offences and when a town or city was sacked, rape and pillage was part of the reward taken by the successful besiegers. But such events were a distraction and a continual temptation that could slow him down; the last thing he wanted was men dropping back to sate their carnal needs when he was intent on making, every day, the locations on Reynard's Roman maps that had been designated as stopping points.

It was at a hamlet surrounded by fertile farms, ten leagues short of the well-defended town of Matera, that Tancred went missing in an area where the locals had shown no desire to do anything but feed and water these mail-clad knights for fear of what they might do if they were denied. But Bohemund, noting his absence at first light, was concerned, as was Ademar, for the boy had been faithful in pursuance of his duties; if anything he had dogged the footsteps of his uncle as if seeking to have some of Bohemund's martial ability rub off on him.

He would not be missing unless something untoward had happened to him.

'Can we delay for one squire?' Reynard loudly demanded as the order to break camp was delayed.

Indicating he should keep his voice down Bohemund answered him softly. 'He is not just any boy, Reynard, he is my sister's son.'

'Who must take the same risks as his fellows and we have to make our next stop while there is still daylight.'

'I cannot leave without knowing what has become of him.'

'And if those pursuing us catch up?'

'We do not know we are being chased,' Bohemund replied, not looking at a man he considered a true friend as well as a source of wise counsel.

'If we are not,' Reynard spat, 'I will eat my gauntlet.'

'Bohemund,' said Ademar, approaching the pair. 'Move on as you must, but I will delay and see if I can find him.'

'No, many men searching will make light work of such a task and I owe you that for so readily coming to my aid.'

'We are far ahead of anything on our trail, Reynard, and can spare a glass of sand to find him.' Then Bohemund dropped his voice to a whisper so Ademar could not hear. 'And let us hope it is not with a knife in his back.'

His father's one-time familia knight had to acknowledge the possibility; not everyone would be happy to give up their oats or their grain and an easy way to make that known would be to attack the people least able to defend themselves, vulnerable when, without properly dug latrines, they would wander off to relieve themselves.

Reynard's expression softened, for he liked Tancred – most men did. 'He would be hard to kill, your nephew. I would pit him even at his age against half the lances we lead.'

'Then let us get searching, for the sooner we know the truth the sooner we can depart.'

The man who found Tancred called to Bohemund and waved, his face grim, that look shared by the half-conroy of his companions with whom he had been searching the western woods, which induced a grip that the leader felt on his heart. The boy was the apple of his sister's eye, and even if she had his younger brother William, the loss would be keenly felt. He joined the man who had gestured, following him and his confrères into the woods, aware that in his footsteps were coming others, Ademar included.

The man, still dour-faced, led him to a woodcutter's lean-to in which were stacked high piles of logs from several seasons, gaps in between them, a perfect place to conceal a body. Standing back, he indicated Bohemund should enter, but their leader knew that to do so on his own exceeded his rights, so he waited for Tancred's father to join him, then made his way between two stacks, one green and recently cut, the other dry and well seasoned.

When he and Ademar stopped, they could not, after a pause, avoid looking at each other, for on the ground lay Tancred, his arm round a young girl, both of them sound asleep. She was on her back, her skirts so raised as to leave no doubt about what they had been doing, and beside her, face down, lay their son and nephew, while beside them, upended and obviously empty, was a wine gourd. Behind them gales of laughter erupted as the men who had guyed a worried Bohemund let their pleasure be known. The noise made Tancred raise a groggy head to look at the two adults framed by daylight.

'Shall I kick your squire, Bohemund,' said Ademar, 'or does that right fall to you?'

'One each I should think.'

The yells of Tancred as the boots went home added greatly to the mirth and that rose even higher as, clutching his unfastened breeches, he staggered out into the open.

The great twin bays of Taranto, really a deep outer cove masking, with a wide island, an inland saltwater lake, were visible from a long distance, for they lay on a flat coastal plain, while the approach from both north and east was from a high elevation. The city was Greek and had been since the Ancient Dorians founded it, part of that one-time Magna Graecia which comprised so much of the Norman possessions in Italy. Ruled by the Lombards, it had not been colonised much and for all it was an attractive port it had suffered since Roman times, given they had laid the Via Appia to Brindisi and directed what trade they had with the East through that port.

Rendered something of a backwater, it had been given to Bohemund by the *Guiscard* because he felt required to present his bastard son with some title, yet he was cautious of appearances to a wider world as well as his wife's sensitivities. By allotting to him such a lordship he gave him recognition without much in the way of power; the true strength of Apulia lay further north in Bari and Melfi. Yet the surrounding plain was fertile and with good husbandry could produce two crops a year, the sea was abundant with fish to salt, while the pans on the shore produced an endless supply of that commodity, so the revenues were far from meagre. It had too, as did all Greek ports, a castle that protected the basin, albeit one in great need of repair.

Being given overlordship of such a place did not oblige the person holding it to reside in his possessions, so Bohemund had made only two fleeting visits since it had been granted: the first was to appoint a steward to look after and if possible grow his revenues, and to ensure that the stud was not only working but that breeding of foals should be increased; the second, when he had been close by in his sister's castle, to see how the improvements he had ordered made to the castle were progressing. This stood on the southern tip of the island and blocked access to the inland lake by the only route that had a depth of water to allow entry and egress by ships of any size.

'What Taranto has, you young degenerate, is people and supplies.'

'Not lances,' Tancred replied, smarting from the pointed allusion to his nocturnal misdemeanour, which he had been ribbed about for days.

'We have lances, what we need are *milities*. Those we pass working the fields will soon be bearing arms.'

'My father says they are often of little use.'

'Well led they can set up a battle so the mounted men can decide it. Even of little merit, they cannot be ignored.'

Word having gone ahead that a large party of knights was approaching, news was, as always, sent to the city by the fastest runners the outlying settlements could despatch. This set off a general alarm in Taranto and led to the hurried closing of the gates. They stayed that way when Bohemund sent his own herald to announce his arrival, for these were folk well accustomed to trickery from the kind of men approaching – even in mail they could be Saracens – so it nearly fell to their liege lord himself to command them to be opened. Yet such was his remarkable appearance that as soon as the citizens saw it was truly him word was sent to unbolt them so he could enter.

Count Radulf, who overlooked Taranto three days later, was obliged to accept that he had failed; there was no point in pursuing his quarry to the walls, he lacked the means to even contemplate a raid, never mind a siege, and besides, having pushed his force hard in an attempt to catch up, his horses were in danger of being blown, while his lances were worn out. The thought of sending a messenger to challenge Bohemund he dismissed, for the giant would likely suggest single combat; having seen him in action on the field of battle that was not a contest in which he had any desire to engage.

Despite what he had said to Tancred, Bohemund reposed little faith in those he caused to be conscripted, for he had too little time to train them. What he needed most were fresh cavalry mounts and packhorses – the destriers had not been ridden or carried any load since Capua – as well as a body of *milites* who looked threatening without actually being of much use in battle. His strategy was speed, for there was no chance of his defeating *Borsa* if his half-brother brought the whole might of his dominions to bear.

So, once he had raided the castle armoury and denuded his domain of suitable horses – the locals could have those mounts he had brought from Capua – he set off for Gallipoli, the southernmost port on the Ionian Sea, which had little heart for a fight and fell to him as soon as he demanded that the citizenry do so; they did not even flee to the fortified island. Next he crossed the Salento Peninsula to Otranto, which, being the major port on the Adriatic heel of Italy, was of strategic value, it being the only haven south of Brindisi into which *Borsa* could land an army.

It was there Bohemund found out how feeble was his relation: *Borsa* had done nothing to reinforce it, or to put in command of its

313

large fortress a man he could both trust and who would never, for the sake of his pride, surrender – a mistake his father would never have made. Certainly they resisted, but Otranto was taken by a *coup de main* when Bohemund led a party of his knights against a weak part of the walls. Having passed through Monteroni and Lecce on the way from Gallipoli he had not only visited his sister but had raised a fresh supply of both lances and *milites*, and those, mixed with the conscripts he had been training on the march, added up to a force he thought he could trust in battle, provided the odds were not too great. More encouraging was what success brought: more lances came from the Apulian ranks to swell his force of mounted warriors.

'Where are they?' Reynard asked, looking all around him as if there were foes hidden in the ground.

'Never fear, friend, we must meet a real enemy soon.'

At the head of what was now five hundred knights and a thousand foot soldiers, as well as the carpenters, woodcutters, cooks and camp followers of a proper army, Bohemund marched north, heading for Brindisi, and with him he had the means to contemplate a siege. Yet he knew, as did Reynard and everyone else he had designated as a lieutenant, that they would surely never get there without they met a host determined to prevent them from even reaching the outer walls of such an important goal.

On a flat and seemingly endless coastal plain it was impossible to see any more than the horizon would allow; there were few to no hills and Ademar was of the opinion, given that this was a part of Apulia he knew well, that the only way they would see any force that lay ahead of them was by the light of their night-time campfires. For that purpose Bohemund sent ahead a number of squires, Tancred amongst them, who, innocent-looking, could act as his eyes and ears.

In his desire to impress, Tancred spread his reconnaissance further than intended and by luck found that Count Radulf was concentring a mounted force at a small town called Squinzano to hit Bohemund as he marched.

'Who told you to look in that direction?' his father demanded.

Like all boys of his years, Tancred had a scowl that was too often present, but was now deeper given he felt he had good cause to feel aggrieved. 'No one, Father, but it seemed to me that a couple of my confrères riding north were sufficient and that for all of us to head in one direction was a waste.'

'How many lances?' Bohemund asked.

'Eighty conroys under Count Radulf.'

'That seems precise, and anyway, how do you know it is him?'

'I went into Squinzano to ask and to count.'

'Tancred, you are a fool,' Ademar growled. 'What would have happened to you if you had been caught?'

'I have de Hauteville blood, Father,' Tancred replied, with utter assurance. 'I would have been spared and ransomed.'

'Or drawn and quartered,' Reynard opined. 'And no bad thing unless we want to increase the birth rate.'

'Did you observe their readiness?'

'They were sharpening their swords with the smith's wheel, Uncle, so it may be they are ready to move.'

'He will know how we march,' Ademar said, 'lances to the fore, so he means to let us proceed and come up on our rear and surprise us, attack our *milities* with we having to get through them to do battle.'

'And on the wrong kind of mount,' added Reynard. 'Against near twice our number.'

Those thoughts got a nod as well as an appreciation of what it portended: there was no way in such a situation his lances would be anything but disorganised, whereas Radulf would be prepared and that would hand him a great advantage, to be doubled or even trebled by the fact that his men would be on destriers and Bohemund's on their riding horses. Only now Radulf's aim was obvious and the trick was to play him false for, given the numbers, it was risky to turn to face him.

'Then it is as well we surprise him,' Bohemund declared.

It was not a road on which they were travelling; there was a sort of wide track made by traders and their donkeys, but that was insufficient for the number of men seeking to march along it and they had thus spread out over a wide area, one which Bohemund expanded, for in doing so they sent up a great cloud of obscuring dust. He had to hope that Radulf was unaware that his aim had been discovered, yet as in all war situations many things had to be left to develop. But he had one advantage and that was the terrain, especially a flank protected by the almost endless sandy beach, on the shore of the shallow water, occasionally interspersed with rocky promontories.

Once more the squires were employed to be his eyes, this time at the rear of the marching host, set there to warn of the enemy approach and, being mounted on swift ponies, able to tell their commander when he must react. Given the low state of training of his foot soldiers Bohemund stiffened them with extra commanders and gave them a simple instruction to carry out when the horns blew. Had he been at the rear of the host Bohemund would have laughed to see what Tancred had contrived: he had got all his confrères to sit facing backwards on their mounts, wearing cowls in which they had cut eyeholes, so that from afar it looked as if they were facing the right way – forward. There was thus no need to look over their shoulders, an act anyone observing them might have seen as odd and caused them to be more cautious.

Count Radulf saw the cloud of dust long before Tancred and his like saw his men, and such was the dun-coloured clothing of the lookouts they did not show up against it. Thus, having slipped in behind Bohemund, he brought his speed up to a steady canter, though not pushing too hard to keep fit his mounts. It was the dust that set up which caused the alert and the first of Tancred's squires was sent to both inform the men commanding the *milities* and then ride on to warn Bohemund.

To canter half a league, on a destrier carrying a mailed knight, exceeded that for which they had been trained; these sturdy animals were designed for short rides into a fierce battle and if Radulf wondered how fit they would be on contact it was a concern that quickly faded. Horses like to run – they do not have to be taught how do so, only when – and his mounts seemed, as he looked along the front line, to be enjoying themselves, heads up and jerking, nostrils flaring and hooves pounding rhythmically, with no sign of impending fatigue. The time came to put them into a faster pace, which he calculated as the point where those foot soldiers would hear the noise of hooves over that of their own numerous feet.

The blowing of the horns did not come as a surprise; what did was the way these men, who had to be barely trained, spun as one and took up a position to defend themselves, shields up and lance points at the ready in an unbroken line. Being committed, Radulf could not let this deter him and he made no attempt to stop his men, which he could have done with a horn blast of his own. Thus the first line hit the shield wall, then on the requisite command split left and right so the second wave could engage, with Radulf now taking up a position from which he could direct matters.

He was not downhearted; the men he was hoping to meet were behind that shield wall and so solid was it they had no chance of breaking through unless the *milites* opened up to let them pass in file, in which case he would have the fight he wanted: his solid conroys on horses trained to fight, against men yet to form up and very likely on skittish and fearful cavalry mounts. That Bohemund's foot soldiers held their line began to make Radulf curious and then to frustrate him to the point where he began to curse their stupidity; they could not beat his conroys, just delay them, and so, instead of beating against them for his original purpose, he ordered his lances to break their line, for if they did, Bohemund would be obliged to then commit what he was obviously holding back, his own knights, who, even if they had remounted, he knew he outnumbered.

The *milites* having ceased to march, the dust they had been sending up was now settling and the corresponding amount produced by his horses was much less. Because of that the air began to clear, and if it was a ghostly chimera at first, it rapidly began to take form, which led Count Radulf, not an especially religious man, to wonder if God had decided to send his celestial legions to participate in the fight. All along the shoreline, several ranks deep, with some lances up to their thighs in seawater, the first rank on the sand, sat outlines of the disciplined ranks of Bohemund de Hauteville's conroys, all on short and solid destriers, their teardrop shields and lance points catching the sun.

It was their horns that blew now, their destriers that came forward at a proper canter, and they hit his men as they sought to wheel to face them, yet unable to do so in the required orderly way. Count

Radulf had the battle he had envisaged, except that the positions were reversed and his numbers counted for less, very obviously so when his lances began to go down to sword and axe blows, more to couched lances which unseated them. Worse, those stubborn foot soldiers now rushed forward to employ their lances on what was now a flank, then to use sharp blades on the throats of the fallen. He watched as their helmets were pulled back hard to expose soft flesh, and he could even see the founts of bright blood that erupted and rose half the height of a man into the air.

He had ordered the horns to blow the retreat and they soared above the cacophony of noise that came from thousands of men fighting, only to find he faced another predicament: his horses had run a long way, and if they were not blown they were tired, too much so to outrun the fresh mounts now chasing his conroys. They had broken up, there was no discipline, and knowing that he was about to be in receipt of a defeat that might be so total few of his lances would survive, Count Radulf spun his horse round to face his enemies, lowered his own lance and charged with utter disregard into the midst of them.

They found his much-punctured body when the fighting died down, while the *milities* were going around cutting the throats of men not yet dead, as well as horses that would never be fit to use all four legs again. There were some of the enemy still breathing and when questioned they readily told Bohemund that Count Radulf had denuded Brindisi to make up the force that had just been utterly destroyed. With no time to waste, Bohemund set off north at a forced-march pace and that brought the result he desired. With too few men to defend its walls, the captain of the castle of Brindisi surrendered as soon as he was sure his honour had been satisfied.

CHAPTER TWENTY-TWO

While *Borsa* had the support of his mother, he also had the backing of the latest pope, none other than the Abbot Desiderius, who had, after much wavering and indecision, and under relentless pressure from his fellow divines, taken up holy office as Victor III. Not that he was going to enjoy a comfortable pontificate, for the imperial antipope Clement was still alive and contesting Victor's right to the Lateran, albeit from a distance. Rome itself was split, which meant Victor was not in possession of much more than the Castel St Angelo and the Vatican Hill, so much of his rule was carried out from his monastery at Monte Cassino. He was better off than Clement: the Romans had chased him out of the city altogether and that sent him north to Milan.

So, thunderous bolts pronouncing anathema sped south with every advance Bohemund made, papal demands that he desist from his actions and bow the knee to his half-brother. The backing of

Borsa had many strands, which dovetailed into papal policy. When Victor was appealed to – and he was almost weekly – he supported *Borsa*, first of all because he was his vassal and the legitimate heir to the *Guiscard*; secondly, he was known to be pious and, lacking his father's strong personality, would be less inclined to question what edicts were handed down to him from on high.

More importantly the papacy still needed a strong Norman bulwark against imperial pretensions and Jordan was, for Pope Victor, too unreliable, blowing supportive one minute then flirting with Henry IV the next, while Bohemund represented a return to the old days of the *Guiscard*, the man who had sacked and burnt Rome when he had supposedly come to rescue it. Yet even with all of his threats of excommunication the one-time Abbot of Monte Cassino was a peacemaker by nature, and pleading letters also came to Bohemund with threats of excommunication, begging him to desist, for his actions could do naught but destroy the fertile lands of Apulia.

Despite his best efforts it was not papal intervention that brought an uneasy peace to Apulia, but the pleas to the Great Count of Sicily to intervene on behalf of his titular suzerain – requests which long went unanswered, given he was occupied in finally securing Syracuse. After Palermo and Messina it was the most important seat of Saracen power on the island, and more than that to many; it had been said since the time of Ancient Greece that he who held Syracuse held Sicily. Despite Bohemund's continued success over the space of a year – he had advanced past Brindisi to take the hilltop town of Ostuni, then ejected his own two cousins from Conversano and was about to target the rich prize of Bari – Roger would not depart until his goal had been secured.

Being asked to act as mediator between these two warring half-brothers, he had much to consider, not that *Borsa* was doing much in the way of fighting; every time his forces – and he declined to lead them personally – came up against Bohemund's men they were soundly beaten and forced into an ignominious retreat. The only brake on Bohemund's advance and his eventual takeover of the duchy was the disinclination of many of *Borsa*'s vassals to switch their support to him – they were tardy in support for their liege lord also – added to the weathervane actions of Jordan of Capua, who could withdraw his knights at will and did so if his aggressive cousin seemed to be doing too well, too quickly.

None of this boded well for *Borsa*'s future as the Duke of Apulia; he could not win, and in time and by attrition, for all his power and wealth, he might well lose. Yet to abandon him to a slow erosion of his power was not an option that held much joy for his uncle; for many years a near-autonomous ruler in Sicily, Roger de Hauteville had concerns in case a problem he thought solved repeated itself, and that not just the line of his communications to Italy. It was the constant demands he had received to come to his late brother's aid, for he had always been much troubled by Robert's ambitions, which were never seemingly satisfied – one conquest always led to an attempt at another – while at home the *Guiscard* had never had control of his unruly barons. Too many times, and at an important moment in the subjugation of the island, Roger had been dragged away from his own concerns in Sicily because Robert needed his aid. He had no desire to see in possession of those same titles a warrior who sought to match and possibly surpass his father.

He had, of course, his vow of allegiance, made at Bari and repeated at Salerno, yet on a personal plane he could not but admire Bohemund while at the same time view his titular overlord in a different light. Even if he thought himself more free than his confrères of the normal Norman prejudice, he still thought Lombards to be inferior to his own kind in every way. Both nephews bore the de Hauteville name, but only one had a pure bloodline and represented what it had come to stand for in Southern Italy. Roger was no more prepared to become the nemesis to one than the other.

These were the thoughts he ruminated on as his single galley entered the harbour at Salerno, his personal standard at the masthead so they knew who was on board. His first task was to convince his relatives – *Borsa* himself, Guy, now Duke of Amalfi, and his sister-in-law – that what they were bound to propose was something impossible to implement: namely, that he should go to Bohemund and threaten to take the field against him unless he desisted from his incursions and handed back the rightful Duke those possessions he had usurped. It proved to be, as he had anticipated, an uncomfortable meeting.

'Surely, Roger,' Sichelgaita insisted, 'you do not dispute that Robert's bastard is in revolt?'

'You cannot do him the honour of using his name?'

'Should I do so, I would require immediate communion for the utterance of a blasphemy.'

'Bohemund seeks what he thinks is rightfully his.'

'Which,' *Borsa* responded, 'we know not to be the case.'

'But it is not as simple as just saying that he should bend the knee and give up his gains, which is what you wish me to propose to him.'

'Why not?' Guy demanded.

'Because he would say to me what I would say to him if the positions were reversed – he would tell me where to stick my lance.' The disappointment at his attitude was very evident in their expressions, but Roger was not about to be swayed. 'How did our family gain Apulia? Was it gifted to us?' No one cared to answer, only to look away as Roger added, 'We won it by force of arms.'

'And had our title recognised by the Pope,' *Borsa* interrupted.

'I am sure your father told you how much love was in the granting of that.'

'Times have changed, Uncle. Pope Victor writes to me kindly and will be happy, should I journey to Rome, to lay hands upon my head and confirm me to the triple dukedom. He is also close to excommunicating Bohemund.'

Sichelgaita went straight to the nub of the quandary, in truth why he had been summoned to Salerno, not that Roger would have accepted anything other than he had come of his own volition.

'You have the ability to force him to cease his depredations.'

'And what do you offer him in return?'

'His life,' Guy spat.

That angered Roger – if *Borsa* was no warrior, his brother was even less of one. 'Boast of that when you can take it, and if you wish, Guy, I will arrange for you to meet him in single combat.'

'He must be stopped,' *Borsa* said, in an almost pleading tone, this as Guy sought to look martial and ready, so easy at a distance from Bohemund.

'He has Taranto from my husband,' Sichelgaita snapped. 'Let him be content with that.'

'It may be best,' Roger sighed, 'to find out what he will accept.' The way the three of them looked at him then made Roger wonder if they were beginning to see him as an enemy, and that was not comfortable. 'I will travel to see him on the morrow.'

'You will need a strong escort, Uncle.'

'No, *Borsa*, I need only the half-dozen familia knights I have brought with me from Sicily.'

That did not endear him either, underlining as it did that he, unlike them, had naught to fear from Bohemund.

'I know why you have come, Uncle, but I would say to you now, to avoid that I must dispute with you, that I will have my father's title.'

'Which one, Bohemund? He had several.'

'Duke of Apulia I will settle for.'

If Bohemund had the ability to read another man's mind, and it did not take too much to read Roger's, he would have seen in the eyes that such a statement was not to be given credence. In any case, his uncle added words that underlined his disbelief and not without irony. One thing the *Guiscard* never did was settle for what he already had.

'And I thought you might be my brother's son.'

At least Bohemund smiled; he did not try to dissemble. 'Join me and I will give you Sicily.'

'Bohemund, I already have Sicily.'

'Not in your own right.'

'Next you will try to tell me that *Borsa* will take it from me, and if you do I will be tempted to ask you how.'

'And what else will you ask of me?'

They were sat in the round bastion of the castle of Conversano, which had been the seat of Bohemund's cousin, and Roger made much of looking around the walls hung with fine tapestries to break up the stark stone blocks.

'I would ask that you hand this back to Geoffrey.'

'He rebelled several times against my father and supported my half-brother. That cost him his fief.'

'Geoffrey swore an oath to *Borsa*, as did I, at Bari and Salerno.' All that got was a shrug. 'I have not come here to ask but to enquire, but I will say this: whatever it is you ask me to take back to Salerno, do not ask for the Duchy of Apulia, for you cannot have it.'

'Who will stop me?'

'If you leave me no choice, nephew, I will.'

Roger liked and admired Bohemund and he had cause to feel at that moment such sentiments were not misplaced. There was no expostulation, no attempt to bluff and call upon his uncle to tell him he thought he could achieve such a thing. Whereas *Borsa* would have blustered, Bohemund just held his gaze, his face showing no expression, an indication that he knew what had just been said was no idle boast. Whereas *Borsa* would struggle to raise lances against him, Roger would not; men would flock to him. Where Jordan of Capua might continue his tepid support, the advent of a host led by the Great Count would see all his lances withdrawn back to his own domains; he would not risk a battle with such an opponent.

'I am trying to think, Uncle, what you will gain from that.'

'Best you think, nephew, what I will lose for the want of it.'

'Do you fear me?'

There was no threat in the enquiry and Roger did not take it as such, answering in an even tone. 'I fear the turmoil you may bring, Bohemund, that I must confess.'

'Turmoil that would impact on Sicily?'

Roger held up his hand, index finger and thumb near to touching. 'I am that close to having the whole island under my control. I will have Syracuse next and then only the southern port of Agrigento and the central bastion of Enna are of importance and hold out against me.'

'I have heard Enna is a harder nut to crack than Melfi.'

The response was a sardonic smile. 'It is, and if you were not so determined here in Apulia I would be inviting you to join me in the siege.'

Bohemund did not smile; he threw back his head and laughed. 'Grant me the title *Borsa* holds and I will come readily. To fight alongside you, Uncle, I would consider an honour.'

Roger did not laugh. 'Sadly, Bohemund, it is not mine to give, only mine to withhold.'

'When I asked if you feared me a moment ago, I did so because I suspect that being a vassal of my father troubled you.'

'On more than one occasion.'

'So it might not please you to have me if I were Lord of Calabria as well. I daresay you would not willingly admit me as your suzerain in place of *Borsa*, but if I held Calabria I would have you by the throat, for nothing could get you in Sicily that I did not sanction and you would, for the sake of survival, be forced to acknowledge me. That was a power my father held over you, even if he did not exercise it.'

'How little you know my brother,' Roger sighed. 'He knew it to be so true it never had to be stated.'

'Which is why you seek to rein me in.'

'I admit that there is motive in what you say, but there is also one thing you are not considering, Bohemund, and it is something you should. I swore an oath to your father to look after his son and heir—'

'But not to me!'

Roger held up a hand; the anger had justification. 'I feel the same bond towards you, Bohemund, even if it was never asked of me.'

'So you would not fight me to the death?'

'I would grieve if you fell in battle and be mortified if that was in a fight against me. Rest assured, if it ever came to a contest, I would hope you would order that I be spared, for I would certainly issue such a command to those I led to show mercy to you.'

Bohemund nodded; it was nearly a bow, which led Roger to suspect it was time to say what had only been in the back of the younger man's mind.

'But you know as well as I do it will not come to a contest. The force I would lead against you is one you could not challenge. I would have all of *Borsa*'s vassals as part of my host, as well as what I could bring from Sicily, while I doubt even those Apulian lances you lead would stay true and the enterprise would have papal blessing.'

'Popes die.'

'True, but do not assume that anyone who is elected pontiff will happily lay hands on you and grant you a title. If it borders on flattery to say so, you are too dangerous.'

'While you are not?'

Roger, leaning forward in his chair, replied with arms as wide as his smile. 'Do you not know I am a good son of the Church? Is it not I who is busy making Sicily a part of Christendom and subject to the Roman rite?'

'So even if the Pope did not bless *Borsa* in a campaign against me, he would bless you.'

'I am seen as a crusader for the faith.'

328

'That is not how I see you.'

'And you would be right not to do so; but it is time to seek a solution, for I must tell you I have no desire to render you a pauper any more than I have a desire to see your half-brother puffed up with the kind of pride I fear he will succumb to once he feels secure.'

'Much as I dislike him, I do know he will not fall in to the sin of pride.'

'Aye, he is too saintly.'

'But not too much so to be a duke?'

The talk that followed was long and occasionally heated, as maps were produced, even if they were unnecessary – both men knew the lands of which they spoke too well to need them, Roger seeking to curb Bohemund's appetites, his nephew aiming to secure for himself a fief in which he could feel safe. Thus any hope of being given Bari was denied; he had to settle for his present fief of Taranto, with the addition of all the lands between there and Brindisi, which included Otranto, Gallipoli and Lecce, which left the final disputes that lay to the south of Conversano.

'I will not let you take this castle and the county off your relatives and my own, Bohemund, and you cannot use the excuse of past betrayals to enforce it. This was home to my eldest brother and he was a gentle and good man.'

That made the younger man want to stick; the land around Conversano was extremely fertile and the revenues were substantial, but Roger would not budge and finally, after much discussion, a line was drawn south of one de Hauteville family fief to the border of another, added to another to the west, as well as a promise extracted to apply no pressure to his Conversano cousins to cede him any land,

and certainly not an agreement that they should be his vassals. The final hurdle was an obvious one.

'You must do duty to *Borsa* for that which you hold.' Seeing Bohemund about to object, Roger, for almost the first time, was brusque. 'If I find no difficulty in doing so, do not say to me you are too proud to act likewise.'

'And what will be my title?'

The reply was given in an exasperated tone. 'You are Lord of Taranto, is that not enough?'

Bohemund responded with a sly grin. 'You are not content to be a mere count, you are the Great Count.'

'So, tell me, nephew,' Roger sighed, 'how in the sight of God do you wish to be known?'

'Prince of Taranto!' Sichelgaita shouted. 'Does the wretch have no shame?'

'That is his final request,' Roger replied.

He had been through hoops and spent a whole day arguing that they should accede to Bohemund's demands, and had endured the unspoken accusation that he was acting for one nephew too much and for the true heir too little, suspecting it would have been thrown in his face if he was not so vital to their cause. It had been difficult too, having to make plain without it being stated that he was not going to support them without an agreement, and if they demurred then he would wash his hands of the whole business. That it was a bluff, only he knew, but the one thing he determined upon was that the matter should be settled so that, if one was not satisfied, neither side would want to contest it; he had his mind on Syracuse, Enna and Agrigento.

'And you support him in this, Uncle?' asked *Borsa* in a quieter voice, when all the arguments had been, several times, exhausted.

'It matters not what title he has, all will know he is your vassal.'

'Count should suffice,' opined Guy of Amalfi, who was, after all, a duke in his own right.

'Is Jordan of Capua greater than the Duke of Apulia, Guy? It is more vital that the world knows who is suzerain and who is vassal than what they are termed.'

'And for this he will swear fealty?'

Again it was *Borsa* asking and, just as many times before, he could not look his irate mother in the eye.

'Do not grant this,' she hissed.

'For peace, Mother, it is a small thing.'

Roger had to bite his tongue then; whatever Bohemund swore, whatever he had said to him in Conversano, his uncle knew his nature would never allow him to cling to peace. Bohemund was a warrior and through his veins coursed the blood of two Norman parents, one of them the *Guiscard*. The Duke of Apulia would be troubled again by his half-brother and it might be that he would have to come to his aid and enforce reconciliation more than once. The thought did not trouble him greatly; he was, after all, a man well aware of the world in which he lived, one where the only hold a magnate had on his possessions was that which he could enforce. Nothing was granted to anyone to embrace as of right; it had to be won and maintained by the same method: the sword.

Attending the ceremony in which Bohemund did duty for his fiefs was to see open and raw hatred, mixed with enough insincere platitudes as to make a sane man vomit. *Borsa* might stand above his kneeling brother, but it had to be remarked that even then he barely outdid him in height. The Archbishop of Salerno was there to witness what was bound to be hypocrisy as Bohemund swore an oath that no one present had any faith he would keep, and if they wondered at his duplicity, well had they not all at one time made vows that had been subsequently broken? How that would be judged was not in their hands, but in those of God.

CHAPTER TWENTY-THREE

Roger de Hauteville was witness, over the following years, to the proof of his suppositions; if Bohemund's uprisings were not endemic, they were frequent enough to give his half-brother sleepless nights. Any slight, however small, would do and any excuse: a demand for his revenues to be promptly paid, a desire that he submit an account of improvements to anything he possessed from castle to wheat field; *Borsa* had heard of William of England's Domesday Book and wished to emulate it. Part of the reason for so much warfare on Bohemund's part was to keep his knights employed – if they did not rebel with him, they would rise up against his title; that was the Norman way.

Slowly, inexorably, the Prince of Taranto expanded his possessions till he controlled all the land and sea ports from Melfi to the heel of Italy, Bari included. It would only have been remarkable if he had been singular, but he was not; there was hardly a vassal in the regions of Apulia and Calabria in the years following that swearing of fealty who did not at some time feel he had the right to question the rule of the Duke of Apulia. Count Roger had met and negotiated more than once with his nephews and more often than that he had come from Sicily, now wholly his, to put in place – often obliged to spill blood – some rebellious vassal of his brother's heir when it was plain he could not do so himself.

Borsa was not alone. When Jordan of Capua died, the Lombards over whom he ruled, always smarting and ever capricious, overthrew his young son Richard and expelled him from his own domains, which had Bohemund eyeing that great fief as a tempting addition to his own, while his half-brother, who had accommodated young Richard, was in terror that he might try to take it over. Then Amalfi rose up; in the years since the death of Duke Sergius, the infant son whom his people were scared to elevate for fear of Gisulf of Salerno had grown to manhood. Taxed by the Normans, who were assiduous in collection, when he raised his standard, the citizens, thinking to ease their burdens, took his part.

In a patrimony beset by widespread rebellion, it was far from a shock that John of Amalfi should demand the return of what he saw as his rightful inheritance. Unable to enforce his own will and with a deposed brother even less able to do so, *Borsa* had sent a desperate plea to his uncle, fearing that with Amalfi so close to his capital – it was only five leagues distant – it posed a threat that had to be met. The surprise was that, when calling on all his vassals to come to aid, Bohemund too answered the call, bringing with him Tancred of Lecce, now in his twenty-first year and already a warrior with a formidable reputation.

There were few more strange sights than to see Bohemund and his half-brother together, the former full of natural, strutting confidence, towering as he ever did over all around him, while *Borsa*, ever beset by worry and his own inadequacy as a ruler, was made doubly nervous by such a commanding presence. The only person who could match him in that was his Uncle Roger who, despite his sixty-plus years was still handsome, still virile and a match for most of those with whom he still trained daily in the manège.

If the Duke of Apulia was the titular commander of the siege, it was in the tent of the Great Count that control was exercised – indeed, it had to be, for *Borsa*, now without the late Sichelgaita to stiffen his spine, spent much of his time in church praying for a victory rather than actively planning and fighting to gain one. Thus, once the rituals of greeting had been completed, and with a degree of suppressed contempt, the Prince of Taranto and the Lord of Lecce bent the knee to their suzerain, then went to Roger's tent to discover where and how they could be of use.

The man they met was greater now than he had ever been hitherto: not only was he the complete master of Sicily, but he had sailed south as well and taken Malta from the Saracens. His daughter Constance had married Conrad, son of Henry IV, and, even if the two were now in conflict, it was very possible that one day a de Hauteville female would wear an imperial diadem. It was well known he was much cosseted by the reigning pope, Urban II, who, unable to enter Rome and be consecrated, had spent six years wandering South Italy, where he had come to realise that for all their varying titles, only one man stood head and shoulders above the Norman herd.

'It has ever been my wish, Uncle, to fight alongside you,' Bohemund said, after they had embraced.

'A desire I share, Count Roger,' Tancred added.

Returning to his seat and looking up at Bohemund, Roger adopted a sarcastic tone. 'I had conflict in Sicily for both of you if you desired such a thing.'

'You will forgive us for not rushing to aid you.'

'We were not prepared to turn our back on *Borsa*.'

'I cannot think what you had to fear, Tancred. Perhaps a priest's missal thrown at your head?'

'How does the siege progress?'

'It will take time, Bohemund. The walls are sound, the defenders determined and this was not undertaken in haste. The citizens and the lord they want to take back spent much time in preparation.'

'So they are well supplied?'

'With everything,' Roger replied, rising out of his chair. 'Come, I will show you what we face.'

Set between two mountains and in a deep bay, with only one real land route in and out, Amalfi had ever been known as a hard objective to subdue and impossible if the besieger lacked a fleet. A lack of such a weapon plainly angered Roger as he outlined the difficulties, for, less intent on expansion than his father, *Borsa* had let the fighting ability of that atrophy, this while most of Roger's own fleet had the never-ending task of keeping at bay Saracen incursions into Sicily, and was thus protecting that island.

He had managed a blockade, but the Amalfians, sea traders themselves for centuries, had set their own merchant ships across the bay to form an arc of defence and Roger lacked the kind of galleys and the men who manned them to break it. The land defence, a high curtain wall, lay between those two peaks, which formed a steep-sided coombe, while at the top of the two mountains, dotted with steep

336

crags and near unclimbable, the Amalfians had built strong bastions hard to assault.

After a long walk they were shown a donkey track that ran along the coast from the west, but that had been sealed off by another wall, which was joined to the arc of ships the Amalfians had set to protect the bay. In the water were sharp wooden spikes, which had been driven deep into the shallows to prevent the besiegers wading in to an attack, and if they gathered to seek to dislodge them, that brought to this part of the defence the archers of Amalfi to dissuade them.

The return up that narrow valley to Roger's tent was to see how crowded it was with fighting men, and that extended well inland – a sea of tents, fires and fluttering standards, for all the vassals of the *Borsa* were here, and for the same reason. It had nothing to do with loyalty and much to do with gold: Amalfi was one of the richest ports on the Tyrrhenian Sea, its traders were masters of profit and it was very obvious that once taken, there would be abundant plunder with which to justify the time spent in breaking down the walls.

'They will succumb, Bohemund, but I fear we will be here for an age.'

'Perhaps we might see *Borsa* achieving glory at last.'

'Sainthood is the more likely,' Roger replied. 'But enough of this gloom and the difficulties; let us all eat together and you can tell me what mischief you have been about since we last met.'

Bohemund laughed. 'For mischief, Uncle, you must look to Tancred – he is the one wedded to it.'

Much had happened in the world in which they lived. Pope Victor had years before gone to meet his maker – no doubt Desiderius was happy with that, for he had never liked his office – while the man who replaced him, Urban II, had inherited just as much trouble with Rome and emperors, though he had suffered less from the Normans. They had aided his election and joined a coalition to fight the Emperor Henry, once more excommunicated, which had led him to a civil war with his heir.

Between Roger and Pope Urban there was apparent harmony, though they had disputes enough about ecclesiastical matters in Sicily, mostly about clerical appointments, but it had never extended into an open breach, both men being too well versed in diplomacy. Over food and wine, Roger related how Urban had tried to entice him into an attack on the North African coast to fight the Moors, a crusade which would aid the monarchs of Catholic Spain, an offer that had been declined.

'Then I take it you are not tempted by the great crusade Urban has called for to the Holy Land?'

'I have enough on my hands here and in Sicily to keep me from temptation.'

Tancred, hitherto mostly an observer, not a participant in a conversation he found dull, as all young men do when their elders talk of past events, suddenly perked up and cut in.

'Given its purpose, "temptation" seems an odd word.'

'Is it? I do not see it as so. You cannot march on the Holy Land without the aid of the Emperor Alexius.' Bohemund's face closed up at the mention of that name; it was a reminder not only of his defeat at Larissa but the ignominy that followed, but he had to put that aside; Roger was still talking. 'And there is also the small matter of pushing back the Turks, which will not be easy.'

'Agreed.' Bohemund turned to Tancred. 'I have fought them and they are hard opponents.'

'But worth it if you seek wealth.'

'I never saw them as having much to plunder. If they were staunch, they were also poor.'

Roger looked confused. 'Do you not see, Bohemund, that if the Turks are dispossessed how much land will become free for Alexius to distribute, and the only people he can safely give it to are those who have by their fighting taken it from his enemies?'

There was some satisfaction in the reaction from both of his relatives; now he had their undivided attention as he outlined what was possible.

'Put aside all the talk of Urban's call to crusade. There are those truly pious who might take up the cause of the cross for their soul, yet there are ten times as many who would see it as a chance to enrich themselves. Those provinces Byzantium lost to the Turks are among the richest they ever possessed and that pales when you include Palestine and the wealth fetched in by Christian pilgrims.'

'Much-abused pilgrims,' said Tancred.

'Take a pinch of salt with those tales,' Roger scoffed. 'I know Urban well and his stories of pilgrim rapine are as likely to be exaggerations as truths.'

'A pope telling lies?' Bohemund responded, his face alight with a joke he and Roger shared: they had never known one not to.

This was no terrain for siege towers; it was too uneven and rocky, so any assaults on the walls of Amalfi had to be carried out by a combination of ballista and ladders. First the great stones were hurled to seek to create a breach or to take off the higher parts of the walls. The rubble caused provided, albeit with a steep climb, a means to make for the gap and naturally that was where the Amalfians concentrated their defence, so either as a distraction or as a proper attempt at scaling – they would never know which inside – another assault would be launched with long ladders, backed up by archers, with the ballista now employed to send fireballs of oil-soaked hay to clear a space on the parapet onto which the knights must climb.

Gathered in darkness at a point where the curtain wall ran uphill to where the steepness of the mountain provided protection, Bohemund hushed his men to be silent. His next command was to pick up the battened-together planks that formed a heavy screen that would protect them until they got close to the walls. By weight it took strong men to carry it, for hooked on the back were their climbing ladders. As soon as they made the base of the wall, the archers and ballista would come into play, seeking to drive back the defenders from the parapet. If this was an attack that had been tried before, it now had a better chance of success; the defenders must be going hungry despite their once full storehouses, for after eight months without a single ship being able to enter the port, they should be running out of food and with it the will to keep resisting.

A three-pronged attack – *Borsa* was to command the centre before the high breach made by heavy fired rocks, though, as was his way, he would send his knights into combat rather than lead them. At his right hand stood his Uncle Roger to proffer advice – in truth to issue the commands. Never doubting that his half-brother was far from admired, Bohemund had come to realise that there was in fact an even less flattering feeling now amongst those gathered, and it was one which extended to his Lombard and Greek levies. Time had caused that lack of love to turn him into being gently despised, both for his weakness and his vacillation. Such men would rail against a strong hand, yet they preferred it to a weak one, and that applied doubly to his Norman lances.

Tancred and the knights of Lecce and Monteroni were on that donkey track, having taken the whole of a moonless night to get into position. They too had ladders, but the aim was to only begin their assault if the defenders denuded this part of the walls to support those under pressure from Bohemund and *Borsa*. Crawling forward with a local who understood the Amalfi dialect, using the reflected light of stars on the water, Tancred had got close to the walls and was sitting listening for the sound of orders being relayed, hopefully followed by departing feet.

Looking at Amalfi from the sea, there were three mountains, one set back and around which the road split to take a traveller east to west along the rocky coast. Atop that stood a picket with a lit beacon, screened off so it did not show to those in the city. As soon as the man in charge saw the first hint of grey light on the eastern horizon, he slid the screen to one side to show the beacon, hurriedly putting it back once more, which told the commanders in the valley it was time to begin the assault.

Tancred heard the horns blow and stood to better listen, hauling his local up too, this as Bohemund and those under the ducal command began their advance towards that mound of rubble. The defenders were not fools; they knew that first light was the best time for a besieger to attack and they had their own means of countering that as soon as they heard sounds they thought suspicious, and no host could move without making a noise.

Using catapults, they sent out their own bales of blazing hay into the still-dark night, which when in the air showed the men coming to assault their walls, as well as allowing their archers to mark their range. Moving forward behind that shield of planks, Bohemund could hear the thud of arrows hitting home as well as smell the stench of burning as the lit points set the wood to smouldering, while over his head flew the burning wads of his own ballista.

Only darkness gave Tancred a chance; once daylight came his men would be in plain view and at the mercy of archers who would be rushed to stop them moving forward, so as soon as he heard the movement of the defenders he poked his local to tell him what words he could hear from the opposite side of the wall. Men were moving off to face the main assault and reinforce walls, obviously suspecting they would be under greater pressure. It was getting light, though it was only the first tinge, so there was no time to delay: Tancred either attacked or withdrew and he was too much of a Norman for the latter.

Crawling back, he brought his men towards the wall, carrying ladders, he on one himself, which he set down against the base, his confrère silently running it up hand over hand. That fellow was pushed aside; if anyone was going to be in the forefront of the assault, it was the man who led them, and Tancred scaled the rough-hewn rungs at speed to find that the men who had remained were alert and waiting for him. It takes great courage and skill to fight perched on a ladder, as well as uncommon strength to do battle with someone above your head, but that was what was happening all along the wall as the Normans, who wielded these weapons day after day, used the muscles that produced to engage their less able foes.

Bohemund was likewise fighting, though he had got a few men with him over the wall and on to the parapet through a combination of fire, archery and sheer bloody ability. They were now fighting back to back to hold that place, but the same imperative was upon him as his nephew. He and Tancred could only maintain themselves if some of the defenders they faced were drawn off to hold that breach in the walls and that was where the attack ran into the sand. *Borsa*'s men of Salerno had scaled the rubble and were heavily engaged, but the gap was high and narrow, which meant only so many could contest the space and that worked more to the advantage of the Amalfians than the attackers.

Not that the fighting ended quickly; it went on until the sun was full up in the sky, until Roger de Hauteville was certain that today was not the day of final success. He whispered to *Borsa,* who seemed to take an age to pass on his advice to the horns, but eventually they blew the several blasts that in their spacing told all the three attacking parties to withdraw. With the men in the breach that was hard enough; they had to back down loose rubble until they could disengage.

Bohemund needed the crossbowmen to create on either side of him a barrier of deadly bolts that could pierce chain mail, so he could get onto his ladders and back to terra firma. Tancred and his men, who had never made the parapet, had the less than simple task of creating the time to abandon their weapons and, using the sides of the ladder, to slide to safety, recover lances, swords and axes and to run far enough to get out of arrow range before the Amalfian archers arrived, with the only thing protecting their exposed backs their teardrop shields.

Trudging back to their tents there was no despair in the Norman camp; this was a day in which they had not triumphed, but in siege warfare there were many more of them to set against the one day of victory. They had suffered losses and wounds, but so had the defenders, both in numbers and in morale, for while the besiegers sat around their campfires would talk of the success to come, the

Amalfians would be considering how close they had come this day to defeat.

Borsa held his place as those who had fought for his standard plodded back to their encampments, as if he was a great warrior accepting the accolades of those over whom he held command. There were many who did salute him with swords to their nose guards, but all knew there was no respect in it; it was a gesture, nothing more. Once everyone was back and the wounded and dead had been recovered by truce, he took himself off to pray, leaving his three relatives, who were themselves God-fearing men, to seek to glean from what had happened an avenue to end the siege.

EPILOGUE

Amalfi never fell, for as news came of the great host forming from all over Europe, intent on sailing to Constantinople, many minds were concentrated. For some it was the prospect of absolution from sins, for amongst Normans, regardless of how many times they confessed their sins, there were those who could recall deeds of a very black nature indeed – transgressions against God, such as the defiling of churches and the torturing of monks, that might stand outside the writ of a priest to pardon. They might burn in hell!

More potent, as Roger had indicated, was the prospect not just of wealth, but of land; a high number of the mercenaries who had come to Italy were younger sons of large families full of sibling brothers – their sires of Normandy bred well – and they had seen the demesnes on which they had been raised go to the elder of the family while they got nothing, hence the need to come south; that was what had brought the de Hautevilles and most, if not all, of their confrères.

The hankering for a landed possession of one's own was strong in them, yet as they looked around the prospect of gaining any where they now resided was slight – it was in the hands of others. The final strand was plunder, which was becoming harder to find in a terrain ceasing to be the troubled polity of years past; it now had an air, the present upheavals notwithstanding, that denoted a country in the process of settling. Judgements bounced off fantasies, but there was no doubting that in the East there was fabulous wealth to be gained for those lucky enough to be in place to grab it.

Added to that they were warriors, highly trained, and they knew if they were fighting now and had many times previously it was a diminishing role; much more time was spent in the manège than the field. And so grew a groundswell of belief that it was time to move on, to look for pastures rich and new; all that was missing was the spark and the leader. Not the least of the lances who thought that was Tancred, who had the ability to work on Bohemund.

'What more can you gain in Italy? You have all that you can take and your uncle stands between you and any further advance.'

Tancred asked that time and again; indeed it became a refrain, this while he made no secret that he had ambitions of his own. Heir to Monteroni and Lecce and also a vassal of Taranto, he was in line for a truncated inheritance, and while he admired Bohemund and would always put his lance at his disposal, he knew that for him there would be no great conquests lest they crossed to Illyria, and his suzerain lacked the means to either cross the Adriatic or remain there.

'Do you recall what Count Roger said? There are conquests to be made in the East, lands to be taken back from the Turks and the Holy Places to liberate, and Pope Urban has promised absolution of sin for those who take a vow to do that on the cross.'

Bohemund was tempted, but before him was a city ever more close to capitulation or sack and it was hard to turn his back on that, for to do so would imply that Amalfi had defeated him. Yet as word came of those who were, as of this very moment, marching towards his own Adriatic ports, as well as the numbers and titles, it was just as difficult not to admit to temptation. Loyalty to Roger held him back, but it was *Borsa* who provided the proverbial straw, for the Duke of Apulia was never comfortable with his giant of a half-brother around; indeed it was rare for them to speak and even more so that they should dine together.

To sit young Richard of Capua at his right hand was an insult to his uncle, the Great Count; to fawn over the boy drove that home and had Bohemund glaring at him, for the intention was as clear as a pikestaff. If it was only rumour it was one easy to give credence: *Borsa*, once the city had fallen, was lining up this army he had before Amalfi to turn to retaking Capua, where he would reinstate Richard, albeit as his vassal; the drip of the words of Tancred, sitting nearby, suddenly had more and deeper resonance. Where now could he ply his lance? Only, it seemed, in the service of a man he despised! For once less abstemious than was customary – the thoughts he was having preyed on his mind and resolution – he decided to speak where normally he would have remained silent.

'I am obliged to ask if it is true, *Borsa*, that you intend to give young Richard back Capua?'

'I am minded to listen to his pleas that I should, yes.'

Bohemund fixed the youngster with a glare. 'I hope you do not expect it to be easy if my half-brother leads.'

'Nephew,' Roger interrupted, 'this is not fitting.'

'Perhaps, Richard, I should gift you Capua, for I am sure to be able to do that while—?'

'Not many would have you as suzerain!' *Borsa* shouted, for once stung out of his usual complacency.

'Whereas,' Tancred piped up, '*none* would choose you.'

'Remember who is vassal to whom.'

'A convenience, *Borsa*,' Bohemund responded, 'and one that will need perhaps to be corrected.' His half-brother gave Roger a meaningful look, which irritated Bohemund. 'You cannot hide behind an uncle all your days, like our father, and much as I do not wish it to pass, he will not always be there to protect you.'

'I can hold my own.'

'If you mean your pizzle, well all men can do that, but a sword is another matter.'

'Bohemund,' Roger interjected. 'These are words better left unsaid.'

'Until when, Uncle?'

'Till the time, perhaps,' said Tancred with a meaningful look, 'when words turn into deeds?'

'You talk of deeds, do you? One day I have a deed that requires to be performed—'

'*Borsa!*'

Roger barked this, and if he did not say it, in his eyes he was advising restraint, for words once uttered could not be withdrawn. He had overseen an uneasy peace between his two nephews and sometimes had been forced to tell one or the other they had to accept things they would rather deny; it had ever been fragile, too easy to spin into a fight to the finish.

'No, Uncle,' *Borsa* said in a silky voice. 'Let it be known that yes, I, the Duke of Apulia, Calabria and Sicily, will put Richard back on his Capuan seat.'

If he had been looking at his uncle instead of Richard, *Borsa* would have seen that Roger was displeased at the mention of his being Duke of Sicily. It was true that the title belonged to him; Roger had never denied it and had even had him as a guest to tour an island that was, in theory, his domain. But he did not rule, nor could he, and if he tried it would mean war; the fact that Roger was his vassal was one rarely mentioned in public, for the very good reason that he only held his ducal title because his uncle supported him. It was the message sent at Bari and it still held.

'From which I might choose to dislodge him.'

'You will suffer if you do, Bohemund, as you should have suffered many times before.'

'When you have the means I invite you to try.'

'I have them all around this tent,' *Borsa* growled.

Bohemund drained his cup of wine and stood up. 'Do you? You think them loyal, when they are here for their purse. If they had a better prospect, they would desert you in a blink. It is sad that you do not know how much you are despised.'

'Do not put it to the test,' Roger asked, though without much passion.

'I must,' Bohemund replied, his face sorrowful. Then he looked at Tancred, who stood immediately. 'And let me say, it is your continued good health that obliges that I should.'

No one disputed that Bohemund had the right to call for the horns to be blown and the only one who might have stopped him from addressing the host once assembled was Roger, and he was sick to the back teeth of what he had been obliged to do these last ten years, well aware that if he possessed a still-living son of his own instead of daughters, matters might have been very different. *Borsa*'s raising of his ducal title rankled, and when he was asked to intervene, that was his demand. That his nephew give up the title and free him from vassalage. Roger had always suspected that *Borsa* saw him as a less than stalwart friend and perhaps even as an enemy; that was what he called the Great Count now.

'If you see me so, then I leave it to you to contest with Bohemund.'

'Do not seek to fool me. I know why you do what you do and it is all in your own interest, not mine.'

With that, Roger walked out, to find Bohemund standing on the back of a cart, as if he needed to, beginning to address the assembled Normans.

'Our Heavenly Father on Earth has called upon all good Christian knights to lay aside their differences and set out to reclaim for God the Holy Places of the birth, death and resurrection of Jesus our Saviour.'

Every man present crossed himself and what followed was a list of crimes committed against the thousands of good pilgrims who had made their way to Palestine for the glory of Our Lord, and horrible they were, even if Roger, listening, suspected them to be untrue: robbery, blinding, rape, crucifixion, limbs cut off, forced conversions – all the litany that had circulated for years and grown in the telling until they had become, amongst the ignorant, suspected truth, while amongst the pious who sought a crusade, Urban included, a means to generate hatred for the adherents of the Prophet.

'I, with my nephew Tancred, am resolved to join that host, not to seek absolution for my soul, but to serve the God who sees all in our hearts and minds. You, the men of Normandy, know my worth, know that if I go there to do battle with the infidel only doom and hellfire awaits them. I would ask who would join with me.'

The cry that went up was huge and so all-consuming it seemed every one of those lances had resolved to join him. In the end it was not them all; and if proof were needed that the restless were right about the settled, what kept many of their confrères where they were was their wives and children.

'Gather your mounts and your weapons, pack your goods, for we leave tomorrow.'

If *Borsa* wept as half his lances departed to the incantations and blessing of the priests in which he stored so much of his faith, no one saw it, for he sulked in his tent. It was the Great Count Roger of Sicily who watched them depart and indeed, given his religious faith, silently prayed for them to both live and prosper. When they had gone, a very long line of the best men, he looked at what was left, and then made for the tent of his nominal suzerain.

'The siege is over, *Borsa*. With those that have gone with Bohemund we lack the means to maintain it. And cease to weep, you are supposed to be a Norman.'